THESE DARKER SECRETS

AARON ROBINSON

Contents

PROLOGUE

The screams began at the bewitching hour—a harrowing sound that woke two small boys from their peaceful slumber. The smell of long burning wood occupying every inch of their bedroom was the first thing Joseph Price noted. The flames were just beginning to lick at the edge of his bed frame, closing in on his feet and the blanket that was haphazardly placed upon him.

In his tired state, the child removed the blanket quickly, feeling out for his brother in the acrid smoke that was stopped from escaping by their small window. The smoke creating a dark wall between Joseph and salvation to the outside.

A second, blood-chilling scream of a woman came from outside, and even at his young age, Joseph knew the dangers that surrounded him. His eyes caught the view from the outside, and even as young as he was, Joseph wondered, just for a moment, if maybe being in the burning building was better after all.

"Boys!" Their father's voice came quickly through the tiny hovel. A crash came from somewhere Joseph couldn't see, and suddenly, his father, Malik, quickly grabbed both boys and dragged them out of the flame-ridden room with no regard for belongings. He just had to get himself and his children out. "The guild found us…"

"How did they find us?" Joseph heard his brother ask as he nuzzled his face in his father's neck, trying to get a good look at the area that was just rubble and flame-ridden wood. Once their home, it looked nothing of the sort now. "Where's Mum? I heard a scream."

"The guild overwhelmed us instantly; there were too many of them. We tried to fight back… but they burnt everything to the ground and took some people away; I don't know how many or where they are going-." Malik said before he began to cough violently, the smoke becoming too much for him as he broke through the last door of their house into the cold night – but still, the smoke followed them. None were exempt from the cough that seemed to linger and claw at them. "I don't know where your mother went, I lost her in the ensuing fight."

"But how did this happen, Dad?" Finley asked as the trio made it through the torched field close to their home, unable to run with limited visibility and the acidic smoke plaguing every corner of their small town. "I thought everyone was really cautious at trying to conceal this location…"

"We are… but there are always going to be blips. This is a particularly big one. They must have been tipped off somehow." Malik coughed out as he clung to his children, stopping moving entirely in the smoke; he couldn't see a way out; there was no point in trying to move. If he couldn't see, then surely the hunters couldn't either. Joseph gripped his father tightly, not wanting to move his face from the man's neck; the smoke was stinging his eyes, causing salted tears to fall without even trying.

"Where's Mama?" Joseph muttered incoherently, looking up at his father in the night. His dark brown hair was wild and unkempt, and his green eyes were glassy. Malik didn't say anything; instead, a few tears, real tears this time, began to fall from his eyes. But before more could come, Joseph could feel his father take a deep breath.

"She's fine, Joey; just don't look anywhere but my face, okay?" Malik finally said, feeling his youngest bury his head back in his shoulder. Trying to hide his face from the smoke, the smog threatening to become thicker every second. Looking back at the home he had exited, he let out a pained sigh. "It's all gone… come on, we need to get out of here before they find us in the smoke."

This was no longer a home or a town. It was not their salvation anymore. It was a mound of decay.

As they ran, the smoke began to clear slightly, allowing Joseph and his family to finally see the midnight town but also opening them all up to danger. To their left, a dilapidated cornfield burning to the ground was all that Joseph could see as he clung to his father.

"Corn…" Joseph mumbled sadly; he liked playing in the fields and eating fresh corn. He remembered how sweet it was as he picked at it. There would be no more fun days like that. His groggy state had now dissipated, and he was wide awake now. Awake to the horrors of the world. "All gone."

"They were close. I could hear them, but we've had people come close to the area before; I thought they wouldn't find this place or move on quickly…." Malik said through baited breaths as he stopped running; his stamina was not what it was before the smoke reached his lungs. Malik's senses were at the next level, able to hear anything and everything from across the mountain that hid their home. Finley and Joseph could try to hide the biscuits they would take on the sly, but Malik would always know. His sight was enhanced to a degree, but his vision was useless through the smoke.

Malik knew how to be a 'know-it-all' father, and boy, did he do just that. But it did come in handy. He was able to find the boys in the smoke and flame-ridden home. If it wasn't for his magical ability, the boys might not have escaped in time.

Another harrowing scream invaded Joseph and his family's ears, coming closer and closer as the trio ran through the area. Whole families were fighting back against the hunters. This place, this hamlet, was everything to the people who lived here, so to destroy it and capture the people was like rubbing salt in the wound.

"Dad, did you see any of my friends?" Finely asked. He knew this was not a top priority, but he needed to know that anything could have happened to them with this level of destruction. "Cousin Maya or Saurin?"

"Sa...Sawin." Joseph said he hadn't got the hang of the boy's name yet.

"I don't know. I can only hope some people made it to the waterfall like we planned, yeah?" Malik looked down at Finley as he crouched, still holding Joseph in his arms. He dug into his pocket, procuring two necklaces, wrapping one around Finely, and then feeling his father place it around his neck; Joseph looked down at the shining gold object on a silver chain. "I was going to give them to you both on your eighteenth birthday. It's your mother and I's engagement and wedding rings. One set for each of you on a chain... to remember us by."

"What do you mean, remember you?" Finley asked, the panic rising as he let the reality set in. "Dad?"

"I need to go find your mother. I need to know where she is," Malik said. The large screech from Joseph's mouth as Malik tried to put him down was probably enough to alert the hunters to their position. Malik flinched, his ears sensitive already. Somehow, he had to convince the boy to let go.

"I'm sorry, Joey. I'm sorry, Shhh. You need to be quiet as a mouse." Malik cooed. Trying to separate his younger son from his body. But Joseph didn't want to move. "I need to find mummy."

"No!" Joseph shouted again.

"I need you to be a big boy, okay?" Malik asked, finally subduing his son and getting the upper hand. The mud was warm, the heat from the flames that surrounded them had melted it, turning it into goop.

"Dad. I can help. I can use my ability; you know how good I've gotten recently." Finley protested as he grabbed for his younger brother's hand. "I'm getting better and better every day."

"No. You two need to go to the waterfall. You know where that is from here. The Hunters won't find you there." Malik said as he stayed crouched down at his son's level and quickly planted two kisses on each of their heads, his face wet from sweat and tears. "Finley, you need to take care of your brother, whatever the cost."

Malik then began to run the way that he had come into the heart of destruction around them. Finley could do nothing but watch as his father disappeared back into the smoke. A second later, a scream of frustration came from his lips, the clanging of metal and the whiney of a horse. Neither Joseph nor Finley could see what was happening, but whatever it was, it was not good.

"Stop!" Someone from the smoke commanded. Further clanging came, then another scream, definitely their father's. A pained scream, like he had been hurt. Maybe it was a good thing that neither boy could see anything.

"Papa!" Joseph said quietly as he let go of Finley's hand and began toddling over to where their father had run off.

"No, Joey. We need to go this way." Finley managed to reach for his brother's hand and grab him, dragging him towards a patch of the corn fields where the flames hadn't reached yet. "We need to get to the waterfall; we'll be safe there."

"Fo-Foxy." Joseph stuttered as he looked back at the broken mound of a home, the smoke clearing to make it much easier to see the devastation. Realising that he had left his favourite teddy bear in the house. Finley knew the fox would be gone now, burnt to a crisp along with everything else in the little hovel. "Want Mr. Foxy."

"I'm sorry, Joey. We must leave Mr. Foxy behind." Finley said it was hard taking care of a child, much more so since Finley had seen what he had. The waterfall wasn't too far away, but getting there through all this chaos and the patrolling Hunters was hard.

"Feet hurt." Joseph cried as Finley picked up the pace, seeing the end of the corn fields in their sights. The more they stayed in this place, the more dangerous it was – the smoke was getting closer, and the flames always lingered. "Finny-."

Finley felt like he had run into a brick wall. The two boys fell with a large 'thump' onto the grass and stone floor. The physical pain they felt was no match for the emotional pain they had just been through. However, Finley had to admit that it still hurt – he hadn't even known what he had run into; the path had been clear moments ago.

"Well, well, well." A woman's voice tutted as she reached eye level with Finley, who still gripped Joseph's hand. "What do we have here?"

Finley stayed quiet as he looked at the woman's face. She was blonde, her hair cut into a short bob-like style, and she was smiling— but it was not a comforting smile. This was something out of a nightmare like all her birthdays had come at once. She was not to be trusted. The large 'H' on her chest told Finley everything he needed to know. He had run straight into Hunter, a hunter who hadn't been there seconds before.

Now that she had seen them, any chance or hope of escape was gone.

"Get off me," Finley shouted.

"Hurt... hurting arm," Joseph screamed as the woman gripped tighter than she had before. Fearing if she let go, they would be gone.

"The commission I'll get off of you two will be wonderful," the woman said, her voice grainy and not kind at all. She was smiling brighter now, but not to comfort the children; just thinking about the money she would get was bringing her joy. "Be thankful I don't kill you two now. Remember: The Hunter's Guild is merciful."

Being dragged towards where their home was, the sad pile of wood now just smoke and ash, Joseph and Finley came face to face with another hunter, a taller man – a scar covering the left side of his face and blood pouring from another, more minor cut that must have been made through sheer luck from someone in the town.

"What have you found there?" The man asked, his voice slightly dejected as he looked around at the carnage he and his team had created.

"I found two youngsters by the cornfields. They made a sizable distance trying to escape; must have been given the heads up by their parents or something." The woman spoke loudly, a sense of grandeur in her voice, like she was proud of her job. "Unlike everyone else here, though, they aren't giving much of a fight; they must understand what's at stake."

"Sarge isn't going to be happy about this; we got overwhelmed, " the man grunted. "We'll have to report this... failure."

"What would you have me do with these two?" The woman asked.

"Take them to Tildra; we need to question and process them. I'll report this to the Sarge and explain what happened here… with a bit of a white lie sprinkled in. Saves our necks." The man said, shaking his head as he let his colleague pass. As he passed the man, he heard something from his lips, confirming his suspicions. Everyone was gone. "Out of all these people… two boys. They shouldn't have fought back; all this blood was for nothing."

As they were dragged away, Finley placed his hand over Joseph's eyes to shield him from the carnage that was in front of them; blood covered the floor, flames and broken timber scattered out, and as he watched on, more and more Hunter's finished what they were doing: Hurting the people that he loved. Taking a deep breath as he looked around at the bodies that littered the grassland, Finley saw one, then ragged his head away moments later, knowing that who he had seen – the body that was on the floor at his feet now… was going to be burned into his memory for the rest of his life.

Finley knew his father's hand by the imprint on his fingers from removing the rings he had given to the boys. The words of the woman who had found the two boys in the fields swirled around his mind as Finley peered down at his father's body.

The Hunter's Guild was merciful…

ONE

Breathe.

Breathe.

Joseph needed to breathe.

Disillusioned and disorientated, Joseph pushed himself up from the depths of where the portal had dropped him; the darkness, in its inky black glory, was acting like a brick wall, stopping Joseph from moving quickly. The saltiness of the water surrounding him stung his eyes as his hands pulled him up. He wasn't deep in the ocean by any means, but the shock of the cold, the darkness and the lack of breath made a sickening cocktail for a nightmare.

Then his face crashed through the thick wall of water, and Joseph let out a long-awaited gasp as his lungs filled with what they needed. Crisp air had never felt so good. But as happy as Joseph was to be alive after escaping the dungeon… he found that he was now presented with another problem whilst bobbing in the vast open water.

He was all alone.

He held Alex's hand before they went through the portal together. Where was he now?

"Alex, Maura!" Joseph shouted into the open air, a mouthful of salt water landing into his mouth as he tried to keep his head above the water, being reminded of why he never got into the water in the first place. The waves were strong tonight, lapping at him and pushing Joseph further out into the water, away from where he had just crashed through. Joseph couldn't swim. He had never learned. He had never been allowed to.

No one replied, but maybe he needed to be louder. They couldn't be too far away if he had landed in one spot. "Maura, are you there!" Joseph called out into the deep, dark abyss. A sound could be heard a short distance away, like a scream of shock. "Alex, is that you?"

"It's me!" It sounded like Maura's voice. As she spoke, it sounded as if she had taken a large gulp of the seawater around her, coughing slightly before getting the strength to once again. "I'm over here; oh my god, where are we?"

The panic in her voice was evident, and Joseph understood it completely. He could hear her, but he couldn't see her. The waves falling and crashing into him were covering his vision too much. While he couldn't see Maura, he could *hear her and* use that to locate her.

Pushing himself through the water wouldn't be nearly as problematic if Joseph knew how to swim correctly. So, as he traversed the rough sea, he struggled as his hands dove into the water to propel him forward, his legs doing a little bit of the work, splashing the water over his head and around him like a dog trying to paddle in shallow water. "I'm... on my way, sort of." Gulp, the shock of the seawater as Joseph practically chugged it by the bucket load as he 'swam' was enough to make him retch. But he couldn't stop now.

"Are you okay?" Maura called; she sounded slightly closer, though stationary in her location.

"Yes!" Joseph called, sticking out his tongue in disgust but quickly retracting it, fearing the water could meet it again. "Keep talking so I know where you are, I can't see anything!"

"I'm over here! Over here!" Maura continued to shout over and over again into the open water. Her voice was getting tired and raspy, and it became apparent to Joseph that, since meeting in the dungeon, none of them had actually stopped to rest. They had always been doing something, always on the run from Caulan or Calvin. Turning the key, leaving the dungeon for dust. Honouring Henry's life. Henry, Joseph hadn't even correctly mourned him; he didn't have time. In his thinking, his daze, he kept pushing forward until.

Crash.

He and Maura collided in the dark. A slight screech of horror and relief came from Maura as she reached for him. "Maura?"

"Oh my god, Joseph, where are we?" Maura asked, her voice ridden with anxiety. She was asking a question, but not one that Joseph could answer, and she knew it.

It was still hard to see her in the dark. Joseph could see the outline of her once frizzy hair, which had long since become sodden with seawater. Her hair clumped down, resting on the water around her. Joseph could feel the strands sticking to him as he tried with all his might to catch his breath and position himself in the water so that he wouldn't sink.

"Have… you seen… Alex?" Joseph choked out, trying not to swallow more rancid salt water. "He was… holding my hand."

"No," Maura said as she began to cough up something fierce. It was clear that the salt water was making her stomach churn, much like Joseph's.

"Alex!" Joseph's voice was hoarse and deeper than usual. A guttural noise that he had never heard before escaped his lips as he tried with all his might to call out to the darkness. Joined by Maura this time, the two's voices echoed, bouncing off the water. "Alex, where are you?"

A cough. It was hardly audible, but it was there. It was like someone had just broken through the water and finally gotten their first breath but had somehow gotten some water lodged in their mouth before they did. The cough echoed out again; it sounded close. Then, a loud screech came—a deep voice, distinct, a confused screech.

"Joseph, Maura!" The voice broke the silence; it was Alex. There was no one else it could have been, but the voice confirmed it.

"We're here!" Joseph shouted, and for once, his hearing was clear; he could hear Alex gliding through the water to reach them, holding onto Maura; Joseph searched through the darkness to see the silhouette of Alex coming towards them. He was a much better swimmer than Joseph ever was.

"He tried to kill us!" Alex shouted as he reached the duo and quickly wrapped his arms around them. Keeping them both close. "That old man in the dungeon, he tried to off us!"

"He saved our lives." Maura rebutted. "He got us out of that cesspit. Probably giving his own life to get us here."

"Saving us? By dropping us here? In the middle of the ocean, there's no way out, nothing around us." Alex asked. He didn't raise his voice, but Joseph could tell he was worried—all of them were.

"He probably couldn't control his magic very well. It wouldn't be a unique situation; the guild didn't let people develop their talents." Joseph replied, snuffing the conversation out like a candle. "He did the best he could with the situation. Just like we will."

Joseph looked around himself. The only thing he could see was the occasional star hiding in the inky blackness of the sky above them. The moon was nowhere to be seen. This whole area was devoid of colour and life. Even he didn't feel alive right now. It was like he was living in a dream, but not a good one.

"There's nothing out there," Maura said, her voice low. It was pitch black, but it didn't mean *nothing was* out there. There had to be some life out there; he just hoped that whoever it might be – they would be friendly.

"I told you it was too good to be true." Alex's voice snapped Joseph back to the matter at hand. His hair covered most of his face, not that Joseph could see much of it, just a small hint of blue from his eyes reflecting off the water. "Basically, we were dead before we got here, and we're still dead now."

"There has to be a reason why we were dropped here. That man, Ol' Sampy, he might not have had control of his magic, but like me and the rest of the people trapped at the guild – we did have intent. I had intent when I would shift into different people; he must have intended to try and send us somewhere safer than that dungeon." Joseph explained as they stopped, feeling the water bob him up and down. The waves slowly crashed into the trio; he found breathing hard, but this time, not because of the water around him. It was like old air was struggling to remove itself from his lungs. His body became heavier in the water, like a stone ready to sink towards the bottom. He seized up, trying to be positive, but it hadn't worked. "There… there has to be something out here,… we just started. It's not fair for it all to end now."

"Well, hey, let's not panic more," Alex said, but Joseph still couldn't see Alex's face in the darkness; he couldn't see the man's expression – or what he was thinking. The words were not as reassuring as they should have been. Everyone was panicking, but Alex was a little better at hiding it. He hid most of his emotions, which were part of him after what happened with the guild training. Alex began to rub Joseph's shoulder, silently attempting to calm him down. "There might be-."

"What was that?" Maura interrupted, dragging the attention

back to her.

"What was what?" Joseph asked, finally catching his breath. The new air in his lungs was like gold dust.

In the dark, he could hardly make out Maura putting her finger to her lips. "I thought I heard something." The sloshing of the water was the only thing that Joseph could hear. The sudden calmness of the waves shocked him slightly as he settled into the water, Alex still having his arms wrapped around himself and Maura, keeping them close for dear life. "There, I did hear something!"

It sounded like a whisper at first—whimsical, magical—like the sound of a windchime or a gust of a morning breeze through an open window, both eerily quiet, just like this noise. It came in a burst, singular, unexpected in the vast open water. But it was there. Maura was right; she had heard something.

"I heard it," Alex said, a slight twinge of glee escaping his lips. "I'm not sure what it was, but it came from the east. I'm sure of it."

Another noise rang out, this time a lot closer – an actual whistle coming directly from Maura's lips. She placed her two fingertips by her lips and then blew. The echoing whistle invaded Joseph's ears and mind. Then she shouted out, almost screaming. Hoping and wish for a response. Right now, it didn't even matter from who. "If anyone is there, please make a sound again!"

Chime.

Whatever it was had to be moving at top speed. It sounded much closer than the first chime from their mysterious visitor on the sea.

"See, I told you!" Joseph said, letting out a large sigh of relief. The old man did have intent. He did send us somewhere safe; the safety just hadn't reached us yet."

Further noises, larger and drawn-out chimes, rang out into the inky darkness. Joseph still couldn't see what was making them, but they were soon replaced by Alex and Maura's shouting, guiding them closer.

"We're over here!" Maura called. A small light began to glide over the water close by. A dark mass was moving forward now, camouflaged, but still, the light got closer, darting right and left forward until it reached Maura's face. Joseph squinted at the brightness of the light. It was like nothing he had ever seen before. There was no candle or oil to make this light; it was white, stark white.

"We've got you!" It was other people. For a moment, Joseph couldn't hear or see anyone. He thought that, once again, they were alone with just the light on their faces, but as the voice cut through, the wash of hope came back.

It was a ship, and it was a beauty at that. Even though it was dark, as it got closer, Joseph could see that it was made of wood, not unlike the ships that frequented Freydale. By the light shining down on him, he could just make out some writing—the ship's name.

Loreli's Wave. A strange name for a ship.

"It's a ship, it's a ship!" Maura shouted in excitement. She then began to swim, slowly at first. Then, as something was dropped into the water—like some sort of swing—she got faster, gripping hold of the rope and pulling herself onto the wooden beam.

"We've got you. Be careful of your legs!" a voice from on top of the ship called out, and with that, Maura was ripped from the water and up into the air. The light still shining into the open water blinded both Alex and Joseph from seeing where she had gone.

"Maura!" Alex called out; as the second passed, Joseph and Alex waited for an answer. "Are you okay?"

"I'm fine!" Maura shouted back, though they could not see her. There is a metal swing that will come down in a second. They'll bring you up onto the ship."

A splash came a second later as the wood collided with the water below them. Joseph and Alex hesitated momentarily, bobbing in the water as the swing floated there, waiting for one of them to take it.

"After you," Alex murmured. Though it wasn't courtesy, it was nervousness.

Joseph pushed himself forward. His legs were tired, but he knew that he had to make it to the swing. This was the salvation they had been waiting for. He grabbed it, feeling a little bit of resistance on the other side as the light shone down on them—as if it was keeping an eye on the two.

"It can hold both of you!" a male voice shouted out as Alex floated by himself in the water, waiting his turn. Joseph felt Alex move quickly towards him, the water sloshing around, covering his back slightly. Gripping onto the rope, Joseph felt Alex's hand steadying him as he grabbed the bottom of the wood with his hands and legs. "Hold on, going up!"

All the water that had stuck to their clothes and bodies suddenly dropped as they were pulled out of the water into the open air. Joseph had never felt anything like it; it made his stomach roll. The metal wasn't entirely stable on the rope; it was mainly just used as a landing platform. As they found the contraption was moving forward, Joseph was glad Alex was steadying him now.

"Woah," Joseph murmured, his movements almost making him hurl. His legs dangled off the side of the contraption; he couldn't see anything underneath him yet.

"We've got you." Suddenly, two pairs of hands gripped over his, pulling the contraption and rope towards them. Quickly, the contraption was removed from their grips, blankets were thrown over them, and Joseph found his feet firmly on the ship, all in one moment. "Stand over there; yer friend wants to get off the pulley."

Joseph moved, turning his head to look in Alex's direction; he looked down at the small drop from the contraption to the ship's floor. One of the men Joseph hadn't even gotten to see yet offered his hand for Alex to take.

"I'm fine," Alex said, hovering over the ship. It was a slight drop, but Alex would need some help, even if he was as tall as he was. Again, one of their saviours, a woman, offered her hand this time. "I said I'm fine."

"Well, each to their own." Their saviour grumbled as Alex jumped from the swing to the floor below, landing with his boots and making a sizable boom when he hit it. Seconds later, Alex joined Maura and Joseph to the side, a blanket wrapped around his body too – it was a cold night, but the water was much colder.

"Are you okay?" Alex asked, his teeth chattering now that he was out of the water. The air wasn't warm by any means, but the blanket did help. Neither looked at him, almost as if Joseph and Maura were in shock like the cold was dragging out all sense of self. "Maura?"

"Hm?" she asked, moving some of her hair out of her face. It stuck to her like it had in the water, the curls now almost non-existent. "Yeah, I'm okay, just a bit cold."

"And you?" Alex turned to Joseph. In the light of the ship, he could finally see Alex's face. It was soaked, beads of water dripping down from his short blonde hair. He pulled his shaking hands from the blanket and moved a piece of hair from Joseph's face.

"I've been better," Joseph said, finding himself shivering too.

"What in the world were you three doing out there?" one of the women on the ship asked. She came into view, her short black hair coming down to her chin in a kind of bob. She smiled warmly, though behind the smile and her eyes was utter confusion. "It seems like a bad night for a swim. We're far from any distinct land masses, too."

Before any of them could reply, a large boom of a door opening and slamming against the side of a wall sounded throughout the open area.

"What is all this ruckus?" The person who had just entered the conversation asked. Joseph felt as if he had heard the voice before, though he wasn't sure without seeing the man's face. It wasn't so much the tone of voice but the accent. "I just had one of the men come into my office to say that we had three people in the water below us?"

"Yes, sir." The woman pointed at Joseph, Alex and Maura. The blankets covered most of their faces to keep the cold off them.

The man's heavy boots came closer and closer until he was facing the three. He stood with his own sizeable blanket, his breath turning to mist in the dark. With him was another somewhat young man.

Joseph didn't recognise the man who had spoken, but he did recognise the younger man. Standing right in front of Joseph and his team on a ship miles away from where they last met was Pierce, the 8th Duke of Rivetia—the very man who had commissioned a job from him not too long ago.

The Rivetia Pendant. And by Pierce's clothes, this wasn't just any old ship that had saved their lives.

No. It was a pirate ship.

Tension. You could cut it with a knife.

"You know not to let anyone on or off this ship without my say-so, Cressida." The older man, who Joseph assumed was the captain, spoke loudly. Cressida stood to the side, slightly shying away, sheepish.

"They were bobbing in the water, sir; we couldn't just leave them." Cressida rebutted quietly; her voice was soft. "I'm sorry."

"Let's get a good look at them then." Pierce then spoke up, the knife having been removed from the cutting board – the tension all but lifted with just a few words. He yawned, though he tried to hide it. Clearly, having been asleep before he was woken up. "After that, they can get back into the water. If they were floating around in there, they wouldn't have much issue with doing it again."

Pierce then grabbed for the closest blanket that he could and ragged it off Alex, almost pulling at some of his hair as he did so. Pierce stood back, shining the lamp he held in his arms at Alex's face, admiring the man before nodding and going towards the following person: Maura.

Holding up an oil lamp towards Maura's face – she winced slightly before Pierce grabbed her face and pulled it back. "It hurts my eyes in the dark."

"It's just for a second. Just to check who you are." Pierce said, sounding a little annoyed in tone. A complete contrast to the person who Joseph had met in the tavern a while back.

"But what are you looking for?" Maura said in retaliation.

"No speaking." Santos scolded as Pierce ragged down her makeshift hood as well. The water from Maura's hair pooled on the floor and covered his hands.

Joseph wasn't sure what Pierce was looking for as he flashed the light in her eyes. Pierce stopped, shook his head, and then sidestepped to stand in front of Joseph. As Pierce got closer, he was inspecting who was in front of him. Through the blanket and the light that was still shining on his face, Joseph couldn't see much, but then, as quickly as it had appeared, the light disappeared.

He didn't feel his hood being ragged down, either.

"I know you," Pierce said as he pointed towards Joseph. He inspected Joseph's face closer, then from further away, then the light appeared again, but when Joseph finally saw Pierce's face, it was full of smiles. "Joseph Price, as I live and breathe! It's me, Pierce, from the tavern!"

"You know this man, Joseph?" Alex questioned, still clutching the blanket and the part of his hair that Pierce had touched when he took off the blanket from around his head.

"I... got the pendant for you," Joseph recalled, and Pierce nodded.

"That you did," Pierce said as he snapped his fingers, commanding everyone around him to look in his direction. "This here is Joseph Price. He is a friend of mine. He is a guest here and will be treated as such by everyone on board. Be kind."

"What about my friends?" Joseph asked as Pierce looked back at the two other people who stood by Joseph's side. "Do they get the same treatment, too?"

"I suppose," Pierce said as he flicked his hand, giving minimal regard for the other two. The truth was that Joseph could tell the type of person Pierce was when he first met him in the tavern. Someone who would only give you the time of day if you did something for him. And Joseph had. Maura and Alex... hadn't. "Do you understand me?"

"Yes sir-." The crew shouted out quickly. It was a tight ship and a tighter captain duo.

"I hope you are not giving these people, whoever they are, safe passage on my ship without my say-so, son." Joseph had almost forgotten that someone else had entered the conversation with Pierce, and it was evident by the expression on his face that Pierce had forgotten, too. "Because I want to remind you that I am the ship's captain, not you. I do not allow stowaways of guests, not when we have such a large mission at hand."

"You'll want these ones," Pierce replied as Santos stood, puffing his chest – in the dark, he seemed a lot bigger than he actually was, but he was hardened by the years on the sea. "Please, trust me."

Santos didn't give any indication that he didn't trust his son. He walked, a slight limp – but not enough to need a crutch as he towered over Joseph, looking down at the boy with confusion. "What's so special about this one? I heard the boy mention the pendant. The pendant that only we were supposed to be aware of. How does he know, Pierce?"

"I might have told you a little white lie when I said I'd gotten the pendant alone. Whilst I was in Freydale at the port, you and this lot were drinking… I might have commissioned Joseph here to collect it for me."

"He has magic?" Pierce's father pointed towards Joseph, looking him up and down, but not with the same hatred that those in Freydale did, not even with hatred, just confusion. "Is he a servant?"

Pierce nodded. "Aye, but he is why we are on this ship now. So, if you throw him and his… group, whoever they might be, off this ship, you're going to…"

"I'm what, Pierce?" His father stood over him, Pierce not looking back, hiding his face. "Going to hurt their little feelings, going to squander this mission? Tell me what I am going to do! As far as I see, I asked you to get the pendant alone, and you failed me. I expect that if he has magic and is away from the kingdom of his 'ownership,' we will have some problems already. Didn't think of that, did you?"

"I'm not tied to any kingdoms, sir. Not anymore." Joseph replied, looking at Pierce's father in the face. Determined to make the man understand their predicament, he really didn't want to get back in the ocean. "I'm not afraid of hard work if it means getting away from Freydale – I'll do anything to stay on this ship. I'd rather not get back into the water if it's all the same to you. We'll do whatever you need to do, clean, cook, just…"

"We have no room. No beds." Santos began. "And no food to spare you."

"Actually Santos, sir. We have a free room; Bernard was dropped off in Freydale; he didn't return to the ship." Cressida butted in but quickly shied away when Santos looked at her.

"One room. There are three stowaways." Santos replied, smiling – he had won again.

"I have a whole room to myself. I'd be happy to give it up." Pierce replied, knowing his father couldn't deny him that. "I mostly sleep in my office now anyway."

"That still leaves one room," Santos replied.

"I'd be happy to share, sir," Alex replied loudly. I'm sure we all would. Maura can take the spare bunk; I can share it with Joseph. Or vice versa."

"There is still no food." Santos shook his head.

"I have a small stomach." Joseph smiled; this was a fight that he would win.

"It's not the cushy life you're used to." Santos was now pulling at straws. He wasn't going to win this fight. Joseph had too much practice annoying people in authority, and it was his only saving grace to make it through all those years at the guild. If he couldn't annoy

Alex, Caulan, or any of the other Hunters, what else did he have?

"What cushy life?" Joseph shrugged. "I've slept on the floor, slept in the streets, I've been beaten, bruised and forced to do things so dangerous that you wouldn't even have a dream about."

"Well…" Santos knew that he wasn't going to win this fight." The work here is hard…"

"Please, I was a servant for the Hunter's Guild for fifteen years; you don't know hard work!" Joseph was enjoying this too much.

Santos wrinkled his nose, sighing. "You don't like authority, do you?"

"Tell me about it," Alex grumbled to the side of him. But Santos didn't take the bait, keeping his eyes on Joseph. Annoyed.

"Listen, Joseph. You need to understand that I run this ship, and I say you can stay." Santos said, but before Joseph could even say anything that sounded like a 'thank you,' he continued. "I don't like noise, I don't like waves, people who question my authority, and if you're on my ship, on this journey with us, then you do as I say. You will mop the floors, you will clean, you will scrub the barnacles off the side of the ship if I deem it fit. But the moment you or your little friends mess up…"

Pierce slowly leaned into his father, but Joseph could hear what they were saying. "Dad, remember he is the reason we are here in the first place if it wasn't for Joseph. None of this would be possible." Pierce interrupted, and even though he had the authority, Santos just nodded – understanding.

"That may be so, Pierce, but-." Santos again leaned into Joseph, the man's beard tickling his ear. "My words still stand; you make any waves or noise. You'll be off this ship quick, and it doesn't matter to me if we're nowhere by land or if it's dark. You annoy me, make noise, distract us from our mission, and I will do what is necessary. Do I make myself clear, Joseph Price?"

"Yes, sir." Joseph nodded.

"Good, I'm glad we understand each other at last," Santos said as he turned around and looked his son in the face. It was clear that everyone here feared Santos; whether that was a good thing, or a bad thing was yet to be determined. Pierce, show them to their rooms. They are your responsibility. I'm going back to bed."

Santos was undoubtedly charming. But the one good thing about this ship, and the fact that they were found by none other than Pierce, was that the boat wasn't going back to Freydale – the crew had no interest in dropping the escaped trio back there. And one other thing – their destination perfectly aligned with where they needed to go next on their journey to find the following key:

"Lift the ladder, Cressida," Pierce said before he opened a large wooden door leading inside the ship. Before turning towards the trio to his right. "Next stop Rivetia."

Pierce's office, stationed at the bow of the ship, was a large but cramped area, oil lamps strewn around the room, lighting it up as much as they could on the rather dark night. Papers strewn all over the room told Joseph all he needed to know – Pierce was a busy man, and if his father was anything to go by, he understood why.

Pierce stood at the front of the room by a large desk and turned to look at the three people who had just entered his domain with complete confusion on his face.

"So, what were you three doing in the water?" Pierce asked as he crossed his arms and looked directly at Joseph. It was more of a question for him rather than Alex or Maura. "Do I have to worry about people following us? You were a servant the last time I saw you. A contract servant at that, too."

"It's a long story," Joseph said; Pierce simply raised his eyebrows and leaned back into the desk.

"I have time," Pierce replied. "Do tell me how you managed to escape. You must understand that despite being in my high graces, I don't want my family and crew to be in danger by you being on the ship. My dad wouldn't let it go if I didn't ask my questions."

"I understand. I managed to escape after we used one of the keys connected to the magic beacons around the realm. We discovered that the lack of magic in the world is starting to cause the world to decay; everything in this decay's path dies, and the beacons are attaching those without magic." Joseph explained that Pierce's eyes didn't display emotion; it was hard to read him, and maybe he was just trying to listen. "Magic hasn't been present in that side of the world for fifty years; when we turned the key, it was like a complete reset; the people in the comas all woke up. A helpful old man managed to create a portal for us – sending us where you found us."

"I'm not following." Pierce began trying to understand to the best of his ability, but Joseph could see it on his face now; it was overwhelming. "Dumb it down for me. I'm not the brightest."

"What Joseph is trying to say is…" Maura piped up, and instantly, Pierce turned his head towards her. Even though she wasn't from this world, she was brilliant and seemed to have picked up a lot already. "He managed to turn one of the keys and return magic to a kingdom called Freydale and some other places, too. We are now on a journey to return magic to the whole world before this decay he mentioned destroys everything and everyone."

"Maura, right?" Pierce pointed to her, earning a slight nod from the girl still wrapped in the blanket. "How do you plan to return magic to the rest of the world?"

"There are more beacons. More keys. We plan to locate them all and use the keys to unlock magic from all the beacons. There are four in total, we believe; one is already unlocked. We just need to locate the other three." Alex piped up when it came to the beacons and the keys; he was probably the most knowledgeable. "We read in a book we found that there was a key in a kingdom called Rivetia. That is where we are going on this ship, correct?"

"Correct," Pierce said as he pushed himself off the desk before zoning in on Alex's face. "I recognise you. What is your name?"

"Alexander Von Loch." Alex replied quietly.

"Yes, I remember you. You were at the tavern to the night Joseph got the pendant for me, causing a right stink about him leaving your guild, didn't you?" Pierce said, his voice laced with a discontent that wasn't present with the other two.

"I-," Alex replied, but Pierce just held up his hand so he could stop.

"You are a Hunter. A general. You hurt countless people, him included." You could have cut the tension with a knife once more. Pierce pointed towards Joseph but kept his eyes square on Alex. "If I found out that you have hurt him, either now or ever again, from this point forward, there will be hell to pay."

"I defected. The Hunter's Guild is not my home anymore." Alex replied; his voice was low, eyes cast down to the wooden floor below him. "I've left the guild. I will make up for what I did for the rest of my life. But I want to help. I want to prove that I can be a better person."

"My point still stands," Pierce said as he grabbed a small knife in his pocket and pointed it towards Alex. "I promised once that I would pay Joseph back one day. I would not hesitate to do some damage control if it suited me. Do we understand each other, Alexander Von Loch?”

“Yes.” Nodding, Alex replied, but he didn’t raise his eyes off the floor.

“Good answer,” Pierce said, still firm, but he removed the knife from the situation, slinking it into his pocket, blade side down. “So, after a short deliberation, I will help you three.”

“Help us?” Joseph asked.

“I said I’d find some way of paying you back one day; that day has come sooner than we both thought. Maybe this can be the payment, helping you save this world.” Pierce said, folding his arms again. “You said it yourself. There is decay following us, and it sounds like you’ll need all the help you can get yourselves.”

“Well… thank you and all for the offer, but we have enough problems without adding you to the mix. We can barely care for three of us, let alone four.” Alex said, but Pierce just let out a short exhale in reply. A grunt almost.

“It’s not like I was asking. I’m helping whether you like it or not, Hunter General.” Pierce said, finally looking over at Alex. It was clear that this man was not going to let it go. He was helping, but Joseph couldn’t even say no. “Now that the questioning is all cleared up and I’m satisfied, I’ll show you where you three will sleep. I’m sure you’re tired. I certainly am. Come on.”

T W O

One singular bed.

"It's not much, but it's home." Pierce said as he barged through the small opening towards the 'bedroom' – a bed, a small window to the outside, and a pot on a stool with a rather sad-looking plant that had seen better days sat at the edge of the room. "Now, Maura has taken the other room, so this is your place for the duration of the trip. However long that might be."

"There is only… one bed," Alex said as he pointed towards the four-poster bed in the corner of the room. A small candle at the edge flickered, but it was barely giving off much light in the dingy room.

"Yeah, sorry about that. You'll have to sleep in shifts; you take the floor, or you both sleep together; it's up to you two." Pierce said as he patted Alex on the shoulder; it was clear that Pierce was enjoying teasing Alex. Joseph was glad he didn't have to sleep with the fish tonight. "A word of advice or a warning. Don't sleep too late; my father is there for punctuality. He wants you three bright-eyed and bushy-tailed for work of his choosing tomorrow. You'll need to work for your meals and bed and make our time worth it. Sleep tight."

Once Pierce had left, Alex dropped the damp blanket to the side and let out a large sigh. "I don't think he likes me very much."

"Really? I wouldn't have guessed." Joseph said as he chuckled to himself. "He told you off like you were some pestilent child."

"I can't believe he pointed a knife at me." Alex let out a further breathy sigh, a small laugh escaping. You, however, have some leverage here. He said you were in his good graces; you could use that to our advantage."

"With Pierce, maybe. But his dad?" Joseph replied. Alex simply shrugged. "If he had a knife when I challenged him with all the 'issues' I'd face on the ship. He would have pointed it at me, too."

"Getting along with authority figures isn't your strong suit. I don't blame you with the people in those positions you've actually had. My father, that baron that took you for that year, me." Alex replied as he moved the pot with the plant and sat down on the stool to rest his legs. "I know I'm the last person you might want to speak about things with, but I wanted to check in with you. How are you feeling? We've barely had a chance to sit down in days."

"I'm fine," Joseph replied, but Alex tilted his head. An action he used to do when they were younger when he knew that Joseph wasn't his usual self. "I'm annoyed. Annoyed that we don't have the book anymore, I'm annoyed that we now don't have any way of knowing where the key might be. I'm disoriented and tired, and I'd really like to sleep in a normal bed for once."

"Lucky for you that we found this place then," Alex said as he looked around the small room. And we're on our way to Rivetia. We'll find the key, even if it is hard to locate. We're one step further than Calvin ever was, and neither of them knows we are on this ship."

"Do you really think Calvin is still hellbent on following us?" Joseph asked; the notion made his skin crawl.

"I wouldn't put it past him. Calvin was always… determined to finish a job when he started it. I feel like the plan to hurt the princess was pre-meditated. He knew he had magic; maybe this was all just some sort of sick, twisted plan his mind concocted up." Alex said. Though he knew precisely who Calvin was, it was clear that losing his friend hurt the man deeply. Joseph could see it in his face. "Why would he join the Hunter's Guild if he had magic? Surely that defeats the purpose of being a hunter in the first place?"

"Maybe he thought he could hide it better, know your enemy," Joseph replied, and with Alex's nod, he knew he was right. "Learn how to act around those you're trying to conceal a secret from. Calvin did say he had hidden it for years; I guess he hid it too far down that he began to believe he had nothing to hide… well, until the outburst at that party. The princess stole from me. Calvin hated me; I don't know why he would defend me that way."

"Indirectly, maybe, he said he was stolen from himself. Maybe seeing someone else get scorned, even if it was you… awakened something inside of him. An anger he couldn't shake." Alex mumbled, looking down at the floor this time. "Pain makes people do things they didn't even know they could. Trust me, I know more than some."

"You're working on it, though," Joseph said as he sat down on the left side of the bed.

"Finding these keys and helping solve the mystery of why the world is slowly destroying itself will help me focus on myself, channel my anger, and make the wrongs right again," Alex said as he interlocked his hands but didn't look up from the floor.

"What wrongs?" Joseph asked, not because he didn't think Alex had things to atone for; it was just which ones.

"What I did to you," Alex said. "I was supposed to be your friend. I was supposed to get you out of that horrible place; we were supposed to escape together. To have a life free of Freydale, my father, the guild, and anyone who ever hurt you."

"Alex…" Joseph said quietly before he watched Alex stand up, beginning to pace slightly. "We both know what happened at the training camp. You were tortured. What could you have done?"

"To protect you better? To fight against what I had been forced to believe? To be stronger?" Alex replied, his voice becoming lighter, not louder, but Joseph could tell that the man was getting upset with himself. Like sitting down, reflecting brought it all back. I was supposed to protect you until my last breath; I failed in that task."

"Come on, Alex, that was in the past," Joseph replied, his voice but a whisper. He needed to find out how thick these walls were; he didn't want anyone else to hear this conversation. "You're different than you were in that last year; just being here now on this ship shows me you're capable of the change you want."

"Maybe…" Alex replied before he stood up from the bed quickly and began to collect the two blankets that he and Joseph had dropped and lay them out on the floor to make a makeshift bed for himself. "I'll-."

"What are you doing?" Joseph asked as he began to get into the bed.

Alex looked confused as he fluffed up the blankets – they were still damp. "Making a bed for myself so you can sleep in that one."

"Why don't we just share?" Joseph said as he looked at the bed – it was the size of a double bed, and then some three people could have probably slept there with no problem at all. "The bed is big enough for the both of us,"

"Won't it be a bit weird?" Alex said – laughing to himself a little, a nervous laugh. "I mean for you…"

"Look, it will only be weird if you make it weird. Sharing rooms with people at the guild makes you a little numb to it all." Joseph shrugged. "We're only sleeping, and if we are doing the same work tomorrow, which I assume we will be, doesn't it make sense if we both get a good night's rest in an actual bed instead of sleeping on the hardwood floor with a couple of damp blankets?"

"I suppose that makes sense, yeah." Alex nodded. As he removed his jacket, the blood-soaked vest was the first thing that Joseph saw. It was old blood, certainly not new, from where the sword had pierced his abdomen almost over a day ago. Quickly pulling off the vest, he laid it out over the stool that his body had just left before he turned around – realising what he had just done. "Oh. Sorry, force of habit."

"It's fine," Joseph said, trying to divert his gaze and managing to look at the sheets that were looking very inviting right now.

"I hope you don't mind," Alex said as he stood, still turned around, facing the wall. "I'd rather not spend the night in a blood-soaked vest. I've already spent more time in it than I would like."

"You don't need to be worried; I've seen worse…" Joseph said before he looked up to meet Alex's face as the man turned around. His face got hot suddenly; maybe it had been the candle by the bed. "I mean, I've been in worse situations."

Watching as Alex sauntered towards the bed slowly but quickly, diving into the bed and wrapping the covers around him. The duvet provided almost smothered Joseph in warmth; he knew this would be the best sleep ever. An actual bed.

"I can't wait to sleep," Joseph said as Alex got closer to him by the second, the hair on his bare arms touching his own. "You're frozen."

"You're like a natural heater; you're so warm," Alex said, but he wasn't complaining. "Listen, I know it's probably not the best time to bring it up. But I heard you in the dungeon. What happened between you and your father before we attempted to escape?"

"I don't know why I did it. Dad caught me rummaging through his money, well, your money. I resisted telling him at first, but he was persistent. He made me recount every plan I had about running away, what I would do with the money, where I would take you. Then he asked me a question. A question I couldn't lie about." Alex said, gripping the covers; the thought of being transported back to that moment made his skin crawl, the coldness of his skin suddenly becoming warmer as his mind raced.

"What was it?" Joseph asked.

"He asked me if the rumours were true about our friendship," Alex replied. "I said they were. He beat me to a pulp, a few blows to the face, and then bundled me into a carriage and sent me to the training centre. They conditioned me to believe you were the enemy until I believed it. They wanted to go a step further, to make me feel it too, to make me associate you with pain... they would have to unless I had lied to their faces."

"Lied to them?" Joseph began, but Alex interrupted him to continue.

"Every morning, they would ask me if you were my enemy. I used to say no. Then, one morning, after a brain-scrambling evening, I woke up, and I just could not take another beating; I told them what they wanted to hear. I was defeated, broken down. They stopped the conditioning there and then. I lasted almost an entire five months." Alex recounted. "I didn't think of you as my enemy; I just wanted to make it seem like I had joined them. It wasn't until you began to treat me differently when we both returned to the guild that I... suppose I did fall into their trap. I became bitter at the thought that we had lost each other. And we did."

"I'd like to mend what we have now, whatever this is. You said it yourself: Your father can't control you anymore. Without his influence... you can just be Alex," Joseph said with a smile.

"I don't know who Alex is anymore," Alex said, shaking his head.

"Anything you want to be. Absolutely anything." Joseph said, putting it plainly. "Yeah?"

"I'd like that," Alex replied, forcing a smile, his pearly white teeth shining in the dark. Then he blinked and looked as if he was ready to change the subject altogether. Being vulnerable was not something Alex had the privilege to be in his line of work. "You're sure you don't mind us sharing?"

"No, not at all." Joseph shook his head. "Do you?"

Alex shook his head.

Joseph continued, trying to calm Alex or at least get the point across. "Like I said, it's of no bother to me. I wouldn't have suggested we share if it was. Just don't wake up hugging me for warmth, okay?"

It was a joke. Joseph hoped Alex knew that, but in the dark – Joseph couldn't really check his face. But Alex began to chuckle seconds later before countering with his own quip, laughing as he said it. "I'd be tempted by how cold I am, but that *would* make it weird."

"Trust me." Joseph began, letting himself get comfortable with Alex being this close. "I've seen worse at the guild."

"I bet; well, good night, Joey," Alex said before his eyes grew wide in the dark, the whites of his blue eyes being the only visible thing Joseph could see. "I'm sorry, I know you don't like that nickname by people who aren't family."

"It's-." Joseph began, but in a panicked state, Alex continued, sitting up slightly – letting in some of the cold.

"I mean, we're not family, just friends, kind of friends, I want to be… friends, yeah." Alex chuckled nervously before quickly turning on his side, his eyes closed – but keeping as close as he could possibly be to Joseph for his 'natural warmth'. "Okay. Good night."

"Yeah." This time, when Alex said the nickname, Joseph felt different; he really didn't mind. "Good night, Alex."

"I woke up this morning to you hugging me for warmth!" Joseph shouted as he, Alex, and Maura stood on the main deck of the ship.

The sun was out today, and it was as beautiful as it was hot. The ship looked a whole lot different in the light. Rust covered most of the side of the outer shell; it looked old—very old. The open sea was vast, seemingly never-ending. Miles and miles… it really put into perspective how in danger they had been last night. If Pierce and his crew had not stopped when they did… well, Joseph didn't like to think about it.

Maura was the first to speak, trying to hide her amusement. "You two shared a bed then?"

"The bed was big enough," Joseph said as he looked over to Alex as the trio looked over the open water. "Or so I thought."

"I'm sorry!" Alex exclaimed, though he was laughing at the same time. "You were so warm; I couldn't help myself, I woke up earlier in the night, and you had your head on my shoulder."

"I have no idea what you're talking about. I don't move in my sleep," Joseph said, knowing it sounded farfetched. Alex began to laugh. "You're getting a kick out of this."

Alex's smirk grew larger before he continued to tease Joseph. "I only wrapped my arms around you after you did that to keep you close to me; that warmth would have gone to waste otherwise."

"That definitely is a point to Alex, not that I'm keeping a tally or anything," Maura said; she was enjoying this a little too much, giggling to herself as she listened in. She kept her vision on the ocean; her dark brown eyes and light copper-brown skin shimmered in the sunlight. Away from Freydale, she seemed happier, even if she was far from home. This ship was good for her despite the harsh start and prospect of more complex work. This was suitable for all of them. "I ship you two together."

"We're on a ship… yes," Joseph said, confused. Maybe this was another language barrier between people from their realm and Maura's.

"No. No. It's a saying. When you…" Maura said before looking at the two of them, before realising that they probably wouldn't understand anyway, even if she explained it. "You know what, I'll just say it's cute."

"I can always swap with Maura if it's going to be that much of an issue with you, Joseph?" Alex asked softly. "In all seriousness, I don't want to make you uncomfortable. Even if you looked very comfortable this morning…"

"No. I'm fine with sharing the bed with you." Joseph sighed. "I meant what I said yesterday; it's better if we both utilise the bed. And I don't feel uncomfortable; when I woke up, I found your shoulder *was indeed* very comfortable… best night's sleep I've had in a while."

"I guess it's not all that bad then." Alex was now chuckling with Maura. "I won't do it again… unless you want me to."

"Don't tease him." Maura scolded but started laughing seconds later, again finding it too funny not to. Joseph rolled his eyes at Alex's words. Maura began to howl with laughter, and Joseph wasn't sure what was so funny, but whatever it was had really tickled her. "Look at his little face."

"Attention!" A voice broke the trio up. Joseph looked up at who shouted; Santos and Pierce stood close by. Santos cleared his throat, looking directly at Joseph as he spoke. "If you're not busy 'chit-chatting', – I have a few jobs for you today; as I said yesterday, you three need to pay your way here until we dock at the port of Rivetia, whenever that is. If you wish to stay here and take up the much too valuable space that we have here, then…"

Santos passed some parchment around to both Maura and Alex, who quickly scanned it. Based on their reactions alone, whatever jobs they had been assigned were not good.

"Cleaner?" Maura asked disappointment in her voice. "With these hands? I've had crystals and diamonds on these hands; they're not for cleaning."

"Is there a problem?" Santos asked, though if there was, he wasn't going to be accommodating about it.

"What exactly am I cleaning?" Maura asked, her disdain for this work shining through now. She held her hand on her hip and looked at Santos almost disapprovingly.

"The ship. Mop, polish, scrub. We all have to do it once, so it's best to get it out of the way quickly." Pierce replied with a short smile, though he knew that Maura did not see it as 'quick' work – the ship was massive, and there was no way she would do this all by herself. "Whatever you can't clean, you must report to me tonight."

"I'm a celebrity; I have my own cleaners. I don't do it myself." Maura replied, but then a look of confusion dawned on her as if she had finally realised she couldn't use that as leverage. She wasn't a celebrity in this realm, and Santos wouldn't care even if she was.

"Whatever you were before this ship, throw it out. As of right now, you are part of my crew, and what I say goes." Santos said in a very unfavourable, gruff, and standoffish tone. He gave them all a glare—he wasn't just talking to Maura; he was talking to the group as a whole. "Got it?"

"Why exactly am I being put on... barnacle duty?" Alex groaned as he looked over the edge of the ship. It was pretty self-explanatory what Alex was to be up to today: scrub, scrape, push, and pull. "Don't tell me I've got to get rid of all of them?"

"Yes. You're strong. You need strong arms for that work." Pierce smirked, once again proving to everyone around him that he didn't care for Alex much. "Be careful of the smell, though. It sticks to you."

"Throw me back into the water," Alex grumbled quietly.

"What was that?" Pierce put his hand to his ear. "I thought I heard you speak."

"No." Alex lifted his head, dejected, then smiled a toothy grin; sarcasm laced his lips. You must be hearing things. It pays to clean out your ears once in a while. A buildup of earwax can be a horrible affliction."

"Just get to work!" Santos interrupted, shouting at the top of his lungs, stopping Alex and Maura's complaining immediately. "Anyone else with a problem with their work for the day can come and speak to me, and then you can go in the water!"

Santos had begun to walk away when Joseph finally piped up. Alex and Maura had already scattered to their respective stations, scared out of their wits about what the man might do. "Um, actually."

"What now?" Santos turned on his heel and met Joseph's face with a rather unsavoury expression.

"I have no job. What am I doing?" Joseph replied.

"Pierce, I've changed my mind after all," Santos said flippantly before turning to Joseph, the boy not sure what the older man was talking about. Pierce only nodded as Santos continued. "Go over it with him."

"Yes, sir." Pierce agreed before grabbing Joseph's arm, not hard, but enough to drag him away.

"Ah, ah. Hang on." Santos said in their direction. "Before you do, a warning, Joseph. Tell anyone what you see here, and I will kill you."

"Come this way," Pierce said, letting Joseph pass him. The man was practically herding him towards the office they had been in the night before.

Pierce brought it forward, holding what he had found. Joseph recognised it almost instantly, though not in the setting it had been when he received it; the bright blue gem shone back at him in the light room.

"Is that the pendant?" Joseph asked as Pierce quickly passed the gem over. "But I've already seen this; why is your father so bothered if I lay my eyes on the pendant?"

Pierce held something else in his hand – in a small vial, a bright blue liquid, the same colour as the encased pendant. "It was actually this that I wanted to show you. Though it does extraordinarily connect to the pendant."

Joseph admired the vial in Pierce's hand—it was the brightest blue he had ever seen, like the colour of the sky and the sea all rolled into one like every hue of blue was trapped inside that bottle.

"What is it?" Joseph asked, enamoured, almost having to stop himself from reaching out to touch it.

"It's called Cerulean's Tears; that's what the old people of Rivetia used to call it. A type of magic used as a lifeblood for the people of Rivetia years back, it covers the entire pendant and the stuff. The tears also keep Rivetia cloaked, as it were." Pierce explained as he, too, looked intently at the pendant in his hand. "The magic is strong, and we think it pre-dates the beacons, which may be why it wasn't affected by the breakdown of magic fifty years back."

"It's beautiful," Joseph replied, unsure why Pierce showed it to him. "When you say lifeblood, what do you mean by that?"

"It helped move the kingdom to bigger and better things, helped it develop," Pierce explained. "Where places like Freydale and Tildra have stayed static, unchanged for hundreds of years, Rivetia flourished with the help of this lovely little liquid." Joseph turned around as the heavy boots that Santos was wearing came up towards him.

"Well, what was it used for?" Joseph asked. Neither could answer; he didn't have a preference; he just wanted to understand.

"It was used for many different things, make plants larger, bring more fruit and vegetation to the kingdom, was used as a natural healer, and sometimes, could extend life to those who it deemed worthy, keeping people alive for decades, even a century over their original lifespan. But overall, it was a weapon." Santos relayed back the information he knew. "A small amount goes a long way, let's just say. Cerulean's tears are in their basic state, just water with amazing properties. Still, given the right intervention, it is the most powerful weapon that the world has ever seen."

"I don't follow," Joseph said as he looked down at the pendant; the bright blue was enchanting. "What does the pendant have to do with this?"

"The water can be made solid. Like that pendant, for instance. Imagine swords, knives, battle gear, spears, large barricades to stop enemy troops from getting in", Santos said, with a sense of pride in his voice as he spoke. "Cerulean tears can be moulded in any different way a person can think of."

"I suppose kind of like you," Pierce interjected. "You can

mould yourself in any way you see fit, too."

Santos looked at Joseph with a different look than he usually did. He always looked annoyed, but now, all Joseph saw was intrigue. "Yes, Pierce here told me all about the magic you possess. Very interesting indeed."

"It's correct that you can shapeshift into others at will, but to be able to control this?" Joseph replied. Looking at the vial, it didn't look like something he could control—and if it was a weapon, he didn't want to, either. It seems a little different to what I'm used to."

"Just give it a try," Pierce said as Joseph felt the pendant being swapped with the vial.

"Well, what do I do with it?" Joseph looked at the two men but found no answers on their faces.

"Close your eyes and visualise something, maybe something small to start with – if, and only if, you truly can control it, then the cerulean in your hands will change into the shape you want it to," Santos explained. "All you have to do is close your eyes and think of something."

Joseph did as he was told. Closing his eyes as he held the vial out – all he could think of was Finley and how happy the little fox was whenever he saw Joseph. He visualised Finley standing in his hands, how he would wag his tail like a dog would whenever Joseph would talk to him in a funny voice – and how the fox would always be there for Joseph whenever he needed him.

"I think we have our answer," Pierce said with a rather triumphant tone. Joseph quickly opened his eyes. He didn't feel anything in his hands, much less a rather large fox. But floating ever so slightly off his hands, Joseph could see the fox he loved staring back at him. "You can control it."

"Finley!" Joseph shouted out; he had missed him so much. He

wanted to hug him, but despite all the feelings he had, all the emotions welling up inside of him, he knew that this was not Finley and knew that unless he wanted to get wet, soaked, there was no chance of hugging him. "Can the real fox see me, too?"

"No. Unfortunately not. It's just an illusion; you can interact with it, though. For instance, you can create anything you want; a sword, like a normal sword, can cut through the flesh; you could use cerulean tears similarly." Pierce replied as all three of them watched as the fox began to disappear. Joseph was glad, though, now that he knew it wasn't the honest Finley; he didn't want a copy of him. He wanted the real deal, wherever he was.

"So, now that we've determined you can control it like Pierce thought you might, we can get started," Santos said as he took the pendant from his son and looked at the gem that looked to be full of liquid. "As I said, Joseph, if you tell anyone, including your friends, I will kill you."

"What do you plan to do with the pendant?" Joseph just nodded in reply. If this magic was so important, then there was no way he would tell anyone; it would be too dangerous to lose such a weapon. "And why do you need me to know about it?"

"We're going to use it to get into Rivetia," Santos replied. "And you, my new best friend, are going to harness the power of the pendant to get us through that barrier."

THREE

Hours had passed, and Joseph was more tired than he had been the night before. Sitting in the communal area, which seemed increasingly crowded as time passed, Joseph, Alex, and Maura sat down with a glass of some sort of beverage, ready to wind down for the night.

"I cannot believe you didn't have to do anything today. You have no idea what I've seen." Alex complained. "Pierce was right; the smell sticks to you. These people have never even touched the bottom of the ship. There are barnacles on top of barnacles."

"I swear, this ship hasn't been cleaned for years. The amount of dirt and mess I had to sweet up, mop and do who knows what was astronomical." With a drink in her hand, Maura looked at the people on this ship with disgust. "It really was a ridiculous amount. I don't think scrubbing will ever remove the dirt from my fingernails... I just had them done as well. Look!"

Maura held out her hands for the boys to look at. An array of colours was splodged on her nails. Joseph supposed it should have been some pattern, but he needed to figure it out. "It's colourful?"

"No!" Maura roared. It wasn't anger, more... anguish. "They're chipped. My mom and I used to go get them done every week. By the looks of this place, I don't suppose anywhere will have a nail salon to get them done."

"Calm down, it's fine!" Alex began, but he and Joseph could tell this was stressing her out more than it should have. Compared to a lot of their other worries, this seemed minor. "When we get you home to your world… you can get them done then."

Maura then pointed to her hair. The coils were all out of shape; the sea water had really messed them up. "And my hair, too. This needs professional work done to it." Maura ran her fingers through her hair and sighed. "Sorry… All of this has really stressed me more than I thought."

"Maura. You travelled through worlds; neither of us has done that, not properly, anyway. It's natural to be stressed out and shocked. The culture alone is different; the world around us isn't something you're familiar with…" Joseph began trying to alleviate some of her struggles. "But we're going to get you home. We don't know how yet, but we will figure something out. We're all in this together."

"Thank you, both of you. You're totally right." Maura sighed again as she spoke, a much-needed sigh. Itching to be let out like old air was lodged in her windpipe. "What were we speaking about before?"

"You two were saying how much work you had done today. And I told you already. I also did some work today; I just can't tell you what it was. It's top secret; Pierce and his father don't want anyone else knowing." Joseph replied as he, too, took a sip of a drink that he had been given. The taste wasn't as pleasant as he thought, but it was better than having nothing.

"Sounds cryptic," Maura replied, a slight twinge of worry in her voice.

Though he knew the alcohol would go straight to his head if he let it. Both Alex and Maura simply looked at Joseph with expressions of confusion. "Okay, well, let's just say Santos told me he wanted no one to know until the proper moment," Joseph said. Suddenly, the concern in her eyes changed slightly. Santos said he would kill people on this ship more times than anything else. Joseph had heard him say it in passing on the first day after they boarded the boat, but it seemed that no one had actually seen him make good on that threat yet.

"I'm glad we had a safe ride, but he is rather scary… don't you think?" Maura asked, and Alex nodded in agreement. "I caught a look at both Santos and Pierce's clothes; they don't really look like pirates… do they?"

"Hm." Joseph drank from the cup again; he knew that the more they pressed, the more he would struggle not to say anything. Joseph knew Pierce and his father were higher in class than they said. Joseph had to change the subject. "Anyway, we need to speak about what we will do when we get off this ship. We have no book to guide us this time."

"We first need to locate the beacon; the key comes after; if we can't find it, then we cannot say if it is affected the same way the Rose beacon was. If the decay hasn't touched the island yet, we might not have to worry about rushing around like headless chickens." Alex explained that he was right. "My guess is that this time, with it being an island and a small one at that – it might be a little easier to find the key than it was for the one we did find."

"That book said there are four keys but five beacons. Why do you think that is?" Maura asked; it was a question that had also been itching Joseph's mind.

"I have no idea," Joseph pondered. Do you know anything, Alex? You seem the most clued up on these things."

"Very little, all the information I had was passed down, so it may have got lost in translation, but my father mentioned once that there was a report years and years back, centuries perhaps, that one day an earthquake occurred, and there it was, a fifth beacon, different from the others – but there is no evidence of this, just that singular report."

Alex began, taking a sip of his drink to clear his throat. "Maybe the people that wrote that book had more information than we did, who knows."

"Different from the rest?" Joseph asked. They really needed to get that book back. How much information they had missed by losing it to Caulan was unimaginable. I assume you don't know how?"

"No." Alex shook his head. "If dad did, he never told me."

"How long do you think it is until we reach Rivetia?" Maura moaned. "I'm not going to lie, and I'm grateful I was saved from the water, but I'm not really enjoying this voyage. I feel kind of sick occasionally, and the work they put me on today is rather unfavourable."

"Only Pierce and Santos know the true location. So far, the crew has no clue; they are just sailing into open water. It's not getting to the location… more inside it will be the issue," Joseph said before shutting his mouth. "I said too much."

"I… no, we won't pry. But at least be honest." Alex said as he placed his mug down on the rickety table. "Is what they showed you dangerous? Are you putting yourself in danger, Joseph?"

"Not really," Joseph replied, shrugging. He didn't want to mention that the cerulean tears were a weapon. "You don't have to worry about me, I've faired in worse situations."

"I made a promise back at that sword fight with Calvin. I would protect you better than I did before. I failed before; I won't again," Alex said as he sipped his drink but kept his vision on Joseph. "I need to know if it's dangerous so that I can step in if needed."

"Why do you need to know so bad if I'm in danger?" Joseph asked, a little taken aback by Alex's tone. He sounded really, really worried. "I get that you want to make up for lost time, but up until a few weeks ago, we didn't speak, apart from the odd morning meeting where you took the money I earned the night before. It's just a bit... much, you being all protective. I just need a little time to process the change."

"You took money from him?" Maura asked. "Sorry to interrupt, but what does that mean?"

"Every morning, after working the night before, Alex would wake me up and take a cut of the money I earned. A large cut." Joseph said sheepishly, realising Maura needed to be more up to speed with how the guild worked.

"I'm not proud of it," Alex grunted back, now sipping at the drink and averting his gaze before Maura tapped the table with her right hand.

"Whilst that is barbaric, taking money from people you have basically enslaved... it has brought up a surprising thought," Maura said, not removing her gaze from Alex. "Do you have any money? Either of you? I don't, obviously."

"Should do. Three gold coins, two silver and six bronze pieces in my..." Joseph began as he felt around for something before sighing. "In my satchel that I do not have with me because your father took everything I had when we went to the dungeon... Including the book."

"I have about fifteen gold pieces, but I hardly think that will help us out in the long run; that's not going to buy us much in terms of food," Alex replied before looking around at the room that they were in, it had very much become vacant. Everyone had gone to their bunks, ready for a hard day's work tomorrow. "And almighty knows that 'our savour' won't pay us for the work that we do today, tomorrow, and however long we are on this ship, will he?"

"Hm, no, I suppose not. We must stretch that gold over until we figure out how to make more." Joseph said as Alex placed the gold onto the table and separated it into five groups, three gold in each pile. One piece each for one day. "I lived on rations for years at the guild;

my appetite isn't that big anyway."

"Well, that might just be enough for us to make it through about five days or so, but we'll all need to pitch in to try and gain more capital. I didn't even think about the prospect of money; it had never been that much of an issue at the guild – they provided all meals for the hunters." Alex said before he realised that he was talking to two people who could not relate to what he was talking about. "What I'm saying is, so far, it's doable. Mostly."

"As much as I enjoy talking to both of you and trying to figure out a budget, can we figure it out when we are off this ship? It's not like we will spend anything in this place anyway?" Maura asked as she stood up from the table, having finished her drink long ago. The silence in the room was quiet. Joseph hadn't even noticed that the room had emptied as quickly as it did – he had seen people leaving instead of stumbling through the room. "All that cleaning has really made me tired, and if it's going to be anything like today, tomorrow, then I want to sleep beforehand."

"Aye, let's call it a day. I could use a good sleep, too." Both Alex and Joseph stood up from the table, too.

"It's nippy tonight. "Maura said, though he knew she was about to make it into something to tease Joseph again. "Enjoy your cuddle, boys, snuggle close."

Taking the bait, Alex slinked his arm around Joseph's shoulder and pulled him close. "Oh, we will." This close, Joseph could smell the slightly familiar scent of the cologne Alex usually wore; even now, it was still there after all his body had been through – the salt water, the barnacles. "Won't we, Joseph?"

"Stop it." Joseph swatted Alex's arm away. As the three departed and Joseph and Alex found themselves in their own room, Joseph kept his eyes on the window that the room had. Looking over the horizon, he still couldn't see any sign of any land. The darkness was setting in, and the sun all but disappeared—it really was pitch black out there. It was a wonder how anything survived out here, let alone a whole kingdom locked away for years.

"Oh, you have got to be kidding me!" Alex said as he flopped onto the bed and grabbed his parchment, which Joseph assumed was his job for the next day. "Bloody barnacle duty again! How many more of them are there?"

"He really doesn't like you, does he?" Joseph laughed as he walked over to the bed, too, noticing a small piece of parchment on the bedside table on his side.

"What's not to like?" Alex exclaimed. "I think I'm pretty likeable, aren't I?"

"Well-." Joseph began before a pillow was thrown at him.

"Don't answer that." Alex shook his head, knowing he would have to wait for Joseph's answer. Alex slumped back onto the bed before turning his attention to the small parchment that Joseph was now holding. "What does yours say?"

"He needs to see me again." Joseph scanned it – the small writing was hard to read at first, probably to keep it away from prying eyes. Almost instantly, he knew Alex would be disappointed – he still couldn't share what he was doing with Pierce and Santos; he didn't want to start this friendship, or whatever it was, off on lies. "Sorry, I can't say, not even in our room. You have no idea how slim these walls are or who could be listening."

"Well, I'm sure you'll tell me eventually," Alex said as he began to prepare for the night's rest, quickly finding his body covered by the bed sheets freshly changed by someone else in the crew. Joseph discovered his eyes becoming heavy, too, and he found himself tucked up in bed moments later, Alex still as close as possible to conserve the warmth that Joseph emanated. It, indeed, was a cold night tonight. "Good night, then, let's get to sleep. Some of us have busy days tomorrow."

If the note had any merit to it, so did Joseph.

'Price,

Come to my office tomorrow for more training; you'll need to master how to use the tears if we are ever going to get into Rivetia. We're counting on you.

Santos.'

Why did this feel familiar?

"It's too tricky!" Joseph said as he slammed his hands on the table before him, annoyed. Both at himself and his lack of ability to make the tears do what he wanted. Try and try again, he could not get the tears to form into a shape more significant than the mirror image of Finley he had made the day before. If they needed him to cover this whole ship… it was not happening. "It's really hurting my head, I can't do it, Pierce."

"We need to make this work, Joseph. Please, can we continue? Can we try again?" Pierce, wide-eyed, asked; he hadn't anticipated the anger that had flown out of Joseph in that second; he stopped, looking at Joseph for a moment as if he was inspecting him. "That anger… your emotions are heightened right now, partially because you can't get this to work but also because of all the changes that have happened in the past few days. We could use it to our advantage… let's, for a moment, look at it from another angle."

"How do you mean?" Joseph asked, removing himself from the table and began to pace around the small, cramped room he was in. It was like a broom cupboard, but Pierce had said they needed somewhere small, out of sight. The cerulean tears' brightness could be contained here; there were no windows, and no one could see in… or out.

Pierce dug into his pocket and procured a small round silver coin. "Take this coin, for instance. Now, by all standards, this is tiny compared to this ship. But what if…" Pierce began as he dug in his pocket for something else. He found a larger coin, gold in colour; he flipped it and caught it in his other hand, then swapped it for the silver coin, hiding it away from view. "What if it could become larger, change its very being before our eyes."

"I'm not following," Joseph replied. He had watched the spectacle, but he hadn't taken anything in. It was like Pierce was talking in riddles, not ones he could eventually understand.

"You could scale this coin up if you created it with the tears like you did with the fox yesterday… or you could scale down this ship, make them the same size," Pierce said as he pointed at the small vial of water in the pendant in front of Joseph on the table. "You could try that with the tears we have there when you've had enough practice."

"I don't know… it really is taking a lot out of me." But Joseph noticed how Pierce started to look at him, like some sort of hurt puppy – his eyes were pleading for agreement. "I suppose I could try one last time before I need a rest."

"Okay, one more try," Pierce said, his eyes glinting with admiration. Think of something small and visualise it getting larger. That's all you have to do today. We can work on changing the shape later."

Joseph grabbed the vial close by next to the pendant. The tears themselves had become the glass on the outside, too. Each time Joseph failed, it always reverted to its previous shape. "Okay", Joseph said as he looked down at the bright blue water. He closed his eyes, holding it out in his open palms, and visualised something, anything he could put his mind to.

The coin.

"Good Joseph!" Pierce praised.

As Joseph opened his eyes, the small amount of water had shifted and changed into the coin, albeit its colour was different. It couldn't be used to buy anything… but was a coin. That last little push had finally given results.

The Cerulean's tears, indeed, were beautiful. Joseph looked at the coin in his hands, feeling the energy it both gave and took away from him; he cupped the coin with his other hand and felt it grow, slowly removing his hands to provide more space. Joseph watched as the coin began to fill his entire hand, spilling over, making it heavier to hold even with both hands. He visualised it getting bigger and more prominent, much heavier, too. The blue hue came increasingly into focus, brighter than ever before.

"Bigger…" Joseph said this change was taking a lot out of him; the breathlessness that he was feeling was never quelled, but as long as he was holding the tears, he could not falter. Joseph stopped visualising the coin growing bigger; it was now triple its original size and weight, and it was hard to hold with two hands. The added weight was a shock at first, even though it was water. The magic that Joseph could perform with this water was exactly the same as his own; it was like the two were meant to be. He closed his eyes, needing to relieve some of his pressure. "And smaller."

"Amazing!" Pierce said as he watched, eyes wide and a smile plastered.

Joseph felt the coin in his hands again. Even though he had been able to do it, his headache was growing. He placed the tears back onto the table, and the moment they left his hands, they reverted back into the vial they had been before he touched them.

"Good work, Joseph." A voice came from behind him. Santos stood there, and a familiar smile was on his face, too. "I was wrong to treat you as I did when you arrived on this ship. I was also wrong to doubt your capabilities with the magic you possess. Pierce told me how you acquired the pendant."

"Thank you, Santos, sir," Joseph said as he gripped the table for balance. His head was really hurting now, making him feel a little dizzy. "Can I... have some water?"

"Here", Pierce said as he passed Joseph a cup. It was different from the wood pails that Freydale used. This was made out of something different. It was cold to the touch—as if it was used to keep the water cold. It was made from metal. "Take a swig. You must be tired."

Santos then sat down as Joseph was drinking. He looked the boy up and down. "What exactly were you and your gang doing in the water, Joseph?" Santos asked. It was then that it occurred to Joseph that Pierce hadn't told his father anything. "It seemed like a very strange occurrence. Not many would want to find themselves out in the open like that. But there you were, miles out from any known shore."

"We were trying to escape from Freydale. We weren't seen too favourable there at the time." Joseph explained. Santos's facial expression changed from one of concern to one of curiosity. "It is truly a long story."

"I assume it was Caulan Von-Loch?" Santos began. Joseph nodded.

"Leader of the Hunter's Guild," Pierce recalled that although he had used their services, Pierce hated everything Hunters were. This hatred was also evident in the way he treated Alex: "Nasty business."

"Aye. I'd heard Caulan was a nasty piece of work, but I never saw him myself. Rumours abound on the seas and on land, too." Santos replied before turning his attention back to Joseph, who was inquisitive about knowing more. "I mean baring the obvious use of magic... Pierce told me that you were a servant and useful to them. Why did they want to kill you?"

"My group and I reintroduced magic to the continent. There was this decay, black spikes that covered everything, leaving destruction in its wake. It didn't matter if it was a kingdom or a small hamlet." Joseph explained, and once again, concern dawned on Santos and even Pierce's face. "We learned that if we were to locate this key and unlock the magic stored inside these old disused beacons, we could stop the decay before it destroyed everything."

"By everything, I assume you mean the realm?" Pierce asked. Joseph nodded.

"The beacons were sending us warnings, almost. Raw blasts of magic from the base knocked anyone without magic into a coma. Still, it was also throwing the decay around at every moment. It was chaos." Joseph said. Hearing it now, it sounded mad; it sounded made up, but it was all true. Joseph had lived it and more. "The coma patients, they awoke when we unlocked the power of the beacon; they all gained their own magic."

"They did?" Pierce asked. "But I thought you had to be born with magic; you can't just receive it…"

"Why are those beacons fighting back now, though?" Santos asked. Maybe deep down, he knew that Joseph couldn't answer Pierce's question—that is why he had interrupted. But Santos wanted to hear now. The expression on his face told Joseph everything. He wanted to know exactly what they were up against, what Joseph's team was running from, and what they were willing to do.

"I wish I could tell you. Alex monitored it for the longest; he'll probably know more," Joseph replied.

"Alex?" Santos asked, and Joseph heard Pierce make a slight tut sound. "I assume that's one of your friends?"

"His name is Alexander Von-Loch," Joseph replied, and

Santos's face changed again, now to one more akin to bewilderment. "He is Caulan's son."

"He was the Hunter assigned to 'look after' Joseph in his servant life, paraded over him like some sort of lord. Why do you trust anything that he says, truly, Joseph?" Pierce asked.

"I don't see how that's much of your business, but-" Joseph said, but then his tone softened – he understood why Pierce might ask something like that. He had been an outsider, too; he had seen how Alex had treated Joseph even if he hadn't been there for that conversation. "We used to be friends a long time ago; I was a servant, and he became a hunter. We had different priorities, and now, they align again. He's trying to work on himself; he put his life on the line for me. That wouldn't have happened if he hadn't changed his heart."

"Hm," Pierce said, as if he was weighing up what to say.

"Sure, he has flaws, but..." Joseph began. "I've yet to meet someone who doesn't."

"Fine," Pierce said, tutting slightly. "You might trust him, but it doesn't mean I have to unless he gives me a reason to."

"You don't have to. I never said you did." There was undoubtedly tension now. Pierce was annoyed at the answer Joseph had given. "Why are you so... bothered by my friendship with him? You don't know him; you hardly know me!"

"Okay, back to the topic here," Santos said, raising his voice and scolding the both of them. "When you get to Rivetia, what exactly will you do?"

"There's a beacon there, isn't there?" Joseph asked. "And a key, we're going to reintroduce magic there too and stop the decay from appearing there, providing it already hasn't. You don't understand how fast it spreads."

"Well, if that is truly what you want to do, then you'll need to run it past the ruler; things work differently in Rivetia from what I can remember. The ruler, whoever they are now, will know where the key is; they will also know where the beacon is, but it's best I not tell you more." Santos said. Joseph almost sounded like a dying rat at being denied the information he needed – information Santos clearly had. "I'm sorry, I'm sure they wouldn't like an outsider knowing too much without the people of Rivetia's approval."

"You can't just tell me something juicy like that and then withhold the rest!" Joseph exclaimed, folding his arms over his chest.

"I can, and I will." Santos let out a small, stifled chuckle at Joseph, trying to challenge him. But he seemed a lot less harsh now, like, for once, the two understood each other. Now, Santos wanted something Joseph had so they could get along better. "Now, Joseph, I expect you are tired; the Cerulean tears are taking a lot out of you. I need to discuss some things with Pierce here, so take the rest of the day off; we can revisit this tomorrow; I do not want to hear another peep out of you until we meet again tomorrow."

Joseph nodded, understanding that this was his time to leave. Santos wouldn't give him a chance again. "Yes, sir. Thank you." Somehow, everywhere he was helpful, the guild, on this ship, so why, Joseph wondered – why was it that people disliked him as a person so much? Maybe it was a 'relationship of convenience' type of deal? It indeed seemed that way with Pierce and Santos. They got something in return for safe passage away from Freydale; it seemed they were getting way more than Joseph was.

"One final thing," Joseph said before he left the room, Santos tutting in his general direction – Joseph wasn't sure if the man was genuine in his praises because it didn't seem like the two got along too well; Santos was a confusing man.

"Go on." Santos groaned.

"Can I relieve my friends of their duties for the day?" Joseph asked, hoping for a quick answer. He wasn't sure what Maura was doing today—probably bottom-of-the-barrel work—but he knew that Alex would want a break. The sun was hot today, and he knew what barnacle duty entailed. "I need to go over a few things with them."

Santos looked as if he were thinking, he. He looked over to Pierce, who simply shrugged. Pierce had given out the jobs for the day—it only seemed fair that the two would discuss it together.

"Yes. I suppose you can." Pierce replied. "Seen as you have done good work for us today, I'll let their jobs slide, but as long as they are on this ship, this opportunity will not happen again. We all work for our meals, our beds; we don't do things by halves either."

"I understand, Pierce. I'll leave you two to speak." Joseph replied, thankful that the two had agreed on something that was beneficial to him for once. He needed a release—the cerulean tears. Though he couldn't speak with the duo about it due to Santos's threats, he very much needed to speak to them about something, anything.

Too much had happened in the past few days not to.

No matter what, controlling the cerulean tears and finding the key in Rivetia were going to be hard work, and Joseph had to be prepared for what was to come at every moment—even for the things he didn't expect.

Barnacle duty did not look fun at all. Armed with what looked like a small knife and dangling on a small swing-type apparatus at the bottom of the ship, Alex worked away, scraping and pulling at every speck of dirt and object stuck to the bottom of the wooden hull. Joseph watched him as one after the other – Alex worked like clockwork, scrape, pull, let it fall into the ocean below, and then, without breaking away for one moment, he went straight to the next.

Joseph hasn't said anything yet; he just watched Alex. The blonde man, with his cut-short hair and the now slight stubble forming on his face from lack of upkeep over the last few days, was a look Joseph had never seen before.

He remembered how they used to be when they sneak around, Alex bringing Joseph food down at the dungeon he called home. The older boy was the only one in that whole guild who held any sense of empathy. Alex kept it a secret from his father.

Caulan wouldn't have allowed a friendship anyway.

Joseph leaned over the ship's edge, looking down at Alex as he worked, trying not to be seen yet. Despite his initial hesitance the other night, something strange was happening in Joseph's mind.

He didn't mind that Alex had called him 'Joey' – something he had even told Alex days before. It was a bit of a shock at first, but it sounded good. He remembered why.

Alex had called him by that name as children with no care in the world. And he noticed something else, too—Alex had been nervous about Joseph's reaction as if he was trying to be careful and attentive. Joseph had very few people he would call friends. Maura, even if he hadn't known her too long, was a definite yes—she was kind, kinder to him than anyone had ever been. Pierce was a close second.

There were a few kinks to work out of both of them. Joseph had never really had friends before—barring Henry, but even that was strained due to the fact that 'servants weren't allowed friends'. Henry was always kind, even if he had lost his whole family before he arrived months before this all began. Joseph thought back—maybe that was why they worked together so well: they had both lost more than most. They related to one another on a personal level.

Alex was tricky because they had been through so much. Joseph didn't like to be vulnerable around anyone, but Alex used to be the person he went to. Whilst he did feel like they had slotted back into that role for the most part, there were still the unsaid things, the moments they didn't get to experience together.

The moments that Joseph really wanted. And after last night's talk – it was clear that Alex was still holding onto the guilt and, more so, the want for those moments again.

Maybe they could, Joseph wanted to. Even how complicated the whole relationship between the two was.

'I was supposed to love you until my last breath.' Those words swirled around him. Both of them – unsaid but true, just wanted to be loved.

"Joseph?" A deep voice broke him away from his thoughts. Alex looked directly at him with a somewhat confused expression. "You're staring. Are you doing okay?"

"I'm-." Joseph finally broke away. He imagined how strange it must have been for Alex. "I'm fine, yeah."

"Do you need anything? I've got a lot of bar-." Alex said as he returned to the job at hand, scraping at a barnacle right before him. "A lot of barnacles to get off the ship before sundown."

"Actually, I came to tell you that you have been relieved from your duties. Santos and Pierce have said you can have a break for the day," Joseph said sheepishly, having been caught staring even if he didn't realise it.

"Really?" Alex's voice verged on excitement and tiredness. "Get in!"

Joseph watched as Alex grabbed a rope and began to pull, hoisting his body off the swing contraption that he had been sitting on. Slowly and with very little ease, even if he had been working since sunrise, Alex pulled himself up towards where Joseph was standing. "Do you need any help?"

"No, no, I've got it," Alex grunted as he swung forward., grabbing onto the side of the ship for support.

"I really think you just need to ask for help," Joseph said, concerned as he watched Alex's mishaps. Pulling himself up a rope was one thing, but back onto a ship with very little support was another. "Here."

"Joseph, I know my own strength. You'll fall if you help me," Alex said as he felt Joseph's hand grab his. Alex tried to swat it away as he got his bearings. "Stop, you'll lose your own balance. Don't get so close to the edge."

"I won't fall. You just don't want to get help; stop being stubborn." Joseph said as he gripped Alex, pulling him up with all his strength. He didn't even realise that he was falling; the that he should have felt didn't even have a chance e to set in. It was a slippery slope; the floor and the water he had been brought up from a day's worth of sailing did indeed make it very dangerous. But Joseph didn't fall, not correctly anyway; he had begun to, the water at the bottom of the ship getting closer every second, but he had stopped as if floating in mid-air.

Looking up at what had stopped him falling, Alex stood, his feet firmly on the ship, holding onto Joseph's hand – keeping him from dropping any further, a look of 'I told you so' on his smug face. Sighing, Alex began to lift him up – like everything he did, it looked as if it took very little out of him to do so. When he got closer to the top, Joseph felt Alex wrapping his arm around his waist, his cold hands touching some skin – making Joseph shudder as he gripped Alex's hand just a little too tight. He didn't want to risk falling. There was no way back onto the ship without someone jumping in to save him, and he knew no one would like to do that.

Joseph kept his eyes closed through it all, not once wanting to look—just in case it all went wrong. He wouldn't be averse to thinking it would—somehow, things always went bad for Joseph; it just became second nature to believe it always would.

Alex grunted slightly as Joseph finally found himself being placed on the floor just in front of Alex. The man now lets go of his hand and wraps his hand around the other side of his waist to steady him. Before flicking the upside of his cheek, forcing the boy to open his eyes to see the smiling face of Alex on the other side.

"Hey there," Alex said, bringing Joseph closer from the edge. Beaming from ear to ear as he did. "I thought you said you wouldn't fall."

"It... was slippery," Joseph said, still slightly bewildered. "Sorry."

"No need to apologise; I'm glad I caught you when I did," Alex said as he let go of Joseph's waist but had a little hesitance to do so. "So now that we are both back safely on the ship, what do you want to do with the new free time?"

"Go find Maura; we need to speak about some things. I'm sure we are all itching to get out." Joseph said before lowering his tone. "I learned some stuff about the key, but I don't want to speak about it in the open."

"Okay, well, let's go find her then," Alex said as he began to walk towards where he believed her to be. We can save her from this 'work' that we have been doing since we got here; it's hardly fulfilling at all."

Now Alex understood what Joseph went through daily at the guild, doing work he didn't want to do. It was hardly the same, but now he was looking at Alex a different way altogether, the way that he had spoken to Joseph softly and with care in his voice. And that smile the man had held when he saved Joseph from falling – it's one of those smiles that I've just not to feel awkward.

No, it was a genuine smile.

FOUR

Sitting on a stool in their bedroom, Joseph looked at Alex and Maura as they digested some of the information he had just told them. Having omitted to tell the two about the tears and what Santos wanted him to do with them, Joseph sat and watched Alex pacing around the room, and Maura just looked lost. Moving from one realm to the other wasn't the only reason that expression was permanently etched into her face.

"Santos said that only the monarch would know where the key was located and that we needed to get permission to collect the key," Alex asked. Joseph had to admit, it didn't sound hopeful. "I lived in Freydale my entire life, I've met the princess of Freydale, but never the King nor the Queen, and the only reason I met Princess Dana was because of my position in the guild. If we need an audience with the monarch, someone who is an outsider, then it's hopeless."

"Maybe," Joseph said, shrugging. "Maybe not. If we somehow manage to get the ship through the barrier, maybe they will want to grant an audience, find out why and, more so, how we managed to do it."

"I've got a slight problem with all of this. Correct me if I'm wrong for assuming." Maura began. "How do we even know…"

"Go on," Alex said as he looked over to her. By the look alone he gave her, it seemed that he was feeling the same exact thing. Joseph was, too. "Say it because we're all thinking it. An island kingdom locked away for fifty years, no one is allowed in or out…"

"How do we even know if anyone is alive?" Mura said. "How do we know that the barrier preventing them from leaving didn't just kill them off, or they starved? If that's the case…"

"If that's the case, we'll be on our own. Like we were last time. But we still have to try and get into the kingdom either way, whether there are people there or not." Joseph explained. "But if they are by some miracle still alive, that is how it works. We must ask the monarch for approval before finding the keys. We probably need to do the same for the beacon too."

Alex then piped up. Both of them had the same mind about this. "I don't care what type of place Rivetia is or how set in its ways; if it means that we break a few rules just to save the world, then I'm all for it. We've done it before; I'm sure we'll do it again." He said before once again realising something. "How do we know that people in Rivetia will accept magic?"

This was true. The rest of the world views magic as skewed. "I have no idea. If we want to save the world, we will have to decide to ignore those people who say no." Joseph said. It felt wrong, like he was taking away their choices. "But… those who won the war, the humans, they locked away magic in the first place. They took away people's livelihoods. It's the same thing… if you think about it."

"People won't be happy either way," Alex began. Joseph could tell that he was nervous about this, the slight shake of his hand as he fidgeted with his shirt, pulling at it. To do this, to return magic, was creating a world that had not existed for a long time. The very notion of this could cause a war, a war that none of them wanted to be part of.

"They never are; it's the way reality works. No one will always be one hundred per cent happy; my daddy taught me that for free. Trust me, being a politician is no walk in the park, especially when he was in the running…" Maura said that whilst Joseph didn't understand some of the words she used, he understood the message – she continued a moment later, solidifying both of their understanding. "But if it means that there is still a world around us… and a chance for me to get home. I'll take that unhappiness from a couple of naysayers."

"I agree completely." Alex agreed. To think that day before, he wouldn't have. Being away from the toxicity of the guild and his father did wonders for him. "But first, we need to actually get into the kingdom full stop."

"Yeah. We're getting there," Joseph said as he found all eyes on him. He had said too much, but what had been done was done now. It was out in the open.

"Oh yeah?" Alex asked, raising his eyebrows and keeping his arms crossed. He sounded almost excited in tone—just a smidge of information was enough to set him off now. "Spill."

"I can only assume, and like I said, I won't pry, but I assume that is what you have been working on with Santos and Pierce?" Maura asked, and Joseph nodded to give her a bit of satisfaction. But he wouldn't say any more than he already had. There was too much at stake. If he told them – they might make it to Rivetia, but Joseph wouldn't. He would be off the ship before he could even blink. "I was cleaning outside one of the rooms, and I heard them both threaten you not to tell anyone; it must be top-secret information for a threat to be made."

"They threatened you?" Alex exclaimed; Joseph knew this was coming from when the words left Maura's lips. "What do you mean, Maura? What exactly did you hear?"

"Santos said that if I told anyone what was happening in Pierce's office, he would kill me. I don't think literally; it was a figure of speech. Honestly." Joseph explained. He could feel both sets of eyes on him; Alex's were particularly piercing. Not out of anger but more of concern.

"Okay, you lied to me when you said it wasn't dangerous." Alex pinched the bridge of his nose as he spoke like he usually did when angry, upset or frustrated. Joseph needed to find out which one he was at the moment.

"I'm sorry, alright, I'm not good at this. I'm not good at relying on people for help." Joseph explained, wanting the stool he was sitting on to fall into the void with him on it. "I was alone for a really long time, I learned how to take care of myself and prioritise survival over relationships."

"I was with you. I was with you the whole time." Alex stopped pacing, looking a bit confused. "Bar that year, I was always there."

"You were, yes, but not on jobs. Not when I was working. I was always alone whilst working, never having any help. I learned long ago that I could only rely on myself to do the jobs I needed to do…" Joseph explained. "You were there, but it doesn't change the fact that I was alone as a servant for fifteen years or so."

"We should be far away from here. I should have gotten you out." Alex said. Again, that guilt was there.

"This would all still be happening around us, though. The decay would still happen whether or not you got me out. We would still be in danger." Joseph choked out. "The work we are doing in that room is dangerous, yes, but not in the way you may think. It's not dangerous to me. I'm not sure they want me to take down the barrier, to break through it."

"That pendant," Alex said as he clicked his fingers and pointed towards Joseph. "It's all about that pendant you got them. I won't pry, but I assume it has something to do with the pendant being the key to getting us through."

"Well…" Joseph began. But Alex held his hand up.

"I don't need confirmation. It's just an assumption that I'm sure Maura is also thinking—" Alex said before he was cut off by a pair of heavy-footed feet clomping down the hallway close to the room that they were in.

"Land!" Joseph looked up at Cressida, who had just run into the bedroom, her breathing heavy, sounding like she had just run a mile to get here and find the three people huddled together. Joseph had seen her around the ship in the past few days, though he wasn't sure what she actually did. Her short blonde hair was cut into a bob, and she was missing a few fingers in her right hand. It looked a pretty clean cut, almost as if they had been chopped off with precision rather than by accident. She was usually seen shouting orders, pottering about the ship, and constantly shying away from Santos mostly.

Joseph wondered why she was on this pirate ship—to be honest, why any of them were—especially if she and the rest of them were so terrified of the man who ran it. The payoff must have been the only reason—to get to Rivetia, to see it firsthand after 50 years.

It certainly wasn't Santos's charming personality, despite the changes in tone in the last few days when talking to Joseph. Santos was now getting something out of Joseph – only he could provide.

"What did you say?" Alex asked – it was a rather rude intrusion into the conversation. "Land?"

"Yes, Alex," Cressida said as she searched the trio's faces before stopping in her tracks, trying her hardest to catch her breath. Joseph needed to figure out how she had learned their names. He had never spoken to her when he was on the ship. Cressida doubled over slightly, taking a sizeable deep breath but finding no sense of urgency in any of their faces; she must have felt the need to elaborate because she continued to talk. "We've found land; Pierce and Santos told me to find the three of you. Santos needs to see you, Joseph. Much importance to his request, I would think."

As quick as Cressida came, she left, running off, probably to tell some other people about the remarkable discovery she and the crew had found. The trio looked at each other as the reality set in.

Joseph said nothing as he began to walk, not run, towards where Cressida had gone. He needed to be prepared if Santos and Pierce had requested him this close to where they attempted to get into. He hadn't even got any sleep like he wanted to.

"Do you think?" Alex began, his interest and emotions flooding back to him as soon as he spoke. He looked at Maura as Joseph passed him. "Do you think we should go?"

"Yes." Maura nodded, watching Joseph leave the room. "I think we should. Let's follow him."

Up onto the deck, the warm air hit Joseph almost immediately. It hadn't been warm before, but he assumed, this close to the barrier, it might be a natural response – a deterrent, make it too hot for people to handle, and they'll leave. But Joseph felt this crew wouldn't back down without a fight; Santos and Pierce certainly wouldn't. Far out in the distance, Joseph could hardly see the piece of land that the man had mentioned, but it was certainly out there; it was unmissable; there was nothing else out there in the rather barren-looking ocean; it stuck out like a sore thumb.

The crew celebrated greatly when the trio made it onto the middle of the deck, among a sea of people who must have been glad that their days of travel and work were over and they could finally get off the ship.

"We've made it boys!" Cressida shouted – earning catcalls and cheers from her fellow crew. She began to laugh, as if manic, as she held onto the side of the metal barrier. "Rivetia!"

For a place that no one here, not even Pierce, had set their foot on in fifty years, they were excited beyond belief. They hugged and made a ruckus around the deck, jumping around like animals, and they hadn't even made it through the barrier yet. If they were this excited so far from the island, Joseph would hate to imagine what it would be like on the ship once they touched the land.

Joseph could work the cerulean tears the way Pierce and Santos wanted him to, but that bit remained to be seen. He was still shattered from the small amount of work that he had done hours before.

"Joseph!" Pierce ran up towards the trio, stopping to catch his breath. "I came to get you; my father needs to see you…"

"Why?" Alex interjected. Once again, assuming the protective nature that he now had.

"Now." Pierce ignored Alex and reiterated. "You know what we discussed."

"I know what we just said about not prying, but I want to know," Maura said as she looked at Alex. The man was practically aiming to jump at Pierce.

"Not happening." Pierce scolded, not once looking up from Joseph's eyes.

"Fine, don't answer me or her. Pretend we are not here, but I am not letting Joseph go without knowing what he is walking into. I know whatever you have planned is dangerous." Alex interjected again, not once caring that Pierce was the boss. "You wouldn't be keeping it this hush-hush if it wasn't."

"Why do you care about what he does?" Pierce scoffed as he squared up to Alex. "Less than a week ago, you were parading over his life. Now you're what? His protector? Give me a break, I bet you have him under one of those contracts…"

"No. No, I don't." Alex said, forcing a gulp down. He had, of course, before he got off the ship had, in fact, had Joseph in a contract. "Even if I did, it's not like you're so blameless. I saw a contract between the two of you the night he got that pendant for you. You're a hypocrite, Pierce. That's what you are."

Pierce shrugged and ignored Alex's words, instead turning his attention back to Joseph. "As I was saying, we're coming into port. You and only you know what we discussed. I need you in my office now."

"Okay," Joseph said as he began to follow Pierce before turning around and holding out his hand to stop Maura and Alex from moving further.

"Why are we stopping?" Maura asked, the concern growing again. It came from a good place; Joseph knew Maura didn't want him to be alone whilst he got them through the barrier.

Joseph shook his head before he spoke. "I know you both feel the same way, *protective*. But really, I need to do this alone." Joseph said. The two understood, even if they didn't want to. They stood outside Pierce's office, but only he could go inside. "Santos's… threats, I wouldn't want to find it they were real. I'm sure you wouldn't either, because if I'm gone… there would be no need to keep you two on the ship either."

Alex then looked as if he had some clarity about how he was acting. His eyes glazed over, and his expression grew softer, though it still held the same look of discontent he had before. "I'll be just outside the room then," Alex replied. "Just…"

"Just what?" Pierce asked, rolling his eyes as he opened the door to his office. "Time is of the essence here."

Alex sighed and then replied, looking at Pierce like he was pleading. "Make sure he's safe."

"I'll promise he will be perfectly fine." Pierce's face softened slightly. "Now, come on, please. We have very little time."

FIVE

Joseph found himself being bundled into the office relatively quickly. Standing there with the pendant already in his hands, Santos gave a sigh of relief as Joseph and Pierce entered. "Finally." He said. "I didn't think it would take you too long to get here after I sent Cressida to get you."

"It's hectic out there; maybe you can hear it?" Pierce commented as he pushed Joseph closer towards Santos.

"You know what you have to do. To protect the ship as it goes through the barrier, you need to change the composition of the water. This is the real deal, super strong stuff." Santos said as he passed Joseph the gem, his hands shaking slightly as he did – he was nervous, but no more than Joseph was. "I know you didn't get any sleep after our last meeting… but please, this is important."

Joseph looked down at the beautiful blue object in his hand, the water inside sloshing about, inviting him to look at it further and for longer. But suddenly, a sound came rushing past the office window; the frosted glass was impossible to see out of correctly, but Joseph could see someone, or many things, running past the window in a frenzy. Excited at finally finding their destination and getting the hell off this ship.

His eyes kept darting between the window, the people running past it, and the gem in his hand. He was completely inexperienced at using the water, and somehow, they expected him to be able to take down an entire barrier?

"Joseph?" Pierce snapped Joseph back to reality.

"I've got it," Joseph said with a smile, though he couldn't shake the uneasy feeling that there was something more to the screams outside. That it wasn't all cheerful.

Joseph hadn't noticed it before, but at the tip of the pendant, the gem had a small valve at the top, sealing the tears inside. But this, inside here, was a much more robust and thus more volatile version of what he had controlled. This was the real deal.

The Rivetia pendant began to glow – the bright blue invading every space he could see. Joseph knew what he had to do – placing it around his neck like he had been instructed before, he quickly opened the pendant lid, letting the light touch him for the first time in the flesh. As he poured the liquid out of its prison, something happened that he, Pierce or Santos wasn't expecting. The water and the tears began to react with Joseph – enveloping him in more than just light this time.

"What's happening?" Pierce asked as he looked at his father.

"It was said that this might happen. When the tears met someone or something they deemed 'worthy', that was old stories, myths even!" Santos replied as he stood up to inspect further. "It can't be true. It's never been proven. It's part of children's fairy tales back in Rivetia. It... can't be real."

"What are you talking about? What is a myth?" Joseph asked as he felt the water shift, it started at his hands where the water had been poured out. This was more than just the light now; the water itself was beginning to envelop Joseph; it moved slowly towards his arms, shoulders, and torso. It wasn't stopping either. Santos moved quickly, grabbing a pile of old books to his left, and began to flick through them furiously, only stopping to give Joseph a slight grimace or pity. "Santos?"

"The Cerulean Tears have moulded with your magic," Santos explained. "You are the human embodiment of the tears. Which means that you can control them a whole lot easier now. You're very powerful, Joseph Price, with or without them... but you are the owner of a potent weapon right now. It was said in old myths that the one who bonds with the tears in this way will become the messenger for the Rivetia goddess of rejuvenation and creation – Lumin."

"So... it's moulded with my magic," Joseph said, from the overload of information, that was all he could muster out. He felt, however, that Santos was keeping something from him. "But what are you hiding from me?"

"Well..." Santos began before returning to the books, almost hiding his face from Joseph as he tried to look busy.

"What the hell is happening?" Pierce then alerted both of them that the tears had not stopped moving. The tears had taken over most of Joseph's lower body now. They then moved, forming a ring around his neck, encasing his entire body, including his face and feet, in the water.

"Santos?" Joseph said, panic welling up inside of him again. It was hard to remember when he wasn't panicking. Still, as Santos continued to ignore and flick through the books at his disposal, he got angrier. "Answer me!"

"It makes you a target. You are very powerful, as I have said. People are going to want to exploit that for personal gain," Santos began, the once strong man flying into a blind panic himself. "I have the diary of the last messenger of Lumin here somewhere... somewhere."

"People already use me for personal gain. If you forget where I came from before I stowed away," Joseph asked. He didn't want to move just yet. The tears were teasing him, making it hard to think about anything other than the fact that water had encased him. He didn't know how powerful they were. One wrong movement… who knows what could happen?

"Yes. I do, I understand. It was bad… barbaric." Santos said as he rummaged through the books but couldn't find the one he was looking for. "But they say that the Luma has a twin, a shadow, an opposing force. Never seen it myself, of course, but it says that the two have worked in tandem with one another – one light, one dark. When the tears have a host, so does the Shadow…"

"Who is it?" Joseph asked.

"No one knows. It could be anyone." Santos said as he finally found a small piece of paper. "It's found me. The shadow demon walks closer; it wants to snuff out the light of the tears, to destroy all I've made. The war is returning; I can feel it in my bones, but this time… I don't think I can win; we're not this close to one another. The Shadow is too strong, and the world has to be ready to stop it when this is not around."

"What?" Joseph and Pierce asked as Santos read.

"It's just what this scrap of paper said to be the last account from the host of the tears last time. But you can see that the Shadow hunts the light, snuffing it out. You can fight it all you like, but the hosts will meet one day, and it won't be a pretty sight." Santos explained that, as he showed Joseph the paper, he was careful not to touch the tears around Joseph's body. "It's a bloody war waiting to happen…"

"I don't want to be in wars." Joseph snapped. He understood what Santos was speaking about, not a literal war with bloodshed and loss, but between the light and the dark; it was unfortunate that one of those people happened to be himself. "I just want to be safe from people trying to hurt me. I just want to feel safe in a world that hates my existence. I don't want a war, I don't want this pain anymore, I just want to be free."

"Okay, okay, I understand," Santos said, stopping Joseph. "You are safe as long as you're on this ship, and we are on our way to Rivetia, where you will be extra safe. No one can hurt you."

Joseph felt an overwhelming need to look down, to move his head slightly. The tears had stopped at the ring around his neck – like it was waiting for Joseph to reach his full potential. He just had no idea what that really was.

"We're getting closer to the barrier; any closer without the tears working their magic, and it won't be pretty," Santos said. Turning his head to look back at Santos once again, Joseph found himself peering over towards the window. The sea of people running past it was still occurring, if not even faster now. The noise was getting louder and louder... until it seemed Santos had enough. "What is going on out there in Lumin's kingdom?"

Suddenly, as if they had heard Santos ask the question, Alex and Maura burst down the door, looking somewhat frazzled. "Sorry, I-," Alex announced as he looked upon the annoyed faces of those around him and Maura. "Um…"

"Leave!" Pierce shouted louder than he should have. Leaving his spot and practically manhandling Alex to his feet, quickly grabbed Maura and Alex's shoulders to usher them out of the door. "Leave now. Get out!"

"But-." Alex began as he looked over to Joseph, a look of confusion covering his face. Before he could ask any more, Pierce pushed forward with his hand again, guiding Alex and Maura towards the door.

But Pierce was not having it; he was getting louder as he spoke. "Did you not hear me? I said get out!"

"But Santos. There is a problem!" Maura shouted out.

"What do you mean, girl?" Santos asked, raising his eyebrow and leaving Joseph to get closer to the two intruders. "What is going on out there? It sounds too loud to be harmless excitement?"

"They found us," Alex said as he locked eyes with Joseph. That gaze and the tone of Alex's voice told Joseph all he needed to know. The Hunter's Guild had found them. "*He's* just outside."

"How?" Joseph asked, the stress from the tears getting closer and Caulan's reappearance making things much harder. How could he possibly have known we were here?"

"The branding tells the guild where you are without even needing a contract, so they can track you," Alex explained as he pointed towards his own arm where Joseph's mark was, though he couldn't see it currently. Sadly, it was still there, and it could still be used against him. "I can't believe I didn't think of it before."

"Who is out there?" Santos asked, and it suddenly occurred to Joseph that he wouldn't have known —despite hearing stories of Caulan and his misdeeds, he had never experienced them himself, and neither had Pierce. "Is anyone going to answer me?"

"Caulan Von Loch. Alex's father. He's probably here to collect and take me back as a prisoner to Freydale." Joseph said, finding the courage to move a little bit, taking a small step towards the door. "He said he would always find us. Whereabouts is he?"

"On a ship, it's literally meters away from us. It came out of nowhere, like magic." Maura explained. "It's one of the boats from Freydale, I think, I saw one of them, the large wooden ones- when we were being dragged towards the dungeons – it's much smaller than this one by far, but it's still a problem."

"Well then…" Joseph said that as he regained his limbs, the cerulean tears were not hindering his body use; they only covered it.

Once he got moving again, he could hardly feel them, even if they were still getting closer to covering his entire face. "Let's go tell him what for, eh?"

"What are you doing?" Pierce asked, stopping Joseph in his tracks, careful not to touch him or the tears as he did. Just standing in front of him like a brick wall. "We must get through this barrier; everything else can wait."

"Caulan won't wait," Joseph replied before Pierce and Santos looked as if they were collectively going to argue. Still, Joseph held up his hand, the watery blue illuminating both faces. "I'm not asking; it's a necessity. If we want to overcome this barrier, we need to speak to him. No. I need to speak to him."

"What on earth is that?" Maura asked as she pointed towards the tears surrounding Joseph's body like armour. She didn't dare touch it. "Is that your body?"

"No. It's just water. Magical water." Joseph explained, trying to keep the conversation light; if he were to speak to Caulan again, he wanted to be relaxed when he did. He tried to stay calm and articulate what he wanted to convey. Then, he could get them through the barrier. "I'm not quite sure myself what it is… but there is it, attached to my body… to my magic."

The light from outside the room was nothing compared to the brightness of the tears, but Joseph found himself wincing at the sight of the sun. He moved slowly, careful not to touch anything prematurely, just in case. Joseph took slow steps as he reached the ship's side, looking out into the ocean with Alex and Maura at his side.

There it was. Joseph recognised one of the ships from the docks in Freydale was the Dalian. Formally, a warship used to fight against rallying kingdoms… since then, it has just become a fishing boat. Bringing most of the produce to Freydale and the smell, too. The Dalian was mostly wood but with a hard rock attached to the front of the ship, used to ram into the opponent in the way. One bang from the Dalian, with the metal on Santos's ship, might not go down, but it wouldn't make a fast getaway after being hit, that was for sure.

"What in the bright blue is it doing?" Santos asked as the Dalian approached the ship's bow, where most people were. Santos got up high, grabbing the side of the boat and hoisting himself up before guiding the attention onto him and shouting as loud as he could. "Hey, Captain!"

Of course, with the two ships being close, he didn't need to shout. Joseph could see Caulan, and Caulan could see him; the man didn't even look up at Santos, who was begging for answers and attention. "I don't need to speak to you. Just to him, and I expect to find him on this ship before I am yours."

"I'm sorry, but I cannot allow that," Santos said in disagreement. He clearly thought that Loreli's Wave could stand on its own. He wasn't scared of Caulan, which was a change. "Joseph is part of my crew, an integral part of it, so I cannot let him leave."

"You mustn't have heard me, captain." Caulan began, throwing Santos's words back at him. Caulan's voice was full of anger; if Joseph was standing in front of the man, he would probably feel spittle on his face from the seething, boiling rage the man had. The Dalian inched closer, enough for Jospeh to see Caulan's wild grey hair from lack of upkeep, the wind blowing it up, out and every which way. "I'm not asking for him to be returned. I'm telling you, he needs to be. Joseph Price is the property of Freydale. And, when he returns to Freydale, he is in for a punishment like he has never seen!"

"You can understand why that won't happen, Dad!" Alex began, earning a look of disapproval even from his distance.

"And you, Alexander, you are relieved from duty altogether; you are grounded… forever!" Caulan shouted. "Both… no, all of you will be punished for this treason!"

He had shouted that last part louder, ground his foot into the floor, and told everyone here what he planned to do if Joseph ever went back to Freydale under Caulan's watchful eye. Those gritted teeth must have hurt as well.

Treason. There wouldn't be a kingdom if they hadn't turned that key. But Joseph chose to hold his tongue. It was no use speaking to Caulan sensibly now. He wouldn't listen anyway.

Santos, however, doubled down.

"And I'm telling you, Caulan. You see, he is not your property anymore; we're a long way from Freydale, and your laws do not hold up here. So, if you believe you are getting Joseph back – you're the mistaken one." Santos shouted before his attention was cast away from Caulan and his boat; instead, Santos looked behind him to where their destination was. "In fact… you're actually in another kingdom altogether, a new kingdom, with different rules – and I'm sure they would agree that Joseph is a refugee. They won't let you take him even if you beg if you plead."

"Oh yeah?" Caulan asked as he looked out into the open blue water; there was nothing but a small island that nothing could really inhabit. "So what kingdom is that?"

"Rivetia!" Santos shouted triumphantly before getting down from his perch and running towards Joseph, careful not to touch him. "Do it now, Joseph. Cover this ship in the tears if you can. Get it through the barrier whilst I have Caulan talking."

"So, Joseph, are you going to come willingly, or am I going to have to sink this ship for you to understand how serious I really am?" Caulan asked. Joseph didn't quite understand why Caulan wanted him so much, why he wanted Joseph back in Freydale. It was like a need rather than a want. Like Caulan needed to know where the boy was at all times. "What – what is that swirling around your body? It looks like… water."

"This?" Joseph asked as he looked at the tears and got a quick idea. If the tears could surround him… they might be able to surround the ship, too. With a smile, Joseph was sure that Caulan could see, Joseph slammed his hands onto one of the barriers on the vessel's side. "These are Cerulean Tears."

"What are"—? Caulan began. He watched with wide eyes as Joseph touched the side of the ship, the tears reacting to the movement quickly, connecting with the metal of the ship, melding with it just like they had done with Joseph. "Joseph Price, I invoke the decree of the Hunter's Guild. You are to stop!"

Finally understanding that he was losing, Caulan clutched at any straws that he could grab. In the Cerulean tears around his body, Joseph looked down, noticing that the mark on his arm from the guild was glowing the ever-familiar purple. Suddenly, he found that Alex was beside him again. Though he didn't want to touch the tears, he stood as close as he could, so Joseph knew he was there.

"Joseph, you understand what the decree is… don't you?" Alex asked. Joseph simply nodded. "So… you have to stop."

"That is enough." Pierce interrupted, stepping forward, grabbing Alex's shoulder, and turning him around to face the man. However, Alex was taller and more muscular, ragging Pierce off. Joseph knew this was not just because of Alex's need to keep Joseph safe. It was more than that this time. "You have been trying to sabotage the mission and get him to stop at every moment possible. We are so close, and now, just because your dear old dad is here, you buckle?"

"Don't act like you know me. You don't." Alex spat before reigning it in, enough to explain. "The decree of the Hunter's Guild was created to neutralise those with magic. It's not used often, but when it does… well, each servant's marks on their body are connected to the decree; if someone with authority states they invoke the decree and Joseph doesn't stop what he is doing and my father states the password…"

"Password?" Santos interjected.

"A jumble of words, then the branding begins to syphon all of their will, all their energy until there is nothing left but an empty husk, waiting for orders," Alex said, his face grim as he spoke.

"Which means…" Pierce began, but Joseph cut him off quickly. His hands were still on the ship's side; the Cerulean Tears did not care about a decree of passwords. They still worked their magic as the seconds passed.

"If I don't stop, I lose myself, completely, forever," Joseph said. Suppose the Cerulean tears weren't moving around his body like a coil, draining him anyway. In that case, he might have said that the decree was already working, too. "And who knows what Caulan would make me do."

"Justice." Caulan began his sequence. But Joseph didn't stop.

Justice was what the Hunter's Guild thought they were giving the people of Kalem by rounding up the people with magic.

"Dad," Alex shouted between the two ships. The ships kept moving, neck and neck—the meters between them were slowly disappearing. Caulan could have probably boarded Santos's ship by now, but he looked perfectly comfortable where he was. Alex, however, and everyone around them were not. "Dad, please don't invoke it."

"All he has to do is stop and come with me," Caulan said. He didn't even have to shout this time. Joseph could see the smile on the man's face as he continued. "Obelisk."

Joseph assumed the Obelisks were the beacons—those shining bright beauties that were destroyed in the war long ago. With them gone, magic was sealed away. Each word told a story, which Joseph remembered more and more as each word was revealed.

"Joseph, stop", Alex pleaded, but he still didn't want to touch the tears. Joseph could tell that Alex wanted to grab him, to shake him, to make him understand. But Alex couldn't bring himself to reach out. It didn't stop him from speaking, though. "You don't have to do this."

"But…" Santos began, but then he looked as if he was doubting himself.

"Dad. He just escaped the guild. If this degree is completed, he loses himself all over again." Pierce interjected his father before he could continue, and it looked as if Santos was understanding.

"Joseph… just step away from the side of the ship," Maura said as she moved forward from where she had been standing. Moving her hands reluctantly, she dove into the tears and grabbed his hand. Squeezing it tightly. She looked slightly uncomfortable as the water moved around her arm but said nothing about it. Instead, she chose to speak quietly, tentatively. "I don't care what it takes, but we will find another way. This is not worth your life."

But Joseph did not lift his hands from the side of the ship. The tears were advancing, reaching the bottom of the vessel and branching out to other parts, touching every patch of rust and barnacle. A blue hue replaced the bright sun, reaching out to cover even Caulan's ship in the glow.

"Slaughter," Caulan said, souring the moment. "We're halfway there, Joseph. Make up your mind!"

Slaughter. To remind Joseph of what the guild did to his people… and his family long ago. And what they could still do to him given the right incentive.

"Please." Alex began, but he didn't move; he didn't attempt to reach into the tears; Alex stood on the sidelines looking in, a grimace on his face. "I've seen what happens when the decree is used… please, I don't want that for you… for someone that I-."

"For someone that you what?" Joseph asked, finally allowing

himself to speak. He had been watching the tears spreading around, getting faster and faster as the surface space grew smaller. But he had heard every argument, every pleading word.

"Someone that I…" Alex said, struggling to form the words. "Someone that I deeply… care for."

"Touching as it is to see, next comes…" Caulan said – as if theatrically he clicked his hands, the two ships now so close Jospeh and Caulan could look into each other's eyes. Neither was willing to back down, even with people asking them to stop on both sides. Then Caulan let the word go out into the open. "Empower."

Empower for what the guild became. Drunk on power with every person who became a 'servant' at their guild.

Pierce moved closer, pushing his hand through the tears and grabbing Joseph's other hand. There was almost an unspoken understanding between them – that Joseph wouldn't stop even if it meant that he would die. He wasn't returning to Freydale, and he wouldn't let Caulan win the way he wanted.

"Painful," Caulan said through gritted teeth.

Painful for what the guild did to servants every day – causing pain. Ripping them from friends, family, and their cultures. Each person had their own belief and story, nullified and shaped into one mind – a servant's mind. No individuality, no rights. Just a painful life.

Alex was to the side of Pierce. He took a moment, ducked underneath Joseph's arms, which were still outstretched, and popped his body back up so he was in front of Jospeh now. Caulan wouldn't get the satisfaction of seeing Joseph's face as the last word was spoken.

"I'm sorry," Joseph said as he looked at Alex. Alex looked at him. They saw through each other, words left unspoken, moments never had, and for the first time in their lives together, they understood each other completely. "I can't go back-."

"I know," Alex said, this time not hesitating. He forced his body through the tears that covered Joseph's, reaching forward and wrapping his arms around Joseph, pulling the other into a hug. Joseph looked down at his wrist, the slight glow of the mark on his arm fading as more words were spoken. "If this is the last time you'll

hear it, I just want to say... I-."

"Home."

A home. What Joseph would never have, thanks to the guild.

The last word.

But Joseph didn't fall. He didn't even falter. For a moment, Joseph believed it was because Alex was holding him, keeping him from falling; death was supposed to be instant once the last word was said. But there he was, still standing; the tears were almost covering the entire ship, and Alex, Maura, and Pierce still held onto him for dear life.

"What?" Joseph said quietly. He had heard stories of those who died to their 'password' – how horrible it was, and Alex himself had seen it with his own two eyes. It happened to people... so why wasn't it happening now? "What happened?"

"You're still... Joseph!" Alex replied as he moved his head to look at Joseph. It was both a question and an answer.

"What? How?" Caulan growled loudly as if a man was possessed; he moved – looking like he was running towards a draw bridge-type contraption, probably used to dock with other boats. "Justice. Obelisk. Slaughter. Empower. Painful. Home."

He grabbed hold of the draw bridge, which was just a piece of wood, gathered his strength to place the wood on a barrier, and tried to hoist himself up just enough to see Joseph.

"No," Joseph said – all he had to do was keep Caulan distracted for a moment more. The tears were moving towards their feet now, covering everything in a bright blue hue – shining out. It was a wonder anyone could see at all.

"Justice. Obelisk. Slaughter. Empower. Painful. Home." Caulan said as he finally got his footing on the wood but had not quite gotten up. He was angry and was messing up as a result. "Justice. Obelisk. Slaughter… why won't it work, damn it!"

"Maybe I'm more powerful than you thought I was!" Joseph shouted, his own anger shining through as the Cerulean tears finally touched Joseph, the people around him, the crew, Santos, and Cecelia. They all squirmed slightly at the tears moving around them. They were alive—tiny tear-shaped beings moving around their feet. "And with that… Santos, you can get this ship away from him before he boards."

"Orders noted." Santos grinned as he ran quickly to the wheel, tears splashing around as he reached and gripped hold of it. He turned it quickly, changing the trajectory back towards where Rivetia was, moving closer towards the small island that didn't look like it should hold a kingdom.

"Hey, where do you think you're going, Joseph?" Caulan shouted as Loreli's Wave moved away from the Dallian, forcing the slab of wood Caulan had moved to connect the two ships to fall off into the ocean below. Caulan knew he had lost now, but he didn't stop shouting as the Loreli got further away. Leaving Caulan alone with no way to follow. "Justice. Obelisk. Slaughter. Empower. Painful. Home."

As the ship moved closer, the Cerulean Tears began to react, jumping almost – forming a barrier around the entire ship as it passed through something hidden, like a forcefield. At first, Joseph wasn't sure if the boat would hold up, but the more it made its way through, the more hopeful it seemed. As he, Alex, Maura and Pierce passed through the barrier simultaneously, Joseph clearly knew they could all see the same thing.

The island changed shape entirely, having grown by about ten times its normal size. From what Joseph could see, it was mountainous, with ruins at the bottom—ruins of the great kingdom… This shattered much of the hope he had just gained. It didn't look like there was anyone left to greet them.

"We made it!" Pierce and Santos began to shout with glee. "He bloody did it; the boy did it!"

"I feel a little…" Joseph began as Alex moved himself back to look at Joseph.

"Joseph?" Alex asked, his voice not yet filled with concern. "Look, we made it. You did it!"

"I feel a little tired…" Joseph said. He was looking for Alex and Maura's faces but just saw blurs—a mixture of colours all forming into one… and that sun beating down. "I might just…"

"Hey, hey!" Maura shouted as she tried to help Alex support Joseph. The confusion between the two was dwarfed by the sounds the crew was making, all the happy cheering, all the excitement. "Joseph?"

"Santos, sir!" Alex called, stopping all the cheering momentarily as he laid Joseph down on the wooden floor. The tears formed back into the small blue gem at Joseph's feet. "We need some help over here!"

They had made it to Rivetia.

But what had it cost Joseph Price?

SIX

Inky darkness.

Shadows.

Blackout. Joseph could hardly make out what was in front of him. The darkness concealed a brown-haired man's secret; he couldn't see any distinguishing features of the man's face, just his piercing grey eyes, a light grey, unnatural, his left eye, covered by a scar, causing one of the irises to turn milky white. Maybe his eyes weren't grey after all. Just altered.

Joseph didn't understand what was happening or how he had gotten to this strange place with a man who spoke no words, but he did smile. Not a happy smile, smirk, or all-knowing type – the one that really got under your skin. That wrapped around you like a snake, a smile that bore into your existence.

"What-." Joseph managed to let out a singular word before he felt his words almost jump back inside of him. "What?"

"Lu…" The man began, stuttering on words but still keeping that smile on his face. He tilted his head to the side, almost as if to look at Joseph better. "Luma."

"What did you say?" Joseph asked as he tried to move closer to the strange man. But as he tried to take a step, he felt like he was being pushed back by some invisible force.

"I was like you." The man said quietly, finally finding his words. "I could control the magical water, fought battles, won wars. The power of the Luma is a great adversary. Enjoy it."

"I don't understand what I'm supposed to do with this power," Joseph said before the man began to move. Unlike Joseph, he could actually walk and fast, too. He reached Joseph in under a second. The same smile was still ever-present. "What are you doing?"

"Offering you… this." The man said as he reached around his neck and revealed what looked to be a necklace, counteracting the darkness; the blue hue of the cerulean tears lit up the whole space. It was no man's land, a blank canvas, but Joseph could see the man's face better now. Fashioning it into a bracelet for Joseph, the man quickly wrapped it around Joseph's wrist. "This is the talisman I wore my entire life as the Luma. You will have it out in the real world when you exit this dream. This will help you channel the magic better."

"Who are you, though?" Joseph asked as he admired his new piece of jewellery. "Why are you helping me?"

"I was never here. I shouldn't be visiting, but know I am a friend. As I said, I used to be you a long time ago, " the man said before he turned around. "I have to leave now."

"No, wait, I still don't understand," Joseph said, a small laugh escaping his lips.

"That's the curse of the Luma. You never quite know what's coming next." The man said, slightly turning his head around, but his body stayed turned. "I can leave you with one bit of information before I go. A critical piece of information."

"What is it?" Joseph asked, eager for anything to help him

understand what was happening.

"The decay that's flowing around the world, its dangerous stuff. Now that you are Luma, you are responsible for stopping it, including returning magic to the world around you. This is your mission; you were always heading for this. The prophecy was always about you." The man said sternly.

"What prophecy?" Joseph asked, confused. "I-."

"Your parents were told a prophecy that their youngest would save this world one day, that you would be the catalyst for change. That you would return magic to a broken world. It was never set in stone; things can change through our actions, but now you are the Luma..." The apparition said as he turned back around fully, facing Joseph again. "The prophecy is set in stone now. You are the one that needs to turn all the keys. No one else."

"Well, now I'm even more confused than I was before," Joseph said before the man reached for Joseph's hands, holding them in his own.

"You are strong, Joseph, stronger than I was. I failed to reunite the power of the shade and the Luma. When the opportunity arises, I hope you are worthy and stronger than I could ever be." The apparition said before he turned around again and began to walk away.

"Wait!" Joseph said – trying to reach out to the other man. The man did not explain what he meant. This was not the moment to clam up for someone who clearly loved to talk.

"Joseph…" A female voice different from the man's came through the dream. "Joseph, wake up!"

The man stopped walking and turned on his heel, staring at Joseph with the same smile.

"Joseph, can you hear me?" Another voice chimed in around

him, more profound and concerned.

"What is happening?" Joseph asked as he covered his ears from the surrounding sounds, echoing off each other, around his soul.

"Joseph?" Clear as day, that was Alex's voice. Guiding him out of the dream world in which he was trapped.

Before his mind cleared, the bright light from the cerulean tears bracelet faded, and Joseph saw the same smiling man standing near him. He cocked his head to the side again like he had before, getting a good look at Joseph, his eyes darting from the bottom to the top of his head.

Then, his smile fell. "You are in danger."

When Joseph woke, he wasn't quite sure the meaning of the dream or who the man he had been shown was, either; there was a slight familiarity to him, but his face didn't make sense like it was all jumbled up like a dream or whatever it was hadn't shown Joseph the whole picture. There was no urgency to open his eyes as he lay down— the sun was warm, still beaming down on him as some noise became more audible by the second.

"Jo…" the voice began. It was like the words were jumbled up, too. The word was repeated repeatedly as if guiding him towards opening his eyes. "Jose… Joseph?"

When he opened his eyes, all Joseph could see was a blur of a face looking down at him and a few others moving around him in tandem with one another. There was a sure commotion as more sounds became audible, but someone kept him propped up enough that the sun stung his eyes as he tried to open them properly.

"What happened to me?" Joseph said as the words spoken came into focus before the rest of the world did. "Where…?"

"Just don't move, okay?" The voice said. It was Alex. There was no mistaking it, and if he tried hard enough, he could see the blonde wisps of his hair in front of Joseph's face. The blurry image of the hair sticking up was clearer now that Joseph knew who was holding him. "You took a tumble, and we're not sure why. We made it to Rivetia. We're off the ship and on the beach."

Were they on dry land? Finally.

Joseph only realised how tired he was again, struggling to keep his eyes open. He wasn't in pain; those words Caulan had strung together hadn't affected him at all, and rather than worrying why they hadn't, Joseph was just glad that he didn't die in the process. Dying was not good. Or so they say.

Finally coming into focus, Joseph could see a few extra people in the background. Maura and Pierce were speaking with one another, and both had what looked to be sombre expressions on their faces. Worried, probably. Joseph didn't like people to worry about him; he had lived his whole life in the dark with a tiny list of people who cared for him – he didn't want the extra baggage, even if it was lovely.

Santos and his crew looked busy unloading their various items off the ship as the group of four stood or laid to the side instead. As Joseph adjusted his head to see more, he noticed that Rivetia wasn't exactly as he imagined. The small island was all but gone, replaced by this large mountainous clump of land masses.

It looked like the beginnings of some old ruins—broken down buildings that looked too old to even classify as habitable, marble statues covering the floor, all shattered and covered with what looked to be moss and weeds. No one had inhabited this area in a long time, maybe even before the war. The decay and the growth looked too far gone to be just a few mere years.

This place did not seem to have such a 'formidable army or ruler'. Joseph just hoped he hadn't made a mistake in helping the crew get here because now that they were in Rivetia… there was only one way out. Back through that barrier, Joseph wasn't sure if his body could do much more.

It looked like a place that was war-torn, even now. But the few people who had made it towards the docks didn't look too hard done by, if not a little flabbergasted. Joseph knew that if he saw a large ship dock at their harbour after so many years of no one coming in and out of the barrier, he too would be just as concerned, confused and nervous as they were. And currently, he was feeling all of those, rather sick to his stomach.

Joseph moved his body against Alex's instructions to see Cecelia and the rest of the crew. They looked as if they were unloading the ship entirely, bringing barrels and clothing that must have been loaded on—Joseph had no idea what was inside. It looked like they were planning to stay now that they were here.

Even though he had helped them get into Rivetia, he had no idea of the crew's intentions once they arrived; so far, though, Pierce and Santos seemed too busy overlooking the unpacking to care that there were a bunch of new people slowly making their way to the docks over the horizon. But Joseph noticed. The weather was different inside this 'dome' as well. It was hotter than it had been outside of it, the heat getting to Joseph a little more than the exhaustion right now – he needed a drink, something, anything; he was parched.

"Drink?" Joseph asked. The small noise alerted all three of them and some of the crew, who were moving things and piling them up on the beach nearby. Some of the natives moved closer, bewilderment covering all of their faces.

"How did you-?" an older woman asked. She looked a little older than Santos did. Her eyes darted from the new group of people and the ship. Her skin was like old leather, frail and lightly tanned from the harsh sun, just like the rest of the small unit of people who found themselves still living in this kingdom even now.

"I need a drink, please?" Joseph asked again. He didn't have time for the woman's questions, and it seemed that neither did the other people around. They were all too preoccupied with their various unloading and worrying.

"Okay, I'll find something." Maura nodded, leaving Alex to hold the fort while she searched one of the barrels that some of the crew had brought off. She was sure they wouldn't mind—after all, Joseph got them there in the first place.

"Here, Maura, there's water. I think it's a natural spring." Pierce said as he pointed to a small pool of water close by to where the two had been stood.

Maura walked over and quickly procured some water for him to drink. Joseph weakly gripped the cup, drinking down every ounce of the water swiftly provided, forcing his head up so he didn't choke. Freshwater had never tasted so good before.

"He should not drink the water, " the old, bewildered woman warned, pointing towards Joseph, who was already drinking it as she spoke.

"What, why?" Maura said, her eyes bulging out of her head as she looked down at the cup that was all but empty. Maura then stood up, her fists cast down. A flurry of anger, spittle, and fury came from her tone, a version of Maura Joseph had never seen before. "Thanks for the warning, lady! Could you not have told us before I gave it to him?"

"Is it poisonous?" Pierce asked, stepping away from the 'natural spring' he had pointed out.

"He is not native." She spoke, scolding all the new people on the beach but keeping her eyes solely on Joseph. She did not have a worried expression but rather a hopeful one. Joseph just didn't understand why. "Who knows what it will do to an outsider like him after so long..."

"What do you mean-." Alex began, but before he could ask anything more, the weight he felt on his body from carrying Joseph subsided. Concerned about what the woman had just said, he turned to Joseph – tightening his grip on the boy. Now, even the crew were taking note of what was happening.

As Joseph turned his head, he saw Santos no longer looking at the pile of items already unloaded off the ship but rather joining everyone by Joseph's side.

"Joseph? Are you okay?" Santos's voice called from close by. He could hear footsteps coming towards him from the small deck area where he and his crew were loading their various items.

"I'm… fine," Joseph said as he managed to push himself up from the ground he was lying on; with assistance from Alex and Maura, he was upright as rain almost thirty seconds after drinking the water. "I don't feel weak anymore… what was in that water?"

Santos stepped forward to offer some information. He kept looking at the older woman who spoke, but she didn't look at him, instead keeping her eyes on Joseph. "The tears, they live in the water surrounding Rivetia, even in the small pools that Pierce found for you to drink out of. I'm glad to see that even here, above ground, the tears are still active and working in harmony. They still wish to heal."

"Above ground?" Maura asked as she turned her head, squinting slightly in the bright light.

"Did I not say?" Santos asked, looking around at the ruins, squinting slightly to see further against the sun. The ruins spread for miles, and a beautiful kingdom would have been reduced to rubble. "Rivetia is mainly underground, with vast waterways and aqueducts scattered above the ground, but they lead down. Or at least, that's what I remember."

"Who are you to have such knowledge of Rivetia?" the woman asked. She was older than Joseph initially thought she was, holding some sort of stick to keep her upright. Now that he was standing up properly, she was dwarfed by many of the people around her. "You're just a simple outsider, are you not?"

Santos looked at the woman, studying her face. His eyebrows raised. Then, in an act Joseph hadn't seen after spending his days with Santos, the man looked on the verge of tears, the most emotion the man had shown.

"Hello again, Kala," Santos said, his voice warm and soft. The woman narrowed her eyes as she heard her name on his lips. "Even now, I recognise you. You look no different, even fifty years later."

"How dare you address the Queen with such informality!" a younger man with equally tanned skin and jet-black hair shouted out towards Santos, a look of obscene shock on his face. You are to address her as Queen Kala and nothing more!"

"Queen?" Santos replied, taken back, chuckling quietly, taking no heed to the man who had shown such hostility. "You're a queen, Kala? That's sure impressive. You always wanted to outdo me in every way possible. I got stuck with the ship; you must run a kingdom!"

"I demand that you show the queen some respect!" The man once again shouted at Santos.

"No, Salador, it's fine." Kala spoke calmly, soothing the man next to her. Before she stepped forward, placing her cane before her, she looked at Santos with a curious expression, a small smile forming on her lips. "So, you know me?"

"Very well, indeed, yes." Santos smiled, getting closer to her. Kala kept her eyes narrowed as she came closer, studying the face of the man who had confused her so much. Before she exclaimed. Suddenly, the similarities made sense. "I wondered how long it might take…"

"Oh, my dear baby brother," Kala exclaimed once more,

earning confused, shocked whispers from the crew, and Pierce stood next to the trio.

"I wasn't a baby even when I left the island." Santos chuckled as she pulled him into a hug, all the frailness in her body disappearing as soon as she held her brother in her arms. More chattering occurred between Santos's crew and Kala's people. All wondering just what they had missed.

"You'll always be my baby brother, no matter how old you are… or how old I am, for that matter." Queen Kala said, her voice lightening slightly as the emotion took over. "You disappeared just before the eve of that terrible war ended. What happened? Neither you nor your father came back. I thought you had perished."

"I followed father against his wishes. He was going off to fight, and I thought I was a big boy, too big for my boots. I snuck onto his fleet of ships, and when he found me, there was no way to turn back. Then, the war ended out of nowhere, and magic was banished." Santos said as he embraced his sister once again. Joseph looked at Santos, inspecting him; if he had gone to war with his father, just by looking at him – Joseph would have said that Santos would have only been a child at most. "We couldn't make it back to Rivetia even if we wanted to; the only way that we could get back was to break down the barrier with you know what. And we only recently had access to such a large suppository worth that could do the job."

"And father?" Kala asked. "Is he with you?"

"I'm sorry. He died a long time ago. He was old when we went to war; the war aged him too much. I was only nineteen when he died." Santos said Kala had some sadness in her eyes, but she sucked it up, though her eyes were still glassy with tears. "Father would have loved to see this, to get back to Rivetia."

"Yes, how did you get in?" Kala said, looking around at everyone standing at the docks. "That barrier has been a right pain;

we've been unable to go in or out, and trade has all but stopped. It's been hard for a while."

"Meet Joseph Price, Kala," Santos said as he brought the boy over, though he didn't explain how Joseph had managed to get through the barrier. Truth be told, neither did Joseph. "He is the very reason I am standing here today."

"This is just a mere boy." Kala scolded her brother as she looked upon Joseph, realising that he was the same one who had drunk the water that had apparently healed him. "Don't tell me you drafted a poor boy to get you here."

"Kala, he could use the cerulean tears, absorb them, and channel them into his body. It was magical. Like everything we thought would happen when we found 'the one'." Kala's face changed. It was like she knew what Santos was talking about.

"That will be why the water did what it did to him. He was weak before, but now he isn't even when he is not native," Kala explained before she went slightly wide-eyed. "The Luma has returned."

"The Luma?" Joseph asked. Santos had said the word before, and though Santos knew of it, he didn't seem too clued up on it; Kala did seem clued up. It was time for some answers about what was happening to him. "Can you please explain what that is?"

"The Luma was a warrior, created by the Goddess of Rejuvenation and creation Lumin. Stories go that she bestowed the power to harness the Cerulean Tears for the good of the world. To create, rejuvenate, and heal after a catastrophe hundreds of years ago." Kala explained, her voice croaky. She held onto her walking stick as she looked at Joseph, her thoughts whirring as if trying to delve into every detail she could. "For many years, the Luma was a title passed onto the next generation, used for the good of the world, at least when the world was harmonious with one another. Two siblings were up in the running for the power. Only one prevailed; he received the gift of the Luma. The other got nothing."

"Well…" Salvador interrupted, then shook his head as if unsure If he wanted to continue.

"Well, what?" Joseph asked. "If I am the Luma, don't I need to know?"

"The second sibling didn't believe it fair that her brother got the power. The Luma always had this pendant. We called it the Rivetia Pendant; it's been lost for a long time." Salvador interrupted, and Joseph's mind was cast towards the gem of pure Cerulean Tears he had used. "Before the bestowing ceremony, she stole the pendant and broke it in two. The anger she felt, the betrayal. It darkened the pendant she took, creating…"

"The Shadow…" Kala said, her voice grim with worry. "Neither has been seen for a long time, so if the Luma is back… so will the Shadow return. The decay, everything destroyed. Not just here but the world."

"Do you think…?" Alex began as he looked around at Joseph and Maura.

"I do think," Maura replied. "I might not have seen it, but the decay following the two of you… it might have something to do with this."

"Explain?" Kala began, bug-eyed, looking at the two of them. "What are you two speaking of?"

"There is already decay following us around. It's already destroyed a kingdom on the Juna coast. It started from an old beacon, and we believe that the decay will follow us here." Joseph began, explaining to the Queen what their travels were all about. She listened intently, nodding. "Do you happen to know of any beacons here at all? Or any keys?"

Joseph already knew there was. He just hoped that, given that they were already speaking about it and that she was the Queen, she might just let it slip off its location and how hard it might be to find the key. This island looked far too big to traverse all on their own.

"Ah. I do." Kala replied. She looked like she might say this, but then she pursed her lips shut, looking around at the many people who had yet to announce themselves. "But first, you all need to rest. The King will want to speak to all of you individually, just a simple assessment. You can ask questions later."

"But-." Joseph began but then realised it was best to do as he was told. This was a different place than Freydale – different customs. Santos had warned him that he needed to speak to the ruler – so say, he would have to do.

"Back to work, get all the cargo off the ship while we speak amongst ourselves!" Santos called out to the crew. Cressida, overlook it for a moment. I need to be alone in private with my sister and these lot."

"Yes, sir." Cressida smiled. It was probably the first time he had seen her smile in the entire three-day journey—probably the stress lifting off her now that she was safely off the ship. Joseph understood that completely.

"So, Santos," Kala said as she moved closer to the group of five. "Do you really think he is the Luma?"

"I do. I have seen it with my eyes; your nephew has, too. Ask him." Santos explained, dropping a further bombshell onto Kala.

"My nephew?" Kala asked as she searched Alex's face and then Pierce's. Pierce took this as his opportunity to take her hand and meet her for the first time.

"I've heard so much about you; my name is Pierce," Pierce said as he shook the woman's hand, towering over the small woman. She didn't look much like a queen from where Joseph stood, but maybe things were different in Rivetia.

"I wish I could say the same." Kala began to laugh as she embraced both men who towered over her. She had gotten her family back, which seemed like a long time coming. "It's very nice to meet you, Pierce!"

"Can I ask you a question, Queen Kala?" Joseph began, earning a nod and an eyebrow raise from the woman. "The Cerulean Tears. Do they... can they save someone from dying?"

"They're said to be able to rejuvenate someone in their last moments, but, I don't know, I've never seen it." Kala shook her head, an aura of cynicism about her. "Why do you ask?"

"I was supposed to die on the ship... back in the kingdom I'm from, I was a servant, and the man who ran the guild I was assigned to had a rather special way to kill me. He had to say a string of words, and once said, those words would activate something inside of me – it would kill me." Joseph said before he realised that he didn't fully know how the decree worked. All he knew was that it would kill him, or rather – how it wouldn't now the tears had bonded themselves to him. "The tears were surrounding me, and it was as if they were able to keep me from succumbing to the effects; I only wondered if maybe they had stopped it from happening?"

"It could be that... The Cerulean Tears protecting their host." Kala said as she rubbed her chin with her free hand. "Leave it with me; when you come and speak to the King, I will provide more information to you."

"Thank you," Joseph said. For right now, he was just glad that he was alive.

"Okay, listen up! We have guests. They are allowed safe passage into the kingdom. Let them pass. Take them down, turn on the underwater heated spring, and inform King Fennick, someone. We're having a party tonight in honour of my family returning!"

"Yes, Queen Kala." Salvador nodded as he began to walk towards where the group had come from. Down below.

Kala then turned to Joseph, eying him up. "So, if you're really 'the one' as they say, I want to see it myself." The Queen said.

"He's still too tired. That barrier really took it out of him. Can he rest first?" Alex interrupted. Kala looked displeased that she had to wait but then nodded in agreement. "Thank you, your majesty."

"Oh, I like this one; he has a real nature for royalty, doesn't he?" Kala laughed quietly; the people were slowly moving throughout the area, and Queen Kala's group was all moving around to help Santos's crew move the boxes inside where Joseph couldn't see yet. "I've not been called Your Majesty in years. It sounds right, don't you think? Take note, people, take note!"

"So we can stay?" Joseph asked. People were already getting unpacked, but the Queen hadn't confirmed it. She raised her eyebrows and nodded quickly.

"If you are who my brother says you are, Joseph, then you are the one to bring this kingdom back to the light," Kala said as she reached for Joseph's hand and began to shake it, a smile forming on her face; this time, it was different—a happy smile, a smile she had clearly not done in a long, long time. "It's very nice to make your acquaintance, Joseph Price."

SEVEN

When Joseph finally woke up for the third time that day, he was in an unfamiliar place. Waking up in a new place was always scary, but this was something else entirely. He hadn't even recalled falling asleep in the first place.

The room was small, like some sort of bunker. The only light came from what looked to be a familiar blue hue flowing through it— like a stream heading out through a small hole into the wall leading to somewhere he couldn't see.

The room was not visible to his eyes; there were no candles, no flames to make fire-light, and he couldn't even see anything in front of his face. The blanket on his body was weighted, like it kept him down, strapped and stuck on the bed. It was hard to move under, probably to conserve warmth underground – very little heat would make its way here; there had to be other ways to stay warm in the winter months, maybe even into the summertime.

Joseph lifted his arms – feeling for something, but nothing was before him. Nothing was behind him apart from the walls keeping the room upright. As he let his arm fall, he felt something at the side of the bed other than the weighted blanket. Hair, fluffy, short. Moving further down, he felt skin, cold to the touch but soft too, the light sense of breathing, the warm feeling of air being breathed out of the lungs of whoever it was next to him. Whoever it was had also been asleep but seemed to be in a rather uncomfortable position doing so. Like they had fallen asleep keeping watch.

Joseph pressed into the person's cheek, feeling a slight stirring from the person – like they had started to wake up from their sleep.

"Hm?" The person made a slight, tired noise as they raised their head, a yawn escaping their lips. "I fell asleep."

That voice, the faint scent of the cologne he knew so well, and as the person moved closer, Joseph realised who it was, and he was somewhat relieved. Alex's face became visible seconds later when light flooded the once-dark room after he grabbed an oil lamp on the wall and lit it quickly. Joseph could see for the first time since he had fallen asleep.

He could see Alex's hair, slightly unkempt from Joseph messing it up; he could see the blanket, a thick, wiry cotton-type throw – large enough to cover three bodies at least; it must have been wrapped around his body at least that many times, too. And he could see the extent of the room, white walls with a beautiful flower border, all individual flowers illuminated by the same blue hue he was so familiar with – like they had been crafted out of cerulean tears themselves.

"Can you help me up?" Joseph asked as he zoned in on Alex, the man's face coming into focus as he got closer. "Where are we exactly?"

"Here," Alex said as he took some weight off Joseph, dropping some of the blankets to the floor at his feet, letting him move and breathe appropriately. "Do you not remember? We're in one of the rooms in Queen Kala's home. This underground area is massive, and I think it spans the whole island. Maura went out to explore hours ago when this party honoured Pierce, and Santos's return began. She's there now; I've not even left this room."

"You didn't want to go to a party?" Joseph asked, yawning himself – looking at Alex, who grabbed a match and lit one of the candles on the side of the bed. Bags under his eyes showed Joseph why the man had fallen asleep whilst 'on watch'. "Why not? I thought you were the life and the soul of the party?"

"Pierce and Santos clearly said they don't like me. I don't want to ruin their style; I also want to stay with you. I wanted to ensure that you were okay before I even attempted to step out of this room. Maura offered to stay too, but I told her to go and explore." Alex explained as he came to sit on the edge of the bed. "I think she just needed some alone time to think, breathe, and do whatever she felt like doing. It's been tough for her, an unknown realm in constant peril, magic; even just speaking about it overwhelms me. Imagine how she feels."

"Yeah, good idea, actually. I can't imagine what Maura is going through." Joseph replied as he felt his body become heavy as it caught up with the fact that he was awake. "What do you think dragged her here? It seems odd that someone from another realm would appear in ours."

"Maybe she's here for a reason." Alex offered, clicking his tongue. "I'm not sure of the reason, but maybe she just is; whatever laws the universe had – they've all been thrown out recently."

"That's true. I can't believe how much has happened since we left Freydale that one time. When you're cooped up in one kingdom for most of your life, you forget that other people out there don't harbour ill will to magic." Joseph said, fiddling with the blanket. "I never thought I'd find people who don't care that I have magic, people who see me as a normal, everyday human being rather than a shapeshifter."

"I got speaking to someone just before you fell asleep. The people of Rivetia didn't harbour ill-will to those with magic like the rest of the people in the war. In fact, Rivetia were fighting on the side of magic itself, even those who didn't have it themselves. Those tears things are too important to both the people here and the entire ecosystem; if they lost that in the war – they'd lose their livelihood." It sounded a lot like those in Rivetia had their heads screwed on. Alex cleared his throat; maybe he had realised the same – that magic wasn't the enemy, but the people who thought themselves so fragile that they had to destroy something that made them feel inferior. Everyone with magic knew that because that was what the war was about. "I guess I'd never thought of it that way."

"You're relearning many new things, the same way I am. You were brainwashed; your father branded you a hunter before you even learned to walk. That was always going to be your destiny for him." Joseph said, reaching out to grab Alex's hand. "You can change your destiny now like we were going to before we were both shipped off. You can start again."

"Do you think…" Alex began. Before he held himself back, Joseph could see him fighting against himself as his thumb traced around Joseph's hands. "Do you think we could start again?"

"I'd like that. I don't know how yet. There are so many unsaid things between us, people like us, we don't have the luxury of speaking about them, we don't think we're owed them." Joseph said, Alex began to nod; he understood completely. "I say screw that ideology; I want to break those rules; I don't want to feel helpless anymore. I think that to start out, we need to be open with each other and say things we previously never could. We both owe our past selves that."

"I agree," Alex replied, gulping slightly as he prepared to say something. "The dream when we were by the lake when I said I loved you. I meant it. In some twisted way, despite everything I did in that year, taking the money from you, acting out against you, cooping you up in the guild… deep down, I think I was trying to get rid of those feelings for you because of everything that was drilled into me. This is me being as open as I can be, I love you, but I hate what I did to you. I hate myself."

"I love you too; I think I always will to some capacity," Joseph replied before he felt Alex's eyes bore into him.

"Do you mean that?" Alex asked.

"I wouldn't have said it in the dream if I didn't mean it," Joseph said as he propelled himself forward in the bed to better look at Alex, who still held Joseph's hand in his own. "Listen, it's complicated. We both did things we will always regret, but I think that's just part of every relationship, platonic or otherwise. We both misunderstood each other; we were told lies about one another to convey a narrative that your father wanted to thread into our lives. He didn't want us to be friends, let alone anything else, so…"

"I think we both need to throw anything he told us far away," Alex said. "He can't hurt you, me or us anymore."

"I'll hold you to that," Joseph said as he heard Alex let out a small chuckle.

"Can I do something? You can tell me no if you don't like it." Alex asked before Joseph felt Alex's large hands pulling him into a hug. Joseph felt himself wrapping his own hands around Alex's body, the two of them turning their bodies so that they could be more comfortable. "Are you okay?"

"Perfectly content," Joseph said as he buried his head into Alex's shoulder. "Can we stay like this forever?"

"I'll clear my schedule," Alex said, chuckling.

"You're wearing different clothes." Joseph lifted his head from Alex's shoulder, though he did not remove his hands from the cuddle. He knew it wasn't relevant to their conversation, maybe inappropriate. Still, Joseph couldn't help but notice the lack of the blood-stained vest that Alex had worn since they escaped. Now, he looked like he was wearing something very similar to what one of the natives had worn when they met them by the docks.

"Oh," Alex said as he looked down at the clothes that he was wearing. The two of them broke the hug for a second. "Yeah, they sort of made me change clothes when that Jericho guy noticed the blood stain and the dirt the jacket was covered in – Queen said if I was to be a 'gentleman' and look after you whilst you slept, I had to be dressed like one and not a 'mess'. I don't really understand what she meant by that. They gave Maura a dress, too, but she almost refused to wear it. Apparently, it's customary, especially on party days."

"You look good," Joseph replied. "Though, now I feel a little bit underdressed."

Alex reached to his side and procured some clothes at the edge of the bed. "They gave you some stuff to change into when you woke up. If you can stand, I can leave the room to let you change if you want?" Alex said as he removed the last of the blanket, letting it aimlessly fall to the side of the bed.

"I can stand, yeah," Joseph said as he threw his legs over the side of the bed and stood up. A little wobbly at first due to the lack of walking for however long he had been out, but not wanting to be proved wrong to someone like Alex, he regained composure—he didn't even need to hold onto the bedside table this time. "See?"

"Good." Alex smiled before walking towards the door at the back end of the small room. "I'll let you change. You can use a mirror on that wall. Then I thought we could explore the 'town' together. Really, take it all in?"

"Sounds good to me." Joseph nodded as he managed to take a few steps away from the bed. Alex hesitated, grabbing the door handle as if he didn't want to leave. Joseph looked over at him, smiled, and chuckled slightly as he reached the mirror. He had seen himself for the first time in a while – he looked like a mess, too. "Go, Alex, I'll be quick."

Now he was alone, Joseph looked around the room properly.

The walls looked as if they had paper on them, something entirely different from the brick walls that Freydale had. And the flowers looked painted on. Great care had been used to individually detail even the smallest of areas—Rivetia truly was something out of this world.

As he looked at the paper, feeling its softness and reaching out to touch it, he could better understand why Pierce had referred to Freydale as primitive. Compared to this kingdom and this room alone, it was.

Finally, looking back into the mirror, the glass slab handing over what looked like a much larger bedside table, Joseph glanced at himself. Instantly, that whole sense of wonder, the amazement on his face, suddenly changed. He looked dirty, his clothes were messy, small holes covering his shirt that he hadn't noticed before and as he looked at them, really looked at them – he realised that he wouldn't be able to tell someone what colour they might have been when the guild gave them to him. The sense of wonder had entirely gone now; Joseph had never seen himself like this before, even the cuts to his face, the bruises that covered his arms and his chest as he lifted the bottom half of his shirt – it turned his stomach, he hadn't noticed them before. He had felt them but noticed? *No.* He was too wrapped up in other things to care.

Joseph had never seen himself like this before. Maybe Alex and the people in Rivetia were right; he needed to change clothes.

The shirt he was wearing was oversized, too big for him. The guild didn't care for the sizes of its servants; they gave out clothes rarely, and it was the pick of the litter; wait too long, and you got the hand-me-downs that had seen better days. Sometimes, much better days. His old clothes slipped off his rather skinny body quickly enough; a leaf came loose from the fabric as he did. Joseph watched it fall in the mirror, drifting towards the floor like a feather would. It held meaning for Joseph – he was falling into an unknown realm, a new sense of self.

A reflection he had never seen before.

Looking down at the larger table below him, he saw what looked to be a basin, some clean-looking water in it – having not washed his face and cleared it of the dirt and, much more importantly, the cuts on his face, one by his lip and another by his eyebrow, small enough not to notice, but they needed to be cleaned, he didn't want to have more problems on his hands than he did now. Cupping some of the water, Joseph splashed it on his face quickly, feeling the effects of the coldness – shocking his body awake properly; he just had to keep going.

He kept his face, peering into the mirror to see where he was scrubbing with his hands. Slowly, the dirt subsided, and he could see himself clearly. Great, big bags under his eyes, he still looked a mess, but Joseph knew no amount of scrubbing in cold water would change that fact.

That was a whole other can of worms to open altogether.

Now that his face was clean, Joseph began putting on the clothes he had been provided: a new shirt, trousers and what looked to be a jacket. As he slipped on the sweater, Joseph noticed it had the same blue he was familiar with etched into every fabric thread. He had never felt something so soft, something so new,… since he was a free man, back living with his parents and brother in that town he couldn't even remember the name of now.

Back when he was happy.

Gathering up the old clothes, Joseph placed them on the bed and laid them out on the duvet. The guild always taught him to make his bed from a young age; they always wanted it done, so now, as he quickly made the bed that had been provided for him, Joseph realised that it was a habit he would never break.

"Alex?" Joseph sauntered towards the door the man had walked out of moments before. "I'm ready."

There was a slight clicking sound as the door opened, and Alex entered with a smile, looking Joseph up and down. "It looks good." But then he walked up to Joseph and began to take the jacket off him, shaking his head. "I don't think the jacket suits you…"

It definitely didn't.

Joseph had never worn a jacket before and wouldn't start now. "Me neither." Alex, on the other hand, suited one, especially the one that he was wearing now. The dark purple colour of it complimented the bright blue made from the cerulean tears—it made him look smart—and, as Queen Kala had said, gentleman-like.

"Shall we get going, then?" Alex said, smiling at Joseph with his signature grin. We can explore all we want. As we walked towards Queen Kala's house, I saw loads of food stalls lined up inside. We could always try those first. There is always the idea of going to the party, too, if you feel up to it."

"You don't need to worry about me; I'm fine; I just need a bit of time to adjust to moving around again," Joseph said with a smile. However, Joseph moved quickly before the two left the room, grabbing Alex's left hand. "Is this okay?"

"It's perfect," Alex said before he raised their hands together and quickly moved his fingers to interlock them instead. This did feel much more comfortable. "Are you ready to go?"

With his free hand, Joseph grabbed for the door handle and opened the door quickly, ready to take his first steps into the unknown. "I am indeed."

EIGHT

The underground city of Rivetia was a wonder to the eyes. Black cobbled streets, white sandstone walls, cerulean tears, and light blue light shimmering everywhere made the somewhat dull area a marvel. Without the tears, the hallway, which Joseph would describe as cold, dank, and rather dark.

"How far down would you say we are?" Joseph asked as he and Alex moved around into a large circular area where the food stalls that Alex had mentioned were held. Still holding Alex's hand, Joseph dragged Alex towards them quickly, like a happy child. Rivetia was a lot different from Freydale. It had items on the stalls that he had never seen before, or rather, never allowed close enough to.

"I'm not sure; we were walking down the stairs to get to the city for a while," Alex said as he gripped Joseph's hand and happily dragged through the weaving city. "Despite the burst of energy you had above ground, it all seemed to disappear once you entered the underground. It was like the tears were less potent down here or something. But I'm glad you've found the energy again."

It did make sense why the tears, though they looked bright, didn't nearly look as blue as they did outside – the sun was shining down on them, almost as if it was revitalising the tears. Down here, it was just like magic was diluted. Joseph looked down at where his feet stood, one on each side of the small river of tears; inside the water – small teardrop-shaped items floated, but they didn't look as active as they did above ground. They didn't even look alive.

Every piece of the stone walls was covered in greenery, delicately placed there on purpose to spread throughout, so it didn't seem so dull down here. Joseph wasn't sure how long they had been down here, but he could tell they were planning for the long haul. As Joseph and Alex made their way through the sea of people moving forwards and back, he noticed people to the side – shouting out words, trying to get the passers-by to come over to them, much like the fairs in Freydale.

But this felt different—this was everyday life, this was people trying to make a living. So far, this place had checked all the boxes of where Joseph had wanted to find himself. The sun was an issue, though; he did like to see the sun. Despite the vast size of the tunnels, he felt claustrophobic. But that was really the only downside.

"Strawberries!" A man shouted to the side of them, shocking Joseph slightly by the loudness of his voice. "Get your fresh strawberries right here, fresh from Rivetia soil up top!"

Joseph watched as Alex fumbled through his pockets, procured a small bonze piece coin, flipped it in his hand and walked over to the stall. The strawberries were indeed the largest he had ever seen, like the size of a tangerine, forming a perfect point at the bottom – the vibrant red staring back at him. Alex picked up four large fruits and threw one in Joseph's direction. "Think fast!"

Joseph had never had the luxury of tasting one—in Freydale, strawberries were the 'gods' nectar'—and they were hard to come by, so they were never eaten by anyone who wasn't a royal or at least very high up in social status.

"I've never tried a strawberry before..." Joseph said as he

looked down at it and quickly took a bite.

"What do you think?" Alex asked, studying Joseph's face as he tasted the 'god's nectar' for the first time. Alex had probably eaten hundreds in his life, but even he was excited to eat this one – freshly grown by the looks of it.

Joseph thought back to the year he was working for the baron. He had tried new foods due to the work he was put to, but he had never tried fruits like these, even though they were above the barons' standing in social circles.

"It's so sweet," Joseph replied, letting the juices run down his hands and biting into it again. Savouring the sweet taste. "I love it."

"I forget sometimes that you are doing many things for the first time. What else, if you could, would you try?" Alex asked as the two walked. Alex placed the two other strawberries in a small bag that he was carrying on his side. They were walking closer towards where the music was playing from, a light song, like a drum beating in a celebratory tone. Tapping feet could be heard as if hundreds of people were dancing in tandem with one another.

"Chocolate," Joseph said, feeling his mouth water. That was another thing that he had never had the luxury to try. "I used to see these chocolate tarts at the baron's house; the baron always had parties. He forbade me from trying them; he was kinder than the guild, but his word was gospel regarding food and what he didn't want me to eat. So simply because I was denied, I want to try chocolate."

"There are different types of chocolate. Dark chocolate is bitter, milk chocolate is what it says it is, and it is made with some milk. I've tried both." Alex began before he stopped walking and turned to face Joseph with a slight smile, squeezing Joseph's hand. Joseph was happy that Alex was delighted; clearly, being away from Freydale was also doing wonders for him. Alex looked around momentarily, his eyebrows lifting slightly as if he had spotted something. "In fact… stay there and close your eyes."

Joseph did as he was told; he could feel Alex removing his fingers from his own and leaving for a brief second. As he waited, Joseph listened to the noise that surrounded him; he could pick out certain sounds: people calling out for attention to sell their various wares, footsteps on the tiled floor clanking as they were hit over and over again by all types of shoes. And then there was the water; small waterfalls all around the room made for a calming sensation.

He zoned in on the water for a moment, more so, what was inside it; he could almost hear the clanking sound of the cerulean tears in their natural habitat, hitting one another as if they were like little globs of metal. It was a faint sound, barely audible to anyone here, but maybe because of who Joseph was – the Luma, perhaps that was why he was more in tune with the tears than everyone else. It was a fun sound, not distracting. It made him feel strangely safe. Safer than he had ever felt on dry land before.

Then, Joseph felt someone reach for his palm, placing a medium-sized item in his right hand and allowing Joseph to close his fingers around it. It felt like a parcel of sorts, cloth wrapped around it to keep it safe and sound, whatever it was. Alex then grabbed Joseph's other hand as if it was always meant to be there and squeezed it once.

"You can open your eyes again," Alex whispered into Joseph's ear, and even though Joseph couldn't see him, he could tell that Alex had a massive smile on his face. "I found you some chocolate."

"You did?" Joseph asked as he looked down at the item in his hand. The white cloth concealed six light brown chocolate shapes. They looked tasty, and each one looked slightly different, but all in the rather famous shape of the tears that were scattered everywhere around this underground paradise—Cerulean tears-shaped chocolates. "Thank you!"

"It's the least I could do. You deserve it all and more." Alex said as he studied Joseph, looking down at the tear-shaped chocolates in his palm before Joseph reached down, picking up the smallest piece of chocolate and popping it into his mouth. "What do you think?"

"It's not as sweet as the strawberry; it's a different type of sweet," Joseph said as he savoured the chocolate, letting it melt slightly. "In a way, I'm glad I didn't get to try this in Freydale; I'd use all my money on it if I could. It really is that lovely. Do you want a piece?"

"I couldn't possibly take-," Alex said as Joseph cocked his head to the side and looked at him with a squinted look.

"You bought me a wonderful gift, Alex; I can share it with whoever I want, and I want to share it with you," Joseph said, knowing Alex couldn't possibly say no to that ideology. "I insist. Please."

"Thank you, Joseph." Alex grabbed a small piece himself, but he wanted to leave the larger ones for Joseph.

"And another thing," Joseph said as he squeezed Alex's hand in his own, copying what Alex had done. Alex looked at Joseph, confused, as he stuffed the piece of chocolate into his mouth. "I have a request that I hope you will grant."

"Hm?" Alex asked as he chewed on the chocolate, eager to know what Joseph would say.

"I want you to start using my nickname again," Joseph replied, and he could almost see Alex's eyes bulging out of their sockets for a second.

"But your rules..." Alex stuttered.

"I know of them, yes," Joseph said as he placed the chocolates on the side of a table close by before grabbing the man's other hand. "Alex, you saved my life in that sword fight; you have proved time and time again you are not the person you were in Freydale. I meant what I said in the dream, and back in that bedroom, I want to start again with you. What better way to begin than using my nickname? Like we did up until we were separated. Even though we both know it happened, I want to sidestep away from it and prove that that horrible year no longer dictates my life."

Alex looked as if he was deliberating with himself. He stared down at Joseph for a few moments before that signature smirk appeared on his face. "Okay," Alex said as he moved his left hand away from Joseph, scooping up the chocolates and placing them into his jacket pocket before resuming his position by Joseph's side. Shall we keep walking, Joey?"

"We shall indeed," Joseph said as he smiled to himself. It felt good hearing Alex call him by his nickname. He knew that it would be a hard slog, but maybe one day, the year that never was could be a distant memory—a blip in their story—a time neither could remember.

Joseph vowed in that carriage he could get 'his' Alex back, and with a few small days away from the toxicity of Freydale and Caulan's grip, he almost had. Joseph didn't know where it would go, but he was here for the ride.

He just hoped Alex was, too.

Joseph was glad for some respite as he made it up the last step of the underground city. It was dark outside, which was odd – down to the town, Joseph realised he had no idea what time it was. The cold air breeze swirled around him, and he and Alex stood basking in the freshness of the wind, which lashed at his face.

"That's a nice breeze," Alex commented as the two began to walk away from the staircase, still holding onto his hand.

"Was I asleep for this long? It was morning when we got to

Rivetia… it's pitch black outside now," Joseph said as he surveyed the area, Alex simply nodding to his left. He couldn't see much else than what he did when he first arrived on this beach. Large stone pillars still stood in their rightful place, leading to what Joseph assumed was a castle, the large stone floor still sitting there, with abstract drawings and mosaics, beautiful sculptures half broken. Still, the walls were no longer there, leaving the only trace of someone who had ever lived there in those identical statues, faceless, armless, sometimes even just a pair of legs attached to a pedestal.

Whatever caused this, whether time or a war, had not been favourable to the kingdom of Rivetia. No wonder they all lived underground. Life seemed better that way, if not a little backwards.

"Hey, you two!" Joseph heard someone call the two of them over. As Joseph looked over to where the voice had come from, he could see two figures in the distance: Maura and Pierce stood together, looking as if they had been mid-conversation—standing amidst the statues, the broken monoliths of time long since passed. "Joseph, you're awake!"

"Hey," Joseph said as the four convened, moving closer together. Maura had a massive smile on her face. "Fancy seeing you here."

"You're looking a whole lot better. I'm so glad." Maura said as she went to hug Joseph briefly. The two had never hugged before, but it felt good as she wrapped her arms around him. Maura gave warm hugs, something Joseph had never really had before.

"What are you two doing up here? Pierce, I thought you were at a party celebrating your return." Alex asked. Pierce simply nodded, and a brief smile appeared on his face.

"Well, it was more to celebrate my father returning, but remember, they never even knew I existed until today. My father was a high-ranking official, even though he was young when he left. He's well-known in the kingdom by a lot of its older denizens. Me, I'm just his son." Pierce said as he looked around the area. "Not that I don't matter, y'know. But I don't know the people I'm partying with. I saw Maura wandering around looking a tad lost, I thought I'd come with her."

"I was exploring, and Pierce doesn't know the island himself, so I offered for us to go together rather than alone," Maura said as she stepped back from the hug to admire Joseph in all his awakened glory. "Did you two do the same?"

"We went to the market first, and I heard the music coming from this great hall—but I felt a bit overwhelmed. I needed some fresh air. Thankfully, Alex knew where to go. Those stairs are a killer." Joseph replied before realising they were still holding hands, and Maura and Pierce were catching on.

"So, you two…" Pierce began a slight smirk appearing on his lips in the dark. It was hard to catch, only there for a moment, but it was gone quick.

"What exactly is going on?" Maura said; her smile was far more evident, and Joseph didn't quite understand the excitement in her voice. "Are you two…?"

"We've decided to give it a go," Joseph said before looking at Alex confusedly. Still, when Alex nodded in his direction, all confusion left his body immediately.

"After everything he's done… Joseph, you should be." Pierce began, but before Pierce could get any more words out, Alex held up his free hand to silence the man.

"We're trying to figure it out. After everything I've done, it might seem odd, but we've realised life is too short; with this decay following us, we want to make the most out of every moment we have. Now that my father has no control over us…" Alex replied quickly, a flurry of panicked words exiting his mouth. "I know that you will never see us as a conventional couple and that we don't even know how it will work. We are former hunters and former servants, but we want to try to get past who we were and, more so, what happened that year. Neither of us wants it to control our lives anymore. We both want to be free of the torment."

"I was going to say…" Pierce said as he reached out to touch Alex's shoulder – stopping the flurry of words almost instantly. The man then turned to Joseph, the smile returning. "Joseph, you should hold his hand with pride. I had my misgivings at first, of course. But Alex has shown in these past few days that he truly cares for you."

"It's very complicated, but we're trying it out. Living our lives the way we wanted to back then, even though those times are gone, we want to make up for it." Joseph said as he gripped Alex's hand tighter. "He's a bit different, but so am I. Alex is returning to the person he was; the anger is gone. I realised we were both victims in all of this, and despite what happened between us, we've somehow slotted straight back into the roles we had before. It feels right."

"You don't have to explain yourself; you're both adults. You have your history; I shouldn't have been hard on either of you on the ship. You both look lovely together, and however fast or slow the relationship goes, I will support it… We both will," Pierce said as Maura smiled, nodding, and sat close to one of the statues. "It's good to see you happy, Joseph. I did mean what I said on the ship, though, Al; you hurt him; there will be hell to pay."

"I'll never make that mistake again," Alex said as he chuckled nervously. He looked over to Joseph with a quick flash of a smile.

As the four conversed with each other, a few people passed Joseph and his group as they caught their breath at the top of the staircase, all filing out into one big cluster – he hadn't seen these people on the stairs as he came up. It was a long way down, too.

"What's happening out here? Why are there so many people?"

Alex asked as the four congregated in the area, keeping Joseph close to him as best as he could.

"Hello everyone!" A voice called from the front of the now rather large crowd. The whole island had come up to the surface at once. Santos stood at the front on a large pedestal. He cascaded his voice down, weaving through the people eagerly awaiting his following words. "I would like to direct everyone's attention up to celebrate mine and my son's safe return; the King has graciously agreed to bring back an old tradition we had as a child. So please, cast your vision up, and enjoy the show; it's pretty... colourful."

"The party must have moved to the surface," Pierce said as he stayed back a little. "Wonder what they're planning."

A loud bang rocketed through the area, shocking everyone in the crowd. Joseph could have sworn he had jumped out of his own skin for a moment, but as he looked up towards the sky, an array of beautiful colours replaced his fear.

As the crowd moved, Joseph felt his hand slipping from Alex's. It was not a panic, not a hold-on-your-grip moment, but rather, as the bangs got more frequent and the sky filled with colours, Joseph got lost, immersed in the bright lights around him.

"Wow!" some people shouted towards the front of the cluster. A few more jeers and calls came from the crowd as Joseph regained some of his composure.

"What are they?" Joseph asked Maura and Pierce, not knowing if they would know.

"Fireworks," Maura said in awe. She didn't even look back at Joseph, instead keeping her eyes square on the sky where the fireworks were coming from. More and more, they came, filling the sky with all sorts of colours and shapes: purple, white, blue, green, and red. All made for a spectacle against the dark, black sky. Not even the brightest star in the sky could compare to this tonight. "They're beautiful."

Joseph watched as the fireworks flew into the air and burst quickly. The noise they made was like a squeak—then a large boom, hurting his ears as he watched. His eyes drifted towards the open water, the tide falling and rising and waves crashing into each other. His eyes searched the beach where everyone was standing until they landed on a darkened figure—its silhouette only illuminated by the water.

He hadn't even realised that Alex had left his side. He sat down in the sand, knees crouched together – looking out into the waves. Joseph watched as he picked up a small stone from the water and skimmed it.

The stone made two small bounces and disappeared into the ocean, ready to start life in the aquatics.

As Pierce and Maura stood in awe, Joseph walked closer to Alex before plopping his body down into the sand beside him.

"Hi." It was the most normal thing he could say, but Joseph felt he should have said nothing. Alex didn't smile; he didn't react. Only kept his eyes on one spot out into the distance.

"My father is still out there, you know?" Alex said as he picked up another stone but had yet to skim it. "I saw his ship when we first arrived at the top of the stairs; it's the only one out there. He's waiting."

"He can't hurt us, remember? Like you said." Joseph said, and though Alex nodded in acceptance, whatever was going through his brain was bothering him more and more every second. "What's going through your mind? Talk to me."

"I've been toying with it ever since we left Freydale, after what my father said, that I would be dead to him if I left..." Alex said as he turned his head away from the water and straight into Joseph's eyes. "He said before I was bundled into the carriage to the training centre, I had besmirched the Von-Loch name... that I soiled his family. Our family. I don't want to do that ever again."

"You won't," Joseph said, but it seemed that Alex had more to say.

"What you said on the ship about me making my own life, that I can be whoever I want to be..." Alex began, speaking quietly, fumbling with his hands. "I want to make the most of the time I have. Life is so short, and we've been through so much in the short time we've already had; I want to start our life together properly this time."

"How are we going to do that?" Joseph asked. He was on board for whatever Alex could suggest. The truth was, Joseph, too, wanted to get stuck into it. He had already lost so much time, and with the beacons now active around the realm and the vision of Alex's death looming over him, if he wanted any time with Alex at all, he needed to find a way to stop the man's death.

Alex stood up from the ground below him, patting himself down, sand dropping off him quickly as it failed to cling onto him. He turned his face towards the waves, just thinking. "I have no idea, but I do know that wherever you go, I want to be with you every step of the way," Alex said as he turned his body towards where Joseph sat at his feet. "You know, when you were in the guild, before we were separated, there were a lot of ways I thought of how I could get you to escape."

"Oh?" Joseph asked, interested. There was nothing to lose now; he was free. "What were they?"

"The obvious, running away like we planned. That was the main one; it had a lot of different iterations throughout the years. We'd jump on a spice ship at the festival and ride the seas. We'd find a secret tunnel in the sewers of Freydale and crawl our way out, or..." Alex said before pursing his lips shut and turning his head away again towards the water.

"What is it?" Joseph asked, chuckling to himself – he could tell Alex was flustered at whatever he had just remembered.

"It was a fleeting idea; I don't think it would work, to be

honest," Alex said, saying that the way his voice was raised confirmed to Joseph that he was indeed flustered.

"Tell me," Joseph said.

"I'd marry you, and then they'd have to let you free," Alex said, still not turning his face from the sea before him. His voice was quiet. "I don't know the logistics, but I was a teenager and had no idea how the world worked then. Please, just scrub it from your memory."

"Who knows, if we had escaped when you said, we might have been married," Joseph said. "Stranger things have happened."

"I think that would have been nice," Alex said as he turned his body again to look at Joseph before offering his hand to bring Joseph to his level. "Would you actually have married someone like me, though?"

"I think it was when I turned eighteen that I first noticed I had feelings for you. I think I had for a while, maybe years. It was at the festival after we had gotten the lemon pie. I marked my face with the powdered sugar, and you wiped it off with your thumb. I don't know why that was it; I couldn't tell you. But I knew I liked you then." Joseph replied, Alex still didn't lift his head. "My feelings grew occasionally; I thought of the life we could have had if we had escaped. I think I would have been happy to marry you, yes. Away from the guild and its influence, who knows what might have been?"

"Hm," Alex said as he lifted his head again, looking at Joseph in the eyes. "Would you marry me now?"

Underwater. Jospeh's ears suddenly clogged; it was like he was underwater. The question swirled around him like a fish in a fishbowl. Joseph looked at Alex, but it was like his eyes were going in and out of focus; the banging of the fireworks above him, combined with the words that had just exited Alex's mouth, was a hard pill to swallow.

"What?" Joseph found himself asking out of pure confusion.

"Alex, are you asking…"

"It's not the way I envisioned it. In all the scenarios I concocted in my head, I didn't envision myself having a mini panic moment, spurting out incoherent ramblings and then just asking you to marry me…" Alex said; he sounded shocked at himself, annoyed even. "Please, ignore me. I'm so embarrassed to even suggest it. As you said, it's too complicated. How would it even work? Up until a few weeks ago, we didn't even talk. We didn't get along. I hated you, and you hated me, and now I'm asking you to marry me on a beach in a kingdom we know nothing about. Honestly, how silly can I get?"

"Alex…" Joseph began – once again, the man's head was cast down, and he was mumbling.

"I shouldn't have even started that conversation; who do I think I am?" Alex began. "I'll never bring it up ever again. I'm sorry. Marriage is a massive commitment, and we've just restated this relationship; part of me wants to jump straight in and make up for the lost time, but I know you have your boundaries…"

"Alex," Joseph said as he removed his hand from Alex's, quickly grabbing the man's face to bring it closer to his own so they could see each other's eyes again.

Joseph felt a spark as their lips touched in the dream, as if everything made sense. This was what he wanted; this was always what he wanted.

"What is it?" Alex asked. Noticing Joseph staring at him, probably with a goofy grin.

He wanted to be happy. In Alex's arms, he could be. No one's judgment could tear them apart anymore.

"Life is too short; we've had too much taken from us already – let's make the most of what we have," Joseph said as he looked back at a somewhat stunned Alex, who was just trying to comprehend what was happening. "It's risky, but what's life without a little risk. So, ask the question. The way you had it planned."

Bewildered, Alex fumbled with a ring on his right hand – one he had owned for years. Joseph watched as the man bent down on his right knee and held the golden ring. He was a bit scared as he spoke and still a bit confused.

Alex asked the question.

"Joseph Maynard Price, will you marry me?" Alex asked. He sounded confident as he spoke but was still nervous and conscious, too. He looked up at Joseph with a hopeful look, awaiting his reply.

"He-hem." A noise interrupted them a second later before Joseph could even reply.

"What is it?" Joseph asked, raising his voice slightly at the person who had just interrupted their moment. "Can't you see we are in the middle of something?"

With her eyebrow raised, the queen stood with her walking stick dug into the sand, looking at Joseph with a smile. "Hello again, Joseph Price."

"Your majesty," Joseph whispered as he laid eyes on the queen, who stood with her walking stick, digging into the sand below her feet. Joseph stepped back and wiped his mouth, trying to make himself look a little presentable. "I'm sorry, I wasn't expecting you."

"I'll forgive you, I'm sorry for interrupting, but Joseph, we need to speak. The demonstration of your use of the cerulean tears – the King has requested an audience. As much as I don't want to break up the celebration, I need you to follow me." Queen Kala said as she moved her walking stick in the sand, trying to get a better grip on the floor below her. "My brother was forthcoming in telling me your price to give us the demonstration. You want to know where to find the Rivetia key, correct?"

"Yes," Joseph replied quickly, eyes casting from Alex to the queen. "We want to return magic to the realm."

"A noble quest, I'm sure." Queen Kala said as she began to turn around, the sand getting stuck between her sandals. "Before I give up this information, however, I need to know if you are truly the one we seek. So, please."

"Okay," Joseph said as he began preparing to follow her. The nervousness he had not felt for days suddenly started to creep up on him again. An audience with the King – it was a big deal. "Can Alex come too?"

"Only you were requested." Queen Kala said quickly – not turning around to look at either of them. "It is only you with the power over the tears. Only you are allowed in that throne room."

"Please hold that thought, Alex," Joseph said. He felt terrible as he rushed off. He wanted to give Alex his well-deserved answer, but certain things had to wait, even if he didn't want to.

"I'll be waiting for you out here…" Alex said as Joseph felt Alex's hand leave his. The mere thought of being alone in that room with an all-powerful king made him nervous; the more anxious he thought about it, the more he thought about it. "Good luck."

He was going to need all the well wishes he could   get.

NINE

The grand throne room was much less imposing than its name. It looked built quickly, with one enormous chair placed haphazardly in the middle of the room. With its large back and what looked to be beaded jewels, the chair was adorned with the same fabric from which Joseph's clothes were made. The Cerulean Tears were here as well, swirling around in matrimony with one another in two small rectangular ducts, brightening up the room that would have been dark without them.

"Joseph Price, I presume?" The King was young, different from what Joseph thought he might be. As Queen Kala was an older woman, he had assumed that the King was her husband. But this man, with his wild black hair and copper brown eyes, staring intently at Joseph as he stood in the middle of the room beside the two pools, was maybe only a few years older than Joseph at most. "King Atlas. My mother has told me much about you."

"Hello, Your Majesty," Joseph said quietly, unsure of himself and why he was there. "I'm sorry, I thought-."

"I understand. Do you want to know why my mother is Queen and I am King?" King Atlas began, a smirk on his face. "I also bet you want to know how I know your thoughts?"

"Yes," Joseph said.

"To which part?" The King asked, still, the smirk was plastered on his face. His voice was soft, not at all intimidating.

"Both," Joseph replied quickly.

"My father died a few years back; as per royal tradition, I took on the role of King. However, my mother is known as Queen only by name, not rank. It's rather trivial." King Atlas said flippantly, waving his hand. "The mind reading came with the job; my father had it before me, and my grandmother had it before him. It's an offensive tactic; always know what the person before you is thinking. Gifted to us by the goddess Lumin herself."

"I see, that's quite impressive," Joseph said, now feeling a little on edge; he also felt like he wasn't allowed to think – just in case it came back on him. "I-."

"Yes. Yes, it is." Atlas agreed, shifting slightly in his chair to get a better look at Joseph. "However, that is not why we are here; we are here because of your magical ability. I want to see it; I understand you are a shapeshifter. But I want you to demonstrate your apparent control over the Cerulean Tears."

"What would you have me do, Your Majesty?" Joseph asked as he looked down at the two small pools of tears by his feet. Something told him that the tears here were what he would use for the King's request. He just hoped that whatever it was wouldn't be too strenuous. He was still a little breathless, looking at the tears in the pool; they made Joseph nervous. The King knew this, too.

"Nervous?" The King asked as he hopped off his throne and took two cautious steps. He stood, arms behind him as he looked Joseph up and down for a moment before his signature smile reappeared. "Joseph, I would have you create something for me, a staff for myself. I would like it to be long – I would like the top to form a point, so I may use it for anything I need, a weapon, a walking stick for mountaineering, or anything. Do you think you can do that for me?"

"Yes," Joseph said, nodding. "I think that would be easy enough."

Anything was easier right now compared to getting through that barrier. But he didn't want to seem too cocky about it. At last, King Atlas didn't want too much of a specific design. All Joseph had to do was think of a normal-looking staff, like one he had seen so many times in Freydale. Working for the upper class meant that he knew the ins and outs of their society – he knew what an 'expensive' staff would look like, right down to the type of wood used. Using the cerulean tears was not the same as carving wood; if anything, it would make the 'crafting' of such an object easier.

Joseph thought back to the staff the old baron who took him on had used: firm wood stained dark, with what looked to be glass, like a sceptre, just less ornate. His mind pictured the staff, how, when he would go out in the night parading as the baron, he had to hold the staff a certain way, never touching the top, always keeping his hand about three-quarters up the staff.

Small notches where his old hands had gripped the wood over time made it easier to find where the man wanted it held. Joseph went down towards the pool on the left, feeling the water surrounding the tears flowing quickly towards him as he closed his eyes. It was still strange not knowing how these little beings worked, how they could change their shape at will, how they could harden like crystal at a single touch.

Joseph felt some of the tears get stuck around his fingers. He knew this was the moment he needed to create the staff, first in his mind, and then, just like magic, it would appear in the water. The staff would start slim but robust and get thicker at the top towards where the egg-like shape top would end at a minor point, a sceptre by any other name. But these tears felt different to those on the ship, less diluted, stronger. In seconds, Joseph could feel the weight of something new in his hands.

The shining dark blue object shimmered in the water as Joseph gripped it and dragged it towards the surface. Careful not to scratch the object before he could crystalise it, Joseph reached with his other hand towards the staff. The water was still flowing, the tears moving around their new home—it felt almost cruel to seal them in this stuff, but Joseph knew that despite being sealed, it would not hurt them.

It was almost as if the tears could feel how Joseph felt, and Joseph could touch them. This is what they were made for, to be used to become items that could help the people of Rivetia.

"Extraordinary," Atlas said as the blue covered some of his face. His mouth was agape as he looked at the staff that Joseph had created. He walked closer and reached out to touch the staff.

"Not yet," Joseph said; he didn't look at Atlas; he just kept his eyes on the swirling tear-shaped items in the water and how they danced in the water. "It's just water at the moment. I must find a way to cure it and make it tougher."

How he was going to do that was another problem altogether. Joseph had forced a ship through a barrier; he had created this stuff, but to make a tangible object out of this water was uncharted territory—all of it, really.

Joseph stared intently as the tears began to whiz around in the water as if they were replacing the water that was sloshing around; every inch turned that same bright blue. The tears got faster by the second until nothing of the clear water was left. Instead, they left an almost icy blue hue over the staff.

In certain angles, it would look stark white. Then Joseph moved it, and the cerulean tears activated inside the barricr—specs of the blue colour they emitted were evident as he moved it.

"There you go, Your Majesty," Joseph said, slightly confused at how well that went even though he was going into the unknown. If Atlas had asked him to do it again, to create him another – Joseph wasn't sure he could. It had just happened; nothing was by his design except the tears. The tears controlled everything. "One staff made of the tears."

"May I?" King Atlas said as he reached forward; Joseph gracefully passed it over. Atlas gripped the staff as if he were feeling it out, ensuring it met his desires. He twirled it as if it was some sort of baton and then slammed the bottom on the floor, making a large boom; the tears inside the staff activated at this moment, and a flurry of colour erupted in the room. Lighting up all nooks and crannies. "This is good. Great, even. Perfect."

"You've proven that you have the control the Luma always presents. It does seem that the tears might have melded with your magic, which makes it slightly easier to control, but… that's good. Very good." Queen Kala said as she stood up shakily; it seemed she needed the staff more than her son. "Do you think you could, I don't know, try and take down this terrible barrier? If you have the power of the Luma at your disposal, surely it means you can try."

"I could try… then, you'll tell me the location of the key?" Joseph said, looking both the monarchs in the eyes as he asked this. They both seemed genuine. He didn't know why he felt this way, like an innate sense that they could do no wrong, that they would always tell the truth.

"Of course." Queen Kala said. "You must understand, I just want the security in the knowledge that we will be free after this; the people of this kingdom deserve that. They've been sealed in darkness for far too long."

"No, no, I get it. You don't have to explain yourself; I understand all too well what it's like to wish for freedom." Joseph said, understanding before he looked around the small room, nervous to speak his mind, but he knew he had to; King Atlas could hear his thoughts anyway. "I'm not sure how long we have left with this decay following us. I don't know how long it will take to reach the island."

"If you can just try, that's all we ask. If you can't do it, we can return to it later. A few days won't hurt when we've already endured fifty years." King Atlas said with a smile as he held the staff happily. "I'll even take you to the location myself if necessary. But if you can try, it would be much appreciated."

"I will give it my best," Joseph said as he nodded and left the two alone. But before he reached the door, he felt a hand grab for his shoulder. King Atlas towered over him, a warm aura surrounding him, in no way intimidating.

"I'm sure you'll do your best. If you were, I can offer one thing, a trick." King Atlas came close to Joseph's ear, making the hairs on the back of Joseph's neck stand up. "Drink some of the water, let it meld with your body, your soul. It may give you the strength that you need to remove it. I'll leave you to your team now. When you have it all figured out, please let me know."

"I will, Your Majesty." Joseph smiled as the man leant on his new staff, using it as a crutch and a walking stick, finally able to move around the way that he wanted to – his old age was stopping him from doing a lot of things, but now, with this new staff – it meant a whole new plethora of opportunities had opened. It had for Joseph, too. "Thank you for the advice."

"Now go, I feel you have unfinished business with your partner." King Atlas said with a smile; it was warm, knowing. "I do hope I did not ruin the proposal."

"How did you know about that?" Joseph said, but then he remembered what Atlas had told him. King Atlas tapped the side of his head twice—all-knowing. The King's power was a force to be reckoned with. He could and would know everything if he dove down deep enough.

It reminded him of his power to dive into people's memories, which had become stronger recently after he had been hit by the blast. He wondered if he was hit by the beacon in Rivetia... his magic would grow even stronger.

Joseph smiled at King Atlas, then Queen Kala, and turned on his heel, ready to return to the beach. Suppose Joseph was going to attempt to remove the barrier. In that case, he would need all the help he could get from everyone and everything around him. The entire realm was counting on them getting this key, and they didn't even know it. He could not fail to impress King Atlas.

Disappointing the King was never an option, not if he wanted to save the realm from utter destruction.

TEN

Outside, on the beach, the crowd had died down. As Joseph exited the underground city, the night sky was still lit by the fireworks' last dregs. Large booming noises covered every area, but the excitement had died down. People were tired, all partied out.

Towards the beach's south, Maura and Pierce stood talking with one another; the darkness surrounding them seemed like an old friend. They were laughing at something, proper belly laughing. Alex was close by, though not in the conversation, prodding holes in the sand with a stick he held in his left hand. As Joseph got closer, it seemed like he had been playing a game with himself, more out of boredom, but he had been at it a while... there were a lot of holes in his feet.

"You're alive!" Maura's voice was the first thing Joseph heard as he got even closer to the trio. "You were speaking with Alex, then the queen arrived, and you two disappeared. Alex wouldn't say what happened."

"Because I didn't know myself," Alex muttered in response. "She showed up and whisked him away for that demonstration of the tears; that is all I know."

"As Alex said, it was for the demonstration she asked for. The King wanted to see what I could do. Glad to say, I passed his expectations." Joseph explained. "I also told them about the journey we are on and what the plan is."

"So, what did you tell my aunt... and cousin?" Pierce said, hesitantly speaking about the King. Not too long ago, neither knew each other existed. Maura and Alex looked at each other, as did Pierce, the nervousness in their voices and faces. It was clear that Alex had spoken to them about his fears about telling more people about the journey they were on.

"I told them I needed the location of the key, and that was that. Many lives, including theirs, hung in their decision to help me. I didn't sugarcoat the truth." Joseph replied plainly.

"And what did they say to that?" Maura asked.

"They had some... requirements," Joseph said as he looked out towards the ocean, noticing a slight shimmer of light – the barrier. Even in the dark, the faint glow of the tears was evident. "They wanted me to try and remove the barrier; they said if I at least tried, the king himself would take me there."

"Remove the barrier?" Maura asked, concerned; they had all seen what happened on the ship. "But Joseph – you struggled with getting through the barrier, you collapsed. To take it down, that would be so dangerous. Do you think that your body could handle something like that?"

"I have to try. Not just because I want the key. But think about it, these people are stuck here – can you really say you'd be okay with leaving them locked here, forever?" Joseph asked, and her face softened as she shook her head in reply. "I was cursed to be a servant for a long time, locked in my own personal hell every day. I can't, in good conscience, let someone else suffer, let alone an entire kingdom."

"What's he like?" Pierce interrupted, his eyes downcast. "The...

king."

"I didn't get to speak to him much, just enough to get my point across. He's brash, a little rough around the edges, tall, and must run in the family with you." Joseph replied; it then became apparent that Pierce had not spoken to his cousin, let alone seen him. "He's very confident, or at least seems so. Oh, and he can read minds. Probably where he gets the confidence from – know his enemy."

"Well, that's not terrifying at all," Pierce said. "I don't want to read people's minds."

"It would be a burden for sure," Maura replied. "Imagine knowing what everyone thought about you at all times."

"How exactly does he want you to remove the barrier?" Alex asked from the ground below them. "It's alright doing a demonstration for them, and after what happened on the ship, I don't want to take the risk of you hurting yourself again. Not after what we spoke about before you were whisked away. I don't want you to risk it…"

"But we need the key," Joseph argued, interrupting Alex before he could say anything more. "All they need me to do is try it; if I can't get it down, they said they'll still give me the information I need. I just need to give it a go."

"If you had let me finish, I think it goes without saying…" Alex said, stopping himself again, hesitating. His voice was soft, coaxing Joseph into a sense of security. He was fiddling with a ring on his finger, the golden one he had received for his eighteenth birthday to celebrate becoming an adult. "Whatever you need me to do, I will. I'm sure all of us would say the same."

"You… You'll help me?" Joseph asked as he looked towards the group, sighing and smiling. He knew that despite their misgivings, Alex would follow Joseph into oblivion. Maura needed a way home; she needed the group to succeed, and Pierce was just along for the ride, but even Joseph could tell he believed in their cause. He was also paying back a debt… for getting the ship through the barrier. "Of course… of course, you guys would."

Joseph moved, looking out over the ocean again. The glimmer of the field around the island glinted, reflecting the rise and fall of the water. He breathed in the air, the coldness catching his breath for a moment—there was nothing else for it. He just had to go full throttle, not just because this was going to be a massive undertaking but because there were real lives at stake.

These people celebrating their fireworks wouldn't know what hit them once they were allowed outside of their little island. Joseph knew how it felt to be locked in a cage, with no way out and no one to help. He never wanted another person to go through what he had. Even though it was differing circumstances, the meaning of freedom stayed the same.

It was a need. It's not a simple want. Joseph needed to give them freedom.

"So…" Pierce broke the silence; everyone's eyes were on him instantly. "Where do we start?"

"I'm not even sure what I'm supposed to be doing!" The sound of sand hitting the sea was audible as Joseph stood just before the water's edge, looking out into the barrier. He had tried crouching by the water to try and get it to move in the way he wanted it to. The barrier needed to be removed; that was clear as day.

How – that was the question. "Removing the tears from the equation might be the trick. Think about it; they were the ones that created this barrier; maybe you can't use the tears against each other." Pierce said he had the most experience with the tears apart from Joseph; taking his advice might have been the best thing. "Maybe you've got to draw the energy from the water, hoping to reunite them as one entity."

"One entity," Joseph said, nodding his head before realising something that frustrated him even more. "That would be helpful if I knew how the tears actually worked. Every time I've done this… it's been a complete fluke! We need this key. We need it."

Eventually, the barrier would have to come down, no matter if the King told them of the location of the key for simply 'trying'—he was sure, without a shadow of a doubt, that the King would not let them leave without taking down this forcefield. They had gotten in, but there was no way out—not without consequences.

Like last time, he overexerted himself.

"When we were on the ship, what did you do to let us through that barrier? You might be able to recreate it." Pierce said, continuing with his questions. There it was, the thought that plagued Joseph – that he might, once again, have to put his own life in danger. He had already forfeited his freedom by accident; the tears had bonded to him – another cage for his magic.

"You do remember what he was like after he did that, though, right?" Alex piped up, shaking his head. "He was practically legless; he couldn't walk or really talk. We don't want to repeat that; it would put him out of action for days. We might not *have* days."

"As far as I know, it was like I was in a trance; it was completely involuntary. It was like the tears were controlling me, like they wanted me to do it, to get through." Joseph shrugged as he stood up to look further out into the ocean. The start of the moon's rise was just over the ocean level. Despite everything, at least it was going to be a beautiful night. "I'm not sure how, or rather if I can control that or if I can recreate it."

"Do you think…" Maura interjected, stopping as if she was thinking. "Back when we were on the ship, the tears protected you. I don't know how the whole invocation Caulan was speaking about works, but by all accounts – you were to die. You didn't."

"Okay, you're onto something," Joseph said, agreeing with her. "Go on."

"You told us earlier that the King mentioned drinking the water. When you were on the ship taking down the barrier, you were holding the tears, being surrounded by them too... but what if you drink some of it." Maura replied, leaving her spot on the beach and walking towards the water; as she did – the tears began to react slightly, lighting up – illuminating the dark area. "Maybe with it inside your body, it might be far more effective. The King must think there is some merit to his claims, or he wouldn't have offered such a compelling find."

"I can give it a go," Joseph said as he walked towards one of the springs close to where they stood and got some of the water in a small cup that was sat next to it; the blue hue from the tears swirling around it was much more evident in the dark as it was in the daylight, it was strange to drink it, he could feel the tears moving around in a flurry, they wouldn't be hurt if he swallowed, but it felt odd none the less. It took a moment as Joseph downed the small amount of water in one gulp, but the tiredness that he felt subsided slightly.

He didn't feel better about taking down the barrier, though.

Maura took Joseph's hand in hers. Her beautiful silver ring on her right hand felt cold on his hands, and her nails painted a ruby red, were chipped. She breathed in and then out. "Breathe in," Maura said, and as he was told, Joseph did. "Breathe out. Close your eyes; we won't talk, and there will be no distractions. Try, like before, to visualise the barrier disappearing and see the shimmer fade with every growing second.

"Okay," Joseph said as he exhaled. He let her hand slip through his own as he stepped closer towards the water.

"We will be right here next to you." Maura's voice swirled around him, and he did as she had told him. He closed his eyes, feeling the energy the tears had given him. The borrowed energy was rocking back and forth between the tears and Joseph, both taking something from each other. But together, they could be a phenomenal force.

Deep in his mind, he could see, no, feel the barrier. He could feel it breaking as his vision woulded it to. The barrier was fighting back, the tears unwilling to take their rightful place in the ocean below.

His mind was working on overdrive. He could see a bright light as the barrier split in half, and the tears connected to one another began to fall, like how a glass would shatter. He couldn't hear anything related to what was happening in his mind. Hence, as he opened an eye to peek at the fruits of his labour, he was sourly disappointed. Nothing had changed.

"No," Joseph said as his arms drooped beside his body. "It's not working. I... I can't get to the same state as I did on the ship. Which means I can't even begin to tap into the power they give and take away from me. I can't feel the tears; I can't will them to do as I want." Joseph said as he stood back, leaving a small trail of footsteps where the water hadn't quite reached the beach.

"I don't know what to suggest..." Pierce began, his voice grave. "If drinking it doesn't help... there must be another way that we can-."

"I can't do it. No one can. Not me, not you, not even the King!" Joseph shouted in reply, feeling an anger he hadn't experienced in a long time, not an anger at Pierce, Maura, or even Alex. No. He was angry at himself, at his inability to help.

"But maybe if you-." Maura began, but she was stopped momentarily when Joseph turned around to face her.

He looked at his feet, gripping a small black rock and threw it into the ocean, close to the barrier. "Don't you see, I'm not strong enough for this, which means we are trapped here and can't save the world outside? We've failed before we even start."

It was no surprise that he had two very stunned faces looking back at him in the dark. Their eyes told Joseph that they both understood his frustration, but he had never had an outburst like that before in front of them. On the other hand, Alex did not have the same shocked expression.

He had seen this anger before. The first time that they met, he had shied away from Joseph just because of how damaged he had become back in that dungeon – it took a while for both to warm up to each other. So, when Alex made a beeline for Joseph, his face was as hard as a stone, and Joseph didn't quite understand why. Alex gripped Joseph's arm softly but hard enough to have some leverage to drag him.

"Come with me," Alex said as he began to drag Joseph towards the water.

"What are you doing?" Joseph protested as he felt his clothes begin to get wet and heavier. The Cerulean Tears were moving rapidly around him as the water reached his middle, covering his legs entirely.

"I need you to get angry," Alex said.

"What?" Joseph asked, stunned. "I don't like being angry, you know that."

"But your magic, it works via emotion. You have anger, lots of it, most of it from the guild and from me. Right now, I need you to be angry. Don't you remember what my father said when you were in the castle?" Alex asked. He, too, was onto something himself. But Joseph didn't remember much from that night. "He told people not to get you angry. Now, I think that means your magic gets heightened when you are. I've never seen it, but something tells me *he* has."

"When I was a little kid. Your father was there the day I was processed into the guild in Tildra. We were in the dungeon, and he was being cruel. He separated me from Finley, my brother, the only family I had left. He tried to take my brand new pet fox. I didn't fully understand much; I was too young. But I did know distress when I saw it. Finley, my brother was distressed, thrown to the ground... I lost it. I grabbed Caulan by the wrist and unknowingly dove into his memories."

"What did you see?" Alex asked. Thinking back to what Caulan had made him sign back in the dungeon. He couldn't tell Alex. He had to make up a lie, something. Anything to deflect.

"I can't remember. I was only young. But I was so angry, the anger boiling inside me spilt over; I suppose you are right. Emotions heighten my magic. It's why he never wanted me to get angry..." Joseph explained as Alex continued to drag him further into the water. "He was scared of me. He was scared of what I had shown him. He was scared of what more I could do."

Joseph kept this rhythm up as he and Alex stood in the water. Joseph could feel the water around him, waves lashing at his body as he tried to focus on Alex's voice. The words didn't matter, but the tone, the noise, echoed in his head repeatedly.

"Let it all go, Joseph," Alex said as they reached a good spot, the water getting just to Joseph's middle. Let all your anger and all your grievances spill over again. Channel it; if it doesn't work, we can try something else."

Breathe in, breathe out.

Breathe in, breathe out.

Joseph didn't need to vocalise what made him angry; all he had to do was think. Many things made him angry: the guild, how Caulan had manipulated everything from the day he had arrived at his guild, how he had been separated from Alex and Alex from him.

How he didn't have Finley, that he had run off in Freydale, and they still hadn't found him. That as far as he was aware, his brother was dead. Lost for a cause that neither of them signed up for. Even now, as they stood on this beach, the world worked against them in ways that Joseph couldn't understand. All this war stemmed from people's inability to feel whole within themselves, and jealousy caused all this.

"Step back." Joseph snapped, not at Alex mainly, but he felt that if the man was close, whatever anger he felt, whatever power Joseph would gain from this – it would hurt him. "I don't want to hurt you."

"I'm staying with you until the end," Alex said quietly, disobeying Joseph. "Breathe in, breathe out. Let all your emotions go."

The ever-present humming from the cerulean tears was swirling around him, too. Still, Alex's words playing in his head were much louder and more evident, keeping him calm even though Joseph couldn't control his movements.

Breathe in. Breathe out.

Then, as if a switch had flipped in his brain. He didn't want to be angry anymore. He wanted to feel a different kind of emotion.

"I love you, Alex. I want to spend the rest of my life with you," Joseph said before he felt himself becoming lighter, like the air was grabbing him and pulling him out of the water.

His brain showed him images, working on overdrive. The barrier, how it was formed, the cerulean tears clumping together, thinking they were protecting the people of Rivetia when magic was sealed away. Forming a permanent barrier around the kingdom and its people, stopping them from ever leaving.

But also stopping threats from coming in. More images flashed by: two siblings, both with chestnut brown hair, twins perhaps, one boy and one girl playing by the waterside. They grew older and more mature as time went on. The waterside was always their place to go to feel free.

Then he appeared in Joseph's mind, the man in the vision after he stepped off the Loreli's Wave. The same scar plastered across his left eye. He was the Luma; his sister was the shade.

He could hear it in his head, the man's final warning.

"You're in danger." He said, over and over again, anger in Joseph rising and falling, anxiety and worry all combining into one as he felt actually being lifted up into the air, leaving Alex's grip and the water around him.

What came next was the sound of breaking glass, like a hammer was being thrown at it repeatedly – even louder than Alex's words playing on repeat and the tears that kept passing by him in that tower of light. But the Luma's words were the noisiest of all. He was in danger, though Joseph wasn't sure from what threat.

Joseph could feel the water around him, though he couldn't tell if it was coming towards or away from him. But as he opened his eyes to peek at what was occurring, he noticed that the tears were being removed from the barrier. A small hole was beginning to form, almost in the same place that the ship had come through days before.

The water coming towards him from the hole was getting faster. Larger droplets hit him, and Joseph began to feel eerily tired as if every bit of energy was being ripped out of his body. But he had to keep going.

"Come on, Joseph!" Maura shouted out. Through all the noise only he could hear, he could still make out Maura's voice, which encouraged him—he had to do this; he had to make them all proud.

The barrier had to break. As usual, Joseph wasn't controlling the cerulean tears, but they were controlling him. The trance-like state guided him to complete this task, even if he didn't understand it.

"You can do it!" Pierce shouted, his voice was calm as always, but Joseph had never heard him this loud, even on the ship when he was commanding his people. "Just keep pushing through."

"We all believe in you!" Alex shouted out in one final act to try and make Joseph understand they all had his back through this. "I believe in you!"

A bright light began to shine from Joseph's body as the cerulean tears disturbed by the small hole began congregating around him. They were binding him similarly to when they were on the ship, and how it kept Jospeh protected. Safe. Untouchable.

But something felt different this time. Joseph felt tired as if every inch of his being was being ripped apart from the inside. As the tears swirled around him, Joseph noticed they weren't under his control.

They were draining him. He was under their control.

Then, the light spread out like an explosion, and Joseph began to feel the wind on his body as if he were falling through the sky. He looked up, seeing the shimmer of the barrier still ever present, then down – the water getting closer and closer.

"It didn't..." Joseph let out a hoarse noise as he awaited to fall into the water below – whilst it wouldn't kill him, it would have hurt a lot, falling from the height. The pain he was already in... but the splash and the pain didn't come. "Work?"

As he opened his eyes, stomach deep in water, Joseph found he had been caught. He hadn't even realised that Alex was running towards him. He had been the one to see Joseph, at great stress to his body. "You're okay. Whatever happened just now was spectacular."

"What did happen?" Maura asked. After she and Pierce had joined Alex in the water, she waded further, trying to reach them.

"I have no idea. I could see things in my head; it was like the barrier was a glass dome, and a hammer was slamming down on it; I could visualise it breaking!" Joseph exclaimed as Alex began to drag him out of the water towards the beach where Pierce and Maura were standing with a blanket to wrap around him. "But that light grew brighter, and then I began to fall… I felt the tears draining me."

"But you did something…" Pierce said. "That light, the whole island must have seen it; I wonder what it did, that magic, whatever it was, I can tell it was strong stuff."

Seconds later, a rumbling sound erupted throughout the area. Joseph and Alex looked out over the water at the small hole Joseph had created – noticing small cracks beginning to show.

"Is that…?" Alex asked as he squinted.

A moment later, the ground began to shake violently. Maura and Alex grabbed Joseph and pulled him out of the water and over to the safety of the beach, away from the water, which seemed to be sloshing around—shaking with the rest of the island.

On the beach, he could see the statues, which had once been a beauty to behold, smash down and fall, breaking further as the ground reacted to whatever Joseph had done with the tears.

"What is happening?" Maura asked as she pulled Joseph and Alex further away from the water. But she never got her answer.

The shaking stopped just like that. It was as if seconds before there hadn't been an earthquake. Then, the sound of glass breaking rang through the entire island, down below the ground, in the aqueducts and maybe even as far as the queen's home. Joseph was already wet, but he felt as if he was becoming dowsed in the stuff – like a flurry of torrential rain, but not coming from the sky, rather – the barrier itself.

It was gone.

"Did the barrier just… break?" Alex said, bewildered, wide-eyed, and looking at the water before them. The shimmer of the barrier – the blue had now transferred to the water and at their feet, illuminating the entire island in blue cerulean tears. If people were looking – they could have seen the island for miles.

"It would seem…" a voice began. Joseph looked over to where the voice came from; he recognised it. Walking towards them with her cane two steps ahead, Queen Kala had a bright smile as she looked out into the ocean. "You are a force to be reckoned with, Joseph."

"By the gods." Another voice came deeper, and Joseph recognised it. King Atlas stood with his staff, not too far from where his mother stood. He stared at Joseph with admiration and fear at what he had experienced with his own eyes. "You did it…"

"I-." Joseph began, feeling a little bit sick as he stood using Alex as a crutch. The sand was wedged between his toes. "I brought it down… for you."

"You did much more than that, boy." Queen Kala replied as she raised her eyebrow and scooped up some sand, the water gleaming in her hand. She inspected it closely, bringing it to her eyes. "You gave the tears something up there… you imbued them with the power of the Luma. That explosion of light brought the tears back to their rightful power."

"Which means?" Alex asked.

"This means we can also bring Rivetia to its rightful place and power." King Atlas interrupted and walked towards the group, arm outstretched to shake Joseph's hand. "I owe you a thanks. A great debt. Tell me if I'm wrong, but Joseph, you were a servant for the Hunter's Guild, correct?"

"That's correct," Joseph replied. "But if Rivetia has been locked away, how do you know what I used to be?"

"I know many things, remember?" King Atlas said as he towered over Joseph, that faint smile still evident on his face even in the dark. "Forgive me again if I am overstepping, but I can see why they kept you around for so long. You're useful and strong. And with these tears at your disposal, you can create. You can be anything you want now; you are free."

"Thank you, your majesty," Joseph said. He wanted to be free so severely; maybe these tears could be a blessing rather than the barrier that even he believed they were. Being the Luma and using the tears for good things was all part of Joseph's new start, even if this wasn't according to plan.

"Are you part of Joseph's group?" King Atlas asked. The trio next to Joseph nodded. "What are your names? We haven't been formally introduced. I also thank you if you helped him get to this point."

"My name is Maura," Maura said, holding her hand – King Atlas reached for it to shake.

"Nice to meet you, Maura. I'm hoping that you like the island." King Atlas said, taking his time to speak to her. He had been trained on how to talk to people. Or maybe it was just the mind reading. "My my, you're far from home, aren't you? I'm assuming there is a story there?"

"A bit of a story, yes," Maura said, chuckling to herself. "It's a very long story."

"I'm sure you can tell me all about it tomorrow." King Atlas said with a smile. "And you are?"

"Pierce," Pierce said as he reached over and offered his hand to the King.

"Yes, the cousin I never knew I had." King Atlas said as he swatted away his hand rather than pulling Pierce into a hug. Joseph could tell shocked Pierce; he didn't look uncomfortable, but rather unexpecting of the hug. "We were both kept in the dark. I assume our parents were as hurt as each other, but I'm glad to meet you finally. I would have showed my face sooner, but I have a lot of important business."

"Likewise, getting through that barrier has been pretty much my whole life's work," Pierce said as the hug ended shortly after. "More so for my father than anything else. He wanted to get home so badly; now I know why."

"Indeed. Please, come to my throne room when you get the chance. We will speak more." King Atlas said as he patted Pierce on the shoulder. He then turned to Alex and held out his hand.

"Alex," Alex replied quickly as he took King Atlas's hand and did a quick bow – he, too, had been trained to deal with royalty. A trait that, even now, he couldn't quite get rid of.

"Ah, the fiancé, " the king said, looking Alex up and down as he propped Joseph to his side. I hope I did not ruin the proposal earlier with my intrusion; I hope you understand."

"Fiancé?" Pierce asked as he looked at Joseph.

"You proposed to him? What is happening?" Maura asked, looking as if she was mulling over the information that had been told to her. "Oh, my. God."

"I never got to answer properly," Joseph said before Alex nodded, removing the gold ring on his finger, the one he cherished, and holding it in front of Joseph.

"I hope you understand I'm not about to get down on one knee again, not with all these people in front of me. Plus, the sand would stick to me, and you know, annoying that would be." Alex said, holding the shining golden ring with his pointer finger and thumb. "So, Joseph Maynard Price, will you marry me?"

"I   will.”

ELEVEN

"I cannot believe you are engaged, Joseph…" Pierce was the first to barge into the bedroom where Joseph had fallen asleep the night before. The side of the bed that Alex had been sleeping on was cold. Joseph remembered hearing him move about; if he knew Alex like he thought he did – the man would get breakfast. Pierce surveyed the room as he entered, looking for something, or rather at the lack of something. "Good, we're alone so that we can talk properly."

"What about?" Joseph asked as he propped himself up in the bed. The flame from his bedside lamp flickered as Pierce picked it up and turned a valve on the side of the lamp, making the flame grow in size. "You said you would support the relationship no matter how quick it went; those were your exact words."

"I did… I do." Pierce combatted as he sat on the end of the bed, placing the lamp back in its usual spot. "Is it not just *too* quick?"

"Well-," Joseph said, but Pierce held his hand. He wasn't quite finished.

"I understand you both feel the same way; you both want to make up for lost time, and I get that, I do. Despite my hesitance in trusting the man, I know Alex has been through a lot." Pierce began, looking Joseph straight in the face. "But there has to be something else there; there has to be some other reason on top of those I mentioned why it is so quick. Why a rational guy such as yourself is agreeing to all of this."

"What if there isn't a rational reason why? What if I want to make up for lost time? What if I missed out on so much that every second counted?" Joseph asked. He wasn't being accusatory, not angry. Still, he wanted to explain himself to Pierce so the man would understand. "I have loved Alex for a long time. I never got a chance to tell him back then, but it was clear. The whole kingdom knew before we did. I hated his father, but not him. It's why I never told Alex about the vision I had…"

"What vision?" Pierce asked.

Suddenly, Joseph realised who he was talking to. It was like a switch flipped, and his mouth shut once again. Pierce wasn't part of the contract he signed; Joseph could tell Pierce about the vision of Alex's death. He could.

But he didn't want to. He didn't want to make it feel real.

"A slip of the tongue," Joseph said quietly. "Forget what I said; that wasn't meant to come out."

"Well, that now makes me more curious…" Pierce's voice was low, deep, coxing Joseph into saying more. "Whatever it is, it's got to do with why you're agreeing to marry so quickly, doesn't it?"

"No," Joseph said. Pierce, please. I don't want to talk about it. It was a long time ago. It was a slip of the tongue."

"I don't think it was. Suppose you're keeping something bottled up. It won't be good for the team." Pierce said. "It's better to be honest and open with people. Why not lighten the load a little bit? If it was long ago, you've been hiding this for so long. It might feel good to tell someone finally-."

"He died!" Joseph shouted. Loud enough that Pierce stopped speaking almost immediately.

"What?" Pierce asked; his voice was quiet and soft, but Joseph was angry.

"After my brother, Finley, and I were captured by the guild, we were taken to a dungeon in Tildra to be processed. We made it through their tests. But there was a man in the dungeon with us, the one who took me to Freydale and separated me from Finley..." Joseph began.

"Caulan?" Pierce asked; Joseph affirmed with a nod.

"As he pulled away, I got angry, upset; I couldn't tell you. A power I didn't know I had manifested. I grabbed him by the hand and dove into his memories, showing him something... a vision, a memory from the future – I wasn't sure. It showed destruction off the scale, the beacons blasting people with their magic, the decay overflowing and somewhere in the chaos... Alex died." Joseph began, calming himself down as he looked down at the ring on his hand, which Alex loved so much. "In the vision, it happened after the beacons activated again."

"So, you don't have much time left..." Pierce began. "I'm... I'm sorry. I shouldn't have pushed you. That was wrong of me."

"Hm," Joseph mumbled, nodding as they settled into the silence—the awkwardness.

"Does Alex know about any of this? I know you said he didn't know about the vision..." Pierce asked. "Does he know he is going to die?"

"No," Joseph replied quickly. "I can't tell him. I have a contract bound to me. Caulan forced me to sign it so as not to tell him of his demise. I signed it just before we left Freydale. You are the first person I've... reluctantly told. Because the moment I speak about it is the moment it becomes real. I have to confront the fact that the person that I love is going to die sometime soon, and I have absolutely no idea when that is going to happen."

"You might be unable to tell him, but I'm not bound by contract. I can tell him for you." Pierce replied, and suddenly, Joseph's eyes shot up. Hoping that it was some sick joke, but Pierce wasn't joking. His eyes alone told him that.

"No, no, you mustn't," Joseph said, fear in his voice. "I want to be able to save Alex, and if he knows about the vision and his death, it might make it worse. It might make it happen. As much as I hate the man, Caulan might be working on a way to save him, too."

"His father put a contract over you. He's separated you and him. What's to say this isn't another ploy to separate you?" Pierce asked, his voice was firm. "Put so much pressure on you to keep the secret that you drive him away? Because you would be too scared to commit properly, I think Caulan knew that you two would fall back into the roles you had before you were separated. That he could see the bond between you. He knew this contract and burden would make any relationship hard."

"What if you're wrong, though, Pierce?" Joseph asked as he stood up from the bed, pacing across the small room.

"Well then, we will figure it out. We will find out the cause of his death and stop it before it happens." Pierce replied. Joseph went quiet momentarily as if thinking, but Pierce had more to say. "I will tell him if you want me to. I will tell him alone if you don't want to be present."

"Hm, maybe that's the right course of action. You are always better at articulating yourself…" Joseph said. "You're right… he does need to know. I hope he doesn't hate me for keeping it a secret for so long."

"He won't. You two, you're survivors. You've both found each other in a world that would much like to see you not communicate. The world is in constant peril, but you two, you're stronger than most."

Pierce said as he stood up and wrapped his arms around Joseph, pulling him into a hug. The two never hugged; they had shaken hands, but that was as far as it had gone. "I hope you don't mind, but sometimes a good hug is what someone needs. And you, Joseph Price, are someone that needs a hug."

"Thank you," Joseph replied, leaning on Pierce's shoulder.

"When do you think you'll get married?" Pierce asked as the two strengthened the hug. It was true; Joseph did need a hug.

"We haven't spoken about it, but ideally, before we get to the next beacon... you know, just in case." Joseph said, and he could feel Pierce nodding his head. He understood—finally, someone understood. So, what happens now?"

"Where is Alex?" Pierce asked.

"I think he went outside; I heard him moving about a while ago. I assume he went to find some food. King Atlas said there would be a feast." Joseph said as he pulled away from the hug.

"There is, people are already up there," Pierce said. "I'll go find Alex, and you needn't worry about anything."

If only that were true.

The people of Rivetia had worked tirelessly all night to restore the kingdom. As Joseph walked up the staircase, he could see broken parts of the stairs and their moulding, which were all fixed. As he got further up the stairs leading to the main square, Joseph could see tall limestone structures standing in the air in a semicircle around the castle that Joseph had imagined the day before.

He couldn't see them entirely due to being far down, but they towered over the staircase—a natural beauty.

As he and Pierce made their way up a staircase that had been a large incline hill the day before, Joseph could see the marble floor with the statues on either side leading towards where the party was being held. It wasn't too far from the beach they were on yesterday night, in the eye line of the water – the best way to see if people were coming in and going. It was a beautiful sight of the open waves and blue ocean – empty and barren- if not a little daunting. Joseph wondered how long it would take before someone knew the barrier had been broken down and how long it would take before someone with an opportunity would make their way here.

He just hoped they wouldn't be bad people. There were many of them around Freydale, so Joseph knew the world would be just as bad.

Joseph kept his eyes on the illuminated path as he strolled through the long line of people, raring to go outside. From the inside of the cave-like structure, the bright light from the morning sun was finding its way into every crack.

Pierce had left him in the dust as he had run up the staircase on a mission. "I'll see you in a bit, Joseph. All will be fine." Pierce said as he reached the top of the staircase.

He hoped so. Feeling himself getting warmer the further he got up the stairs, the morning sun bleared down at him. He was glad that the sun finally reached this place. The barrier being gone was going to be good for the kingdom. It seemed everyone was enjoying it, too. Everyone had massive smiles on their faces. Joseph got to the last stair and basked in what he could see.

"It's beautiful," Joseph said as he looked around. Everyone seemed in such high spirits, as did he, but his conversation with Pierce soured that feeling a smidge.

"I'm glad you think so," Queen Kala said to the side of him. It was as if she had appeared out of nowhere, standing off the side of the staircase, like she was waiting for them. You made all this happen."

The smell of food was wafting from somewhere Joseph could not see, knowing that much of it would be seafood. Joseph was already excited; he hadn't tried any seafood since he had been a 'free man' all those years ago; he remembered, even back then, it was a delicacy; his mother made shrimps once – he didn't know where she had found them. Where they lived, east of Tildra, was a grassland, and there wasn't much ocean around it. So, this party and all the food was a treat Joseph had wanted for a long time.

"I took down the barrier, but you all slumped hard. How did you do this in one night?" Joseph asked, earning a small, knowing smile from the woman.

"The power of the Cerulean Tears is a wonderful tool. We used them to recreate what we had lost. It makes for quite a picture, doesn't it?" Queen Kala asked, and Joseph nodded. "That Maura, your friend, was helping us last night, too. She put in as much effort as the rest of us. She and the King seem to get along quite splendidly."

"Do they?" Joseph asked. Queen Kala only winked at him once.

"I expect you want to find her and your team, so I will let you go. Enjoy it, Joseph. You've also earned a little relaxation—and with the engagement." Queen Kala said before letting Joseph pass her.

"Before I do… the location of the key?" Joseph asked, knowing that simply asking broke that relaxation rule she had just bestowed. But Queen Kala nodded.

"I'll take you to the key, or at least to its location tomorrow morning, but today, I want you to enjoy yourself; it seems very rare that you get that chance with what you've described as your life before you came here." King Atlas had just appeared out of nowhere, still wearing the same clothing as the rest of them, but now adorning his new staff, the King smiled and nodded. Maura had come with him, all smiles, and her smile widened as she looked at Joseph. "The key is in an old cave system – the beacon can also be found there. It's a dangerous feat, but I'm sure you can traverse it; I'll explain on the way there, but as my mother said, for now, enjoy this. Please."

"You don't have to tell us twice..." Maura said as she linked arms with Joseph and began to drag him off towards the buffet tables.

Joseph had never had a party just for him. There had been birthday celebrations before he was captured, but he couldn't remember them. Alex had brought a piece of cake once for them to share when they were younger—that had been the first time that he felt happy.

He felt happy now. He just had to keep telling himself that something wouldn't come by to ruin it all. He just had to keep telling himself that it wouldn't happen.

Maura ran over to another table close by, dragging him along with her.

"So, you're engaged." Maura began as she picked up some of the fruit on the table. "That's different, that's new."

"I've already had the whole spiel from Pierce. He thought it was too quick." Joseph explained, but Maura placed a berry in her mouth and listened. "I explained my reasons, and he seems more on board with the idea now."

"Good. I was on board with it from the get-go, so no reasons were needed. From the moment I saw you in that dingy club in what I can only assume was a dream, you were cute together. The way you held hands, it just looked... I don't know. Like your hands belonged together." Maura explained. "I sound silly, but that's what I saw in you two. My parents married very quickly and were madly in love."

"Yeah?" Joseph asked, finally learning a little bit more about Maura. Even though the two had been travelling together for a while, she didn't open up very often, or they never really had a free moment before something else happened around them to distract them. "How did they meet?"

"You know, I don't even know. But my parents were young, I know that. They were both working on their careers, but Mom always said that he just got her from the moment they laid eyes on each other – it was like they were made for each other, like everything made sense all at once, like colours became more vibrant, music became louder." Maura began as she fumbled with another bit of fruit in her hands. "When dad died, she was inconsolable for months, never got out of bed, hardly ate. Then, she dove into her work and became a monster to the cause. She wanted to make me famous; I don't know what strings she pulled. But before I disappeared, everyone knew me and my business all at the same time."

"Do you miss it?" Joseph asked. He knew it would be a sore topic, but Maura dug her hands in her pockets and shook her head.

"I don't miss it at all. I like having some secrets to myself. Everyone, and I mean everyone, knew everything, sometimes even before I did. I thought I'd miss my mom, but after Dad died, she withdrew from me. She only cared about making me famous, not what I wanted to be or do with my life." Marua said, her eyes squinted as she thought back to it all. "I miss my phone the most."

"That brick thing you had that day you woke up?" Joseph asked. He remembered she had asked to get it charged. He didn't understand what that meant, but maybe he wasn't supposed to.

"Hm. It ran out of charge a while ago." Maura said. "I lost it a while back when we went to that beacon. It used to hold my entire life. I used to be able to talk to people about it, you know, rather than sending a letter. If I wanted to know something, I didn't have to look at books; I could find out instantly using my phone. I could always watch everything on that screen and take photos to have the memory. That's what I miss. The simplicity of it all."

"We'll get you home, Maura," Joseph said as she snapped her head to look at him. "I mean it; we will find a way, no matter the cost. It's not fair that you were snatched away from your world whilst ours is being slowly destroyed."

"Sometimes I do wonder... why me?" Maura said. It wasn't a question but more of a statement. "Like, what have I ever done that would warrant this? I'm not special; I'm just an ordinary girl with normal parents... mostly."

"Whatever the reason, we'll figure out how to get you home," Joseph said. So what's this about you getting cosy with the King?"

"We were just talking last night. I thought I'd help restore the kingdom like the others. He wanted to hear more about my story..." Maura said, a small smile erupting on her face. So, I did. Our conversation didn't go... unnoticed."

Joseph and Maura laughed as they popped more food into their mouths before Joseph saw someone in the corner of his eye—or rather, two people.

"Hey, you two," Pierce announced, speaking loudly as he and Alex began to walk over. "We're Sampling the food, are we?"

"Hm yeah, it's lovely," Maura said as she stole another piece, something with chocolate on it. Joseph wasn't sure what it was, but she looked like she had enjoyed it nonetheless. "I can't believe all this was made from the Cerulean Tears. It's incredible."

"Maura, can we just chat alone for a moment?" Pierce asked as he looked at both Joseph and Alex. She caught on quickly and began to walk towards him.

"Of course," Maura said as the two began scurrying away.

Leaving only Jospeh and Alex by the buffet table, Joseph felt a dark cloud of unease. He wondered how Alex felt about receiving that information and how he had reacted. But as he looked at Alex, he couldn't see much emotion. He couldn't see anything in the man's eyes.

"I'm sorry for keeping that from you." Joseph started strong, trying to keep his composure as he spoke. "I couldn't start our life together without telling you, though. I'm sorry it came through Pierce's mouth, but I cannot speak. Your father forbade me; he had made me sign a contract before we went through that portal. I hoped that, given time, the vision I had… my vision wouldn't come true, that if we had managed to escape together, we wouldn't have that hanging over us. I know I held a massive secret, but I should have told you. This isn't what you signed up for when you asked me to marry you, me lying to you, knowing something life-changing like that. I would understand if you wanted to call it quits. I would accept it."

But Alex didn't say anything. Instead, he moved quickly, wrapping his arms around Joseph and pulling him into a hug—a most unexpected move.

"You were doing what you thought would keep me safe, Joey," Alex said as he rested his chin on Joseph's head and pulled him closer. Joseph could feel himself settle, but his eyes were welling up with tears. He didn't want to cry, but he could feel himself start.

"I'm sorry," Joseph said as he let some tears fall out of his eyes, wetting Alex's shirt. I should have told you and made an effort to loop you in. You should be angry at me."

"I'm not angry at you, Joey," Alex said as he let out a breathy sigh. It was clear he had also been crying before. "I'm angry at my father. He was the adult; you were a child. It would be best if you hadn't been the one to reveal that information; it should have come from him. But he kept it a secret as well."

"But you're going to", Joseph said before he felt the mark on his arm begin to glow. It told him all he needed to know. He could not speak about it; Caulan would know by now.

"I know what's going to happen," Alex replied quickly. "I'm going to die… eventually. We don't know when, and we don't know why. But I do know that I want to make the most of the time I have left."

"Which means?" Joseph asked as he moved his body away from Alex to look him face to face; the man was smiling from ear to ear as if he had concocted something in his mind.

"It was Pierce who suggested it… I didn't think he was that on board with it. But he knows the gravity of the situation…" Alex began as he was moving around the answer he wanted to give; Joseph just stayed quiet, waiting. "He suggested we get married before we go in that cave. He suggested today, whilst there is a party going on."

"I did indeed," Pierce said interjecting. You have no idea how much time you've left, Joseph. You said it yourself: You wanted to tie the knot before we got to the beacon. If what I heard my cousin and Aunt discussing with you earlier is authentic, that's tomorrow. The party is all setup, and it is a party for you. It wouldn't take too long to set it up differently."

"I want to, guys, but it doesn't change the fact that we don't have anything to get married with, for instance, rings, an officiant… family," Joseph said. His head was swirling. How much has his life changed in the past few days?

"Those… around your neck." Maura pointed towards the two wedding rings he had forgotten all about that had been hung around his neck for the past fifteen years. He never took them off.

"My parent's wedding rings?" Joseph asked as he clutched at the silver and gold objects. His father's was the bigger one. "I can't even really remember them giving it to me; they've always been with me… I suppose I forgot they were there."

"You can't have your parents with you… but you can have a symbol of them every day. Simply by wearing them, Joseph." Maura explained. "What better way to honour them?"

"The officiant?" Joseph asked as he removed the necklace from his neck.

"My father. He had many weddings on the sea if you can believe it. He would be happy to, I'm sure. It's the least he can do." Pierce explained, and suddenly, all was coming together.

Joseph's head was spinning, but he was happy about it. He wanted to get married to Alex on a beach in the newly constructed kingdom that they, as a group, had helped come to fruition. The first wedding on the beach was probably in a long, long time.

"So, we're actually doing this?" Maura asked. "They're actually getting married today?"

"We need to make the most of life whilst we still have it," Alex replied as he reached for Joseph's hand and again interlocked their fingers. "Are you okay?"

"Perfectly content."

TWELVE

A wedding. No time to prepare. Joseph did feel nervous now.

Not cold feet, he wanted to marry Alex. He wanted to be with him, and now, with Alex's imminent death hanging over them, the notion of 'rushing into it' didn't sound so bad right now.

Queen Kala had bundled Joseph and Maura into the bedroom that Joseph had slept in and given strict instructions for King Atlas to do the same for Alex and Pierce. Separating Joseph and Alex, the tradition of not seeing each other before the wedding was still a thing in Rivetia.

"For weddings, we have the traditional dress. Usually, there aren't two grooms. It's a bit short notice, but we can work with the clothes that we have." Queen Kala said as she dragged in a rather large trunk; even though she was old, she seemed spritely enough to pull it independently. Wiping down the trunk, all the dust fell off it. It flew into the air, causing her to cough slightly before she opened it up, flipping the lid to reveal beautiful satin clothing, reds, blues, and purples. "Here we are. I'm glad it survived all this time."

Queen Kala brought the suit out of the trunk and held it up. The suit was in two pieces: a jacket and trousers. Each thread was adorned with light blue thread placed onto black satin fabric, with dashes of red and blue throughout the darkness, like the sky was changing colour from night to morning.

"It looks beautiful," Joseph said as he stepped forward, feeling the fabric; Maura did the same.

"So soft… even when it's been here for so long," Maura said, commenting as she looked at the intricate stitching.

"The best part…" Queen Kala said as she placed the trousers down and held the suit jacket higher. "Maura, if you can, please turn down the flame on the table. I want to demonstrate something."

Maura nodded and quickly did as she was asked. The room instantly darkened, and Joseph could see it. Each thread was shining bright blue, like the cerulean tears did in the water, like all of their clothes, but so much brighter.

"Woah," Joseph said as he admired the light the jacket created; they no longer needed the flame. The room was cast with a light blue shine, covering each inch of the small room, lighting it up in a way that a flame couldn't. "It's so bright."

"It's imbued with the strongest form of the tears. This was the first Luma's wedding suit." Queen Kala said as she admired the bright light; almost immediately, Joseph removed his hands from the suit; from what he had been told – this suit must have been old… ancient. "He got married to a local girl, and we had this suit specially made to honour the Luma and what he did for the kingdom. It felt befitting that you would wear it; after all, you've done an awful lot for us, too."

"Can I really wear this, though?" Joseph asked. "It's a relic; the first Luma was… a long time ago, wasn't it?"

"You forget that the tears heal; they keep this suit in perfect condition." Queen Kala said as she picked up the trousers again, draping the suit over his shoulder. "It might be a little tight around the edges; you're a string bean, but the Luma… well, he was something else. No matter, the tears will work their magic."

"What do you mean?" Maura asked. "Sounds a bit ominous."

"No, no, rather the opposite." Queen Kala chuckled. "They adapt, as you do, Joseph. The suit might be small on you, but once you've got it on, the tears adapt the shape of the suit, making it so it would fit the wearer perfectly. Don't ask me how it works; it has something to do with how potent the tears are; they are the real deal."

"I wonder what Alex will wear," Maura said. She was thinking out loud, but Queen Kala replied anyway.

"I left him with the King. I'm sure he has many clothes that Alex could wear. They are the same build, same height. He'll find something to fit him, something befitting of marrying the current Luma." Queen Kala said as she passed Joseph the trousers, then turned on her heel with a short smile.

"A second question, will you take his last name?" Maura asked. "You know, it's sort of a traditional thing, but… I have no idea how things work around here."

"Despite it being my family name, Price has always held a bit of a… bad taste in my mouth; it reminded me that I had a price tag over my head, sold to the highest bidder. My last name will always remind me of who I was before I left the guild", Joseph said; he didn't confirm a yes or a no. But Maura nodded, understanding, nonetheless. He understood why she had asked; she wanted to know what to refer to him as after. She was naturally curious, and that was a good thing, too.

"Come, Maura, let us go, let Joseph change, " the queen said as she opened the door and walked out quickly, still spritely in her older age. "We will be just outside. Let us know when you are ready," Maura said as she gave Joseph a quick hug, which he reciprocated before she left the room.

Joseph quickly put the clothes on the bed, turned the flame back on the lamp, and began to get dressed.

Getting himself mentally ready for an event neither party ever thought would happen.

Today was the day Joseph Price would show Caulan Von-Loch wrong.

Nervous was no longer the word. As Joseph and Alex had been changing into their respective clothing, the entire courtyard where the buffet tables used to be had been changed completely. Now, standing where one of the extensive buffet tables was the alter – lots and lots of chairs and in the middle, a white velvet rug trailing the entire vicinity of the aisle.

Joseph felt as if the entire contents of his stomach were going to come up and show itself again as he stood at the bottom of the aisle, looking forward at the altar. The three men stood close by, two facing him—Santos at the alter and Pierce with his hands clasped together behind his back. He hadn't changed clothes. But it was clear that Alex, who stood with his back facing Joseph, had changed into something more comfortable.

Queen Kala and King Atlas sat on one of the front chairs, and it seemed that everyone in the kingdom was in attendance. Some sat down, and some stood up at the back due to the lack of chairs.

It seemed everyone wanted to be here to see the Luma, the person who saved their kingdom, get married, even if they didn't know him. Joseph was a private person, but for today, he could let that slide. He wanted everyone to know he was marrying the person that he loved…

It still felt strange to say that after so long, how open he thought about it, how strong his feelings had become, coming back with a vengeance. Or maybe they never went away at all. Joseph wasn't sure, but he was sure that this wedding was happening. He had been in a haze ever since Alex asked him; maybe it was the conditioning that he got from Caulan.

He couldn't and wouldn't ever be loved because of his magic; he had to snuff out those thoughts. As he had kept telling Alex, Caulan couldn't hurt them anymore, and he certainly wasn't going to hurt them on what was supposed to be a happy day.

The music began, playing from an instrument that Joseph did not recognise. It was a much smaller flute-like object that played a wispy tune. Cheerful in tone. There wasn't a pattern in tune, though Joseph didn't claim to be an expert. But it was a calming, familiar tune from the old times, something that might be played at festivals or maybe a nursery rhyme his parents began to sing to get him to sleep.

Moments later, everyone, including Alex, turned around to the back of the aisle.

"Come on then," Maura said as she linked arms with Joseph. "Let's get you down that aisle."

"Okay," Joseph said, his voice breathy, letting out a few puffs of air. The nerves were really getting to him now. Let's go."

As he walked, Joseph zoned in on Alex. He was wearing something similar to Joseph. The blue and red hues of the outfit contrasting with the black were the same, but this time, there were golden hues. The thread that was woven within the suit was golden, fit for a king. This was clearly one of King Atlas's pieces, but Alex wore it well.

He looked just as nervous. His hands held together, waiting for

Joseph to arrive at his side.

The aisle wasn't long, but the courtyard was large and intricate. Flowers that hadn't previously been there were draped over the statue, and flowers made a path following to the bright white velvet carpet at their feet. As he passed them, King Atlas was sitting closest to the aisle. He gave Joseph a quick smile and a curt nod before mouthing, 'Be happy.'

Joseph reached the alter and found himself slotting right where he was supposed to. Maura moved to the right of him, Pierce to the left of Alex. The music stopped as all the chatter died down.

And Santos began to speak.

"We are gathered here today to witness the joining of Alexander and Joseph. Two people amid the world's chaos and the trails they were sent from forces we did not understand found each other." Santos said, his voice was crisp, clear, projecting all over the area – he was different from the man they first met on the pirate ship a few weeks before. He seemed a lot less brash and happier now that he was at home. Santos was all smiles, too; Jospeh just couldn't tell if it was because he was home or if he was happy to be a witness to this event. "I won't go on as I think that Alex has some things he wants to say. So I will pass it over to him to express how special this day is."

Alex turned to face Joseph.

"I never thought I'd be standing up here. When we were separated in the old days, I thought all opportunities to be happy had passed me. I ruined it further by accepting what everyone else had told me, that we were supposed to hate each other. That was the only story I kept telling myself. But you, Joseph, you are a light that shines through even my darkest period. I don't know how you do it; it happens whenever you're around." Alex began as he looked Joseph in the eye; his voice was as crisp as the air around them, clear and conscious; he didn't want to mess anything up. "I want to open myself up to change; I want to be with you every step of the way. I will make up for what I did for the rest of my life, but I would rather be by your side, as your husband, than against you and alone. I meant what I said, I love you, Joseph Price. I always will, no matter what happens. I know that now."

"When I was a child, you tried hard to get close to me. I remember our first meeting; it was a father-son day at the guild, and your father had brought you in. You slipped away, curious as you always were. You found me, a secret in the dungeons only your father knew about. You had no prejudice then; you asked who I was and why I was there. You helped me off the floor and wanted to play with me. I said I couldn't leave because your dad told me I couldn't, and you marched straight up to your father and told him off right then and there." Joseph began as he began to chuckle, thinking back. It wasn't a lovely time, but imagining Caulan being told off by his seven-year-old son was funny. "You persisted in trying to be my friend, even if I didn't want to. You fed Finley, you fed me. You weaselled your way into our lives, even finding out my birthday… you brought a cake for me and even scrounged together a candle for good measure. After that, I knew you could be trusted. That you had a good heart. I thought you were mad when you asked me to run away with you. But now I know, as we stand on this beach miles away from Freydale, that you were right to be. We are together, and I will not take that for granted."

"I will never take you for granted ever again," Alex said as he went to hold Joseph's hand. A smile crept up on Alex's face; it was a bashful kind of smile – a small one.

"As unconventional as that was, we all understand what you have been through. You've both worked hard to be where you are physically and together. You've been through highs and lows." Santos said.

"We hit the lowest point…" Joseph countered.

"Total rock bottom," Alex interjected with a short laugh.

"But my point still stands; you found each other and are willing to work on those lows. You are here today to witness the union of these two people who, through all these trials they have had, have fought tooth and nail to love, care and break the stigma they were both taught… that a magically inclined person cannot love a hunter and visa-versa." Santos said, his voice warm as he looked at Joseph, remembering how Alex's father had been, the wildness, the crazy. "They were wrong… so, the rings."

Pierce walked with the two rings in his hands and quickly slid Alex the silver ring and Joseph the gold one. His parent's ring, King Atlas, had dipped them into the cerulean tears – the cracks they had from years of wear and tear all having disappeared. And on short notice, they had been making the correct size, even though he was wearing the suit that changed shape. He still didn't understand fully how it worked.

"Alex, please repeat after me," Santos said as he held up his hand and gestured for Alex to do the same. "I Alexander Caulan Korin Von-Loch."

"I Alexander Caulan Korin Von-Loch." Alex said with a smile.

"Do take Joseph Maynard Price as my lawful wedded husband." Santos continued.

"Do take Joseph Maynard Price as my lawful wedded husband." Alex copied as he put the ring on Joseph's left hand, next to the engagement ring.

After Alex had finished placing the ring on Joseph's finger, Santos completed the vow. "I will care, cherish, to have and to hold from this day forward. In this life and the next, I will protect and uphold these solemn vows."

"I will care, cherish, to have and to hold from this day forward. In this life and the next, I will protect and uphold these solemn vows." Alex said, letting out a breathy sigh. All anxiety left his body now that it was all over.

But now it was Joseph's turn.

"Now, Joseph," Santos said, holding his hand up. "I, Joseph Maynard Price."

"I, Joseph Maynard Price." Joseph began, feeling his legs turning to jelly; his hands were shaking in anticipation and overflowing with anxiety. He didn't want to get anything wrong.

"Do take Alexander Caulan Korin Von-Loch as my lawful wedded husband." Santos continued.

"Do take Alexander Caulan Korin Von-Loch as my lawful wedded husband," Joseph said, a smile appearing on his face; he couldn't stop smiling. His hands were shaking as he held the ring in his hands, ready to place it on Alex's finger like he had done before. The ring slid on quickly. This is what his parents gave him the rings for.

They hoped he and Finley alike would find someone, someone in this broken world to spend the rest of his life with. Someone worthy of their mementoes.

"I will care, cherish, to have and to hold from this day forward. In this life and the next, I will protect and uphold these solemn vows." Santos said as he placed his hand down on the altar before him.

"I will care, cherish, have, and hold these solemn vows from this day forward. In this life and the next, I will protect and uphold these solemn vows." Joseph said as he let out a nervous sigh. It was strange; he, too, felt the anxiety just disappearing from his body, like a curse being lifted.

"That's the hard part done, lads, so..." Santos said as he laughed, glancing at the two of them. "Both of you may kiss your groom."

And so they did.

THIRTEEN

The celebrations were in full swing. It had been hours since the wedding, and people were still dancing with no signs of stopping.

The music had changed once again, a more upbeat version of the songs that Joseph had heard whilst walking about Rivetia's underground. He was up and down, always dancing with someone, even if it was his wedding; it seemed everyone wanted to dance with the Luma. It was a big deal here. Tradition apparently.

"For the last time tonight, will you give me the honour of dancing?" Joseph said as he sat down in one of the chairs and heard a voice next to him asking him a question. Joseph sighed before he saw the person; he was tired. But all tiredness fell from his body when he saw Alex holding his hand. "We've not actually had a first dance together, just us."

"I will… " Joseph said as he took Alex's hand and was dragged onto the dance floor. Alex was all smiles; it was a big deal for him to hear that from Joseph's lips, but Joseph hadn't got used to it yet. The change in the last name he had always known Alex by was odd but good.

Even if he had gotten married before, Joseph wouldn't have

changed his last name. There was too much history there, too much loss. His name, his family name, was a reminder of the people he had lost, and he never wanted to forget them. Alex's was a reminder of what he had done to people, of what his father had done to people.

The dance floor was empty, or if it had been busy, people had dispersed pretty quickly, and the music slowed. Alex pulled Joseph closer to him on the dance floor, grabbing his left hand and placing his right on Joseph's waist, guiding him slowly into a sort of waltz.

Joseph had seen people do the waltz at the party at the castle back in Freydale. He had never danced before, mainly because servants weren't allowed to, so he wasn't trained. But Alex… was. He was guiding the dance; Joseph was being pulled – but he didn't mind.

As he twisted and turned, Joseph looked at what was on people's faces, all smiles. Some speak to each other. He zoned in on Pierce and Maura with huge smiles, sitting by a giant cake that hadn't even been touched yet. Wedding toppers were placed on top of the cake, Joseph and Alex – standing next to each other, and the words Mr. and Mr. at the bottom.

It was Maura's idea. In her experience, weddings as extravagant and special as this had to have a cake that was just as beautiful. And it was.

This whole day, which Joseph had been nervous about, to begin with, had turned into a beautiful one. He hoped that this was a sign of what was to come—more beautiful days free of the torment that he had experienced his whole life.

Caulan had been wrong, and because of his prejudice, he missed his only son's wedding. Joseph felt a tiny bit of pride in that. That he had won the fight. And that through it all, through all his trials to save his son from 'the monster' that was magic, he had lost him in the process.

"I'm sure you'll tire of me saying it, but I love you, Alex,"

Joseph said as he rested his head on Alex's shoulder. Alex kept doing what he was doing and guided the dance.

"I love you too," Alex replied, kissing Joeph's head. "I can't believe the events since we arrived in Rivetia. You're my husband, and I couldn't be happier! I don't think anything could change my mood-."

"It's a ship!" Someone shouted from the side of the beach. The music stopped instantly, and Joseph and Alex found themselves walking off the dance floor towards Maura and Pierce, who had been joined by the King a moment later.

"These are the first people we've had arrive since the barrier is down. How did they know to come?" Joseph heard Queen Kala ask her son, who shrugged his shoulders. "Have we had anyone leave the island since it came down?"

"Not as far as I am aware. We would know about it." King Atlas finally said, keeping his tone to a whisper as he began to walk towards where the person who had announced the arrival was. Joseph watched as the man's feet almost sunk into the sand as he stepped off the marble floor.

"You don't think it could be *him*, do you?" Alex turned to Joseph, his arm around Joseph's shoulder, keeping him close.

"Your majesty…" Joseph began; King Atlas turned on his heel. Thinking back to what Alex had mentioned about seeing the Dalian before whilst sitting on the beach. Joseph hadn't seen the ship yet but wouldn't put it past someone like Caulan to give up. "Before we came into Rivetia, we were in conflict with someone on the outside, sorry to say, but he's still out there, patrolling the area. He might have seen the destruction of the barrier; there was that blast of light, remember?"

"Right." King Atlas said as he looked over the horizon towards the ship. Its mast was high in the air as if it was expecting to travel a long distance at high speeds, unlike it had been waiting. As Joseph reached where King Atlas was, Alex, Maura, and Pierce looked at the ship on the water. It wasn't the Dalian. Thankfully. "Well, whoever it is, they're coming into one of our ports... I only hope they're here for nothing nefarious."

As everyone watched with bated breath, the ship was moving quickly. Maybe they had noticed people on the beach; they just wanted to get to the port and off the boat. Perhaps it was because a 'new' island smack bang was in the middle of where they had been treading. Either way, these were the first people to enter the island since the barrier was down, and they wouldn't be the last people to arrive unannounced.

King Atlas went first, securing a distance between himself and his people – just in case he needed to step in.

"Move slowly." Queen Kala told the King as he tried to quickly make it down to the docks. "You don't know if they're friendly, maybe just take a step back…"

"I'm fine, mother. I'm King; I need to be able to converse with them without you worrying about me." King Atlas groaned, this time speaking a little louder than usual – Queen Kala just smiled and nodded in his direction – she was just a worried mother; that was all it was. Moments later, a small boom came from the ship as it docked at the top of the beach – a few steps away from where the King stood. "Here we go then…."

No one moved for what felt like hours. At the top of the waterline, Joseph could see barnacles clinging to the ship's side – this ship had been on the water for a while, and there had been no dry docking. The mast came down with little ease; some noise came from the inhabitants, but no discernible words were spoken. Whoever owned the ship… they were coming down to the dock.

It didn't seem like an unfriendly advancement. There were no people on the top of the ship pointing down weapons or looking at the citizens in untoward ways. It looked empty apart from a few people that Joseph could see moving around in some port holes on the side and movement at the top.

"Hello?" King Atlas began, loudly announcing his presence to the new people who had arrived. Someone popped their head over the side of the ship, a youngish man with a scruffy beard and hair; he looked as if he had been on the sea for years.

"Greetings!" The man said he had a light and airy voice; as he spoke, he began to lower a ladder for his crew to use to get down, the ladder landing haphazardly on the dock. Joseph watched as, one by one, about ten people – way less of an amount than Santos's crew all clambered onto the side of the dock.

They looked like boys, children—younger than Joseph by a few years at most. Whoever these people were, they had not been on the ship as long as their Captain. They didn't have bags under their eyes like Santos' crew.

As they stood on the docks, King Atlas didn't budge from his spot, still unsure of their intentions, and now they were off the ship – it made him and everyone on the beach even more wary.

"Who are you?" King Atlas asked as he stood with his staff and all his subjects behind him. Joseph, Alex, Maura and Pierce are standing in front of the crowd.

"Some people have been trying to find Rivetia for a long time." The Captain said. Very vague. Suspicious. But at least it wasn't Caulan." "Boy, are we glad to be here? I thought this place was a myth, but it suddenly appeared to us."

"You're not unfriendly, I hope?" King Atlas asked, making small, cautious movements with his staff in his hands. He was still unsteady on his feet due to the sand. However, if they were unfriendly, Joseph had no problems admitting that the man would probably be able to dispose of all ten of them quickly.

"Not at all. Your majesty." The Captain said, somehow

knowing that he was speaking to a King; maybe it was the makeshift crown or the different clothing, but he greeted the King in a way that made Atlas stop tensing so much, the King relaxing his shoulders and gaining a grip on his footing in the sinking hot sand. "My name is Captain Gerry Darion. I've tried and tried again to get into Rivetia over the years. My family used to live here years ago before the war, and I wanted to see it for myself."

"We had a barrier keeping Rivetia locked down, hidden from the rest of the world…" King Atlas began. "How in the world did you know to come here?"

"We didn't…" Captain Gerry said, a little bewildered at the question. "We set out on the ocean days ago; it was a chance encounter. Here…"

Gerry stepped forward and passed King Atlas, a piece of paper with browned edges stained with mysterious things. Joseph could see it from a short distance away, a map of the island and some numbers at the bottom.

"What…" King Atlas said as he looked at the paper in his hands, but Gerry quickly cut him off.

"They're coordinates given to me by my family of where Rivetia was. I've been coming here for years, around the area – patrolling it almost, waiting for the day I might find it." Gerry said. He did seem genuine, but he was a little nervous, perhaps. "When… when did the barrier you speak of come down?"

"Last night." Queen Kala interrupted, her voice coarse and grainy. She was just as suspicious as the rest of the people of Rivetia. Now you are here, what is your intention?"

"Of course, we just want a room, if we may," Gerry said as he looked back at his small crew. As Joseph looked at them, he noticed a few of them were a lot smaller and younger than he initially thought. "They're refugees, lost folk. I've been training them for a life at sea. We just need to rest in a nice bed and have proper food. Then we'll be on our way back to the sea."

"As long as you are friendly and courteous, I don't mind who comes and goes. We've missed a lot of that while we've been locked in isolation." King Atlas said as he turned towards the group that had followed him down from the party.

"Do you think it wise?" Joseph heard Queen Kala whisper to her son moments later. "To let these outsiders in with no knowledge of who they are apart from being refugees?"

"You let me stay." Joseph interrupted in a whisper.

"Those were different circumstances", Queen Kala replied, leaning into where Joseph and Alex were standing. You brought peace back to the kingdom; I don't want these people to uproot that."

But the King did not heed her words. "I'm happy for you to stay, but what are you refugees from...?" King Atlas turned around and asked Gerry, who looked like he was consulting his crew. "You don't become a refugee from anything... is it conflict? Do we have anything to worry about with your arrival?"

"We were all ex-servants, your majesty." One of the younger boys roared.

"I collected them all from their guilds, some in Tildra, some all the way west in Dalston in the Septica Region. Freydale... has always been tricky; I never got anyone from there. We went to the kingdom many times over the years, but saving someone there was a lot harder. I wanted to save as many people as I could." Gerry explained that as he looked back at the young people before him, Joseph noticed their hair had been cut short, probably to sneak them out and change their appearance. "Trust me when I say no one will know they were gone. There is no danger of conflict. Some have been gone from their guilds for weeks, months even."

"Okay, well, if there is no trouble." King Atlas began, scratching his cheek with apparent nervousness. "Please, come on in. There is plenty of food. We just had a wedding, so please grab a plate. One of my fine subjects will find you a place in one of the newly refurbished inns around Rivetia. But please, come to my quarters later on, I must speak with you regarding a few things."

"Is there a wedding cake?" Gerry asked, curious.

"Yes, but it hasn't been cut yet. We hadn't quite got to that bit." Alex said as he squeezed Joseph's shoulder with his hand and pulled him closer. Their rings are both on full display.

"Well then, we won't interrupt any further. I'm sure these kids would love some cake after such a hard journey on the sea." Gerry said as he nodded at Alex.

Joseph got a good look at each of their faces. One of them stood out to him, though. He was a little older than the others, and he had the beginnings of a beard on his face. Maybe he wasn't one of these new recruits that Gerry had mentioned. Joseph wasn't sure.

As each recruit passed, the man Joseph zoned in on turned on his heel, faced Joseph and then looked at Alex.

"Sorry for interrupting your wedding." The man said – finally saying what his Captain had meant to say. "Captain Gerry can be a little… unaware sometimes. Congrats."

"Thank you…" Joseph muttered back. But as the man turned to walk and follow on with the other boys in his group, Joseph couldn't help but look at the man, his familiarity.

If he was an ex-servant too, Joseph knew that prolonged staring was always a bad sign, someone looking at you for just a bit too long – all the back of the hairs on your neck stand up. It did for Joseph, and he was sure it happened to every person trapped in a cycle at the guild.

"Can I help you?" The man said in a deep voice, and he looked Joseph up and down. In the clothes Joseph had been provided, there was no indication that he was a 'foreigner'. Joseph could almost see the cogs in the man's brain going haywire, trying to figure out why a person 'from Rivetia' would be solely staring at him.

"No." Joseph shook his head, averting his gaze. "Sorry."

"Look at me for a second..." The man said as Joseph did as he was told. The man looked deeper at Joseph than he had previously. Making Joseph a little uncomfortable. "I feel like I know you-."

"What is the holdup, Quartermaster?" Captain Darion asked as he walked back to where the man stood at the back of the line. But the man did not budge on releasing that information. Instead of looking at his Captain, he kept his eyes on Joseph as if inspecting him. "I say, what is keeping you, Price?"

Joseph's eyes darted up towards the Captain a moment later.

"What did you say?" Joseph asked, earning an insightful look from the Captain and an even more confused look from the other man.

The Captain, however, chose not to interject anymore.

"I know your eyes. What's your name?" the man asked. He crouched down slightly, his eyes slightly tearing up as he looked at Joseph's like he was just waiting for confirmation of his suspicions.

"Joseph."

Before Joseph could tell what was happening, the man grabbed him and pulled him into a hug; Alex had let go of Joseph moments before. "I thought I knew those eyes... how are you here? How are you here?"

Joseph was sure now that he was speaking to the person he thought he was. Without any other needed confirmation, he already knew. Joseph buried his face further into the man's chest – letting out a small, hardly heard sob come from his lips.

Alex piped up. "I'm sorry... who are you?" It was clear that even Alex needed confirmation.

That was when Joseph heard it, all the confirmation that he needed. "My name is Finley Price." Finley let out another sob as he hugged Joseph just a little bit tighter. "I'm his brother."

FOURTEEN

Joseph knew Finley was alive. It wasn't just intuition, but when he was shown his family when his parents appeared to him at the Rose Beacon, someone was missing – Finley. His spirit hadn't moved on, and as much as he was told that there was no evidence that his brother made it out of Tildra… he knew. Joseph just knew.

"My brother!" Finley exclaimed as the group of five sat in the courtyard surrounded by wedding supplies and food. The youngsters from the boat stuff their faces with the recently cut wedding cake, and the music is still playing; now, it is a triple celebration. The barrier being removed, a wedding and their first arrivals from the distant lands. What a day. "Let me look at you again. You're all grown up. I expected you to be long dead, what with all the flare and bluster that Freydale had. Oh Joseph, how did you escape?"

"It was a relatively new thing; we're also kind of refugees in a way. We've only been out of Freydale for a few weeks." Joseph replied as he and Finley sat opposite one another. "I thought _you_ had died, Finley! I was told you were missing, presumed dead, five years ago!"

"That was when I escaped. See, I was tasked to flatten a mountain close to Tildra. They wanted to expand the empire and make space for houses. They'd left me alone for a fleeting second, and once I had flattened the mountain, in the dust and decay… I managed to make a run for it." Finley explained that keeping his voice low was a side effect of being trapped in a guild — any conversations with unsavoury topics had to be kept on the low down. Even here, it still bothered him, Joseph could tell. "I found my way onto that ship, said who I was, thankfully Gerry didn't report me… we started out together, earning more and more opportunities to take servants and save them from… well, the life we were living. I had hoped to make my way to Freydale to find you."

"I'm glad to say we're no longer there," Joseph said with a smile of triumph.

"What are you doing here?" Finley asked as he looked around the group. Joseph could tell he was a little out of sorts, looking at the faces of the 'new' friends his brother had made.

"We're on a mission to find those beacons scattered around the realm and return magic stored within them. We've already unlocked the one in Freydale and Tildra, but we are here now to unlock the one in Rivetia." Joseph began, keeping his own voice low. "You see, there is this decay-."

"Joseph!" Maura strained to shout out, stopping herself from being too loud to not draw attention to herself. "Why don't we consult everyone in the group before you just blurt out the entire plan to a stranger!"

"He's my brother; he won't say or do anything," Joseph snapped. He was looking at the situation through rose-tinted glasses, and no amount of scolding from the group would shake that. "He's not a stranger at all."

"To us, he is." Maura countered, folding her arms.

No one said anything. The tension in the air could be cut with a knife; it was so thick. Finely turned to Maura, a smile on his face.

"Who are you?" Finley asked as he turned to Maura.

"Maura." She said, a little stunned, like a deer meeting a human for the first time. "Maura Jackson."

"Well, Maura, you know my name; I know yours. We're not strangers anymore." Finley replied as he took a swig of the drink to his side and dug a fork into the cake he had been offered. "I want to help you if you let me; it gives me a chance to break away from the crew I have for a moment and spend some time with my long-lost baby brother, doesn't it?"

"I suppose," Alex muttered, tapping his fingers on the table, clearly annoyed at Joseph's lack of consultation – revealing their entire plan to someone none knew.

"And what's your name, boys?" Finley sat back in his chair and looked back and forth between Alex and Pierce

"Pierce, 8th Duke of Rivetia." Pierce began. Finley's eyes grew wide, and Pierce must have caught on because his following words came out in a slight sputter. "But I don't use the title often; it's just Pierce. My name is Pierce."

"And my brother-in-law?" Finley said as he cocked his head to the side and smiled.

"Alexander…" Alex said, coughing out his name. Though he didn't even attempt to mention his former last name, the look on Joseph's face gave him all the intel he needed to know.

Do not mention your family name.

Finley leaned back in his chair and clasped his hands. "Von-Loch, right?" Well, that was a useless effort. Alex simply nodded. "Don't worry, Alex. If you were anything like your dad, you wouldn't be here right now, nor would you be married to my brother. Right?"

"No. No, I wouldn't." Alex muttered through gritted teeth.

"So, you said you unlocked the beacon between Freydale and

Tildra?" Finley asked, looking around at all the people at the table. Joseph nodded in reply; a smile crept on Finley's lips when he heard this. "How did Freydale take it?"

"Not great, I'll be honest; it was only a chance encounter, and we managed to escape," Joseph replied. "We arrived here about three days or so before you did, I was the one who took down the barrier."

"You did that?" Finley asked, his eyes like slits, confused. "How? Your magic only allowed you to mimic others. You are a shapeshifter."

"Somehow, my magic evolved. As I got older, I began to show signs of having extra control – I could dive into people's memories with a simple touch. I got hit by a blast of magic from one of the beacons not too long ago, and it developed that further, too. Made me stronger. Taking down the barrier, that power… it's a recent change I haven't quite fully grasped yet." Joseph explained, shifting slightly on his chair; he didn't even want to get into the whole saga with the tears; he wasn't sure Finley would understand anyway – mainly because he didn't himself. "It's a little ironic. Caulan wanted me dead years ago, but my magic was the only reason I am still alive."

"Mum and Dad did always say that you were… special. Maybe this is what they meant." Finley replied. Almost instantly, Joseph remembered his dream when he first landed on the beach, showing the old Luma. How there had been a prophecy told to his parents. Maybe this was all true.

"Do you remember why they said that?" Joseph asked. Hopeful.

"No. Sorry." Finely said as he leant forward in his chair again. "They seemed pretty private about things."

"I see," Joseph said.

Finley seemed to remember something, something he thought

might lift the mood. "Do you still have the fox I made?"

"I'm sorry, no." Joseph shook his head, his eyes cast down. It didn't lift the mood. "More than a week ago, I still had him; I lost him in the woods of Freydale, and he hasn't been seen since. I hoped someone would find him before we left the continent, but we left quickly."

"I'm surprised the little guy survived as long as he did. Fifteen years is a long time." Finley said. He didn't seem disappointed but somewhat happy that Joseph had managed to keep him in good nick for that long. "I'm sure you'll find him somewhere. We can maybe do it together?"

"I'd like that very much." Joseph smiled. He couldn't believe that he had his brother back and a safe place to rest his head – this place, Rivetia, was turning out to be the best place that he had ever landed his feet on.

"Joseph, can I speak with you for a moment?" Alex asked as he stood up from his chair and began to walk over to where Joseph was sitting.

"Hm?" Joseph began, turning his head towards Alex. "Sure."

There was a certain tension at the table like the others were waiting for Alex to speak, but as he came round the table and stood directly next to Joseph, towering over him, he uttered only one word: a question.

"Alone?" Alex asked sheepishly as he offered his hand out for Joseph to take.

"Oh," Joseph replied quickly as he took the hand, standing up and glancing at the people at the table before him. "Just... talk amongst yourself for a second."

Gripping his hand, Alex dragged Joseph towards a little side street, a bit away from view from the other three. "Do you really think it wise?"

"What?" Joseph asked, a little taken aback by the question.

"Well, I'm not sure I feel comfortable with him knowing all of this information so soon," Alex said as he crossed his arms. But Alex held up his hand before Joseph could say anything in defence. "I know how it sounds, but doesn't it seem just a little bit sketchy that your long-lost brother… and I mean lost, shows up on a boat the day after you return Rivetia to its rightful place in the world? And suddenly, he's all up for leaving his group to help us with the quest?"

"I understand your concerns. I do. But maybe it's all a coincidence that the captain said they had been on the sea for days." Joseph sighed. "Of course, he would want to help because he wants to spend time with me. He wants to make up for lost time. So do I."

"Okay, I get it," Alex muttered as he leaned his head on the wall. "I don't want to argue about this, not today. He's your family, the only one you've got. But I can't shake what I feel."

"You're my family too." Joseph gripped Alex's shoulder.

"Yeah, that's hard to get used to," Alex said, slightly chuckling. He peered out of their hiding space. Joseph followed his gaze, looking at Maura and Pierce, who were both apprehensive about the new ally. "I don't think I'm the only one who is worried."

"What is this really about?" Joseph asked.

"He doesn't like me. I can tell." Alex murmured. "The moment he figured out my name, our name, a switch had flipped."

"We can't change who our family is, no matter how hard you try. But we can break the stereotype. You can be different from your family." Joseph explained as he looked out of the hiding hole at Finley. "I might have been looking at it with rose-tinted glasses a bit…"

"What?" Alex asked.

"I don't know Finley. He is a stranger. We've had fifteen years apart; who knows what happened since then. I know I've been through a lot. He certainly will have, too." Joseph said as he turned to Alex, realising something. "But listen, he will be a helpful force in the cave. None of you have magic, and mine, even with the tears at my disposal, I can't imagine it will do much. I can't even remember using my shapeshifting in the past week… but Finley can do things we can't." Joseph explained, but he could see Alex's face looking back at him, almost like he had been slapped, a gormless look etched onto his face.

"No. I don't follow." Alex said, shaking his head, and all Joseph could do was smile. He knew Alex was trying to understand, but there wasn't much going on inside his head right now. "Dumb it down for me."

"Finley has control over the earth, the ground, rocks. It's called Geokinesis. Finley's power might help us in the long run if we go into a cave." Joseph explained, and for a moment, he could see Alex's eyes, an understanding. "I don't know how his magic developed as he aged, but when he was younger, he could cause earthquakes and move rocks with ease. If any paths are blocked, he can help."

"Right," Alex said as he crossed his arms. The night sky above them, the twinkling stars being the only light, made it hard for either of them to see the other's face. But Alex's voice was low. "Okay. You, Joseph Von-Loch, drive a hard bargain. I'll give trusting him a go for you. If… when we have a free moment, we can have a honeymoon?"

"It's hard to get used to that name but you drive a harder bargain," Joseph said as he kissed Alex quickly, a peck on the lips. "The moment we're done, we can honeymoon until our heart's content."

"I'll hold you to that," Alex said as he chuckled before grabbing Joseph's hand, ready to return to the table to join their group.

Joseph smiled in the moonlight as he settled into Alex's

embrace. "I hope you do."

FIFTEEN

Early in the morning, King Atlas came to collect Joseph for the 3-mile-long walk towards the elusive cave where the beacon was. The King walked ahead, using the staff that Joseph had created to propel him further up the steep hill, gaining ground on the group of five just as the sun was starting to rise.

Joseph and Finley slinked back to speak with one another, catching up for all those years lost. Alex was slightly behind the King; the years of leg work and strenuous training for his work in the guild had paid off even here, and Maura and Pierce were in the middle. Pierce helped Maura get her footing occasionally, even with the shoes provided – it was clear that she had never climbed up hills much in her lifetime.

"How far away are the ruins, your majesty?" Alex was the first one who piped up. Being the closest, he was trying to keep pace, and even with his training in the guild, Joseph could tell that the man was out of breath. "I can understand why we are going to the ruins of a city because, honestly, who would want to make the daily trek up here in order to get home?"

"It's not that much further, I assure you. The island is deceptively larger than it looks. There is a lot of history on these shores, but if you're tired now… Imagine what you'll be like when you're in the cave." King Atlas said he didn't turn around to look at any of them, instead choosing to use his staff to make it easier to force his body up. None of the others had that luxury. Joseph almost wished he had made his own staff before making the trek up here.

"What can we actually expect?" Maura asked a question that, so far, the King had avoided. "From the cave, I mean?"

"In recent years, the cave system has only been traversed a handful of times. It's a maze down there, a conglomeration of tunnels and homes all at the same time. People, ancient Rivetians, used to live there so they could be close to the beacon." The King explained, still not stopping climbing. "But just because it's previously a home, doesn't mean it's without fault. Half of the cave is flooded, and different levels have different levels of flooding; you may even need to use the Cerulean Tears to make your way down and further through the cave until you reach the beacon."

"No, you've lost me now." Pierce interrupted. "Different levels of the cave? What are you talking about?"

This time, the King turned around. "This cave, it's a little different – as I said before, it's a maze. It goes up, down, left, right and diagonally. The beacon is down; remember that. You will have to traverse three layers or 'pools' of water from the stories. They all go down, but the cave itself… wraps around itself. Moves."

"Moves?" Joseph questioned. "It's alive?"

"I didn't say that…" King Atlas said, looking like he was thinking of what to say next. "You don't have to worry about the moving aspect of the cave; that's the least of your issues. The issues come with the 'booby traps' the old citizens created to keep intruders out, but…"

"Booby traps?" Finley inquired as he helped Joseph up the hill; both were straining slightly to follow the group.

"As I said, there are a few; I can't name them all, but I know there is one room in particular that you need not give into temptation; I've not been down there myself... This room will show you what you want in life, what you want the most at that moment – you cannot give into temptation." King Atlas explained, looking as if he had seen a ghost drip white in appearance. "Keep one thing in your mind… whatever the cave is, whatever entity it might be, it wants to keep you there. Do not let temptation kill you."

"How does that work?" Maura asked; the King turned to look at her. "Is it some sort of enchantment? Everything seems to draw back to the same thing, magic."

"I don't claim to know how it works, but you need to heed my warning." King Atlas replied, his face grave as he looked upon the group of five. "There have been a lot of people who we lost down there even before the war; I'd hate to have to lose you five as well. But you must beat them all to get to that key and the beacon."

King Atlas turned and began to climb again. He was far away before he stopped, reaching a summit the others had yet to see.

"Have we reached the end?" Joseph asked as he grabbed for a rock sticking out of the ridge they were climbing, forcing himself up to join the others, realising just how slow he had been.

King Atlas did not answer the question; instead, he crouched down and swirled his hand in what looked to be a puddle. "This is the entrance to the cave; in here, you'll find the maze; through the maze, the booby traps appear, and then you'll find the key and the beacon in one place. You should find the key still in the keyhole if you'll believe it."

"You never thought to retrieve it?" Alex asked.

"We tried, but it's grim down there, and we didn't need to. Not really. The Cerulean Tears kept us going; there was no need to retrieve the key." King Atlas explained as he stood up. "I respect that it doesn't sound good, the fact that I am willingly allowing five strangers to go in here, a place so dangerous, but I would be a fool to not allow it. You are here to right a wrong that occurred fifty years ago. I cannot stand in the way of that."

"Er-." Maura began, looking as if she was contemplating continuing. "Are you sure that the cave entrance is here, your majesty? All I see is a puddle."

"I'm positive this is the right place." King Atlas replied as he pointed towards the puddle. "I did say you might have to use the tears to traverse the cave… well, this is one of those times. You need to use the tears to create a bubble; the bubble will drive you down until you reach dry ground…"

"We have to go down to find dry ground?" Finley began. "How does that work exactly? If this place is flooded… surely the rest of the cave is too."

"Like I said, I don't claim to know how the cave works; it's all a bit topsy-turvy. You go down and somehow end up right, like the cave flips upside down. I've only read about it, though, of course." King Atlas said as he looked around. "You're safe for a while after you get into the cave; it's further down where the booby traps lie. You need to go down, always keep going down; you might have to veer off the path sometimes, but always keep it in your mind… to go down."

"Right. Down." Joseph said as he looked at the bubbling puddle before him. It did look rather large, enough to fit one person in it at a time; two was going to be a push.

"This is where I must leave you. I'd like to say I'd help more, offer more insight, but this…" King Atlas said as he again pointed to the puddle of bubbling water, the same blue hue starting to light up the area. "Is uncharted territory for even me. Unfortunately, what you experience here is up to you to figure out."

"Thank you for all your help,, your majesty,, hospitality, and information. I'm sure we'll be fine from here." Alex said as he held his hand out for the King to shake.

The King did just that. "You've hit the jackpot with this one, Alex. Don't forget that." King Atlas said as he smiled towards Alex. Only the King held no prejudice towards Alex for what his father did. He didn't care about what past the two held but what they were doing now.

Moving onto Finley, he held his hand for the man to shake. There were no pleasantries between the two, just a simple smile.

"Pierce. My cousin." King Altas said before he quickly pulled his cousin into a hug again. This time, as Joseph looked on, Pierce didn't look uncomfortable, feeling happy enough to,, wrap his arms around the King. "We didn't get much time together, but once this is all over. I do hope you find yourself back in Rivetia. Despite being King, I hope we can be a proper family."

"I'd like that, Atlas," Pierce replied. "But I must do this and pay back a debt."

"A very noble quest indeed." King Atlas nodded. As he retreated from the hug and moved further down the line. "Ah, Miss Maura Jackson. From a land so far away, so distant."

"Hello, your majesty," Maura said. "I'm glad you saw us off. I'm sure the others will thank you for leading us here."

"I enjoyed our talk on the beach, learning so much about your life before you ended up here. I'm also privy to your own quest to return to said life. There is an old disused portal down at the base of the cave, next to the beacon. If you can get it working, that might be a chance you can take to get home." King Atlas explained, and suddenly, Maura's eyes were wide, and a smile appeared on her face. "But should you decide that you would like to stay in the realm, I do hope you find your way back to Rivetia as well. I'd be happy to make your acquaintance again if you do."

"Thank you... Atlas." Maura said before her eyes went wide again. "I'm sorry; thank you, your majesty."

King Atlas smiled before he reached for her hand and kissed it once. "For you, Maura Jackson, I will forgive the formality."

Now it was just Joseph that the King needed to speak to. The King zoned in on Joseph and motioned with his head towards a spot on the cliff they were standing on.

"Thank you for bringing us up here. I'm sorry for my constant pandering at getting the information, but you can understand how important it was." Joseph explained as he and King Altas turned away from the group of four that were now inspecting the puddle at their feet.

"I'm glad you came to Rivetia, Joseph. You've enriched our lives so much," King Atlas said, smiling, grateful. I need you to promise me something, if you will."

"Anything," Joseph said, a little taken back. "Name it, please."

"Don't give into the temptation to get revenge on those who hurt you. I know that is a big ask. But you're a light in this world, which I want to keep intact. Whatever you do, I implore you to make people hear your voice, but in ways of good, not bad." King Atlas replied as he held out his hand to Joseph. As Joseph looked down, he thought about those words: What would it have achieved if he did get revenge on the people who hurt him? He would become just like them, and whilst he wouldn't be as bad, he wouldn't be good either. He would be corrupted and broken, even more so than he already was. "That's my only wish for you. Do you think you can honour that for me?"

Joseph took the King's hand, something he wasn't used to – shaking hands with royalty. "I think I can, yes."

"I'm not at liberty to say if this is true," Atlas said as he looked around to check if others were listening in. "You're the Luma, so it's imperative, I say. The last Shade to walk the earth hid their part of the gem somewhere safe, so their successor could find it. Tales say the gem is hidden somewhere in this cave… so please be careful. Because The Shade could be anyone, even someone in this group of yours."

"Thank you for telling me," Joseph said, though now the meeting had been soured. The mere mention of The Shade brought it back to his mind, but he had forgotten that this was something he had on his plate, amongst the one hundred other things swirling around his brain constantly.

"One other thing…" King Atlas said before he pointed towards something on Joseph's person. "The gem that you got from that dream, from the previous Luma, the one around your neck, that you keep hidden..."

At this point, Joseph didn't ask how Atlas knew as he gripped the gem, bringing it out to show him. "What about it?"

"Its magic is strong. Stronger than any other form of the tears. I don't know if it's true, but there were stories where people once believed the two gems could be reunited. I don't know what would happen if you did. But if this decay is as bad as you say it is, you might need all the help you can get." King Atlas explained, keeping his voice low. "There were theories that the Shade could be used for good, too. That the power was not all corrupt. It just needed to find the right host. A host with good intent. But each time the Shade appeared, they used it for destruction. Hopefully, this time, whilst the world is in peril, whoever owns the other half of the power can work together with you."

"If they don't?" Joseph asked.

"Then the decay you mention is the least of your worries, I'm sorry." King Altas replied. He nodded at Joseph before sneaking him something, a small seashell-like object. "Use this if you get in trouble. We in Rivetia will heed your call and come down the cave, no matter the perilous journey. We owe you a debt, Joseph. The whole kingdom does. You will always have a home in Rivetia."

With a simple smile, the King left, trudging down the hill quickly with his staff stretched out front. Joseph watched. He was quick at walking on the craggy stones and hilly areas. The natives had learned to adapt, a quality Joseph knew all too well.

"So…" Finley began, snapping Joseph's attention back to the group and the task. "How do you want to do this then? Do these Cerulean Tears just protect us?"

"The king said that we need to create a bubble using the tears, but by the looks of it, only one person at the most could fit down this… puddle at once," Maura explained as she, too, crouched down and swirled her hand in the water before her. "I mean, I can go first; there's no skin off my nose."

The water began to glow brightly as Maura quickly got into it. Her sodden clothes were already pulling her down as she settled into the small area.

"How is it?" Pierce and Finley asked in unison as they knelt to her level; Alex and Joseph stood at the sidelines, waiting to see what might happen next.

"It's warm water. The bubbling from the tears moving around is strange, too, like tiny little objects rushing past you at a hundred miles an hour… it's almost like taking a bath in a jacuzzi…" Maura said before she raised her hand out of the water. "You won't know what that is, duh. Scratch that. But it's fine, honestly. Right, let's get to it."

Joseph watched as Maura closed her eyes. Like clockwork, like the magic was accepting her, the tears began to reach up like a tower. The iridescence of the water as it covered Maura fully shimmered in the morning sunlight. The circle shape was completed as it had just reached over her hair. The tears were careful not to miss out on one area where water could seep to disrupt the air.

Inside the small puddle and into the translucent bubble, which none of them could see very well, Maura looked as if she was floating.

"Maura," Alex called out, being the first to feel brave enough to speak after what they had just witnessed. "Can... can you hear us?"

"Yes, I can!" Maura shouted back. The sound coming through the water was muffled, but her voice and tone were still evident. She sounded nervous, and as the bubble started to sink into the small area, taking her with it, she let out only one sentence to guide the others to follow her: "I'll meet you down there!"

"So, who's next?" Finley asked as he and Pierce both looked back at Joseph and Alex.

"I think I should go last, considering the tears practically do as I say; one of you three needs to go," Joseph replied as he watched Pierce slide himself into the water from his crouched position.

Once again, like clockwork, the tears reacted to the disruption before towering up slowly, creating the bubble as if from thin air, just about missing Pierce's spiked-up hair as he settled into the water around him. Being bulky, the puddle looked much smaller for Pierce than it had Maura, a tight squeeze if Joseph had ever seen one.

A thumbs up from Pierce solidified that he was okay as the water began rising over the bubble. Before long, Finley held Pierce's spot in the water, taking no time at all to hesitate before he too. He was gone into the cave's depths, all three searching for the same thing – dry land at the bottom of the water-filled cavern.

"And so, there were two," Alex said with a nervous giggle as he looked down at the pool at his feet. Joseph noticed something as he observed this version of Alex: He had been a whole lot quieter today, more reserved. Even now, as the man looked down at the puddle before him, it was like Alex was in a trance—one he was going to struggle to get out of.

Nudging Alex on the side slightly, the man sucked up some air as if he had forgotten to breathe for a while.

"Are you doing okay?" Joseph asked softly. Hearing Joseph's words, Alex blinked twice and turned his head from the puddle towards Joseph.

"Yeah, sorry," Alex said, shaking his whole body. "I don't know what came over me there. I felt I couldn't get out of my head for a second."

"You fully zoned out," Joseph said as he knelt at the puddle. "Come on, let's get this over with; as soon as you are in the water and down on dry land, that's part of the problem solved right then."

"Okay," Alex said, nodding as instructed, sliding his body into the water, bobbing up and down as the water settled. "So, I only have to imagine the tears making a bubble over me?"

"Exactly. Just think about yourself being protected. The tears will do the rest of the work for you. It should take only a few moments." Joseph said as he watched the tears begin to react like they had with everyone else. It was like the tears were gliding around Alex, but they did not rise; they didn't look like they were going to create the bubble. "Alex?"

"Is it working?" Alex asked before he opened one of his eyes that had been previously closed to have a peek.

"No." Joseph shook his head as his eyes connected with Alex's. "Try again. Really focus this time."

"I thought I did before. I was imagining the bubble rising around me." Alex said as he closed his eyes once again, his face contorting slightly as he imagined hard like a child might do – but still nothing from the tears that surrounded the pool; they were swirling around him but not creating anything like they had for everyone else, native to the island or not. Alex, it seemed, was the outlier. "No, it's still not working; these things don't want to do their job."

"Hang on, let me try," Joseph said as he got into the water, too. Alex moved to the side, trying to make enough room for Joseph. As soon as Joseph landed in the water, almost immediately, the Cerulean Tears in the water began to react differently, beginning to rise ever so slowly like they were creating a bubble. "Maybe they don't like you."

"Oh great, semi-sentient water doesn't like me either?" Alex grumbled as he watched the water circulate around Joseph. "How am I going to get down if I can't use them like everyone else?"

"We can share," Joseph said as he reached for Alex to take. Quickly, Alex did so, getting as close to Joseph as he could to save space. He held onto Joseph's waist as he watched Joseph close his eyes, and the cerulean tears finally moved around both of them, covering them in a thin layer of water like everyone else.

"It worked!" Alex exclaimed. "So, it's just me then, great!"

Alex then wrapped his arms around Joseph and pulled him close, saving space. Now that there were two of them in the small puddle, it would be easier for the bubble to go down if they were as close as they could be.

"I think that's us ready..." Alex said as he settled into the water. His body had been tense before. Still keeping his arms wrapped around Joseph as the bubble began to sink, he and Joseph looked around. The blue shimmering of the tears as the bubble met the water was so bright that it illuminated their faces, counteracting the dark in which the cave thrived.

"Are you ready?" Joseph asked. He just needed Alex's confirmation—a proper confirmation. "We're going down."

"Not really, but I'll have to be," Alex said as he let out a muffled sigh, one he had clearly been holding onto.

"Three." Joseph began – the light from above was slowly disappearing every moment.

Alex followed suit. Joseph could feel his whole body shaking in anticipation. "Two…"

And before either could say the last number, the bubbles dove into the water quickly, plunging them into darkness, only slightly illuminated by the blue hue from the tears.

The race for the Rivetia key had begun.

Joseph had never been so happy to feel dry land—even if he was upside down and had face-planted it after the bubble popped once it had exited the water.

Finding Alex next to him, Joseph quickly dusted himself off, stood up, and surveyed the area before him. The only part that was slightly light was the tears swirling around the pool of water above them. "We'll need something to climb up to get back up there…"

"Where is everyone?" Alex asked as Joseph's attention was snapped towards the rest of the cave. How silent it was—there was no sign that anyone had been there before them for a while.

"Maybe they went on ahead?" Joseph asked, nervousness and anxiety rising as he and Alex settled into the cave's darkness, dankness and silence. No map in the world could teach them how to traverse this place, so if they had lost Maura, Pierce, and Finley, there would have been no telling where they were or where Alex and Joseph had landed.

Through the dark, Joseph searched for an exit to the chamber they were in; the rock was naturally jagged – and Joseph wondered why anyone in their right mind would want to come and worship the old gods down here, let alone live in the cave. Taking a few cautious steps, Joseph could see what looked to be an opening in the room, dimly lit by the Cerulean Tears struggling against the lack of light down here. Running his hands along the cave walls, he came upon the opening… it seemed a lot deeper than it had looked.

Tapping his foot onto the ground before him to test where it led, Joseph kept going with the cautious steps, worried that one wrong step and he would begin to fall; there was still no sign of where the others were – maybe… they hadn't been as careful.

"Hang on. Is this an old lamp?" Alex said – his voice echoing off the walls as he stood close to the pool of water above the cavern. Hearing the clink of metal as it ground against the rock, Alex picked up the circular object, brushing it off for dust and grime. Before turning what looked to be a small dial on the bottom. "I wonder if it still works…"

Joseph saw the light coming from the lamp a moment later, illuminating the entire cavern in a bright blue hue. Clearly, a long time ago, someone had managed to harness the tears to use them as a light – they certainly needed it down here. "I think you have your answer," Joseph said as he could see the path forward; Alex held it with his right hand, lifting it up high as he made his way towards Joseph. "Do you want to go ahead? It's better to have the light ahead of us to ensure we can see where we're going."

"Yes, good idea," Alex said as he squeezed past Joseph, holding the lamp before them, illuminating the path. As Alex walked, he kicked something in front of him, sounding like another lamp—the same clatter between metal and rocks. He scrambled to pick it up. "Here. Let's see if this works, too."

Passing the old lamp to Joseph, Alex pressed the same button on the 'new' lamp, revealing a similar blue glow. One lamp was helpful, but two was terrific. They lit up the dark cave at every angle as the two walked closer towards a destination neither of them quite knew.

Moments later, they heard another noise further up the path, a voice that told them that, despite the looks of it, they weren't alone down there after all.

"Hey, you guys!" Further down the 'hallway' – Maura's voice bounced off the walls, guiding them towards where she was. Somehow, having gotten further into the cave without the help of the light, Joseph held up the lamp to illuminate the area, and he could see Maura, Pierce, and Finley all standing with their arms linked. "What took you so long? Quickly get over here… this place is fantastic!"

"Sorry, Alex had some trouble getting the bubble to work… we had to come down together," Joseph replied as he and Alex steadied their pace, trying not to run towards the group; there was no telling where they would go if they took a wrong step. "It was a bit of a squeeze with the two of us; it took longer."

"How did you three get down without the lamps?" Alex asked as he, too, raised his lamp higher than before, the blue casting shadows on the dark walls. As they walked, tiny pictures of what looked to be stickmen coated the walls—mainly with stories of times long since gone by. But Joseph had no time to dawdle; none of them did. "I can't see a thing without these…"

"We did it the old-fashioned way… though a lamp definitely would have been helpful; wish I'd have noticed them," Pierce said as Alex and Joseph reached the group of three. The walk towards them wasn't all that long. Still, it felt like miles – every step cautious, every moment nervous, waiting for the inevitable dread to creep back up. Joseph did not like the dark; it reminded him of bad memories and even worse times. "I thought we might just have to trail our hands on the walls the entire way around, but I'm glad you two found an alternative."

"There are more lamps back there, I think, must have been left behind by the previous inhabitants or something… they're full of tears," Joseph said before he noticed that the entire area that they were in was illuminated – the blue hue kind of gave that fact away. The open pocket they had found themselves in was massive, giant carved statues towered high in the sky. "I can't believe all of this is down here… they're like soldiers, don't you think?"

"They certainly look that way. They don't look like booby traps, thankfully, just old statues." Finley said as he looked at one of the statues nearby; her carved face stared back at them all like she was observing them, waiting for the perfect moment to strike. Joseph just hoped this wasn't one of the booby traps King Atlas had mentioned. So far, it seemed like they were just what they were: statues. "They're beautiful, if not a little creepy. Should we continue? I'd rather get out of this room as soon as possible if it's all the same to you four."

"I agree completely; something about them, I can't quite put my finger on it, but they scare me a little," Maura said as she wiped down one of the statue's faces, the dust caking the marble coming off in large quantities in her hands.

"Right, everyone… grab a lamp, turn them on and let's get through this cave whilst we still have time," Joseph said as he trudged on, holding the light high in the air to guide the way. As he walked, Joseph heard the familiar sounds of the metal lamps clanking on the rocky floor, ringing through the room. With five lamps, at least the cave wouldn't be so dark anymore; nothing could hurt them in the light.

He just had to keep telling himself that, even if he didn't believe it. If living as a servant for fifteen years taught Joseph anything – even in the light of day, even in the presence of other people… monsters could be lurking anywhere.

And anyone could become a monster if they were pushed hard enough.

SIXTEEN

Joseph always had thoughts in his head from when he woke up to when he fell asleep. Down in the cave, his thoughts, which Joseph long believed had become out of control years ago, were doubling down tenfold. His mind, senses, and entire body were on high alert, struggling to grasp one thing at a time.

Each room, chamber, and stone allowed one to wonder what exactly the reason was for its existence, why an entire kingdom of people had lived down here all these years ago—it couldn't be just because of the beacon and its proximity. Wondering why they had lived down here wasn't the *big* question, however.

It was why they had left, and by the scattered lanterns and the few 'homes' or as Joseph would call them – dwellings he had been into, they were just as broken, shattered, and dust-filled as the rest of the kingdom had been before he arrived – Joseph's mind wondered as to why they had left so quickly, too.

In one of the rooms, high up in the air, it looked like they were just finishing off a more enormous statue—it was missing a head. The features were all off—unlike the pristine monoliths they had seen at the beginning. Using the tears in the lanterns helped lead their way, ensuring that no one fell any of the deep drops Joseph had seen as he walked through the area. Time had not been kind to this area.

Time was never kind at all.

"I can't believe all of this is down here; imagine all this rich history… no one from home would believe this if I told them," Maura said as she got her footing on one of the slopes leading up towards what looked to be a house – where they had been walking, Joseph assumed it was a street, Joseph presumed, though no carriages would be going down these lanes, that was for sure. Metal poles erected from the ground close by looked as if they had a hook on them. The lantern he was holding – they must have gone there to light up the area. "I wonder why they left if they had all these homes down here… it must have been something big for them to never return."

"I couldn't imagine living down here for your entire life with minimal escape options if things went wrong. It would be too much fun," Pierce replied, reaching out to touch the artefacts the inhabitants had left behind long ago. "I can only assume that demand for food, sunlight, and companionship forced them to leave. It must have been a long time ago, though – those ruins we saw when we first arrived in Rivetia had been there since my father was a child."

"It is magnificent that they could build everything down here without light. My eyes are hurting after half an hour of being down here—the blue light is giving me a headache," Finley said as he opened a wooden door to one of the dwellings. The creek of the metal hinges bounced off the walls as he did, making Joseph realise that they were alone down here, completely alone.

As the group headed into the unknown, Joseph stopped to look around, holding out his lamp to light his way through the small caverns that dotted the old ruins. Something was scuttling around inside, probably not too happy to see the light from Joseph's lamp; it had been dark for years. He looked at it, a bug, and in a way, it reminded him of himself. He had been a servant, trapped for so long, and even with all that freedom he had now, trapped was still how he felt.

Taking a deep breath in, feeling the dusty air surround him,

Joseph allowed himself to breathe out – right now, even though he should not have, he felt trapped due to the impending mission they were on and the fact that more and more, the decay seemed to be spreading. He wanted to sit down, to allow himself to have a brief break – a second's peace and quiet. But he knew that as long as those beacons remained locked and the decay spread, he could not rest. He had to stay trapped. Bound to the contract, even outside of the restraints of the Hunter's Guild. The contract seal was still on his arm, a reminder of his past and that they still had a hold over him, even now.

Joseph hadn't even been allowed to grieve, to allow himself to process all that he had been through. As he watched the bug scuttle around in the bright light from the tears he held in the lamp, he felt a slight panic welling inside him. Though unsure why, Joseph was beginning to feel overwhelmed, as if everything he had been through was coming back to bite him.

Caulan and the guild called Joseph unscrupulous names. He had seen the acts he had completed in the guild's name, all the people he served, and how cruel they had been. The fire—the flames that killed Henry, Henry himself suffering, and not properly being able to grieve about that either—Caulan had taken that away from him when he extradited him back to Freydale for trial.

All those people in the dungeons after the trio left, he was not sure, but in his heart, he knew that if someone like Caulan had anything to say in the matter, they would all be dead, Hunter or civilian. They were a threat if they had magic.

No doubt about that.

A snap of something in the background shocked Joseph's system back into action. He turned on his heel to look at the nature of the disturbance, the lamp still in his hand illuminating before him, throwing most of his body weight into the turn. The person behind him threw their hands into the air slightly as they looked upon the state that Joseph had let himself get into. Joseph was breathing heavily, and his hair spiked up. He would have been a sight for sore eyes.

"Hey, it's just me." Finley stood with his arms folded, concerned as he looked at Joseph's face in the dim light. "Are you okay?"

"No. I don't think I am." Joseph said, stepping back to ground himself and see Finley correctly in the dim light. The cave walls set in on him as Joseph tried to be rational about how he really felt. Weighted. That was what he was feeling, weighted. "Sorry, I just let the world get to me for a moment; being down here, on this mission, I do not know. It had never affected me before, but in the dark, alone, it allowed me to think about things I had been neglecting…"

"I assume it's about the guild and what happened?" Finley asked. He had hit it right on the head, like a hammer to a nail. Finley cocked his head to the side, looking at Joseph a little further. Like he was peering into Joseph's soul. "I think about it too. The stuff they put me through, even five years later. But I suppose it has not been as long for you…"

"I have not really had a moment to think properly. Everything around me zoomed past me like light flashes; I was always doing something. The quietness of this cave, the unnatural stillness, I suppose it unnerved me. Made me susceptible to think, to have thoughts of my own." Joseph explained. Though he felt as if he did not need to explain himself to someone like Finley., He had been through it all himself. He finally had someone who fully understood him. Alex could try to understand, and Joseph felt comfortable speaking to him about it, but Alex's experience differed. Finley was the same through and through. "Caulan sold me once to a baron – but the experience was not bad. It was better than the guild ever was."

"What happened?" Finley asked.

"After a year, the baron died. As all natural things do. But with his death, we all found ourselves in the guild again. My best friend,

Henry, was one of these servants who lived with him most of his life. He was different, more childlike than an adult. He had not had the same experience with life as I had. I tried to protect him all I could. But I failed. Completely." Joseph explained. "Sometimes I feel like it was my fault he is dead. I left him alone with a monster, I should have tried harder to drag Henry away. He went to the pyre because they did not see him as useful. But he was. He really was."

"They sold me too. My longest was for two years when I had just turned eighteen. The guy I was sold to was rich and had various servants at his disposal, but there were always favourites. People he could give special treatment to. You know, let them go outside with no supervision, give them extra meals. You had to work up to become a 'special servant'." Finely hesitated; Joseph could see his lip quiver slightly in the dim light. That was what Joseph was. A star servant. "If you misbehaved… the punishment's – he would work you to the bone, make you do things you did not want to do repeatedly. He would relish the pain you would experience, both physical and mental. People went mad through my 'owner.' No one did anything about his treatment of us. One day, I decided enough was enough. People had tried and failed to escape over the years, but I thought – anything would be better than this, the constant torture… even death at his hands. I just did not care anymore. He had broken me. I was never a contract servant; I was always someone to sell to the highest bidder. My power was too interesting to pass up, apparently."

"What happened?" Joseph asked; it seemed like Finley needed this, too. They had both experienced the horrors of The Hunter's Guild, even kingdoms apart. Joseph wondered if the other continents had the Hunter's Guild, too. Rivetia did not – he asked if the other continents held the same values as Rivetia – who both opposed the war and the locking away of magic. He hoped people would be on his side in the end.

"They found me; it was inevitable. One of the other servants told my 'owner' what I was planning. I do not blame them; that household was a man-eats-man world. He punished me, as I said, forced me to flatten a mountain for more land – it was a massive strain on my body." Finley said, his voice no longer stuttering; he seemed empowered as he spoke about this experience as if it gave him the strength to continue. "If I had succeeded in what he needed me to do, I would be free of the punishment any further, but I would also be out for the count for maybe a few days at most, literally unconscious; flattening a mountain is not easy – my body was so tired. I did as he asked, and when the dust rose in the air as the last stone crumbled to the ground before me, I created a diversion. My punishment became my escape route. Picked this thing up and kept it as a momentum."

Around his arm seemed to be a small band – just an old scrap of metal fashioned into a bracelet – a momentum, a reminder to never let himself be in that situation again.

"I *was* a contract servant," Joseph explained. Their time as servants was slightly different. Finley reached out to touch Joseph's contract mark. "There were times I could have escaped through the contracts I would form. If I completed a job, sometimes people promised me a quick trip out of there at their expense." Joseph replied.

"Why didn't you?" Finley asked; his voice was low.

"They would have caught me before I even attempted to cross the kingdom gates or aboard a ship – the guild tracked me. I had been there the longest and had seen people come, go, disappear, and reappear. As much as I wanted to go, it would not have been worth the risk for me and the person who helped me escape." Joseph explained. "I didn't want anyone else to go through what I had; if we had been captured, someone else would be mixed up in all the mess."

"So, how did you escape this time?" Finley asked.

"When we returned magic to our continent, Caulan captured us, threw us into a cell, there we found a man who could create a portal – he saved our lives..." Joseph replied before thinking for a moment and continuing. "Alex started all of this; he was the one who took me to the beacon in the first place. He was the one who ignited my will to fight again."

"You and Alex, can't believe you two are actually married. Joseph Von-Loch, it's hard to get my head around." Finley said, a little nervous, crossing his arms and looking around the cavern. His eyes darted back and forth. "After everything you two have been through together…"

"What exactly do you mean?" Joseph asked, snapping. Squinting his eyes, unsure of how Finley would know anything regarding what Joseph and Alex had *been through*. "How do you know what we went through together? I *did not* tell you anything about our lives…"

"Relax. It is an observation… obviously things went on between you two." Finley explained, holding up his hand to silence Joseph from protesting. But Joseph was still on edge. It seemed like an odd choice of words. *After everything they had been through.* It was like he knew.

"Sorry for snapping," Joseph said. "I suppose I'm just on edge."

"The guild really messed us up pretty good, didn't they?" Finley said with a small, awkward chuckle.

Scoffing, Joseph nodded. "Almost too good," Joseph replied. "I'll give it to them; they're good at their job."

Finley walked closer to Joseph, pulling the unexpected boy into a bear hug. The man's quivering voice hit his ear. The sorrow that Finley felt for what happened was evident in every word. It was like he was returning to the night the guild captured them both. "I promised Dad I would protect you from all of that…" Finley sounded as if he were really struggling not to cry now. "I failed. I failed the last wish that father wanted."

"Were we the only survivors?" Joseph asked. "What I mean is, did anyone else make it out alive, Cousin Maya? Saurin?"

He had not thought about those two or anyone from the village for years. He did not even know where he plucked those names. It was as if just by being near Finley, memories he had long forgotten were all coming back to him, like flashes of his own magic.

It was his magic. His magic had changed recently; this was just another stage of development. He did not know yet. Finley had touched him, but this time, instead of the other way around, it had only been brief, showing only flashes of the memories that Finley held deep within.

"They died with the rest of them. We only made it because the guild caught us, and we did not put up much of a fight." Finley explained. "If they had made it, I assume they too would have been put through the system, though I can't say I know if they would have survived the test."

"What magic did they have again?" Joseph asked; it felt strange, but those memories did not seem to come too quickly.

"Maya was the one who could control water, make it rain whenever she wanted, our crops never had to go without…" Finley said. "Though he was my best friend, I can't remember what Saurin could do… it's all a bit fuzzy, maybe my mind protecting me from upset… just talking about him and all of them-."

Joseph stifled a breathy sigh as he blocked any emotion from getting out. He had not been sad a moment before. Something was happening; his magic was changing before his very eyes. Mirroring emotions and memories—he had been unable to do that before. Maybe being down in this cave, in the quietness, unconsciously meant that he was discovering parts of himself he never knew existed.

"We should get back to the others," Joseph said. He did not want to speak about what happened; he knew now that was all that mattered to him, and they had been gone from the group for too long.

They needed to get back to the mission at hand. "They will be wondering what we are doing. They might have found something."

"Joey…" Finley's voice was soft, making Joseph's feelings harder. He did not want to let them out, not now. "It's okay to be upset, to be angry."

"I'm fine," Joseph said. It was not a lie. "I accepted that they were gone a long time ago. I do not know why I am crying."

"You can't fool me," Finley said as he stepped back to look at his brother correctly, the same eery look of concern on his face from the start of the conversation. It was a pity look, but Joseph, even though it was a horrible situation, he did not need pity. Joseph had accepted it had happened, he knew in his heart — but knowing and hearing it were entirely different things. He needed to process things the way he always did alone. "I might not have been around for fifteen years to see you grow up, but you still have the same face and mannerisms you had all those years ago."

"I said I'm fine," Joseph said as he shook his head. Finley was courteous, but Joseph needed to do this alone. He did not need or want anyone around him while he figured out where to go next in his journey to understand the grief. "Can't I just be fine?"

"Of course you can. But if you are not. You know where I am." Finley replied.

"I do know," Joseph said as he lifted the lamp in his hands again, illuminating both of their faces, looking towards the cave exit Alex, Pierce and Maura had walked through ages before — that was their next destination. "Now, let's move before we lose our chance to get that key; I don't want to even think what the decay might do if it finds its way here."

"Sh-." A noise came from somewhere Joseph could not see. "Shade."

"What did you say?" Joseph said as he turned to Finley. "Did you just speak?"

"No," Finley said as he held up his arms, clearing himself of any action. "I did not. Why did you hear something?"

"Sha…de." Again, it was coaxing Joseph closer to the voice that spoke only to him. Joseph turned to his brother and smiled, wanting to mention the fact he was hearing voices in the cave might put everyone on edge. More so than they already were.

"No…. sorry, I do not think I did," Joseph said, lying through his front teeth, but Finley must have bought it. "Come on, before the decay finds its way towards us…"

Thankfully, he had not seen any decay yet, but Joseph knew the moment it touched the mainland, it was coming for them—and quick, too. Taking his first steps away from the wall, being careful where he stepped with the lamp outstretched in front of him, Joseph began heading off with Finley slowly behind him, leaving that part of the cave.

What was waiting for them on the other side of the darkness, the next pool, the next level, and Joseph was sure – booby traps to make this journey just that little bit harder than it already was.

Hopefully, Joseph could find answers to questions that had been on his mind since this journey began, why now was the decay plaguing them after so many years, and why Calvin had been so dead set on returning magic in the first place.

SEVENTEEN

Once more, the pool of water leading towards the next level was much smaller than it should have been. With there having been no sign of booby traps in this level of the cave, Joseph should have been glad, if not ecstatic, that they hadn't had many problems down here. Yet, uneasily plagued him with every step, as if the cave made them feel unwelcome. As it had worked before, Maura went first, then Finley and Pierce were just a short behind her.

Once again, Joseph and Alex had to go together. The tears vehemently refused to work for Alex at all.

"They still aren't doing anything for me; it's like they've got some sort of aversion to me or something," Alex said as he splashed his hands in the water as he and Joseph bobbed around in the deceptively deep puddle, trying to get some sort of response, but still, the small teardrop-shaped masses didn't move closer. If anything, they stopped moving altogether. "They bloody hate me, don't they?"

"I wonder what it is that they don't like…" Joseph said as he leaned down to the smaller pool Alex was bobbing in, placing one of his fingers into the water and watching the tears naturally glide towards him. Alex sighed harder as his eyes also glided towards Joseph. "It really is just you... This pool is much smaller than last time, so we might be in for a bigger squeeze than last."

"Are you going to be able to get the bubble up around us?" Alex asked as he pulled Joseph in closer than he was like he had done at the surface, but a lot, lot closer.

"I'm not sure, but I'm going to try anyway," Joseph said as he closed his eyes, visualising the tears creating the bubble; just enough room so that the both of them could fit down the small opening and not get too squished. He could feel the small tear-shaped objects moving around him quickly, and as he opened his eyes to peek, he saw the tears just about closing up at the top of Alex's spiked-up hair. "Right... I think-"

Joseph watched as the bubble started to sink, and as quickly as it was, Alex's head was already at the level that the water had been when they first got into the pool. They were sinking fast.

"We're going..." Alex said as he kept his eyes on the top of the opening. If this bubble popped... it would not be suitable for either of them. There was no telling how deep this tunnel was going to be. It might have been shorter than the one on the surface, but Joseph didn't want to take the risk that it would be a lot longer, either.

Once again, they were in a tunnel-like area, an ample open space of pure water. Still, this time, instead of seeing ruins, broken objects, and statues, there was very little sign that any life had ever existed this far down. Jagged rocks jutted out in strange formations, a rock, a space, a rock, a space, making the tunnel even narrower. Still hovering in the bubble, Alex held onto Joseph, making sure to conserve some of their space.

"So, what were you and Finley speaking about earlier?" Alex asked.

"How do you know we talked?" Joseph asked, looking up at

Alex.

"You both disappeared. I can piece together things." Alex said. "Did you finally get to have a conversation? A proper one? I can tell that's what you want."

"We did. He asked what my life was like in the guild and what led me to this journey. It was an excellent conversation, if not a bit hard. We've both been through so much; just one conversation wouldn't be enough…" Joseph replied as he looked down at the water around them. The bubble managed to avoid the jacked rocks that scattered the pool. "Then it got a bit weird…"

"How do you mean?" Alex asked. His voice was concerned.

"He mentioned something and swore it was just an observation, but I can't get it out of my head," Joseph replied. "He said 'after everything you and Alex had been together, he couldn't believe we were married'. But-."

"Did you tell him of the stuff we went through together?" Alex interrupted. He, too, was clocking onto what Joseph was getting at.

"That's just it. I didn't mention a thing. It was like *he knew.*" Joseph said, shaking his head.

"What was he doing in those five years he was missing?" Alex asked, though he knew that Joseph couldn't reply. "Something tells me he wasn't always with that Captain. What did he tell you?"

"He said that after escaping, he came into contact with the Captain immediately. But remember what Gerry said?" Joseph asked; everything seemed to be falling into place for him. He wasn't sure if Alex was on the same wavelength, though.

Alex hit it right on the head a moment later. His eyes are wide. "He went to Freydale multiple times," Alex said. "If Finley was Gerry's right-hand man or whatever quartermaster, he must have come too.

Which means he could have met you, me, anyone."

"I'm telling you this now before it gets worse, but my magic seems to be… changing down here," Joseph said. "Finley touched my guild mark, and suddenly, I remember things from my childhood, names I've never thought about in years. My emotions changed too, emulating his – when he was sad, I was. I don't know what it was, but deep down, there was *anger.*"

"Anger?" Alex asked.

"He hid it down deep, but it was there. I don't know what he was angry at, but it's hard to be picky with a long list of things hanging over our heads." Joseph mumbled. "I think I should be… no, we should all be a little cautious around Finley for the moment, just until I work him out until I work out his motivation. There is something he isn't telling me."

Pop.

Joseph didn't even have a chance to breathe before being thrown into the cold water. The pressure was pulling him down and further away from where they had been slowly gliding down. Now, he was going way too fast to see where he was going. The bubble was no longer around him, and there wasn't any air in this water to create one.

He had been too distracted.

Alex wasn't there anymore. His fingers were no longer gripped onto the jacket that Alex had been wearing; in fact, he wasn't holding onto anything at all. He tried all he could to shout out, to try and find any semblance that there was a person next to him. Still, as he opened his mouth, the water flooded in, forcing him to shut his mouth again with a moment's notice.

A jagged rock sticking up from a point had been the one to pop the bubble. As fast as Joseph felt the water drag him down, the sooner he found himself upside down, falling onto dry land, struggling to expel the water from his guts.

"Alex, Alex, can you hear me"? Joseph shouted. As if panicked, he stood up almost immediately and rushed towards the closest wall he could find, shouting the house down before he felt a hand placed on his shoulder."

"Hey, woah, it's me." His brother's voice brought Joseph back to reality. Seeing the room he had landed in—the same jagged rocks sticking out of every wall—brought it all home for Joseph. They were getting into much more dangerous territory the further they went down. "Did you lose Alex?"

"Yeah, we were in the bubble and... and this rock popped it, he was dragged away, and I was pulled down here... I don't-." Joseph began as he noticed that he, Finley and Pierce were in the same chamber, but Alex and Maura were not. "Where did they go? We need to."

"I was watching from above as Maura was pulled away by the current; she went into a separate chamber from me. When I was pulled down and landed here, I tried calling out for her but got no response." Pierce said the man was still soaked as if he had tussled with the rock. "I think we all became victims to that rock, this cave... it's truly a force to be reckoned with, and we haven't even come across any booby traps."

"Unless that was one of them." Finley countered as his eyes drifted towards the pool of bubbling water in the ceiling the three had fallen out of. "A jagged rock between two 'chambers' separating people, sounds like whoever created this cave... if it was created, wanted to weaken the people coming down here who didn't know their way around. They wanted to make it harder for them to come down to the beacon."

"Maura!" Pierce shouted, getting closer to the wall that it looked like the jagged rock above them was connected to. "Maura, if you're there, say something."

Nothing. Or at least, they couldn't hear anything in response.

"Alex, if you're there, talk!" Joseph shouted out, banging his hand on the wall. "Say something!"

A muffled sound could be heard a moment later. It was deep—like Alex's—but it sounded distorted. But with no visuals, there was really no way of telling.

Who else would be down here? There couldn't be anyone. They would know about it.

"We're… stuck… on-." The voice became a little clearer now. It was definitely Alex's voice; his accent was shining through as he spoke. "Other side…. of cave… wall."

"They're on the other side," Joseph said as he turned around to look at his brother. "Finley, could you break down the wall with your magic? Get them on this side?"

"I'm not sure what this wall supports; if I break it down, there might be issues; it might cave them in, us, or both. I can't take that risk." Finley said as he looked up at the top of the wall again before touching the rock as if feeling the energy it gave off. He stood there for a second, all eyes on him, before removing his hand and shaking his head. "The king did say there would be two routes; whatever is on the other side is a hollow tract, like another chamber like what we are standing in. We may not be able to see them or communicate properly, but Maura and Alex are in this other chamber – as far as I can tell, they're safe. They can go one route; we can use this one."

Joseph sighed – he didn't like the answer at all. He wanted to know that the two of them were safe on that side; the mention of bobby traps could be anywhere, and with no way to help them, it could be dangerous. "But-."

"I had not the greatest plan, but if we want to be safe, it's all we have." Finley continued, cutting Joseph off before he could make a demand. "I don't want to ruin our chance of getting the key. If I take it down this way, it might crush us all. That would do us no good, would it?"

"No." Joseph thought about it. Like a child being told off, Finley slotted into the big brother role quickly. But do the routes line up? They're alone, and neither have magic. Are they safe?"

"When I connected with that rock just now, yes. We just keep walking, and eventually, they lead to the same place; I couldn't, however, see any booby traps – that's not how my magic works, I'm sorry." Finley shook his head. But Joseph knew it was irrational to ask for Finley to try again. He didn't want to risk the chance that Alex and Maura would be in danger and have no way of defending themselves.

At least Joseph and Alex had magic on their side, and Pierce could also use that to his advantage.

"We'll… meet…" It sounded like Maura shouting out to them. Still, it was again coming out, and muffled and broken sentences were the only thing coming out of the other side of the wall. "At… next pool."

"Stay safe, both of you!" Joseph shouted out, though it was unknown if it would reach the duo.

Alex's deep voice came through the wall, much less muffled but still hard to make out fully. "You… too."

EIGHTEEN

Wraith's run.

Past the chamber the trio had found themselves in led to a long tunnel, the jagged rocks jutting out with every step. A few words were written in red on a small sign just as they entered this tunnel – Wraith's run, a game to reach the heart.

"This might be a booby trap," Finley said as the trio cautiously made their way through the cavern opening. "We have to be careful with every step."

Joseph felt the eery feeling as he walked past the sign, which kept growing – the blue from the cerulean tears in the pool, leaving them and making the room darker every moment. He felt as if he was going to burst, the anxious thoughts and feelings threatening to ooze out of him. There was no telling that this was going to be a booby trap, as Finley had said, but as they hadn't come across any – they were due to find one at some point.

As they entered the room as if by magic – and maybe it was, the room instantly became light with the same blue hue that had just disappeared from the other room. The hue was a lot brighter this time, though, almost white in colour – making Joseph squint as his eyes adjusted to the new light that shone throughout what looked to be lanterns attached to the wall, like the torches that scattered the walls of Freydale but without the flame.

"That's so bright…." Pierce said as he held his hand up to his eyes.

"This place…" Finley began as he made his way over to a large-looking throne close to the entrance and looked out where the throne was 'lording' over. "I think this is a running track of sorts."

"Running track?" Joseph asked as he blinked a few times to clear his vision. Finally, he could see what was before him; it looked like three lanes where someone might run or walk. "Is this some sort of game or something? That sign said this was a 'game to reach the heart'."

"The heart of what?" Pierce asked – providing no answer to Joseph's question but instead furthering the conversation with a question of his own and a question that all of them were probably asking themselves now.

"Wraiths run. Can you make it to the other side?" Finley said out loud, crouched down by the wooden chair-like object in front of the running track. As Joseph looked around the room, he could see that there were, in fact, not one but two thrones—one wooden, one gold.

"What did you say?" Pierce interjected as he and Joseph looked down at Finley, who just waved his hand in their direction to bring them closer.

"It's the rules of the game. Play the lute next to the throne you are reading this on; when the music plays, the wraiths will sleep. Play the wrong note or stop; they will feast. When wraiths sleep, you can move towards the finish line; when they wake, you stop…"

Joseph moved towards the wooden throne, finding the

beautiful lute close to the armrests on what looked to be a metal stand.

"So it is a booby trap then?" Pierce asked as he, too, inspected the throne to his side.

"There is more… If caught by the wraith, you'll find yourself in a dungeon – four walls, no windows, no escape until someone finishes the game by sitting on the golden throne and becoming the ruler. Opposite the other 'ruler' on the wooden throne." Finley continued, tracing his finger along the wood-carved rules; time had clearly not been kind to the room; it was tough to read. "Well, aren't we glad that we have at least three people… it doesn't sound like you can play this game alone."

Joseph thought back to the dungeon in Freydale, how it had made him feel, that panic welling inside him – he didn't want to feel that again. It seemed like everything around him ever since he left Freydale had been a ploy to get rid of him. To finish him off completely.

"So someone needs to sit on this wooden throne, and the others need to go running… can anyone play the flute?" Joseph asked. He knew he didn't – his time in Freydale was spent either on jobs or sleeping. He didn't have time to learn an instrument, he hardly had time to learn how to read and write, and it took him a few months to learn how to spell his own name.

Pierce was the one who raised his hand. He was the most experienced out of the trio, experienced in life anyway. "My father made sure that I learned most things. I can play the flute, but I can hold a tune even though I'm not great at it. Enough that we'd probably be able to scrape by."

"I don't know how good of a runner I'll be… I'm not the quickest and can't keep pace easily." Joseph explained; he looked over to Finley, who looked as if he was ready and waiting – if Pierce was to play the flute and stay on this side, it was clear what he and Finley would be doing. "But I suppose I'll have to, I can't play an instrument, and we need all hands on deck, right?"

"You'll be fine. You've fared through worse." Knowing this was a fact, Pierce said as he walked towards the flute, grabbed it, and took his position on the throne. It looked uncomfortable, bumpy and old.

Gnarly wood turned into a chair in the middle of a damp cave did not make or look, for that matter, a good seat to sit upon.

Joseph watched as Finley took a small step onto the track, just a singular foot, and almost immediately, one of the wraiths came flying towards him – it was close as well, ready to touch him and bring him to the dungeon. Finley then took his foot off the board, and the wraith disappeared; it didn't fall asleep as the rules had said. It just vanished. But the fear in Finley's eyes did not.

"Was that?" Pierce asked, a little stunned at what he had just seen.

"I think that was a wraith..." Finley said, his voice was a lot higher than usual. "At least we know what we're up against once we step on this track… you might have to start playing the music before we start, though. They're sleeping; I'd like to start running before I get brought to their dungeon."

"Right then… let's do this," Pierce said as he moved the flute closer to his lips and began to play a slow melody. There wasn't a tune per se; Pierce was simply playing anything that came to his mind, but it worked. As Joseph and Finley stood on the first panel of the track, the wraiths appeared—but they weren't coming towards them now. They were asleep, just as the rules had stated they would be.

Cloaked in grey and black, with smoke rising off them as if they were burning charcoal, they didn't have faces—or if they did, Joseph couldn't see them.

Picking up into a slow jog, Joseph and Finley both made the

same pace, making a rather sizable distance away from the start, still the melody that Joseph didn't know kept playing. He almost didn't want to look back to distract Pierce, but Joseph wanted to see how far they had made it in the short time.

A high-pitched blow from Pierce was the start of their worries.

It wasn't a wrong note, but it didn't sound great either. Naturally, as he gained his composure, the music stopped, and as a result, the wraiths began to move, clunkily at first but floating towards the two, who didn't even think to breathe in response when the cloaked figures swirled around them, hoping to catch them moving, breathing, or making any movement at all that could set them on a path to the dungeon below.

When they didn't move, the wraiths could not see them. They were invisible to their vision if they had a vision.

"Sorry!" Pierce called out as he composed himself and started playing again. One of the wraiths was an inch close to touching Joseph, and he knew if it had, then the game would be over for him. Just the mere touch of one would have sent shivers down his spine. Standing there watching them swirl around him and his brother was almost enough to set him off.

As soon as Pierce began to play and the wraiths had stopped in their tracks as if they had been frozen in time, Joseph went off in a sprint, much quicker than Finley, who had been left in the dust in the wake of Joseph's slight panic. "Joseph, you're going too fast. You won't be able to stop-."

An ear-piercing loud blow — like a screech came from the flute.

Maybe it was the old wood and the damp conditions, but the flute was not making it easy to play. Trudging onto the dusty floor, trying to stop himself quickly, but the wraiths were already awake.

"Wait!" Joseph began holding out his hands as his body came to a stop.

"Joseph-." Finley and Pierce shouted out as a cloak began to cover Joseph's vision briefly before it was removed again. No longer was he in that chamber, but instead in a somewhat square-looking brick box. There were no windows, no bars, and it was large enough to move around in but no escape—none at all.

He was in the dungeons.

Somehow, they were worse than those in Freydale.

Panic welled up inside of Jospeh again as, in the dark, he couldn't actually see anything.

He could feel the floor at his feet, but as he put his arms out, trying to stretch out, all he got was a wall… and it was pretty close too, like an individual cell.

"Hey!" Joseph shouted out, but the calls fell on deaf ears. He couldn't hear anyone shouting back. "Finely, Pierce, can you hear me?"

"Joseph!" Pierce's voice came through quietly. He was clearly shouting, but wherever Joseph was, it was far away from the running track. "Joseph, can you hear us?"

"Yes, I can hear you. Can you hear me?" Joseph called back, but it seemed like nothing would make it out of the cell when Joseph heard a slight 'tsk' sound.

"It's no use, Pierce, I can't hear him," Finley grumbled, annoyed. Joseph could hear his brother jogging slightly, not too quickly – but not too slow either; he didn't want to be caught. That would be disastrous.

"The only way to get him out is to continue the game. Keep going!" Pierce could be heard giving Finley his encouragement.

"Yes!" Joseph called out even if no one could hear him. "Keep going; you can do it!"

He was alone, in the dark, with no escape. He had been here before when he was younger and then the year before – when he was sent away from Freydale, and all of those combined were not worse than this. At least then, he could see he had room to breathe – here, in this cave, there was no room for him to even sit down; he had to stand, and that was final.

In the dark, Joseph could focus only on what was happening around him – Pierce playing the flute, Finley's steps and the sound of the dust underneath his feet as he tried to keep moving in the small holding. Then, two people talking brought his attention someplace else. Above him – a man and a woman.

Maura and Alex.

"So, what is it with you and the King?" Alex's voice came through. Clearly, Joseph wasn't sure where the wraiths had put him, whether he was in a wall or if the chamber was somewhere between the two layers. Still, he could hear Maura and Alex much more clearly than the music being played by Pierce. "There has to be something he's interested in if you got to call him by his real name."

"I have no idea. I've only spoken to the man once or twice. But even if he was interested, he gave me my ticket out of there. You heard him mention the portal that might be next to the beacon down here somewhere?" Maura asked. "Well, if we can get it working, I can go home."

"Are you sure you wouldn't rather stay and miss *all* this?" Alex asked. Joseph could imagine the man pointing at all the rocks surrounding the two of them. "But seriously, you do deserve to go home. Whatever dragged you here wasn't fair on you. It usurped your whole life, and who knows how long you've been here."

"Your dad seemed to recognise me," Maura said, her voice and Alex's getting further away from where Joseph was trapped, but it was still just as straightforward as before. "But there were an awful lot of people down there; how long has this decay been a threat?"

"At least two years, it started slowly, apparently. I wasn't even a hunter then. The moment I was brought back to the guild after my... training, I was thrown straight into the deep end. Mission: find a way to wake the fallen. My father hasn't really stepped foot in the dungeon for over a year or so..." Alex said. "But you weren't hit by the beacon; you were found outside the kingdom..."

"I don't remember it, so I'll take your word for it," Maura replied – the two had stopped walking. Their voices not getting any further away, but the faint sound of footsteps had also stopped.

"It doesn't matter anyway; whatever the reason, it won't stop us from getting you home," Alex said. He sounded rather triumphant – like he was on his own mission. "If this disused portal doesn't work, we'll find another way."

"Even though we haven't stopped once since I woke up, you and Joseph have been so kind to me, I don't understand everything, but that never stops you from trying to explain. You aren't just people I'm following because I'll get something out of it. I... you're my friends." Maura replied, and though he couldn't see her and she couldn't see him, Joseph smiled. He wanted to shout out to her but knew he wouldn't be heard. These walls were impenetrable. "I'd never really had friends back home, just people who followed me around for fame and fortune, so now, as I stand with you, Alex, you are truly a friend of mine. No matter what happened in your past or what happens in your future. Please remember that."

"I will. Same back to you, obviously. I suppose, barring Joseph... I didn't really have friends either. So this is nice." Alex said, countering what she had said. "Shall we get going through this cave? The further down we get, the less time it will take to return to the surface."

"Yeah. Let's get going." Maura said before she began to chuckle audibly. "The sooner we get out of here, the sooner you can be back in Joseph's arms; you mean making us all sick and jealous of your pining."

"I don't pine," Alex said, scolding her playfully. Joseph could tell by his voice.

"Now that I know it exists, I sometimes wish I had magical powers…" Maura said. "Doesn't mean I do. You pine for him, even if you are married now."

As they walked on, the sound of their footsteps walking away from where Joseph stood made it so that he had to strain to hear what the two were saying; the flute playing constantly throughout the entire conversation below had stopped.

He wasn't sure if that was good or bad.

Something moved from within the small box like a cloth wrapped around him. He'd felt this before when he was taken down here. Joseph wasn't even sure how long ago that was; it felt like hours – the darkness, the small, cramped space, it could have been mere minutes, but Joseph would have had no idea. None at all.

Then, the blinding light struck his face again. Squinting his eyes at the harsh change, Joseph was surprised that Finley was sitting on the throne before him.

Joseph was right back where he had been when he was taken away, in the middle of the track. Despite being stood entirely still in his small room, he found himself in a full-blown sprint as soon as the veil was removed from his body.

"Joey!" Finley called from the throne. "You're safe! Where… did you go? We were calling you; could you hear us?"

With a tirade of questions, Joseph knew that this would be coming. Stopping his sprint, Joseph took a deep breath in and out, regulating his breathing. "I could hear you, I was shouting out to you, but I don't think you could hear me. It was just this small, pitch-black room with no space to move my legs. The sounds were all around me; I could hear you running, Pierce playing the flute, and Maura and Alex walking below me... I think it was below, anyway. It all got a bit muddled."

"You could hear Alex and Maura?" Pierce asked as he reached Joseph and Finley, who had now gotten off the throne. "Were they okay?"

"Hm, fine, I think. They couldn't hear me, but as far as I could tell, they were in good spirits; they're making their way through the cave system – I don't think they've had any booby traps their way." Joseph explained, and it looked as if that satisfied the two of them for an answer. "Lucky, I suppose."

"If they're going through the cave, so should we..." Finley said as he patted Joseph on the shoulder. Joseph felt as if he was in a bubble as if his vision were clouded by something. Coming out of the dungeon felt strange... he couldn't quite put his finger on how he felt. But he was glad to be out of there, that was for sure. "Should we go?"

"Yes." Joseph nodded. He looked around the bright room and then at his brother and Pierce, who looked ready to leave equally. "I want to get out of here."

The next chamber was just like the first one. A large, tunnel-like area with two large encompassing walls on either side. Dimly lit by the same lights in the other room, but these seemed a lot less taken care of. Parts of the room seemed darker than others, and it was then that Joseph wished he still had the cerulean tear lamps from earlier; his eyes were straining to make out much in the darker sections of the large tunnel, and like the room with Wraiths run, it seemed to go on forever, with small openings dotted around to different sections, it seemed that far down here – there had been some life here once. But more so than in the first section, whoever was here once had died long ago.

"Do you think that Maura and Alex are okay on their end?" Pierce asked, turning around to look at the two brothers.

"The King said that one section had booby traps and the other didn't – so it looks like they lucked out on that front. I bet they're completely fine." Finley muttered; he seemed hurried, walking quicker than the other two. "Hopefully, we're almost there, he said three layers, right?"

Joseph simply nodded.

"And we're on the second level now?" Pierce asked, and Joseph nodded again, not speaking. He observed Finley, keeping to his own wits. Joseph just wanted to *watch* his brother; he didn't want to think badly about the man, but that 'casual observation' treaded quickly into 'known information'. He wasn't sure if he could trust his flesh and blood—not yet, anyway.

"We're home free. We should be at the beacon chamber before we know it, then it's onto the next one." Finley replied as he turned back to the duo behind him. "Right, Joey?"

"Yeah, right," Joseph replied. He didn't want to seem suspicious himself; he didn't really want to draw attention to himself. But Joseph couldn't shake what he felt, and he felt terrible.

Really bad.

Joseph broke away from the duo for a moment, stepping back as they walked slowly to look at some of the carvings on the walls. They didn't seem coherent; there were no understandable words like in the Wraiths' run. Instead, they were just markings, drawings that looked like they had been done in a hurry or to tell a story in an old language lost to time.

He could tell someone had once lived down here, but for how long and what type of life they had down here was unknown. That unknowing feeling made him feel nervous. They had no idea what they were really walking into.

It was when, out of the corner of his eye, he saw something move, something familiar, small and dark, like it had been carved out of the stone itself. Joseph observed it as the dark object moved around, scurrying from one smaller tunnel to the other, only peeking out to pop its head out to check for predators, maybe. It was this one moment that Joseph realised who he was looking at.

"Finley!" Joseph shouted excitedly as he looked at the fox-like creature in the small tunnel.

"Yeah?" Finley asked, a little taken back by Joseph's sudden shouting. "Joey, do you need something?"

The fox moved as if he were floating, like some sort of ghost, moving in and out between the cave walls, like he was teasing Joseph. He shook his head at his brother and pointed towards where the fox was. "Sorry, I was talking to the fox... the one you made for me."

"What fox?" Pierce asked. "Where is it?"

"You named the fox I created you after me?" Finley asked. And it was then that it occurred to Joseph that Finley had never learned of that fact.

"He was the only thing I had left of you; it felt right." Joseph nodded before turning towards Pierce, finally comprehending the man's questions. "What do you mean, what fox? He's right... there."

"I don't see anything, Joseph. Are you sure you saw a fox?" Pierce asked as he looked around the floor where Joseph was pointing. "You're not seeing things, are you?"

"King Atlas did mention hallucinations," Finley said as the trio stopped moving throughout the cave.

"He's not there anymore..." Joseph said quietly, confused now that perhaps Finley had never been there. "Maybe it was a hallucination; he said something about showing us what we really want... I just want him back."

As they made it further through the long tunnel, Joseph noticed that Pierce was beginning to show signs that he, too, was seeing things that weren't there. Jerking his head around to follow things, his eyes looked shifty—locking onto things in the room that weren't there until...

"Mum?" Pierce said out loud like a wave of shock had rushed over him. He sounded like a child again, ready to cry out, almost scream. "Is that you?"

"No, Pierce, it's not real." Joseph tried to say, grabbing onto Pierce, who was now thrashing around a little bit as if he was getting ready to sprint out of the room to follow the person he was 'looking' at. Pushing the man up against the wall to subdue him, Joseph held Pierce in place as he tried to get through to the man. "It's a hallucination, remember, you said it yourself?"

"No, it's her. It's her." Pierce shouted as he continued to thrash about. Still, with a slight desperation in his voice as well, like all his emotions were welling to the top, and before Joseph or Finley could even attempt to stop him from doing so, he ran off, using all his strength to push Joseph back, taking one of the smaller tunnels in the walls to follow after her. "Mum, it's me, Pierce!"

"It's making us give into temptation; we cannot allow it to make us do things we don't want. This whole tunnel is another booby trap; it's using the people we miss and need to keep us trapped here." Finley shouted out as he covered his eyes and ears. "We cannot-."

"We need to get out of here," Joseph said as he did precisely as

Finley had done, beginning to run with his eyes closed. Their ears were covered, a bad combination in the middle of a tunnel he knew nothing about.

"Tara!" Joseph stopped when he heard Finley screaming out a woman's name that he had never heard before. He sounded so distressed by it like whatever he was hearing was torture to his ears. "Tara!"

"Whoever Tara is, it isn't her Finley!" Joseph said with pure desperation in his voice. He couldn't lose someone else to this. "We need to stick together down here."

"I can hear her screaming in my ear; I couldn't save her." Finley began to hit his head as to clear it like she was whispering in his ear, horrible things it seemed, and though Joseph couldn't hear it himself, it was causing his brother immense grief. "Stop it! Stop it! Stop!"

He took off, running away from where he and Joseph stood. Off to where Pierce had been. "Finley, wait!"

"I just need to get out of this room!" Finley shouted back, still holding his hands to his ears and running off into the darkness. At that point, he didn't care where he was going; it seemed he could just get some peace from whatever was troubling him. Whatever spell had been put on this place down here was ruthless. It was clear that Pierce wanted his mother back, and whoever Tara was, whoever she had been to Finley, it haunted him. He couldn't save her… Joseph wondered what he meant by that.

Having some clarity at knowing this was all hallucinations, Joseph stepped forward, keeping his eyes and ears covered. Still, he knew at some point he had to open his eyes – he had to be able to see.

This cave system consisted of chambers upon chambers upon chambers, and it never seemed to end. He just hoped they were close to the beacon; he wanted to get out of there and see the light. They must have been in there for hours with little to no break, but at least they weren't tired… yet.

Slowly removing his hands from his eyes, Joseph locked onto the exit, the large hole in the wall leading to a darker area than where they stood. Once he was out of the room, he could gather the strength to go find Finley and Pierce, but he needed to clear his head.

Joseph stayed in the middle of the room, making a good pace and narrowing his eyes slightly to prevent any hallucinations from entering his eyesight. His hearing was another thing; he could hear them first before seeing them.

It was him and his brother, younger versions of the two of them, what they were before they were captured by the guild. While playing games and having fun, Joseph was much smaller than Finley, which still stands true today. It was like he was watching ghosts, moving around slowly, playing a memory long forgotten in his mind, playing it out in a loop. It reminded Joseph of a better time. His parents came next, and though Joseph kept his eyes squinted, he could hear them – their voices soft as he remembered.

"Come on, boys, it's time for bed. Grab your teddies." Their mother, Camilla, came into the room the two were in. "Finley, do you have Duckly Paddlefoot?"

"She's here." The younger version of Finley grabbed the teddy bear that Joseph found himself remembering. Even though he couldn't remember too much, just seeing this dream, vision, whatever it was, made Joseph remember things he had long forgotten about. He remembered how Finley used to take Duckly Paddlefoot everywhere with him.

"Mr Foxy." The younger version of himself procured the fox teddy bear he remembered from childhood. It reminded him of Finley; he had to leave the teddy behind in all the chaos when the town he lived in was sieged. "Superhero, Mr Foxy."

"Oh, he's a superhero, is he?" Joseph's father, Malik, said as he crouched down to Joseph's smaller level. "Well, superhero Mr Foxy also looks tired; come on, get into the bed... do you two want a story before sleep?"

The younger version of Finley squealed out. "Yes, please, mum!"

"Story..." Joseph mumbled. He was only four years old, and he struggled with certain words. "Please."

Joseph stopped walking and opened his eyes properly. The scene in front of him had changed; no longer was it Joseph and Finley. Now, it was a slightly older Joseph, wearing his clothes from the guild and another slightly older boy with blonde hair and blue eyes. It was Alex. The two were playing, talking to each other like friends would. Joseph couldn't help but find himself smiling as he watched it unfold. His hallucinations were a little different to that of the other two. That much was clear.

Joseph watched as the smaller versions of Alex and himself ran together, laughing, running past the older Joseph in slow motion – as was the same in the present; Alex took hold of Joseph's hand as they ran to make sure the smaller of the two could keep up. Joseph turned his body to watch it all unfold. The laughter was lovely to hear, like a distant memory that he slightly remembered, like a lingering scent that brought him all back to the past.

Joseph watched as the memory, the hallucination, whatever it really was, began to fade, disappearing into the rock like Finely the fox had moments ago. Joseph kept a smile on his face. Despite all the issues he had had with this journey, he still found it in himself to smile. It was a happy memory, something he had forgotten he could have.

When Joseph turned around to begin walking again, he came face to face with someone he hadn't expected. Alex stood a few inches away from Joseph's body, towering over him like usual. But this was different; it wasn't Alex, but still, the hallucination guiding Joseph to stay, and as Joseph felt Alex's breath this close and the familiar scent of the orange cologne he wore all the time – he had to admit, staying right there was very possible right now. He wanted something familiar and answers to questions plaguing his mind.

The hallucination reached out, like he or it wanted to touch Joseph. Joseph allowed it, getting closer and closer to Alex; he cocked his head to the side as if he was going in for the kiss this close; Joseph was too confused with all the thoughts going through his head that if it had, he would have let him.

Until two pairs of strong arms wrapped around him, linking Joseph's arms with theirs, Pierce and Finley stood at either side of him, pulling Joseph away as they ran. Joseph couldn't even touch the floor as he was being picked up and dragged out of the room.

"Sorry about that, Joey, but we couldn't allow it to touch you..." Finley said as he lowered down Joseph. The two have come back to their senses. "They were wraiths... those hallucinations."

"Once we left that room and entered the tunnels, the spell broke on us. I could see... my mother, or whatever it was for what it actually was, it was a wraith." Pierce explained, allowing Joseph to fully understand what had happened in there. He did think that it was strange, but with that precision, those wraiths must have been able to read his mind – it looked exactly how Alex used to look when they were younger. "It doesn't mean seeing my mother wasn't what I wanted to see. It was like the wraith could read my mind, but there is no telling what would have happened if it had touched me."

"Once we saw you... that close to one, we didn't care anymore, we just went into action. Are you okay?" Finely asked as he lowered his head to look at Joseph's eyes.

"I'm fine," Joseph said, and Finley knew now not to question it. "Now that I'm out of there. I think."

"Good..." Finley replied with a short smile. "What else can this cave throw at us, eh?"

What else could it throw at them? If only he hadn't asked that question.

NINETEEN

Two booby traps in two rooms made Joseph a little apprehensive when he entered the next one.

As the trio made their way through the cave, they found themselves in an equally large room as the room with wraiths running. This place, with a hole in the floor and the bubbling bright blue water inside, was more significant than Joseph had seen since this journey started. At least this time, they wouldn't have to squeeze their way through to reach the bottom.

"Surely, this is the last pool of water before we get down to the beacon," Pierce said as he crouched down and put his hand in the water, the tears reacting to him almost instantly. "Can we at least sit down before we go ahead?"

"We need to wait for Maura and Alex anyway, so I say go ahead. Who knows how long it might take for them to get here." Finley replied as he plonked his body down on the somewhat sandy floor; it was a wonder how sand like this had gotten down here… or up, maybe. This whole cave didn't make sense. There was a clear indication that magic had been used down here, from the wraiths to the tears being found all the way down here – yet it seemed no one had been down in the cave in a long, long while.

"My legs arc super tired… I might just sit here." Joseph said as he walked towards the edge of the pool of water and found a ledge that he could sit on, sand-free.

Before he could sit, however, two voices echoed throughout the large area. They bounced off the walls, forcing everyone's attention towards where the voices came from, a small, inconspicuous tunnel. It didn't even look big enough for someone to move around safely, but the voices that Joseph knew were coming from – were getting closer.

Maura stepped out first, having been on her hands and knees as she crawled through the opening. Small cuts from the jarred rocks covered her hands. As she planted her feet on the ground, Jospeh noticed that she had tried but failed to wrap something around her hands to stop the pain—dark fabric, like the clothes she had worn in Rivetia.

"Am I glad to see…" Maura said as she locked eyes with Joseph, who was just ready to sit down. "Other people!"

Clearly, those words were not what she intended to say, but the excitement she felt as she ran towards the trio was happy to hear. Joseph hadn't heard much excitement in her voice since arriving in this realm.

As she reached the trio, she quickly wrapped her arms around them, pulling them all individually into a short hug. But when she got to Joseph, she smiled before pulling him into a rather lengthy hug.

"Well, I didn't expect this, but I don't mind it," Joseph said as he, too, wrapped his arms around her, pulling her into a hug. At equal height, Maura's hair tickled at Joseph's nose as he buried his head into her shoulder. He didn't realise how much he had missed her, even if they were only a stone's throw away and not that hard to get to. Despite not knowing her for long, Maura was really getting up there regarding friendship.

Hearing her take on it, too, solidified that. They were friends, no matter how long they had been together or what each other had individually been through.

Joseph didn't really have friends. He had Henry, but that was an exception. Before Henry, there had been Alex, but even then, he tended to stay clear of people – knowing that if he got too close, there was always a chance that they could be *'taken away'* by the guild or disposed of… he didn't want that heartbreak, to lose someone else again and again.

"Did you guys have any trouble getting here?" Maura asked as she moved away from the hug, moving her hair out of her face. The cave humidity was starting to make her hair far curlier than before.

"I got carried away by a wraith, put into a dungeon and could hear everything around me, but no one could hear me." Joseph explained, and for a moment, Maura looked as if she was about to laugh; it did sound like a story, but she knew by now nothing was 'out there' in terms of reality in this world. "It was a booby trap, but King Atlas made it out that there were going to be worse things than that; I didn't get hurt; I was scared, but no injuries… thankfully."

"Only injury is to my ego… maybe I'm not as great as I thought at playing the flute." Pierce joked before he cocked his head to the side, noticing someone was missing. "Where's Alex?"

"I'm…" Alex's voice could be heard from the small tunnel, moving slowly through the tract. Alex's hair was the first thing that Joseph saw. It was slightly spiked up and ruffled from the humidity and being dragged through the jagged rocks above him. It was no longer in the quiff-type hairstyle he always sported at the guild. "Right here… a little help?"

Now able to see his face, Joseph and Pierce rushed over to the small hole – both looking at the man as he tried to get out of the tunnel, with little victory.

"Looks like you've found yourself a booby trap after all."

Pierce chuckled before offering his hand to Alex for him to take. "Pretty stuck there, mate."

"Bloody walls shrunk, didn't they," Alex replied as he took Pierce's hand and found himself dragged straight out of the wall in one quick succession. "Woah."

"Oh shush, you're fine. See?" Pierce said as he planted Alex on the floor, feet first, thankfully. The hole he had been pulled through was tiny, much smaller than Alex's frame.

"I…" Joseph could see Alex trying to form a witty response, but it just wasn't coming to him. "Thank you."

Pulling Joseph into a hug, Alex wrapped his arms around him quickly.

"I missed you," Joseph said quietly.

"Me too," Alex replied, his breath tickling Joseph's ear.

Now that the group was together again, even though they had not been apart too long, it felt right. Everything was now able to come together, and they were going to walk out of the cave victorious, having found the key and returned magic before the decay could reach them.

If only it would be that easy, but Joseph could hope. He could put a lot of things on hope right now. Almighty knew that there hadn't been much hope in his life for a long time. But now he had a purpose, and things were working out again.

"Can we all agree on something right now?" Alex began as the entire group looked at him with anticipation. "We never get split up again. This journey has been… something, and I'd really rather not get trapped down here."

"Definitely…" Finley replied before turning his attention to the pool next to him. "Down this pool could be the end of this cave, the end of the worries of being separated. Should we sit? We're all tired. I think we could all rest, maybe even take a nap."

"Aye," Pierce replied. "I could do with a wink or two; who knows how long we've been down here without stopping. Do you want to take shifts, or should we all just try to get as much sleep as possible?"

"I don't think we have to worry about shifts… who else is down here?" Finley asked as he played with the bracelet on his arm, sitting down by the large pool of water. "I say we all just go to sleep, try and recoup some of the energy."

"Sounds like a plan," Joseph said. As he looked at Finley, he noticed his brother was just staring off into space. Tiredness—that was what it was. Joseph felt it himself.

The ground didn't look very comfortable for sleeping on. Still, as the group got ready to rest, Alex tugged at Joseph's arm, dragging him over to where he was setting up his 'camp'.

"This is a secluded space. What we discussed before the bubble popped…you were with Finley just now. Did you find out anything or discover much else?" Alex asked, but all Joseph could do was shake his head.

"I don't want to think ill of him; something… odd is happening. It's irrational. He might even be doing all this, helping us off his own back because he is a good person. He could literally have meant what he said as an observation…" Joseph replied. "This cave is making me all on edge."

"And your magic?" Alex asked as he grabbed for Alex's hands. "Has it… developed any more since we last spoke?"

"Not really. I think it was simply a situation where I was extra… stressed, and maybe like you said at the beach, my magic is heightened by emotion. Doesn't matter what emotion it is, but maybe different emotions have different effects. My magic has changed since getting hit by the blast in Freydale." Joseph replied as he looked down at his own hands. "You know, I can't remember when I last used the shapeshifting ability; it seems whenever I am using magic, it is subconsciously."

"Because here, since getting away from the guild, you can just be yourself, a normal person who just happened to have magic. You're not defined just by your magic." Alex said quietly. "I wonder what would happen if you were hit by a blast from the Rivetia Beacon... how your magic would develop again-."

"Joey, Alex!" Finley's voice cut through the moment. "Where are you? You two better not be fighting."

"Guys?" Maura's voice came around the corner. Before she stopped – an inquisitive look on her face, as if she was this all-seeing all-knowing deity. She knew what had gone down here, it was written in her eyes. Yet, she said nothing. Not even a peep. "They're um… here."

"I was just helping Alex get comfy," Joseph said as he turned his body towards her. She simply nodded, knowing that the two were having a meaningful conversation.

"Well, come on over, get your beds ready." Finely shouted from around the corner.

"Yeah. Maybe we should go to sleep, just for a bit." Joseph said as he interlocked his and Alex's fingers and began to walk to where the group had set up a makeshift bed in the sand. It didn't look comfy, but beggars couldn't be choosers down here. Flopping onto the floor, Joseph moved himself up to where Alex had laid and wrapped his arm around him, settling into the new quietness around them. "Good night, Alex."

Turning his body to face Joseph and wrapping his own arms around Joseph, Alex spoke quietly. "Sweet dreams, Joey."

Joseph was flying.

He was dreaming, or at least, he really hoped he was. He could feel the wind on his face as he flew through the dark landscape. He couldn't put his finger on anything and didn't recognise the area he was flying through. It might have been nighttime, but the stars in the sky weren't visible, even if they were.

It also made Joseph wonder where he was going. There was no rhyme or reason for his trip, his flying. And if Joseph knew anything, his dreams would be slightly different from those of the average person. Joseph rarely dreamed, not on a typical night anyway. Stress, exhaustion, or something else entirely triggering it would force him to dream.

There was always a story with the dream, and not always his own.

He wasn't even sure what he was looking for. No single tree, person, or object could be seen, just starlight from those oh-so-invisible stars.

Whop. A sound in the silent landscape alerted Joseph to an area to his left… right, sideways; he wasn't sure. The sound was repeating, getting more audible as he flew, though in which direction Joseph couldn't pinpoint. It sounded like leather hit something, hitting skin.

"I told you…" A voice, much clearer now. "I told you there was no…"

The disembodied voice became more assertive as he approached, but Joseph couldn't understand complete sentences. He wasn't even sure who was speaking.

"I told you!" This time, a shout from a deep, loud man's voice. He sounded distressed and burdened. "I told you that there was no escape from me. I didn't want to hurt you, but you forced my hand!"

He wasn't sure who he was dreaming of; there could only be a few people, and only four others were in this cave with him – he had to dream of one of them. But he had yet to see any faces; he wasn't sure.

"I'm sorry, I'm sorry. No, please, I'm sorry! Sorry! Sorry!" The other voice came out quickly, getting louder as they spoke, louder and more panicked. Like they had experienced this before. Brutality at the hands of someone who was keeping them captured.

Familiar and not a unique situation for many in this group.

Joseph's vision did not get any better. He still could not see people but could hear them loud and clear. The raps of a whip or some other kind of weapon hitting the other person quickly must have been the 'hurt' the other was discussing. And it sounded painful.

"Do you really think you and me are equal?" The man doing the whipping shouted. "We both might have the same affliction, but I never got myself caught. I feel sorry for you, and I really do. You had to take a contract from me to get your freedom, but you've never really had freedom, have you?"

It was a barrage of words coming down hard on the other person.

"I'll do whatever you want, please, stop." The other man said quietly, bated breaths, loud then soft, like he was anticipating something else.

Joseph didn't understand the significance of this dream or why he was being shown it. Such brutality wasn't usually what he *wanted* to dream about.

"You're going to get on that ship, I order you to, and you're not going to utter a peep about it until you reach its destination." That told Joseph all he needed to know; it had to be that ship captain, Gerry. He didn't seem brutal or mean, yet Joseph had not interacted with him much, and he knew better than to judge people based on first or even tenth impression. If the louder man was Gerry, the other person had to be… "Do I make myself clear, Finley?"

Before he could learn anymore, Joseph felt the familiar invisible arms dragging him away, signalling that the dream, or whatever it was, had ended. Still not visible to his eyes but louder than ever, Finley's now clear voice rang in his ears. "Yes, sir."

Joseph woke up with a start. At first, he didn't quite know where he was. Then his vision cleared, and he remembered the cave, the cerulean tears from the pool next to them still shining—it was a wonder how they had managed to sleep.

As he looked around, he took stock of who he was with—Alex was to his side, choosing to sleep next to each other and round the corner from the other three out of the other's vision.

Maura was further down, and Pierce was next to her, but there was someone missing, someone not asleep. With his makeshift bed looking disturbed, Finley was nowhere to be seen. Standing up, Joseph looked around for any sign that his brother was in the large room.

"Finley?" Joseph asked quietly, not wanting to wake up his companions. "Are you there?"

Joseph stepped cautiously around the three sleeping friends, the sand stopping any sound from escaping from his steps. He wasn't sure where he was going or where Finley had gotten to, but he couldn't have gotten far in this cave.

He could hear incoherent muttering from somewhere close by. Towards a wall not too far away from where Joseph and Alex had spoken earlier, sitting on the sandy floor with his back turned to the group, Finley cradled something in his hands as he spoke quietly, mumbling to the item.

"No," Finley said, seemingly to no one. "No, he's asleep."

He heard a small voice coming through the bracelet that Finley had always had with him. Joseph turned around quickly, hoping not to be detected. Thinking swiftly, Joseph shifted and did something he hadn't done for a while.

It is small enough not to be noticed with much problem. A small lizard that was native to Freydale – Joseph had seen them a lot in his tenure at the kingdom. Right now, he just hoped this type of lizard wouldn't look too strange in a Rivetia cave.

Scuttling towards the wall where he might be concealed, Joseph just wanted to leave and get back to his bed. He didn't want to listen. He needed to regroup if something was happening—he didn't want to be caught.

"Yes, I've embedded myself within the group; they don't suspect anything…" Finley sighed as he held the bracelet up to his lips. "You said I needed to find the right moment, and this isn't it."

"You need to hurry up. The decay is worsening, and we can't keep holding on much longer." The other person said Joseph wasn't sure if it was a person. He recalled the books in Freydale, how they were lost souls trapped in pages. What if this bracelet Finley was so attached to was just another one of these items?

It wouldn't be out of the realm of possibility. Stranger things had happened. And this …person on the other end of whatever device it was that Finley held around his wrist did seem awfully worried about the decay by the sounds of it. It didn't seem too farfetched. But still, Joseph didn't want to reveal himself.

"I'll sort it," Finley said, sounding dismayed. "Listen… I've got to go."

"You better do. Remember what is at stake." The person on the other end said gruffly. Joseph watched as he scurried closer to the wall as Finley stood up.

He wondered who his brother had been speaking to and why he was keeping it hidden from them. As he watched Finley, the sadness in his eyes, which had been evident since the first time he laid eyes on his brother, was growing. He didn't look like he was going to cry, not by a long shot, but he did look frustrated—like he was between two parts of himself—something Joseph knew all too well.

Joseph, noticing that his brother was on the move, started to run towards his own bed, only changing out of the form he had taken once he was around the corner and out of sight. Creeping towards the makeshift bed, which looked a lot further away than anticipated, Joseph stopped when he felt a hand touch his back.

"What are you doing awake?" Finley's voice cut through Joseph's plan. All he wanted to do was forget what he had heard and get back into bed, hopefully making time go quicker so he could get down to the beacon and out of this cave.

"I… couldn't sleep, then when I saw you were missing, I wondered where you got to." Joseph began, stuttering, though he hoped Finley would just chalk it up to his tiredness. "I couldn't see you, so I thought I'd… try and attempt to sleep again-."

"Yeah, I couldn't sleep either. I just went for a walk to calm my head. This cave is truly a wonder. I found some really cool… rocks," Finely said, his voice trailing off.

"Right," Joseph replied. There was an awkward twinge to the conversation; Finley seemed worried, though Joseph wasn't sure at which part – that he might have been caught or the conversation that just occurred.

Finely yawned a moment later. "Well, I should probably head back to sleep, I'm… pretty tired."

"Well, good night then; I'll see you when you wake up," Joseph said before turning around to join Alex in the corner – the man blissfully sleeping without a care.

"Yeah, good night." Finley said, his voice sounded lighter, like before this conversation—the 'normal' pitch his voice was at. Not this dreary version, like cold rain. His whole demeanour felt cold—almost worrisome. "Sleep well."

"I will," Joseph said as he turned towards the wall, settling back into the spot he had created for himself, close to Alex, a little like a place of comfort. Weeks ago, he would have scoffed at the very notion.

Despite Finley's well wishes for a sound slumber, Joseph didn't sleep.

His chest felt tight; it was hard to breathe. Joseph had felt this feeling multiple times in his life, when things were getting just a little bit too much and stress was filling in. He was anxious. Turning onto his side to try and combat the feeling of claustrophobia and worry, Joseph let out a few short breaths before he heard it—a voice calling to him in the darkness.

"Luma." Joseph wasn't sure who had spoken or if it was a person. The noise had been faint, but the word was distinct. "Luma…"

The call was for him and him only.

Like a coo, it elongated the second time the word was said as if the wind had carried it towards his ears.

Standing up once again, being careful not to alert anyone, Joseph walked towards the large hole in the floor. The bubbling liquid inside was glowing, illuminating the area with the bright blue colour he had become accustomed to seeing.

"Shade… is…" The disembowelled voice spoke slowly, softly, as if the words were coming from the water themselves. The words seemed slightly louder over in this spot. Guiding Joseph to follow it, but he knew, right now, he could not.

"What is the shade doing?" Joseph asked the voice, the wait becoming antagonising like it was luring him into madness – he remembered what Santos had said, how the Shade always followed the Luma, trying to destroy each other. How dangerous it could be if the two met. And somehow, even down here, the word Shade followed him. The very mention of the word got his whole body on edge, anxiety and all. "Where is the shade?"

"Shade… is…." The voice repeated; Joseph waited anxiously, leaning over into the pool – almost touching it with his face. The voice gets louder, morphing into the man's voice in his vision on the beach in Rivetia. He repeated words until they echoed off, vibrating through his mind – replacing everything but those words. "The shade is coming."

TWENTY

Joseph had long feared going mad. But moving down the last tunnel, filled to the brim with water, the voice in his head repeating the same sentence solidified that he had lost it.

Or maybe he never had it to begin with.

"Luma." It is called guiding Joseph towards where the gem might lie. Whatever King Atlas had been saying about the gem being down here was correct—even if Joseph hadn't seen it yet. "Lum...a."

"You've had a spaced-out expression since we woke up. Are you okay, Joey?" Joseph could hear Alex talking, but the voice speaking directly in his head was louder. "Joey?"

"I can hear something in my head." Fearing for what Alex might say, Joseph kept his voice quiet, but also because as he got closer to the beacon, the voice just got louder, so loud that whenever he spoke – his own voice came back muffled. "I can't even hear my own voice... It's like it's warning and guiding me, but I'm unsure. King Atlas said a gem might be related to the Shade down here. This voice makes me feel like my head is outside this bubble, under the water. The pressure is too much."

"Did you tell anyone else that this was happening?" Alex asked before he felt he had to reiterate. "The voices, I don't remember you mentioning it before. When did it first occur?"

"After we got off the ship. I was shown a vision; the previous Luma appeared to me. I couldn't tell you why, but he did. And he gave me this." Joseph said as he rummaged through his clothes to find the pendant wrapped around his neck, pulling it out to show Alex. The bright blue shone and shimmering through the water around them. "King Atlas said that this was the purest form of the tears, that I might be able to use this... to reunite the two gems, this one and the shade gem."

"Hang on seriously?" Alex asked. "What would happen if you did?"

"I have absolutely no idea," Joseph said as he held the gem.

"When did the voices begin last night... if we're close to the gem down here, that could be why," Alex said as he looked down at the cave floor on the next level as it was getting closer and closer.

"It only happened last night after I caught Finley talking-," Joseph said before quickly pursing his lips shut, but by then, Alex had heard enough. "I caught Finley talking to that bracelet he has around his wrist. I don't know who was on the other end or how it worked, but he spoke to someone about the decay. Clearly, we aren't the only people who know."

"We wouldn't be; this decay is worldwide; we would be silly to think that we would be the only people in the world that knew about it; we probably weren't even the first people to notice it, either," Alex said before he looked down at the bottom of the bubble, probably to check how much time he had before they got to the bottom where everyone, including Finley, was standing. "But if your brother is messed up in something, maybe we should be extra cautious. Have you asked him about the bracelet?"

"No. I caught him, but I didn't want to get caught myself; I used my magic for the first time in a while – I think he knows I heard him speaking to the person on the other end. Still, neither of us said anything… it was a little tense; I've not felt that since meeting him." Joseph said, relaying all his worries to Alex, who was listening. "Maybe we're all just a little tired, claustrophobic and anxious, I don't know."

"Maybe, but if he's hiding something, then we need to get to the bottom of whatever that is before we can properly trust him," Alex said; maybe it was the voice in his head guiding him, or perhaps it was because they were so close to being done with this current mission, but Joseph wanted to go in all cards on the table; he wasn't usually irrational. But Alex was right.

"I don't think we can," Joseph said. "If he is hiding something, or rather, someone, we need to know if this person is friendly…"

"Or a potential enemy to the cause?" Alex asked.

Joseph sighed but nodded. He didn't want to think ill of anyone, but he had learned from experiences that he shouldn't and couldn't trust anyone just at face value. People always had motives to change.

"I'll be cautious. I won't mention anything to Finley until I know what is happening. If the gem that the Shade is looking for is down here, if that is what's calling me constantly…" Joseph said, feeling a wave of calm wash over him, trying to figure out how to hide how stressed out he was. Despite not knowing him long, Finley would be able to detect stress.

"It's probably best to keep it between us for now. As the King said, anyone could be the Shade, even one of us; the few people who know what is down here are better. It might give you enough time to figure out what is happening around you." Alex said Joseph noted that Alex didn't say they could figure it out, only Joseph. It dawned on him in the bubble that Alex himself could also be a contender for the mantle of Shade. He didn't even know what it meant – despite having the mantle of Luma… it hadn't been explained to him that well.

It could mean anything.

Joseph sighed as the bubble began getting close to the tunnel's bottom. He knew he would soon be with the other three and couldn't speak much more about the topic. "I feel bad for not speaking to Maura and Pierce about this, but I never seem to get them alone…"

"The fewer people that know of our suspicions, the less likely those suspicions will be revealed," Alex replied. "Hopefully, given time, we won't need to."

Alex then began to move, his legs being pulled out of the bubble—this seemed to be the only tunnel that didn't turn them upside down when they exited the bubble.

"Hey, you two. Took your sweet time coming down… listen, we found what we seek." Pierce announced as they practically fell out of the tunnel, landing haphazardly on the sandy floor below them. As Joseph searched the area momentarily, his eyes landed on precisely what Maura was speaking about.

Towering up into the rock around them was a sizeable pillar-like object; unlike the Rose Beacon, it wasn't as cracked and broken, even if it was far below the earth. Hints of blue rock shone out from small rings on the base – forming brighter light than all the Cerulean Tears put together – it was a wonder how people managed to stay in this room long enough to worship the monolith once a month. Joseph struggled to keep his eyes on one spot or even open altogether, squinting until his eyes adjusted to the new light.

"It's beautiful," Maura said as she approached the beacon. It was higher up in the large cavern than they were. Just below the beacon base was a rocky hill leading towards where Joseph assumed people used to worship the monolith. Just looking at the mountain and its steep incline, he hoped the key was still lodged into the keyhole, as King Atlas said. "There is nothing like this back home…"

"Speaking of home… isn't that one of those portal things you mentioned earlier. I saw one of them back at the Rose Beacon; it was destroyed, but this one…" Alex said as he stumbled out of the way of the hole that the bubble had come out of and towards the circular upright rock in the base of a cave wall. Running his hands along the inscription that covered the entire rock, carved in a language that Joseph couldn't understand, Alex inspected the 'portal' or whatever it was. "This one looks intact; I might just be able to get it working again. How, though, I'm not sure."

Maura took a step forward, admiring the stone circle. It dwarfed her, meaning more than one, at least several people, could come through at once. She reached out in awe, ready to touch the portal, gliding her hands over it before she sighed. "If only we had that book, we might be able to figure out how to get it working."

"Now that we know it's here. We can always come back when we do have it back…" Joseph explained as he touched her shoulder. "When we do, we can come back and reopen this portal, get you home."

"It's a shame that we don't have it now…" Maura said as her voice trailed off.

"Well, blame dear old dad for that," Alex grumbled. "We'll get it back. We'll get you home."

"Hm." Maura nodded; Joseph had not seen her look so glum before. Disappointed. She really had gotten her hopes up. Now, he just needed to find a way to keep that hope alive and burning. "But for now, should we focus on getting the beacon back up and running? The colour of the Rose Beacon was beautiful last time; I think I want to see what it looks like this time, too."

Joseph knew that mentioning the Rose Beacon and speeding

along the conversation was a deflection tactic, used mainly by himself for situations he wanted to escape. He knew she felt disappointed that she couldn't leave then and there. Despite being an asset to the team, he knew within his heart of hearts that she wanted to see her family again. She just wanted to be away from this realm.

"That we should," Pierce said, not picking up on the same thing Joseph had—choosing to lead the way towards the somewhat long-looking path up towards the beacon. The gravel on the floor mixing with the sand made for a slightly unfavourable texture on Joseph's shoes as he stepped, and the floor below him would falter.

The trek towards the beacon was better than it looked. The beacon was a few meters away from the slope, so once Joseph had reached the top, he could see it right in his eyeliner.

"The beacon must reach the top of the island!" Finely exclaimed as the group following Joseph made it slowly to the top. Gathering around the front of the beacon, looking at it head-on, he could understand why it was worshipped. But also feared, too. It did look imposing, something that would be admired; Joseph wondered who had built the things or if they had simply appeared one day, reigning over the world with purpose. Magic.

"There is the key…" Joseph said as he reached out to point at the silver-looking item lodged into the base of the tall tower. "Has no one really been down here for all this time?"

"I remember he said the person who turned the key the last time never made it out…" Pierce said as he cocked his head to the side and started to look around where they were stood.

"If that's the case…" Maura began – she too began to search. "Where is their body… or bones, or whatever?"

"I…um." Alex's voice could be heard from behind the beacon. Joseph hadn't even noticed that Alex wasn't behind him, focusing solely on the key shining back at him in the dim light—the blue hue from the cerulean tears couldn't quite reach up here. "I found her."

"What?" Joseph asked, taking a small step towards where Alex was. The beacon's base was enormous, so getting around it took a little time, but it would mean he would be entirely out of sight of the key. "How did she get over there if she died the moment the key was turned?"

"Maybe she didn't die straight away; no one has been down here since us… maybe it's just an old wives tale, a rumour." Alex said that his voice was concerned before he called for Joseph specifically. "Joey, come here a second, though…"

"Are you okay?" Joseph asked as he began to walk towards Alex around the base, the craggy rocks under his feet threatening to come loose at any moment. "Are you guys coming or what?"

"I'm good. I don't want to see a skeleton if it's all the same to you." Maura said as she shook her head.

"I guess we'll stay with her. Plus… he did call for *you*." Pierce replied. Joseph nodded and followed, leaving Maura, Finley and Pierce to admire the key and beacon.

When Joseph finally reached Alex, he looked directly at the skeleton at the beacon's base. The clothes that she had worn before death, a dirty smock that Joseph was sure probably wasn't dirty when she had died, lay tattered around what looked to be her shoulder bones. Propped up at the base of the beacon, her body at a right angle, facing nothing but the cavern wall.

"I noticed she was holding something in her left hand, a rock-like object… so I checked her other arm, and she doesn't have one," Alex said, fearing that he wasn't keeping on the subject but rather divulging on curiosity, Joseph cocked his head to the side and shook his head. "Sorry, well, I reached for the rock, and it started to glow, not like the cerulean tears; it didn't look blue; rather, it looked… jet black."

"Jet black and glowing?" Joseph asked, confused; those words didn't really go together. "Show me."

"Right," Alex said as he touched the rock. "All I did was…"

"Woah." Joseph began, and the rock started to glow like Alex had said. It was like a subtle glow around the edges, but the rock began to change colour as if it were being imbued with colour and matter the moment Alex got close.

"Joey, is that…?" Alex asked, keeping his hand close to the rock, unsure whether or not to grab for it or what consequences would befall them if he did.

"The gem King Atlas mentioned…." Joseph said as he stared intently at the jet-black gem inside the beacon. "And with it, he warned, the shade would follow…"

"It's reacting to me… you don't think that means-." Alex began, reaching slightly further as if he were being drawn towards the gem.

"No," Joseph replied, shaking his head as he went to grab the object.

"But if it's reacting to me, then surely I need to touch it to find out. If I'm the Shade, maybe I can use it for good this time-." Alex said, causing Joseph to think back to what King Atlas told him about how the Shade needed to find the right host.

Maybe that host was Alex, a married duo, the Luma and the Shade. Perhaps they could both work together. They had undoubtedly faired in worse situations and come out on top just fine.

This could be no different. Joseph was still hesitant to let Alex reach out and touch the gem, but he knew he had to eventually. It was inevitable.

"If you are the shade, then we need to consult the others before you do," Joseph said. He was trying not to be selfish. If Alex was the

Shade, he needed to try it out. "I want you to be able to use it for good. I do, and I think you could… but just in case it does change you… I'd like to have everyone know before."

"Makes sense, just in case," Alex said as he nodded. They both understood what was at stake.

It did make sense. If Alex was the Shade, it would make sense why the cerulean tears didn't work for him and why they were working against him.

Joseph was trying to reason, but he didn't want all the people to be the Shade, to be the person he had just gotten back into his life. Someone that I was now very, very close with. It was almost like fate knocking him around all over again.

Holding the gem, Joseph took Alex's hand, breathed in and stood up.

"Come on then, let's go consult the council," Joseph said as he began to drag Alex towards where the others were and where the key was. "Guys… We found something important to discuss before we turn the key."

"Oh, do we now?" Joseph recognised the voice, but it wasn't that of Finley, Maura or Pierce. When Joseph came round to meet whoever had spoken, he found a sight he didn't expect.

Maura and Pierce were knocked out cold on the floor. Finley was sat on the floor, not knocked out but looking shifty, like he was a naughty child in time out.

"No way." Alex's voice could be heard, but Joseph didn't register that he was talking. It was like he was underwater again. If fate wasn't knocking him down before with the Shade, it certainly was now.

"I said I'd always find you, didn't I, Joseph?" It was Calvin, and with a smile plastered on his face, Joseph's friends scattered on the floor, Finley looking on with no emotion, the Shade gem in his left hand and just a sidestep away – the key both he and Calvin were searching for, Joseph had found himself in a terrible predicament... "So, what did you find then?"

TWENTY-ONE

"Calvin…" Joseph heard his own voice say. Out of all of the things that he thought he might see today, the gem, the key, the beacon lighting up the whole cave… finding himself face to face with someone like Calvin, finding himself back to square one, was not something that he thought he would have to deal with today. "I thought-."

"You thought that Caulan had captured me again after I had been knocked out?" Calvin asked before his face turned into a smile. A knowing smile, a triumphant one. Creepy. "I wouldn't let myself get caught again so easily; I made a mistake the first time. I spent a lifetime running before I joined that cult, the Hunter's Guild, proudly serving a nation of destruction and prejudice. I worked them out, and I worked all those Hunters out. I knew what their next steps would be… so I escaped whilst the ice thawed and the dust settled. I wouldn't have missed this for the end of the world."

"I don't care for your story; I want to know why you are here… how did you get here?" Joseph asked, but Calvin just smiled. That coy smile really irked Joseph and got under his skin. "You couldn't have been following us; we would have noticed Calvin."

Alex moved towards Maura and Pierce whilst they lay on the floor motionless; the way they were laid out, it looked like they had been hit from behind by something or someone. Alex reached for Maura's neck, placing two fingers towards her pulse. The three seconds felt like agony; he knew Calvin was... not all there. But to kill someone? Joseph didn't know if Calvin was capable of that.

Alex muttered as he looked up at Joseph. "She's fine. Pierce too... but-."

"What?" Joseph asked Alex; Calvin stayed quiet as if observing to see if the two could figure out what had happened to their friends.

He reached for someone lodged in Maura's hair; the small pebble looked dusty as Alex held it up and instantly looked at Finely, sitting on a large rock close by, hugging his knees. "They were hit from above... by rocks falling from the ceiling, not enough force to kill, but enough to seriously injure or knock out," Alex said, using his hunter powers of deduction to his advantage, that maybe something good had come from his training, after all. Joseph followed Alex's gaze, staring straight at his very own brother. "...I knew something was off about you."

It all suddenly clicked for Joseph, the dream he had experienced before they came down here when Finley was being berated. It wasn't Gerry who was speaking; it was Calvin who was forcing him onto the ship.

The same affliction.

Magic.

"Finley..." Joseph said quietly as he, too, stared at his brother. Finley's eyes shot up a moment later, but the man didn't say anything in reply; he just stared dead pan at his brother. "You've been lying to me."

"No, no, I didn't lie. I didn't. I want to help you, Joseph. I do." Finley said as he finally broke his trance – staring only at his brother.

"You *did lie*. You embedded yourself in the group, so we didn't suspect a thing..." Joseph said, using Finley's words against him. The man's eyes grew wide as he heard Joseph speak. "That is what you said, didn't you?"

"I-," Finley said, forcing himself to stand off the craggy floor. Calvin drew back as if he was enjoying the exchange. As annoyed as Jospeh was right now, he was just glad that Calvin seemed subdued—almost entertained.

"You were talking to Calvin on that bracelet thing, weren't you?" Joseph asked; his voice was raised; he couldn't hear himself shout, but his voice hurt. "This was all planned, wasn't it? Of course, it was no coincidence that my long-lost, presumed deceased brother would show up the day after I took down the barrier around Rivetia. You've... been watching us. Haven't you?"

"I tasked Finley to watch over you," Calvin said as he leaned on one of the walls. "He would enter into Freydale with that Captain, and whilst he was there, he would just watch, observe. You needed to be ready."

"Ready for what?" Joseph asked before he turned to Finley. His voice was lower now, he could tell, and his throat wasn't as scratchy anymore, but it still hurt. You saw me multiple times and never thought to speak up?"

"You were always our mission; I had to come in contact with you at the right moment, the moment you blossomed into the Luma," Finley said. Joseph wasn't aware that Finley knew what the Luma was, or rather that his brother had taken up the moniker. "Once you became the Luma, we knew you were ready, so I showed up when I did."

"So, you knew where I was the entire time?" Joseph asked, then he remembered what he had told Alex. About Finley's observation. "It wasn't just an observation, was it? When you said that you knew what I and I had been through... because you had seen it all. You saw every single part of our journey together."

"That does not matter. You, Joseph, are the Luma. Your magic melded with the power of Lumin herself. That is a very... powerful asset to have." Calvin interrupted – his voice cutting through the conversation like a knife to butter. "We don't want to hurt you, Joseph; we want to utilise you properly."

"Hurt me?" Joseph asked, scoffing as he turned his attention towards Calvin. "You already hurt me. Many times over."

"Did I really hurt you, though?" Calvin asked, the smile appearing on his face. "If you really think about it, did I ever touch you? I only came to the guild a short while after you returned from your stint away... sure I berated you; who didn't. It was the guild's way. I had to find a way to fit in."

"Sure, you didn't hit him, but neither did I. It doesn't make you special," Alex said as he looked at the man who used to be his brother. Now, as Joseph looked at Alex, all he saw was discontent and distaste for the man.

"What about what you did to Henry?" Joseph asked, earning an eyebrow twitch from Calvin. "You got him killed. You don't think that hurt me?"

"I merely planted the seeds; Caulan was the one who chose the participants; I admit, it was dark and not my finest moment, but Joseph..." Calvin said as he turned to look back at Finely and beckoned him close, noticing that Finley had the glowing mark of a contract on his arm, just like he had seen on his own body every day for the last fifteen years before. He remembered what Finley had said about never being a contract servant; it seemed to lie was second nature to him. "But, come on, let bygones be bygones; we're both looking for the same thing: the return of magic."

"Yes. But why do you, of all people, want magic to be returned?" Alex asked. "You don't seem like the type to care that this decay is destroying the world… you might have been a hunter, but you were always the type to want to see things burn rather than save them."

"You're right, Alexander, yes. I never was bothered about the way the world worked. But with the reunion of the keys in each beacon… I won't have to." Calvin replied. "When I read the book on the beacons-."

"When did… you read the book?" Joseph asked. He had never given the book to Calvin; it hadn't left his side until Caulan stole it along with his satchel.

"I made my way through the guild whilst a certain someone's dad was off gallivanting on the sea trying to find you. I snuck in and, thankfully, knew my way around. The book was on full display…" Calvin said before he scoffed, clearly getting bored of all the theatrics. "The book said that once all four keys are reunited and you stand on the fifth beacon after it appears, the walls of reality would crumble, but only for a moment; the people who reach the top of the beacon when the sun hits it's peak can command the world to their will. I wish to create a world where magic rules all. Where we never have to worry about people opposing us again."

"You opposed me for a long time, Calvin," Joseph said. "You were awful to me, and now, what do you want to be on the same side? You want us to work together or something?"

"I admit it wasn't my finest moment, but Joseph listen…" Calvin said as he stepped forward from where he had stood, looking over at Finley for a moment, who nodded in his direction. "We're family, and family stick together, you know that."

"What are you talking about?" Joseph asked. "You're not my family."

"You never could quite say my name when you were little," Calvin said, keeping his voice low. Joseph was having a hard time hearing the man as he spoke. But you were young, so I can't blame you."

"What are you talking about?" Joseph snapped; he was tired of Calvin's mind games. He was sick to death. "I didn't know you when I was little; I certainly would have remembered."

"You didn't know this version of me when you were little. You're right." Calvin said, raising his voice, exclaiming almost as if he had just discovered something. "But you did know me at one point."

"Enough of these mind games!" Alex countered. "If you're going to tell us, can you not be so dramatic about it, please?"

"What is your name?" Joseph asked. Calvin raised his eyebrow and put back on that smile that bore into him.

"Saurin…" he said, teeth gritted. Joseph could feel his legs getting heavy. His head boomed like a headache was about to come on as he tried with all his might to process the information. As he looked over at Finley, he knew then and there that, for once, this man was telling the truth. "My name is Saurin."

Now Joseph knew what the man in his vision had been telling him all along.

He was in danger. A lot of danger indeed.

"No. You're dead." Joseph couldn't hear himself as he spoke once more. Everything was converging around him, and nothing made sense. As his vision flipped between Finley and Saurin, he couldn't quite comprehend what was happening. "There is no way you would have been able to survive… we hardly did!"

"You were four; what do you know?" Finley snapped, showing a new side to his brother. That anger that he had sensed before was on full display now. "He made it to the waterfall like we were supposed to. He escaped all the torture that we went through, but-."

"The pain still festered within me." Saurin began – holding his hand to his chest. "Everything I have done was calculated in the name of revenge. I lost everything to that night, Joseph, don't get facts twisted."

"You joined the guild so that you could, what? Tear it down from the inside?" Joseph asked; he didn't believe it, but Saurin nodded. It made sense how Calvin had been adamant about being allies in that dungeon *because he knew something Joseph didn't.* But he never offered that information, nor did he back down from the pain he had caused Joseph. It didn't matter, family friend or not. Saurin was dangerous, and Finley seemed willing to be on his side. "Didn't stop you from causing pain, did it, though? You tried to get me on your side multiple times; if you wanted me as an ally, why didn't you start out with that? Keep me in the loop? But no, you decided to be cruel, too."

"I admit it wasn't my finest moment, but it was all an act to stop them from suspecting anything; if they had any shred of belief that I had magic or was associated with it, I'd be stripped of everything, become a servant or worse. I couldn't do what I needed to do, what we all need to do, without being on their side." Saurin explained, but Joseph wasn't buying it, family friend or not; he had to have some real pain and anger behind him to do the things he did and still sleep at night. "Even if I wasn't. I got revenge on that princess for you."

"You only did that because you had been scorned," Alex interjected. "Calvin, you and I were like brothers; you're telling me all that was a lie?"

"Calvin isn't even my name, so work it out for yourself," Saurin said bitterly. Joseph could tell that the other did not feel the same despite what Alex felt. He didn't even once look at Alex, instead keeping his eyes square on Joseph. "If you join us, you can get revenge on those who hurt you… I know you feel the pain too, that anger we all do."

Joseph looked down at his hands. The black gem that he had long forgotten was there in his hands. Something told him that now that Saurin had revealed himself, there was going to be some work involved to escape unharmed and with the gem intact. After the last time, he didn't want to think about what Saurin could do, but he didn't look like he had a sword this time. He seemed generally unarmed… well, apart from his magic.

"You're crazy if you think I would join to get revenge. I don't want revenge; I just want to live peacefully. Safe." Joseph said. "And if you listened to anything I've said since we started this journey, you would know this."

"The only way you're going to get that is if we eradicate the people who hurt us," Finley replied, taking a step forward. In this light, the blue hue he had become accustomed to, he saw Finley for who he really was. He was not a victim in all of this; he was willing. He was willing to stoop to the level of Caulan and the guild just to get what he and Saurin wanted.

"You're beginning to sound an awful lot like someone you claim to hate," Alex replied as he approached the beacon, taking smaller steps towards it whilst Saurin and Finley looked at Joseph. Pierce and Maura were by the base, but Joseph could tell what he planned. That is precisely what they came here to do. Turn the key.

"Eradicate is just another word for exterminated. I remember the night our parents died. You thought you kept me hidden from it, but I heard that word be used. You sound exactly like them." Joseph said both Saurin and Finley looked crazed, their eyes staring blankly at Joseph – like they had thought out everything, they had time to let the pain fester – and had become just like the people they were fighting against. "You, Saurin, Calvin, whatever your name is. I understand you're bad to the bone; you've been unkind since joining the guild. But you, Finley, we've been through the same things. Surely you can understand that fighting back the way those people did is not the answer."

"I believed what you did for a while, but after I saw countless of our people killed… and after I saw all that decay and destruction all because people couldn't fathom having magic in the world, and after Saurin showed me our true nature, what we could actually do with our magic…" Finley replied as he stomped his foot on the ground, and instantly, it began to rattle like the starting of an earthquake; the ground was rumbling, and rocks began to fall from the ceiling, covering a small patch where Joseph and Alex were standing covered in rubble and dust. As Finley held out his arms for Joseph to take, Joseph zoned in on the guild mark on his arm. The contract mark he had seen earlier when Saurin appeared… but this time, the purple glow of the magic hidden inside was growing in the faint blue light. He was being controlled. "You need to join us. We can show you the limits of your magic and how to change those limits. I won't ask twice."

"Tell me something, Alex. What is the main sign that a servant is contracted?" Joseph asked, turning to his husband, who looked confused. He clearly hadn't seen the mark on Finley's arm yet.

"Their mark glows purple…" Alex said, offering insight as he clocked onto why Joseph had asked the question he did. Joseph knew all too well what a contract looked like. But maybe, if this was his first contract… Finley didn't know.

"So, tell me, Finley, if you were never a contract servant, why exactly is your mark glowing?" Joseph asked before Finley looked down at his own arm, trying to hide it from view. "I knew it. Saurin is controlling you… but that mark looks different to the normal guild mark."

Joseph felt Alex's arms pulling him back, his lips close to Joseph's ear – Alex's breathing was laboured but fast, as if he had figured it all out. "Joey, be careful. I know that mark. It *is* different." Alex said as if he finally realised the gravity of the situation and just how dangerous it could be. "Your brother has been invoked."

Saurin was two steps ahead, staring at Joseph with a smile. "I figured it out, did you, Alexander?" Saurin said as he, too, revealed a mark on his arm—the controller mark. It's glowing reddish, just like Finley's. "He's my puppet, but make no mistake; he did all this willingly."

"No one would do that willingly," Alex said through gritted teeth. Joseph had never seen what an invoked mark looked like; it was very rare. But Alex had. You lose all sense of self. No one, and I mean no one, would sign up for that just for revenge for whatever you really want."

"But I did," Finley said, finally speaking up for himself. "I was the one who told him the password. Everything has been calculated and perfectly worked out to ensure we get exactly what we want. I meant what I said; you were always our mission, and now you are the Luma. We need you on our side; you'll understand that soon. You really have no choice but to come with us, Joey."

"Don't you dare use my nickname right now!" Joseph shouted, spittle flying as his voice stretched towards the boundaries of the cave wall. Alex had to hold Joseph back – his arms were flying sporadically. Alex was holding him in place, stopping Joseph from running up towards Saurin and punching the lights out of the man. "Only family get to call me Joey; you, of all people, know that!"

"I am your family…" Finley replied, his voice changed, becoming more recognisable to Joseph, the voice he had used when they first met on that beach, the calm, collected version of his brother. The one who had come clear and transparent about his stature and life. He looked hurt, only for a moment, before his outstretched hand turned to a point, and his finger was directed straight at Alex. "He calls you Joey; he uses your nickname! Alex is not family, Joseph! His father has destroyed everything; you should hate him!"

"In case you forgot, Alex is my husband. These rings aren't just for show. So, by right, he is family. This is better than what I can say for my flesh and blood. Caulan might have destroyed many things, but Alex is not his father. He is a separate person." Joseph said before breathing in and out, Alex letting him go from the grip he had over him.

"The apple doesn't fall far from the tree," Saurin exclaimed, scoffing slightly as he looked Joseph in the eye, wondering just how naïve the boy was. "If you don't come with us willingly, Joseph, I know a little… trick to get you on the side."

"What?" Joseph asked. "You're never going to get me on your side. I know right from wrong, a concept clearly lost on both of you."

"Justice…" Saurin began – shutting Joseph up almost instantly. He took a moment before he recognised what Saurin had said. He played it repeatedly in his head. This cave had done many things to mess with his head, so as he stood staring directly at Saurin, he had to ensure he heard him correctly. "Obelisk."

"You don't know… you can't know that!" Joseph shouted – only he and Caulan, as Sargent of his guild, would know of the invocation.

"Slaughter," Saurin said, continuing through gritted teeth. He was halfway through the invoke. "Empower…"

"Calvin… Saurin, please. Don't do this." Alex piped up from behind Joseph. He knew that it was useless and that either way, Saurin would continue. Joseph knew what he needed to do.

"Painful," Saurin said. His voice bounced off the walls, echoing around him. Saurin was all for theatrics; he held out his hands for Joseph to take, a smile appearing on his lips again as he continued, his voice loud and clear. "Last word, Joseph. You know it, so say it along with me!

"I'll go with you," Joseph shouted, shutting Saurin up immediately.

"Absolutely not. You can't." Alex said, stuttering slightly as he spoke.

"I can't win against you. I can't win against the invocation." Joseph said, his body straining, the invocation having taken some life out of him already, but the more time went on without a word spoken from Saurin's lips, the less his body seemed to react. "I must turn the key. It must be me. If you let me turn the key, I will go with you."

Remembering what the previous Luma had said about Joseph being the only one who could turn the keys and not letting anyone else touch them, he didn't want to disrupt the balance of things even more than he already had. Disobeying those orders… well, he didn't want to see what would happen if he did.

"Fine… but make it quick," Saurin said as he pointed towards the beacon. "Go ahead."

Joseph had a plan; Saurin had no idea what he had just agreed to. As he passed Alex, Joseph turned to him and quickly winked, letting the man in on the plan as best he could. It was like people had been saying they had a secret language only they were privy to. Joseph understood Alex, and Alex understood Joseph.

Joseph quickly did as he was told, grabbing the silver key and turning it clockwise. Unlike the Rose Beacon, however, there was no blast that knocked them back; instead, there was little to no evidence that any changes occurred at all. The cracks, however, did begin to fade. The beacon was coming back to its original state, and the magic was back in Rivetia. It was that simple. No fanfare… this was what Joseph was hoping for.

"Is it done?" Saurin asked, the crazed voice coming back. He knew that he was finally getting Joseph on his side—it was clear that the man wanted to get going. Joseph, did you unlock magic?"

"Yes," Joseph said as he stood and turned towards the man holding all the cards. But Joseph had one of his own. Looking down at the black gem in his right hand, Joseph turned to Alex, who was standing nearby. "Before we go… can I say goodbye?"

"Get on with it!" Saurin shouted. "Time is of the essence here."

He walked over to Alex, under the watchful eyes of Finley and Saurin and quickly wrapped his arms around Alex, letting the man rest his head on his shoulder, his ear close to Joseph's lips.

"So much for a honeymoon," Alex whispered a slight chuckle coming from his lips, but Joseph knew this was a tactic to deflect how he felt. As he looked up at Alex, he could see it in the man's eyes; they were pleading with Joseph to fight. He understood what was at stake, how dangerous the invocation was, and that Saurin was out for himself and only himself. He didn't really care about Joseph, it was clear. "Please don't leave me."

"I don't know where they will be taking me if I leave… or what will happen if I go with them," Joseph said as he pulled Alex into a hug before giving the man a quick kiss on the cheek, the gristle of Alex's beard tickling Joseph's lips. "If this is how our story is supposed to play out, I hope the rumours aren't true, that you won't lose yourself to this darkness."

"What do you mean…" Alex asked. His voice was low, quiet.

"You said you wanted to use this for good…" Joseph said, and before Alex could even understand, he shoved the gem into the other man's hand. "Prove it. You'll find a way to save me. I know you will."

TWENTY–TWO

Thick black smoke began to rise from the gem in Alex's hand. The colour only Alex could see before was now visible to everyone around him. The jet-black gem in his hands turned into a rainbow of colours. Joseph stepped back and watched the smoke envelop the entire space around Alex. He struggled to see the man as the smoke got thicker and thicker. Reminiscent of the decay that had been following them all around.

The thick, acrid smoke was beginning to lose colour, turning a deep black. The smoke reached the top of the cave, cloaking the newly blue hue of the beacon. Joseph could feel their arms pulling him back as the smoke reached them. He caught the face of the person who held him—Saurin and Finley both gripped onto one arm each, pulling him away from the display that was evolving around them.

"Get off me!" Joseph shouted as the black smoke found its way towards some of the rocks that scattered the area. Joseph observed as Alex's hand reached forward from the smoke, breaking the rocks and turning them into dust before his eyes.

"What is that thing?" Joseph could hear Finley ask to the side of him as Joseph was pulled back.

"What did you give him, Joseph?" Saurin shouted through the chaos as he moved quickly towards the rock Finley had been perched next to moments before, his arms wrapped around Joseph, keeping him in place. Saurin was strong; he had to give the man that. "Finley, grab the other two! I ask again, what did you give him, Joseph?"

Struggling to keep his eyes open, Joseph saw his brother moving quickly, grabbing Pierce and Maura's arms and dragging them towards the rock he and Saurin were standing near. Despite being a monster, Saurin held some semblance of a heart. Even if it was black as coal.

Joseph stood eerily still, using his hands, even if bound by Saurin, to slice through the smog created by the gem. Coughing became the only sound he could hear, though he wasn't sure who had made the sound. The smoke took all his senses away, decaying them – even though he hadn't moved from the spot he had been forced into, he couldn't really tell left from right. He knew he was very high, but the danger level was still unknown.

"Alex!" Joseph finally shouted out, coughing through the barrier, taking tiny breaths to try and stop the acrid scent from invading his nose and mouth. "Alex, can you hear me?"

"For the last time…" Saurin said, coughing and spluttering. All confidence was gone from the man's body. "What did you give him?"

"The Shade gem. If you know what the…" Joseph said he couldn't make complete sentences in this commotion around him, even if he couldn't see Saurin's face; the man's grip on his body told him all he needed to know; Saurin was furious. Anxious too. "If you know what the Luma is, you'll know what the Shade is, too."

"You have no idea what you've just gone and done, Joseph!" Saurin shouted; his voice was hoarse, gritty. "If Alex is the shade…"

"Unhand him!" A voice cut through the smoke. As two small white lights dove through the darkness, light from Alex's eyes. The lights zoned in on Saurin, who held dearly onto Joseph. The voice was disembodied, much more profound than Alex's, like it wasn't real, like a nightmare. "You will… unhand him!"

Saurin did as he was told as if he was, and he contracted himself. Like there was a decay of his own free will. "Joseph…" Saurin said as his body seized up. "You don't know what you've done…You didn't want a war; you've just created one."

War. The world was already war-torn. It had been for fifty years. Even longer than that. Every day, a hunter found someone with magic to induct into the guild, a step further towards the war that people long believed had ended.

"If you think that life is perfect and free of war now, you're sorely mistaken, Saurin," Joseph said. They still couldn't see each other's faces, but the smoke was thinning slightly.

"The Shade and Luma are opposing forces; you *can't* work together. The decay plaguing the world, the Shade and it are directly connected. The Shade is destruction in its raw form. You don't know what I read on my journey here, what information I ingested. The Shade and Luma always destroy one another; it's the natural way the two work. Ying and Yang but off the scale." Saurin said as Joseph's vision cleared, and he could see the utmost fear on Saurin's face; every atom of his confidence had been shot. Joseph tried with all his might to process the information Saurin was spilling out for all to hear – thinking back to when Santos read him the piece of paper on the ship, how he had described the meeting of the Shade and the Luma. A bloody war waiting to happen. "Brother and sister, mother and son and now a married duo. The laws of the universe do have a… sense of humour."

The smoke entirely cleared a moment later, the acrid scent of burning wood still lingering in the area as everyone could see each other. As he looked at Alex's face, he could see the man's clothes had changed, the jacket and trousers he had been given on his first day here, the blue and the purple hues being replaced with a deep black colour. Alex's eyes were one of the first things he noticed; the bright white light was coming from his eyes, and Joseph couldn't even see the colour of the man's eyes anymore. Clipping the gem onto his jacket, Alex took a few steps forward from where he had stood, holding his left hand out in front of him.

As he moved, more rocks surrounding his feet turned to dust. Joseph slowly realised the power of the Shade—this was pure destruction.

"You two may leave." Alex's voice was still dark, disembodied. But as Joseph zoned in on his husband's tone, he could hear Alex's voice behind the more profound, almost possessed version. Alex took small steps forward and stared directly at Saurin and Finley.

"What if we don't want to?" Finley asked, getting some form of confidence. Still, all that quickly dissipated as Alex's eyes zoned in on Finley, cocking his head to the side, Alex simply smiled. It wasn't a smile that unnerved Joseph; deep down, he knew that everything Alex was doing now was to protect Joseph and his team from further harm. It took him a while, but for now, he was using the power for good. "Joseph is my brother, the only family I have, I'm not leaving without him."

Alex lifted his hand in the air; Joseph could see Finley moving towards the man, not on his own accord, but like he was being controlled like Saurin had done moments before. A complete loss of sense of self. Decaying his natural sense. "You call yourself a brother," Alex said as he brought Finley closer, the man's ear close to Alex's mouth. "You might not know this about me, Finley, but I made a promise to Joseph a long time ago, a promise I couldn't keep… ever since I've been paying for that mistake. Since then, I promised to protect him no matter the cost…"

"So what, do you want a medal?" Finley asked through gritted teeth. There it was again, that anger that Joseph had sensed. That unbridled, unwavering anger replaced any fear that Finley might have held.

"No." Alex's voice returned to normal, as did his eyes as the gem lost its colour. But Alex still had control over Finley. His voice was evident as he spoke, his vision square on Joseph. "What I want is for you to leave *my* family alone."

"We'll go." Saurin piped up from behind Joseph, his eyes wide as if he had just figured out how serious the situation was. "We'll leave. But don't worry Joseph, you'll see us again, and one of these days, very soon, you'll finally see things from our perspective. When you do, you'll seek us out."

"You'll have a long wait," Joseph said, shaking his head.

"Not really. The decay is upon us, getting closer and closer. A few months is all I give you before you come to find us when the world really begins to die. There is such a bigger game afoot here beyond just you and me. Finley, let go...." Saurin said as he grabbed a small capsule-like object from his pocket and threw it on the ground. A portal appeared moments later; that must have been how he appeared out of nowhere. Finley walked past Joseph a moment later. He didn't look at his brother or Alex; he just did as he was told – the invocation in full force. Unaware of where the two were going, Finley disappeared as he entered the portal, but Saurin hesitated. "See you soon, Joseph, and when we do, that is when you'll finally understand."

"We'll see," Joseph said as Saurin reluctantly entered the portal he had created from nothing. He had never seen such a device, and he wondered where Saurin would have gotten it from. Maybe there was a bigger game afoot, as he had said, but Joseph wouldn't join them just to find out *what* it was.

Joseph noticed the eerie silence first after his captors left. Turning around from where the portal had disappeared, he looked at Alex, who stood there staring at him.

"Did I scare you?" Alex asked as he cocked his head to the side, his voice getting back to normality, but his tone was still a little off. He looked tired; his eyes were droopy. "It was not my intention, Joey."

"A little. I was scared for you. I had no idea what would happen when I gave you that gem. I didn't want you to get hurt." Joseph said, not immediately running up to Alex to give him a hug as he would usually do. After all that, he still had to determine if this was Alex or a different version of the man he knew. "Are you... okay?"

"Perfectly content. We're cool. I won't hurt you; I meant what I said; I would protect you with my life. I feel stronger, but that's about it. I just wanted to make sure you were safe." Alex said that as he took giant strides, Joseph kept his eyes on Alex's feet, and the rocks on the ground were no longer being affected as he stepped closer to them. He reached out and pulled Joseph into a hug a moment later. Joseph first notices the feel of Alex's clothes, like velvet; the jacket is soft, and Joseph just wants to bury his face in it and fall asleep. But after all that, he knew Alex probably needed to sleep more. The man's breathing felt laboured, but he didn't seem too affected by it. The gem attached to Alex's jacket was still glowing slightly as Joseph looked up at it. The shade power was still active, even now. "I couldn't let them take you."

"I know," Joseph said, nodding. Before his eyes scanned the floor at Pierce and Maura, who had been out cold the entire time, neither had moved. If they couldn't get them up and move – Joseph wasn't sure how they would get out of this cave. Alex couldn't use the tears to traverse the cave, and there was no way Joseph could carry four people with him. "I have no idea what the power you gained will mean, but right now, we need to wake the others and ensure they are okay after those rocks hit them. Now that Saurin used that portal to get out of here, it has made me think."

"How exactly did we get out of here?" Alex said, hitting it right on the head with the correct answer. He crouched down, slapping Pierce's face a few times lightly, trying to stir some sort of reaction from them, but as many times as Alex did this, the less hope that Joseph had that they would wake them. "They're out for the count; they probably won't be up and moving about for a while; even when they are, they've been knocked out; they wouldn't exactly be mobile for hours after the fact."

"So, what do you propose? Just sitting here and waiting it out?" Joseph asked. It did sound like the safest option.

"Might be the best point of call. We can't move them, and there doesn't seem to be a way out of here without Pierce and Maura being coherent enough to use the tears to their disposal; almighty knows I can't use them if I couldn't before; I certainly can't now…" Alex said as his eyes lit up again as he looked over to the beacon that was five feet away from them. "Your magic developed after you were hit with the first blast; what would happen if you got hit by this beacon?"

"I have no clue," Joseph said as he stood up from where he had been lying, trying to get Maura and Pierce to open their eyes. He followed Alex, who was slowly getting closer to the beacon.

"It might make you stronger, able to get us all out of here. Don't you remember what the book said? People would worship the beacons and visit all of them. The beacons would bestow their powers beyond what they were usually capable of. It made them stronger." Alex said as he pointed towards the beacon. It all made sense to Joseph. Maybe Alex was right. "Now that the beacon is whole again, maybe it can help us like it was always meant to do."

"I could give it a go," Joseph said as he moved slowly towards the beacon. The monolith standing there, lighting up the area as if it was waiting for him to present himself. "Stand back… we both know what happens if you get hit by a beacon."

"Duly noted," Alex said as he stood back, facing where Maura and Pierce were lying, protecting them. He watched as Joseph got closer and closer to the beacon.

These Darker Secrets

Joseph let out a large sigh as he reached the base of the beacon; in his line of vision, the silver key reflected all the colours of the cave. This deep blue was rising through the beacon to the island's surface. The beacon reacted as if it sensed someone 'worthy' of its power. He thought back to his ancestors, people before him who had stood here, how all of them were lost to time but still with him in ways that he couldn't understand.

He remembered Jerrick's words that those with magic were identical. They were all connected by the same force that kept them strong. They were all family in one way or another. As Joseph anticipated the blast coming towards him, he reached out to touch the beacon, feeling the craggy rock that people long before him had touched, too, held in their hearts. Worshipped. He thought of all the things he had lost, all that knowledge, and the culture he missed out on. The traditions.

Now, he was righting a wrong, but he would always feel a hole in his heart, longing for what he couldn't have.

The beacon looked as if it was beginning to prepare to send a blast, the light shining from the base of the beacon getting stronger, as it had done with the Rose Beacon. Joseph kept his hands on the beacon, willing it to give him its power.

"Joey." Alex's voice was quiet as Joseph instantly turned to look at the man. "I feel a little bit…"

Joseph charged into a full sprint as he watched Alex hit the ground a moment later. Dust rose as his body went down with a bang right next to where Maura and Pierce were laid. The gem on his jacket had all but lost its colour now. Joseph had no idea what it meant, but as he reached Alex, cradling the man in his arms, he found that Alex had already fallen deep into sleep, but what kind of sleep, he wasn't sure.

Metamorphosis or exhaustion? He wasn't sure.

"Hey, hey." Joseph found himself saying as he held Alex's head in his arms, bringing the man up to rest on his crouched legs, but Alex did not respond. His breathing was more laboured than it had been before, a lot slower. Joseph found himself crying out in anguish, confusion and frustration. So much had happened in this one day; this was just another blip he didn't need. "Don't fall asleep on me, please! I can't get you all out on my own. I'm not strong enough! Wake up!"

As Joseph cradled Alex, he looked over to Pierce and Maura; there was no way that he could carry three people up the shafts to the top of the mountain King Atlas had brought them up. There had to be another way that he could get out, a way to get help.

As he moved Alex's head further up his lap, carefully playing with the man's hair, he tried with all his might to think of a solution, but nothing came to him. He was lost.

Then, as if all his answers were given to him, as if karma was giving him something to work with, Joseph felt something in his pocket, the item sticking into his leg from the excess weight being put on it.

The seashell King Atlas had given him.

'We in Rivetia will heed your call and come down the cave, no matter how perilous the journey.' The words of the king were swirling around him as Joseph heard the beacon making a gurgling noise before he even felt the blast hit him square in the chest.

This was not how things were supposed to go. As soon as the blast melded with his body, Joseph found himself feeling the same as Alex had: laboured and tired.

"Please, help me." As he felt himself becoming tired, Joseph felt his own body fall from his position. He kept the seashell close to him and turned his head towards the beacon, which was still lit up—ready to blast a willing participant. The light lit up the entire area as Joseph saw the blast approaching him. Joseph repeated his call, screaming the words through the tiny seashell as the beacon prepared for a third hit:

"King Atlas, help me."

As his eyes closed, he really hoped that someone would come find them, that the call would be heard, if not by the king, then someone. No matter how perilous.

TWENTY-THREE

"Repeat after me." A voice said as Joseph regained a sense of self. He was no longer in the cave, somewhere light, strapped to a bed with some sort of restraint. Joseph tried to move but found himself thrashing around in the same spot; whatever he strapped down with was strong. His vision cleared, and he could see the person who had spoken; he recognised the man – but he had no idea where he was from. The man shined a light in his left eye, the blue light shining in his eyes. He had no idea what the man was looking for, but it reminded him of the night he first came onto the ship and how Pierce and Santos had acted. He wondered what they were looking for, too. "Joseph, do you understand me?"

The man's words echoed around Joseph as he finally looked around the room he was in. It had stark white walls with just the bed and a small window. It was reminiscent of the underground city of Rivetia, but it was a whole lot brighter. How had he got here? He wasn't sure. The only thing he remembered was…

"Where are my friends?" Joseph asked as he moved his whole body to try and get out of the restraints. He needed to find them, make sure they were safe after all they had been through down there, and never lose anyone else. "Maura, Pierce? Did they make it out of the cave?"

"You were badly injured; please do not move, Joseph." The man said as he placed the lamp on the side of a small table. But he did not answer the question, and as angry as Joseph felt, that just made him dive further into the feeling.

"Where are they? Where is Alex?" Joseph shouted, but the tone did not phase the man. He simply raised his eyebrows—he was clearly adept at dealing with this. But Joseph still didn't know how he knew the man, where he had seen the man's face before. "Where is Alex? I want to see him!"

The man tutted, displeased. "Anger levels are *still* heightened, " he said to someone at the side of the room, Someone Joseph hadn't noticed yet. Every time he falls back asleep, he forgets."

"Forgets…?" Joseph asked, his voice calmer. His eyes locked with the man at the side of the room: the king stood with his arms crossed, concerned. "What is going on? King Atlas, you've got to help me."

"We are, Joseph." King Atlas said as he took a few steps forward. "After we found you down in the cave, you… were different. You were all passed out; we brought you up to the surface and woke you all up. You were a bit, well, spotty. You lost all sense of self. You would fall back asleep, and the moment you woke, you would be on the defence; you couldn't remember a thing. We restrained you to keep you safe."

"His anger levels seem to have stabilised." The man, who Joseph assumed was a doctor, said as he began to grab for the restraints that kept Joseph at bay. "I think we can remove these until he falls asleep anyway."

"Oh, I'm still angry. Very angry." Joseph said as the doctor began to hesitate at his next steps. "My brother and his best friend want to destroy the world. Imagine someone who you were told was dead

287

turned out to be alive, and it's the same person that tormented you in a guild you've just spent fifteen years trying to escape from. My brother's best friend got *my* best friend killed. Try also discovering that your brother has lied to you since rocking up here. He and his best friend want to end the world in the name of revenge… and they want me to join them. You'd be angry, too."

"I know how you feel, Joseph." King Atlas said as he held his hand over his heart and crouched by the bed.

"I find it very hard to believe that you would be familiar with that feeling," Joseph said, scoffing. His anger was boiling up inside him; he had never felt such rage. This is what they had wanted, though. This is how they wanted Joseph to act.

"It is certainly a unique situation, and you're right. I'm not familiar with that feeling. But I do know loss; I do know how it feels to be betrayed. I won't explain how you'll have to trust me." King Atlas said as he removed the last restraint, allowing Joseph to get out of the bed and stretch his legs for the first time in who knew how long. "You got hit by multiple blasts of the beacon; we have no idea how it might affect you. We must ensure you are well before letting you move around alone."

"I'll be fine once I stop my brother and Saurin from destroying the world," Joseph said. He wasn't sure he liked this, how his whole body radiated anger. It affected everyone around him—the doctor and King Atlas, who had looked at him with awe and seemed concerned and displeased at the display he saw in front of him. Joseph dangled his legs off the side of the bed and looked at King Atlas.

"We will stop them," King Atlas said before he came and sat down on a stool near Joseph.

"I'm going to assume you have questions. Though you can probably read my mind, so fire away." Joseph said that King Atlas only sighed and did not avert his gaze.

"I can't..." King Atlas began, rubbing the back of his neck. "I can't read your mind anymore."

"What do you mean?" Joseph asked. "You used to be able to with no problem."

"I have no idea why." King Atlas resumed his position with his arms crossed. He was clearly at a loss; the man looked vulnerable and powerless for the first time in a while. "Ever since you returned from the cave, I've got zilch. Nada. For the other, my power still works; you are the only one I can't read. It's like something is blocking me. It's why you've been here for so long, because we can't figure you out, and you've not been as coherent as this in a long while."

"Fire away the questions then," Joseph said – dismayed. "Don't worry. I might not remember how I got here, but I remember *everything* below. Every horrible second of it."

"You turned the key... that much we know. But what happened *after*." King Atlas began. "Maura and Pierce were out for the count; they don't know anything."

"Finley and Saurin had me cornered. They wanted to use the invocation of the Hunter's Guild to control me and get me on their side. Before... before we turned the key, me and Alex found the Shade gem." Joseph said as he looked directly at King Atlas, his face twitched slightly as he mentioned the gem. "I agreed to go with them, but not before I turned the key. They let me. But before I went with them, I passed the gem to Alex."

"Alex is the Shade?" King Atlas asked, his voice concerned. "Is that why you were knocked out?"

"Yes and no, in that order. Alex managed to harness the power of the shade, and this smoke began to rise from the gem, enveloping him. He protected me from those who wanted to hurt me; he used the power for good like you said someone could." Joseph continued, and King Atlas's face softened slightly. "It took a lot out of him; he was exhausted. He collapsed just before I was hit by a blast of magic from the beacon. I realised I couldn't carry three people up the shafts to the surface, so I called you. It worked."

"Doctor, go check up on the ward Alex is stationed in," King Atlas said as he pointed towards the door. When he wakes up, we need to be careful not to get him angry, to trigger a fight-or-flight reaction."

"I want to see him!" Joseph shouted as he got off the bed but almost immediately fell to the ground, his legs not working as they were supposed to. "I want to see Maura; I want to see Pierce!"

"You've not walked in a week. Your legs will be stiff. You're going to need a lot of rehabilitation. That takes time." King Atlas said as he reached Joseph at his level.

"I don't have time!" Joseph shouted, frustrated. He understood why he needed to rest after all that he had been through down there, but there was just a feeling he couldn't shake. "My brother is out there right now, working on a way to get to the next key. I need to stop him and Saurin before they do. They cannot corrupt the world like they want to."

"Okay, I understand, but you must understand me too, Joseph. You'll be able to leave… at some point. We'll start small. I'll go get Maura and Pierce; bring them here so you can see them." King Atlas said, trying to dispel some of Joseph's anger. "We'll bring you to Alex when we figure out how to wake him. But right now, we must work alone and figure it out independently. You need to rest; you need to channel that anger you have. Maybe seeing Maura and Pierce can help, hopefully."

"Thank you…" Joseph said as he felt the king grab him and help him back onto the bed in the middle of the room before he found himself breathing in and out. "I'm sorry for all the trouble… I'm not even sure why I'm so angry."

"No, Joseph. I'm sorry." King Altas said as he moved closer to the door to exit and collect Pierce and Maura. "I'm sorry for all the pain that has befallen you. So much in such a short life. One of these days, you will soon get the peace you have been looking for."

"That sounds nice," Joseph replied.

"I'll go collect Maura and Pierce for you." King Atlas said as he left the room, leaving Joseph to ponder the silence surrounding him. Peace. He was right; it sounded nice.

But what else would he lose for peace to be a reality? Joseph didn't even want to fathom whatever life could throw at him.

"Joseph." A hand shook him awake. Joseph was on high alert the moment his eyes opened. He hadn't even realised he had fallen asleep or knew how long it had been since he had. As his vision tightened on the people standing in the room around him, a smile crept on his face, and he finally saw Maura and Pierce. Awake. Safe.

"Hi," Joseph said as he tried to move his body again, finding it heavy. He wasn't restrained this time, though; for the most part, he remembered why they were there. King Atlas was nowhere to be seen; it was just the three of them in the small, bright white room. "Are you both okay?"

"For the most part." Pierce was the first to say – Joseph got a look at the man, a bandage wrapped around the left side of his head, where the boulder had fallen on his head; it looked as if the bandage had been changed recently, they looked pristine. "We took a bit of a tumble. I still don't fully know what happened."

"One moment, we were talking about the beacon; the next, we woke up here," Maura said. She looked generally unscathed, apart from a small bandage on her arm. This bandage looked slightly askew like it had been on for a while, concealing a cut that seemed to have bled recently. "King Atlas said that Alex is still sleeping."

"He is; I think it's something like what happened after I became the Luma. I don't know how to describe it, but it was like my body was transforming with the magic; deep down, his body was doing the same. Do you remember when I passed out after I got the ship through the barrier?" Joseph asked – he was doing much better now, like the anger was slowly subsiding. Maybe King Atlas had been correct, seeing that Maura and Pierce were okay after all that happened; perhaps it was helping. "He was the one that saved me."

"Saved you from what?" Pierce asked. "I, um… don't see Finley anywhere. Did something happen?"

"Hm, well, you wouldn't do. He's not here anymore. He was working with Calvin, Maura, do you remember?" Joseph asked; Maura nodded. She had been there when Calvin was after the book; she had seen him for what he was: someone untrustworthy. "Well, forget everything you knew about him; his name isn't Calvin; it's Saurin, a friend of Finley' from my childhood. They are working together to… try and destroy the world and reshape it in their image. They wanted me to join them. Finley Price is a traitor."

"I was not there for any of this, but I don't think I need much context," Pierce said as he raised his hand. "So, Finley is someone we cannot trust… that he is working with someone who wishes to destroy or reshape the world, whatever you said. I get all of that. But what I don't understand is, why?"

"Revenge," Joseph said. "They laid out the plans to me there and then. A fifth beacon appears after all four keys are returned to their rightful place. They plan to use this fifth beacon to their advantage. The story goes that whoever finds themselves at the top of the beacon when the sun reaches its peak can command reality to their will. They want a world where those without magic pay for the sins they created. They want magic to rule the world once again."

"I've never heard of a fifth beacon in all my travels..." Pierce asked. "Is it real?"

"My brother and Saurin seemed to find some merit in the story," Joseph replied. "I think we have to take it literally unless proven otherwise."

He felt a little sad that his brother, of all people in the world, was someone he couldn't rely on, that once again, they were apart from one another due to someone else's will.

"Sorry, backtracking a little... you said that Alex managed to save you in the cave. How?" Maura asked.

Joseph gulped as he began to speak. He hoped that Maura and Pierce would react differently to that of the King, but deep down, he knew everyone had a right to be concerned. "Alex and I found a gem that relates to the shade. It was reacting to him, but there had been signs that this was where we were headed."

"The cerulean tears didn't work for him..." Maura recounted; Joseph just nodded, but she didn't look concerned, just confused as if everything she knew had been a lie. And that wouldn't be too far off the mark as far as Maura was concerned. "But I thought... well, weren't we told that the Shade was bad and the Luma was good?"

"Things aren't always so black and white," Pierce explained, a fact that Maura knew all too well. "He saved you... that doesn't sound bad."

"It wasn't. I don't know how Alex did it; he probably didn't. But somehow, he managed to harness the power for a good cause, to save me. He recalled the promise he gave me that he would protect me no matter the cost." Joseph said as he played with the wedding ring on his finger. "He was telling the truth. He got me out of that horrible mess; he made sure that Finley and Saurin left the cave without taking me with them. Who knows what they had planned for me if we did leave..."

"He couldn't fathom losing you, so he willed the power, not to destroy what he loved, but to protect it." A fourth voice cut through the conversation quickly. King Atlas stood tall with his back to the door. "I told you someone might be able to use the power for good intentions; maybe Alex is that person; who knows? I must continue the research."

"Where is Alex?" Maura asked. King Atlas looked at her and smiled, but he didn't say anything—not yet anyway. "No one would tell us anything. We woke up, and the whole island was being secretive."

"Did you manage to wake him?" Joseph asked as he lifted himself off the bed and dangled his legs over the side of the edge. His legs didn't seem very mobile, but they didn't hurt like before.

"It's early days; he's very… on edge but stable. That's good." King Atlas recounted the information to Joseph. "We had to use unconventional methods to treat him; the tears don't work for him; they don't react to him the same way as they do for everyone else."

"We noticed that in the cave. We joked that they didn't like him." Joseph said as he found himself laughing, which he hadn't done in a while. He then looked at King Atlas, who smiled, happy that Joseph's anger had somehow subsided. "Can you take me to him?"

"He's just outside," King Atlas said as he opened the door. Joseph could see Alex almost immediately. The man looked battered and bruised, and he looked tired still. But he was okay. That was all Jospeh could ask for. "When you're stable, Joseph, I must speak to you alone. If you are truly going to leave Rivetia to pursue the other keys, I need to speak to you before you go."

"Thank you, Your Majesty," Joseph said as he watched the King leave and Alex enter the room. At first, he looked shifty, like he wasn't sure of himself. It was clear that he had also lost some time like Joseph had. He looked at the three faces in the room – inspecting all of them as he closed the door behind him.

"Hi, guys," Alex said – as if he had just popped out for bread and milk on a morning walk. His voice was raspy as if he had just woken up from a large nap, but he seemed more stable than Joseph. More agile. "I um… I assume Joseph told you about me, and I would understand if you were a little hesitant to trust me… I would get it completely."

Joseph watched as Maura made her way up towards Alex. He observed her face—no emotion like she was trying to figure something out. As she reached Alex, she smiled briefly before touching his face—she wasn't hesitant. Quickly wrapping Alex into a hug, Maura dug her face into Alex's shoulder.

"Alex, you're my friend. I meant what I said, no matter what happens in the future." Maura could be heard saying.

"If what Joseph said was true, you saved his life…" Pierce said, taking a few steps forward before touching Alex's shoulder. "That's not half bad. If you think this changes anything, you'll be sorely mistaken; I will still enjoy winding you up. No matter what power you have."

Alex let out a small chuckle. "I have no idea what this power even means for me…" Alex began as he zoned in on Joseph, who was still sitting on the bed, observing the three of them converse. He was happy to finally have some people Alex got along with, before all of this, before the year that neither wanted to remember; it was always just the two of them – neither trusting people long enough to add more people to their little group. "I don't even know how to control it…"

"Welcome to the club," Joseph said loudly with a smile. "That's part of the journey. I was born with it because I didn't know how to fully control my power. It's all part of the discovery and is sure scary. You'll have things happen and wonder, 'Was that me?' or discover things about yourself that you never knew you could. But that's all part of the life of someone with magic. You're always evolving."

"Do you think what I have is magic?" Alex asked. "It didn't

look like any magic I've ever seen before, more like a possession."

"It's early days. But there might be something there. But what did I say?" Joseph asked.

"It's all part of the journey," Alex muttered with a smile before he took a few steps forward. Joseph slid off the side of the bed and placed his feet on the cold wooden floor. It took him a few moments to adjust to the extra weight he put on his legs, like a baby deer taking its first steps. But Joseph had been through much worse; he wasn't about to curl into a ball and admit defeat just because his legs seemed much heavier than usual.

He hadn't walked in days, and sure, he wasn't climbing mountains, but he was up and taking small steps towards the path he wanted to be on.

"Please be careful," Alex said as he watched Joseph from close by. "King Atlas mentioned that you had tried to walk earlier with less than stellar results. Please don't rush yourself."

"No, no, it's fine. I've at least made it off the bed." Joseph said as he suddenly felt watched, but it wasn't a bad feeling by any means; each person had a smile. Joseph pushed himself away from the bed just enough that he had nothing else to hold onto; he needed to dive straight into the deep end. If he was going to get out of here to follow Finley and Saurin, he needed to be able to walk at least a few feet in front of him. If he couldn't do that, he was useless to the cause. "See... I'm doing it."

"Do you need any help?" Maura asked as she stood closer than the others. But Joseph simply shook his head.

"I'm fine," Joseph replied as he took his first step forward. It was a small step like he had barely shuffled from the place he had been in before. His legs were shaking, tired from overuse after days of being static. He held out his arms for balance. Joseph watched as all three of them moved slowly—all holding out their arms just in case he was to fall. "I'm fine," he said.

If he said it enough, he might learn to believe it.

"Don't overdo it, Joey. If you need help, please just ask." Alex said, his voice full of concern; he was right to be; if Joseph were to fall down on the flooring that was at his feet, it would hurt, it would hurt a lot.

"You're one to talk." Joseph found himself laughing, and as he looked up at Alex, he could see that the subtle dig was taken in stride. Alex would be the first person to admit that he was stubborn, but as much as Alex could be stubborn, so could Joseph. "Mr, I'm so independent; I don't need help up the pulley system whilst dangling over the water."

But Joseph was about to eat his words. He could feel himself slipping before his body registered that he was; it was like all his reflexes had disappeared. Unable to hold onto anything, he felt himself take a step forward to try and gain balance. Still, he was already on his way towards the floor before he could stop moving like his body had a mind of its own.

But he didn't hit the ground.

"Hey." Joseph heard the voice as his eyes were shut tight.

"Um… oh," Joseph said, still shutting his eyes. He could feel Alex's arms holding him tightly in place. He wasn't going to fall out of them anytime soon. He felt Alex's hair brush against his nose; the man's face was close.

With his breath on Joseph's cheek, Alex giggled slightly before speaking again. His voice was light and happy. "Caught you." A moment later, he opened his eyes to see Alex's goofy grin staring down at him with a knowing look. "I remember you almost fell over that time as well."

"I suppose I might need just a little bit longer to get back to my usual self," Joseph said, a little bewildered as he felt himself be lifted and placed back onto the bed.

"Yes, you do. You need to rest." Alex asked as he sat down on the bed next to Joseph. "Don't the Cerulean Tears heal you? They did before… why isn't it working now?"

"I might be going off experience, but it might be because his legs weren't actually injured; they don't know what to fix," Pierce explained. "I saw it on the sea; my men would be down bad with some sickness, be on bed rest for days, and when they would feel okay enough to move, their legs would just buckle from beneath them. He just needs to keep walking."

"I want to try again," Joseph said as he slid off the bed. "I need to try and be at my best to beat Saurin and Finley to the next key."

"We will," Maura said. "But it does pose the question…"

"Where is the next key?" Pierce interjected. Clearly, she and Pierce were on the same wavelength regarding this.

"I have no idea," Alex replied as he, too, slid off the side of the bed to join Joseph, hovering his hands around Joseph as if to be ready to catch the boy if he were to fall again. He was determined to help Joseph as much as possible; that was clear, and Joseph couldn't even say no. Alex was helping no matter what. "If only we had the book, then this wouldn't be so hard. We'd know where exactly to look. Regarding Juna, I'm an expert, but the other continents, not so much."

"We'll just have to go collect the book then," Joseph replied, earning confused looks from the three people around him.

"But… the book is in Freydale," Alex replied, and as much as Joseph didn't want to set foot in that kingdom again, he couldn't deny that he needed to push down his fears.

"I'm all too aware," Joseph replied.

"Are you quite sure?" Maura asked. "We escaped from that kingdom on not-so-great terms; now you want to go back?"

"It's like I said," Joseph said before taking a significant step away from the bed, planting his foot on the floor firmly; Joseph looked around the room at the faces of the others; they were all smiling at him, proud that once again he had made the first step at getting back to normal. Whatever normal was? "It's all part of the journey."

TWENTY–FOUR

Joseph could smell salt. It was really all he could smell. As he stood on the beach watching Loreli's Wave be loaded up with all sorts of" supplies, food, weapons and who knew what else. It brought him back to when he had first boarded the ship and how much his life had changed since he had. Days had passed since the incident in the cave, and whilst he could now walk perfectly fine, Joseph's suggestion of going back to Freydale was finally setting in.

They did need the book. But Joseph didn't want to have to set foot in that kingdom to do so. He didn't want the bad memories; he didn't want the reminders. As Maura had said, they had tried so hard to get away from all of that, and now, Joseph was going back straight into the belly of the beast.

He wouldn't allow himself to be captured this time, though.

"Put your back into it!" Joseph turned his head towards where the loud, booming voice had come from. Santos stood observing his crew going up and down a drawbridge-like apparatus, taking copious amounts of boxes and crates inside the ship. Two by two, they would walk up and down quickly. "We need to get this ship in good standing before nightfall!"

The sun was still high in the air; it wouldn't be nightfall for another couple of hours. But Joseph knew this was just a tactic to make them move faster. Santos was a formidable captain. He just hoped that Pierce could be, too, in Santos's place.

"Have you got everything ready?" a voice came up from behind him, startling Joseph as he turned his body to see who had spoken. King Atlas moved with grace with the staff that Joseph had created days ago. He stood, placing the staff on the ground to keep him in place as he looked on at the ship and all the handy work the crew were doing.

"Your majesty. Yes, I think so. Alex and Maura are already on board, and Santos is getting extra supplies before Santos hands the ship to Pierce." Joseph replied, but he was sure King Atlas could see that with his own eyes. "I really hope we didn't cause you too many problems over the last few days. What happened after I woke up?"

"Please, do not worry about that. It's all water under the bridge. You were angry; it would be stupid of me if I believed you weren't allowed to be." King Atlas said as he turned to face Joseph.

"You said you wanted to speak to me before we left?" Joseph asked. He could feel the king's gaze on him like he was trying to read Joseph's mind, but nothing was happening. He was still blocked. "What about?"

"I mentioned that you might be able to merge the power of the Luma and the Shade to create the ultimate power. If Alex is the… true embodiment of the Shade and he can use the magic for good, the old stories used to say that the Luma had to destroy the Shade to take its power, or visa versa." King Atlas began.

"So what are you saying?" Joseph asked; he didn't like the sound of this. This couldn't be how the story was going to play out. "Me and Alex must, what? Kill each other?"

"I didn't say that." King Atlas began. "The old stories are based on when the power of the Shade was used for bad; its power was corruptible. If Alex is the one we're looking for, if he can use this power for the good of all, then maybe merging the power wouldn't have to be so brutal."

"And you're basing this on?" Joseph asked, his eyebrow raised. It was not that he didn't trust the King, but life had thrown a lot of curveballs at Joseph recently, and he wasn't sure he trusted the world not to ruin it all for him once again.

"Complete blind faith." King Atlas said with a slight chuckle. "I need to do more research. Usually, the Luma stays put on the island, providing for their people. If I can do more research, I can ensure that whatever befell us before never happens again. I want to provide a good future for my kingdom. If we can find a way to control the power you two have and merge them in the way of good… maybe Rivetia can have a chance in the sun again."

"We can't stay in Rivetia though…" Joseph said.

"No, I know." King Atlas replied quickly. "It's why I'm coming with you."

"Not that I oppose the idea, Your Majesty… but you're a king. You can't just leave your kingdom." Joseph replied, shocked that he was even suggesting deserting the island in such a manner. "You have people to care for; Rivetia needs you."

"My mother was a queen before me; she ran the kingdom for many years. Truth be told, I think she welcomed the idea, but she was getting a little antsy. It won't be forever, anyway." King Atlas said as he began to walk towards the ship, causing Joseph to follow him quickly. Catching up to the King was challenging with all the hot sand underneath his feet, but the King seemed adept at it. "Plus, what good would a king be if he didn't know what the world outside his kingdom was like? I need to experience the world outside; I can't do that if I'm cooped up in my throne room working on policies, can I?"

"No, I suppose not. I must pre-warn you that it might be dangerous; we're heading to a kingdom where multiple people would like to see me, if not all of us, dead." Joseph said as he finally caught up to the King, who had begun to walk up the drawbridge leading to where Pierce, Maura, and Alex stood, dealing with various boxes and crates. "After that, who knows what is out there for us."

"That's all part of life, is it not? We have no idea what is coming for us next." King Atlas said as he and Joseph made their way up the drawbridge and onto the deck, now met with the confused stares of the other three people in the now ever-growing group. "Hi, guys."

"King Atlas?" Alex asked. Dropping a small crate, he had been holding. "Do you need anything?"

"Please, just call me Atlas." He said with a smile as he leaned his staff on the deck next to him.

"Not to be rushing you, Atlas, but… why are you here?" Maura asked, cocking her head to the side. "We've got a bit of a tight schedule with everything going on."

"He's coming with us," Joseph said.

"But your kingdom…" Alex replied. "You can't leave them after Rivetia is back on the map. It's susceptible to people finding it."

"Is in good hands with my mother, I'm coming back eventually, and Rivetia is thriving thanks to you. I need to continue researching the Shade and the Luma; I can't do that from the confines of my kingdom." King Atlas explained, and Alex just nodded. Understanding. King Atlas walked closer to the middle of the ship and looked around, his eyes zoning in on Maura, Pierce and Alex. "Is this the crew? Just the four of you? What happened to the others? The ones that came with you?"

"It wasn't their fight. It wouldn't have been fair to drag them along. The less people involved in the fight, the better." Pierce explained. "But in my father's words, it isn't the cushy life you're used to, Atlas; you'll sweep, clean, and maintain the ship whilst we're on the water as everyone else will. Is that understood?"

"Yes, captain." King Atlas said as he saluted his cousin quickly. He seemed a lot more relaxed than he had in the throne room, like he himself. Without the title of King hanging over him, Atlas could just be himself. "But in all seriousness, I'm not one to shy from work. Whatever you need me to do, I'll do it."

"Good, well, buckle yourself up; we've got a few days on the sea before we even get to our first destination," Pierce said as he leaned over the side of the ship, giving a small salute-like signal to his father and his men on the ground before the group of people dragged the drawbridge like objects from the boat. No turning back now. "Speaking of our destination, just remind me, Joseph, where exactly are we going first?"

"To get the book," Joseph said as Pierce gripped the ship's wheel. He looked at Alex and Maura, looking just as nervous as each other; all three knew what was at stake, and none left the kingdom in good graces. Joseph held his hand for Alex to take, interlocking their fingers before turning his face to look over the horizon before him and saying five words he never thought he would say again. "We're going back to Freydale."

The story continues in Book Three...

Printed in Great Britain
by Amazon

53667474R00179